We are All Normal
(and we want our freedom)

a collection of contemporary nordic artists writings
edited by Katya Sander & Simon Sheikh

Contents

We are All Normal
(and we want our freedom)

Peripheral Insiderism by **Søren Friis** — 8

In the Regional Perspective by **Lars Grambye & Kirse Junge-Stevnsborg** — 10

On Nordicness and Normality by **Katya Sander & Simon Sheikh** — 14

SOCIAL DEMOCRATS LIKE US

Intro — 20

May the Dikes Hold — **Ernst Billgren** — 22

rl-unplugged-power failure? — **Elin Wikström** — 24

To Change the World — **Måns Wrange** — 28

GYNOCRAFT; Jul. Bomholt — **Jørgen Michaelsen** — 32

The Photo Gallery — **Heidi Sundby** — 58

Who's Zooming Who? — **Karl Holmqvist** — 60

Definitely Boxing Day — **Thorvaldur Thorsteinsson** — 62

The Art of Communities — **Minna Heikinaho** — 66

Outro — 70

THE NAME GAME

Intro — 74

PLAN 01 — **Søren Andreasen** — 76

On Designations — **Sara Jordenö** — 78

A 'Young Lady' Protests — **Beate C Rønning** — 82

The Roundabout of Binary Oppositions — **Michael Elmgren & Ingar Dragset** — 88

All Wrapped Up — **Kirstine Roepstorff** — 92

White Cube for Some and White Queue for Others — **Khaled Ramadan** — 96

The Political Artist — **Gunnar Krantz** — 100

Outro — 106

CARE OF THE SELF

Intro 110

The Gym of the Castrated Girls **Tone Hansen** 112

The Charmings **Heta Kuchka** 116

Notes on Self-reflexivity in Art **Peter Land** 120

Public Educational Tours **Annika Lundgren** 128

Ode **Inga Svala Thorsdottir** 132

From *24 Motifs* **Anja Franke** 136

Outro 152

THE POLITICS OF POP

Intro 156

Notes for a Understanding of the *Safe Condition* Project **Lars Mathisen** 158

2x2 **Arturas Raila** 172

Hard Core, Self-organisation and Alternativity **Gardar Einarsson** 178

On Punk Rock **Jan Svenungsson** 182

Formless Music **Bjørn Bjarre** 188

Anne Lee and the Four Women **Anneli Nygren** 196

Outro 202

FROM A MIRAGE TO MIRACLE?

Intro 206

Borderland Double Vision **Claus Carstensen** 208

Refraction **Magnus Bärtås** 224

The Fall of Louisiana **Elisabeth Toubro** 232

"Its Typically Norwegian to be Good" **Anders Eiebakke** 238

Art in the Backwoods **Jyrki Siukunen** 244

We're all Normal (and we want our freedom) (Today) **Asmundur Asmundsson** 248

Outro 250

NORTHERN LIGHTS

Intro 254

The Modern Moodscape, Part 2   **Ingrid Book & Carina Hedén** 256

Boil, Simmer, Seethe and Stew   **Margrét Blöndal** 262

For Survival/Experience/Feeling   **Deimantas Narkevicius** 272

No Questions will be answered afterwards, neither directly or indirectly   **Sophie Tottie** 276

Allotments, Parks and Green Spaces   **Pia Rönicke** 280

The Wild North   **Jussi Kivi** 284

On Returning the Returns   **Matts Leiderstam & Peggy Phelan** 290

Outro 298

THE GREAT INDOORS

Intro 302

The Mess of Life   **Henriette Heise** 304

The Private Eye   **Katya Sander** 308

A new table, which might not be understood as clean in modern terms   **Jacob Jacobsen** 320

The Gaze of Howard Carter   **Jan Hietala** 324

Where is your Identity?   **Frans Jacobi** 332

The Flows of Intimacy   **Christine Melchiors** 336

Extracts from *Chamber Play*   **Kerstin Bergendahl & Eva Löfdahl** 338

Outro 352

INTERACTIONS AND INTERFACES

Intro 356

… are you talkin' to me!?   **Peter Holst Henckel** 358

War, Art and Intelligent Machines   **Mats Hjelm** 366

Art in the Age of Mobile Phone   **Marita Liulia & Geert Lovink** 382

Institution Media Manifesto   **Kestutis Andrasiunas** 392

All Power to the Copenhagen Free University   **Copenhagen Free University** 394

Heterotopia —Art, Pornography and Cemeteries   **Knut Åsdam** 398

Outro 408

Colophon 415

Peripheral Insiderism—A Foreword

In the Nordic region today, there is an ongoing discussion about identity. Is there such a thing as being Nordic, what does it mean and how does this simplified label position itself in relation to being European, International or Global?

The notion of being Nordic, most likely an outdated, now historical, synthetic construction in itself, is rapidly gaining attention as it is currently being confronted with enormous amounts of seemingly 'incompatible input', questioning the very basis of the Nordic project itself: differences rather than similarities among the Nordic countries, different approaches to the European idea, and perhaps most importantly a both real and media-produced confrontation with cultures for whom the question of identity appears to be less problematic.

Founded in the Nordic region, NIFCA, the Nordic Institute for Contemporary Art, recently decided to create a forum for these discussions; we named it *Det Ny Norden, the New North*, not in a naïve belief that new language changes things automatically, but as a clear signal that the current discussion all too often veers towards affirmative national identities and politics, instead of looking into questions of identities in a broader sense, and in terms of hybridity and diversity.

In the arts, and in life in general, identities are not given or fixed, but rather, are in a state of flux and formulation, not least in the visual arts, where appropriation, hybridity and transgression are original sources of creation. In this conflictual set up, artists play an important role, both in the construction, but certainly also in the deconstruction, of any identity, be it national or based on gender, sexuality or social class. And, indeed, this role of the artist in the society as such becomes increasingly important, but also less pre-defined.

When NIFCA initiated this collection of contemporary artists' writings, *We Are All Normal (and we want our freedom)* in 1999, the wish was to focus on the artistic thematics and concerns that have been present in the Nordic region—and in an international setting—in the late 90s. The idea was to look at the ongoing thinking about art from an artistic rather than an art historical point of view, i.e. to present the discussions, investigations and thought processes from the artists' positions.

Reading through the 53 texts in this collection, one immediate response is that any traditional stereotyped notion of a Nordic artistic identity has become inadequate. Issues of gender roles and relations, art institutions and identities, the welfare model, cultural politics and popular culture are recurrent throughout. The artists are concerned with opening conceptions of art, identity and culture rather than closing or affirming them.

At NIFCA we are also committed to an opening and mediation of such categories and characterisations; as a working method, we'd rather question than confirm, rather initiate and engage than adopt preconceived ideas and paradigms. Undoubtedly, this will lead us and others into some dead ends and useless confrontations, but we consider such an approach necessary to bring about a more innovative atmosphere in discussions. In a certain sense, this is also a more productive acceptance of future scenarios avoiding getting stuck in the present, which for many reasons, we tend to measure by past standards.

Let *We are All Normal (and we want our freedom)* act like an opening, an introduction to ongoing debates, discussions and discourses—a becoming rather than being!

Søren Friis Møller
Director, NIFCA

In the Regional Perspective

In the spring of 2000 Øjeblikket approached the Centre for Danish Visual Art with a view to collaborating on an anthology of texts written by contemporary Nordic and Baltic artists. For the Centre for Danish Visual Arts it seemed natural to support such an initiative. The idea of the publication was on the one hand to deal with themes and artistic issues that had characterised regional and international artistic debate in the 90s; and on the other to present various positions in Nordic and Baltic thinking about art, not with an 'art history' perspective but on the basis of artistic practice. The publication *We are All Normal (and we want our freedom)* gathers together for the first time some of the ideas that concern many Nordic and Baltic artists right now. But why is this so important and relevant? The international focus on the Nordic/Baltic region that typified the 90s was theory-based or consisted of isolated 'case studies'. With *We are All Normal (and we want our freedom)* we get a survey of and insight into Nordic and Baltic understandings of art and reality from the artists' perspectives.

With their diversity the texts reflect a number of central approaches to the social reality and conditions that define the contours of the Nordic welfare images and anti-images at this point in time. The anthology has been organised thematically on the basis of eight 'impact points'. The first is dealt with by the chapter "Social Democrats Like Us", discussing the present-day role of the artist, the polarity between welfare subject and state, and the development since the 60s, when the individual was a producer of welfare, to today, when the individual is instead a product of welfare. This is followed by a focus on the specifically Nordic situation in the chapters "Northern Lights" and "From a Mirage to a Miracle": does a Nordic tradition exist? Did we witness in the 90s a Nordic miracle or was it only brief attention? Subsequently the chapter "Politics of Pop" concentrates on the social implications of popular culture. "Care of the Self" and "The Name Game" discuss themes like identity, categories and gender in terms of theses about subjectivisation and the renewed interest in gender-political issues. "The Great Indoors" re-actualises Nordic indoor life and the idea of 'one's own room'. And the installatory, bodily and identity related transformations of technological development are discussed in "Interactions and Interfaces" with a focus on performativity, dialogue and the establishment of networks.

The themes of the anthology are interconnected and redeployed throughout the eight sections and link the various texts and artistic practices across perspectives as well as national differences. The texts are individual and heterogeneous and range from extended articles through commentaries, critiques and statements to brief fragments and notes. A central aspect is the schism in theories of modernity between emancipatory and reflective potential on the one hand and on the other centrist and exclusive tendencies. The social changes and the increased criticism of the welfare state that typified the 90s had their

constructions of self and the politics of identity and identifications. The next two chapters, "From a Mirage to a Miracle" and "Nothern Lights", place such identity questions firmly in the regional, the current 'hype' of new Nordic art in chapter five (Miracle) and the notion af a specific Nordic tradition within the arts in chapter six (Lights). A tradition that locates 'Nordicness' in the landscape itself. From landscape we move back indoors into the (in)famous Northern 'bedroom culture' for Chapter Seven, "The Great Indoors", that discusses interiors, both architectonically and mentally. The last chapter, "Interactions and Interfaces", most directly deals in exits; ways out of both traditions, institutions and locations. This section presents various models of thinking and producing art that can act as intermediary interventions.

However, these topics are, obviously, dealt with in various ways both stylistically and discursively. The essays collected in this book are texts from different places and times, and are not to be read as similar efforts or offerings. They are, rather, grouped together to show differences, a multiplicity of meanings and methods. Together they constitute a field, sometimes harmonious, sometimes jarringly dissonant. A field of cultural production is also a battle ground. In all, this book presents 53 texts of various length and content, ranging in form from longer articles to comments, notions and statements. There are texts that are allegorical, theoretical, poetic and even pedagogical. These differences not only reflect differences in artistic practice, but also in context: some texts were written for newspapers, others for catalogues or books, some for teaching purposes and others as notes or simply just for enjoyment. Finally, a number of the texts have been specifically written for this publication. Thus, *We are All Normal* is a combination of previously published writings and new commissioned work. Our notion of "artists' writings" is rather broad, even grande: we have been interested in the general production of texts in relation to art, be it debates, theory or work notes, or even text *as* (art)work. Therefore all these textual practices differ greatly in both form and content, and their only common denominator is the artist-subject as author.

The themes outlined and addressed in the eight sections can serve as an entrance to the art and thinking about art in the Nordic region, but hopefully it should also be possible to make readings, and thus mappings, across these sections, across the borders, so to speak. Each section clearly overlaps with another in a broad field of possible and impossible meanings and significations. This also implies, that no matter how pertinent and profound some of these themes might seem, they do not add up to a complete or unequivocal picture. Naturally, there are differences within the region as such, making so-called Nordic identity a more multi-cultural construct than one can easily be led to believe through media, myths and official politics. In the Scandinavian countries, for instance, one might focus on the continuous construction and deconstruction of the welfare state and its subjects, whereas the Baltic countries are struggling, after the fall of the former Soviet republics, with the construction of a (neo)liberal, democratic society. Similarly, the notion of 'Nature'—so long an obsession in Nordic painting—has different connotations for subjects in the mountains of western Norway, the large forest of Finland or the endless suburbs of Copenhagen.

It is our contention, however, of there being one particular notion seemingly prevalent in the Nordic region, possibly termed "the confluence of welfare and freedom". Where do you find your freedom(s) and how, be it in the wilds, within a specific notion of society, or internalised in the individual subject and his or her organising of social surroundings. Not only have the Nordic countries since World War II epitomised welfare, freedom, democracy and peace on the world stage, but within this region as in the rest of the West, the role of the artist has signified the ultimate free man. So, the more artists we have in society, the more free this society is—perhaps. The artist is therefore not an inopportune subject and, indeed, site, to discuss these broad questions and notions. To discuss the "phantoms of liberty" that still haunt us.

The purpose of this book is thus two-fold: to focus on some (artistic) thematics and thinking that have been present in the region (but also internationally) from an artistic rather than art historical point of view, and to use art writing instrumentally and allegorically to discuss the politics and subjectivifications of contemporary Nordic, Post Cold War and, maybe, Post Welfare Society. Arguably, this requires reading between the lines as well as across the sections.

The title, *We are All Normal (and we want our freedom)* is an attempt to specify and problematise the current Nordic situation, where both an almost obscene search for "normality" and equally insisting claim and privilege of freedom is constantly formulated in politics and culture. Tendencies dominating the discussion of art, tradition and regionalism versus internationalism, as well as the parallel political discussions about identity and belonging, regarding the Nordic versus immigrants and refugees—Nordicness and normality is always opposed to something outside, something foreign and frightening. The foreign is apparently nasty and undesirable, whether it is the left wing's anti-Europe rhetoric or the right wing's anti-refugee and immigration policies. True, the political wings do not directly share their 'othernesses', but they express the same logic of desire. 'We' have something that 'they' want to take away from us. 'We' are right and 'they' are wrong. And everywhere normality and freedom seems to come up. The phrase "We are all normal and we want our freedom" originates from Peter Weiss' infamous mid-60s play *Marat/Sade*, subtitled *The Persecution and Assassination of Jean-Paul Marat as performed by the Inmates of the Asylum of Charenton under the Direction of Marquis de Sade*, and is a chant Sade has the inmates sing. It is, thus, a chant that stems from the bourgeois revolution and the beginning of the modern, sovereign subject, albeit perhaps perverted by Sade, at once an outdated subject of the Ancien Regime, and on the other hand pointing forward to a more diffuse, postmodern subject whose quest from freedom is not altogether noble.

However, the quest itself continues to haunt us, and the cries of normality and for freedom have been heard many times since. It was perhaps heard almost simultaneously to Weiss' play, in the student revolts of 1968, and certainly in one of the period's famous pop songs, the eerie "The Red Telephone" by the LA band Love, where the chant strangely represented and combined the riots on Sunset Strip with psychedelic fallout and personal, mental breakdown. And it could easily have been heard many times since, it could have been heard in Copenhagen's post EU election riots in 1993, where the police opened fire on the demonstrators for the first time in the history of Danish democracy, and also at the infamous protests at the EU summit in Gothenburg in the summer of 2001, where the world's most 'social-democratic' town was turned into a battle ground, causing a trauma that has shaken the democratic self-understanding of Sweden in particular, and the Nordic region in general. But it can also be heard as a roar at right wing meetings and as a whisper in the silent, as yet still minority of the middle classes that vote for Nationalist, anti-immigration populist parties, and for whom the notions of 'we' and 'normal' and 'freedom' are exclusive rather than inclusive. Could it be that *Nordic* and *Normal* are really synonyms?

In closing, we would like to thank Lolita Jablonskiene and Anna-Kaisa Rastenberger who assisted us in terms of research and co-editing in the Baltics and Finland respectively. We would also like to thank our funders, and NIFCA who initiated this project, and Black Dog Publishing for their effort and enthusiasm, both of whom made us think more about 'the North' than we ever had before, and probably more than we would ever have liked to. And finally we would like to extend our thanks to the following individuals for their help, comments and suggestions, and without whom we could not have done what we have done: Matthew Buckingham, Michael Eng, Kirse Junge-Stevnsborg, Gareth James, Elsebeth Jørgensen, Mark Kremer, Anders Kreuger, Duncan McCorquodale, Sanne Kofod Olsen, Gertrud Sandqvist, Helena Scragg, Helena Sederholm, Paula Toppila, Anne-Grete Toresen, Per Gunner Tverbakk, Jorunn Veiterberg, Sonja Wiik and Cecilie Høgsbro Østergaard.

Social Democrats Like Us

ILLUSTRATION: JØRGEN MICHAELSEN: PSEUDO-PHONE—AN INSTRUMENT THAT DIRECTS SOUNDS FROM ONE SIDE TO THE OPPOSITE EAR, VICE VERSA

One of the foremost chararteristics of the Nordic countries, is, of course, the notion of the modern welfare state. The Nordic state as a utopia, model and everyday life can be said to produce a particular welfare subject, which in turn brings about a particular matrix for the traditional role of the artist. In other words, the incorporation and institutionalisation of modern notions of freedom by the welfare state—with its aestheticised and culturalised everyday subject—have had an enormous influence on the constitution of traditional notions of the avant-garde, as well as for the 'social plastics' of our day, that differs from the art world in general. The welfare subject cannot be separated from the institutions which forms it, and within this ideal 'social democratic' subject, there is never discord between the individual and the community. Welfare and freedom is a communal project. In this way, the role of the artist is not that of an outsider, but rather that of a model citizen, as the embodiment of this perfect subject.

The texts in this section primarily relate to the relation between the welfare subject and the role of the artist, a role that has undergone drastic changes since the beginning of the welfare project the late 1950s. A change, that, perhaps, can be described in brief as a shift from being a *producer* of welfare to being *produced* by welfare: where the welfare state was once a common objective, a project, strived for by most sections of society, it is today an institutional body and historical construct. It can be viewed both as a productive device, the motor of society, and/or as mere representation, even simulacra, but in any circumstances as the matrix for the construction of subjectivity and, in turn, the function of the author and the role of the artist.

Jørgen Michaelsen's conceptual piece of writing, "GYNOCRAFT; Jul. Bomholt", explicitly engulfes the production of art in the social democratic notion of the subject and definition of culture—exemplified by the late Julius Bomholt, former Minister of Culture in Denmark, who defined the cultural policies of the Danish welfare state. In this piece, social democratic, rigid thinking is evident in the work itself. Other writers also appropriate literary forms, such as Ernst Billgren, whose text "May the Dikes Hold" begins this chapter on a symbolic note. "May the Dikes Hold" was originally published as the first chapter of a novel by Billgren that tells the story of two Nordic painters who's development as artists coincides with the emergence of modern society. The building of the dikes themselves can be read as serving as a prerequisite to the modern welfare society as well as the national state, and the controller of these dikes can be seen as the quintessential social democratic constructivist. The control over natural, hostile environments also plays an important part in Elin Wikström's project description "rl-unplugged-power failure?", that suggest a power cut as a site-specific art piece for a location in western Norway. If this signifies a symbolic breakdown of power and order, the darker side of the social democratic subjectivity is also at play in Thorvaldur Thorsteinsson's piece, "Definitely Boxing Day".

Thorsteinsson's piece is, like Billgren's, allegorical, but shows hidden desires and imaginings of the characters in his 'pocket play'. What lies beneath the well-mannered, tolerant public persona is also at stake in Heidi Sundby's account of the meeting between art and its audience in her essay "The Photo Gallery", where she tells the story of visiting a gallery in the company of her father, and their ensuing dialogue around a homoerotic photograph. Contemporary art practice and social democratic subjectivity is also the topic of Karl Holmqvist's concrete poem "Who's Zooming Who", that sees the Scandinavian welfare model in relation to global capitalism and local art scenes. The subjects in the social democratic welfare state themselves are the topic of Måns Wrange's account of a current effort in Sweden to define the 'average citizen' for political polling purposes in his essay "To Change the World". Minna Heikanha also tries to facilitate change and democracy, although on a smaller scale, in her description of her own community based social works in the city of Helsinki, in an entry, appropriately titled "The Art of Communities". In Heikanha's works and writings we are again witnessing the confluence of subjective art practice and communal issues, where the role of the artist is to interact with social life and circumstances, as did indeed the controller of the dikes.

May the Dikes Hold

As usual in the mornings, the fog was quite impenetrable, but the sound of a distant knocking could be heard quite clearly. Something that resembled a black Viking ship glided out of the fog and approached the dikes at Pewsum. The knocking and scraping sound came closer, and now the dike controller's broad-beamed, flat-bottomed boat came into view. The sound came from the long iron bars, which you stick into the wall to find weaknesses and cracks in the dike. Day after day the unpopular, dark-clad controller travelled along the coast in his search for upcoming catastrophes. While working he mumbled little curses at the feckless villagers, predicting, like a raven, future floods which only he could control. The villagers felt uneasy when this bird of ill omen glided past their abodes, and they suspected that it was in fact he who called up the future catastrophes.

The boat was ugly and crooked as a jetty, with circular fenders like a series of shields along the side. It was built to lie steady in the shallow water while the controller, like a hymenopteran prodded and twisted his long feelers into the wall.

"Reinforce while there is time, reinforce before the dikes give way", he exhorted the villagers who were fast asleep in their cottages and did not hear a thing. "Looking porous; it's bound to give way soon; all hell will break loose if it isn't mended." He had mumbled this rigmarole for years and sooner or later events would prove him right.

The controller picked up the iron bar that seemed to be right for the crack he had noticed at that very moment. He started to twist and bend in the hope of discovering a weak spot or dislocating a stone, which had come loose. His logic was simple and straightforward: "If it gives way now, you won't run the risk of unpleasant surprises later on when you aren't prepared. Better face an accident now than have nasty things happen when you're siting down to a nice meal with a couple of friends, thinking that its going to be an ordinary evening."

Nobody cared about the fact that he had often noticed weak spots and had had the dikes mended in time, thereby managing to save thousands of people and their property. Nobody praised him for his foresight.

At even intervals the controller went ashore at dawn to buy supplies. This was a risky business, even in the villages that let him go ashore without hurling stones or words of abuse at him. This time he had chosen the small village of Pewsum, a typical little village where he had stopped many times before.

As usual, on his way to the country shop he passed a little house made of red brick. Only brick can withstand the salt winds of the North Sea. The winds had denuded the landscape of trees, with one exception. Outside this house there was an unusually magnificent walnut tree. It had survived because it had been planted in the middle of the courtyard, sheltered from the wind. This morning a boy was sitting under the tree playing with some animals he had made himself from walnuts, wax, and twigs.

The boy's name was Ernst Wilhelm. His mother had christened him after the emperor of the country, in the hope that he would perform great deeds but the boy under the walnut trees was never called anything other than Wilhelm. When the boy grew up and had children of his own, his son was in his turn given this name, which he in turn gave his son, and so on, into our days.

Previously printed in Ernst Billgren, Sucker and Housecalls, *Stockholm: Lars Bohman, 1999.*

translated by Gunilla Florby

Introduction

I relax at the hotel in Bergen, after a car trip to Øygarden. My first visit to the island. I wonder how it may have been living out there in earlier times, and how the area will change in the future. Stone Age vestiges sit next to modern oil and gas installations. On the way out, there were lots of tunnels cutting through the mountains, very pretty; but giving long periods of crackle if you're listening to the car radio. As I take it off, the synthetic sweater sends sparks all around. My skin is salty; it conducts electricity. I have just enough time for a shower and some reading, before meeting the organisers of Naust again. I start the book *Girlfriend in a Coma*: there Karen and Richard were sitting on a bobbing chairlift above the Blueberry Pist, when "the lights... blinkered, then skittered, then blackened". There they sat, "in the pitch dark... bouncing, stuck, suspended above raw nature", their "faces jeans-blue from the Moon".[1] I read that the electricity in Blueberry Pist comes from dams in northern British Columbia. The light from the reading lamp dims. The ventilation system whistles. How far has the energy in the cables travelled to get here? Where does it come from? How does it all happen? In the restaurant, Solveig talked about the weird mood that had settled in her and her boyfriend's flat one evening when there had been a power cut, even though they had been informed several weeks in advance that the electricity would be cut off, leaving an entire residential area of Bergen without power for several hours.

Back in London, late at night. The sky is orange grey. A sordid, red lamp is lit in the neighbouring house. Green emergency exit signs glow in the stairway inside the office block opposite. The people below me are having a party, "Let's party like it's 1999" on the record player. The pyramid on the top of Canary Wharf flickers hysterically. The computer has remained untouched for some minutes and the screen saver is activated. I stare at the clutter of ducts, thinking about the time between Christmas and New Year's Eve when the boiler broke down. We pottered about, wrapped in blankets, and wearing woollen hats, gloves and three pairs of socks. None of the predicted millennial catastrophes had occurred. Business as usual. War and hunger and air pollution. Traffic jams on the motorways, the tube brought to a standstill, and the line being engaged every time you try to get onto the Internet. Last time I visited the Tate Gallery, to see the *Abracadabra* exhibition, the fire alarm was set off, and sheer panic erupted amongst the crowd by the exits. Last night, in a restaurant in Shoreditch, just as I sat with my friend eating banana and ice cream, there was a power failure. A perfect chance to make a run for it. We remained seated. So did the other guests. When it was over, it felt like coming out from the cinema. A time-space gap. How would the evening have turned out if the power failure had not occurred?

I look at how the lines in the palm of my hand cross each other, larger and smaller grits in the oil, good luck and bad luck, life and death. I think of chance, of fate, of evolution, and of God. I don't know the meaning of the lines. This summer a girlfriend and I were the first to arrive at a car accident; the roles could have been switched. Bang, smash, you're out. It's a quick thing. A man was lying there unconscious, and when I used his cell phone to call the ambulance, the silence between the ringing signals seemed to last forever. In the preface to his novel *Crash*, J G Ballard reflects on how the relationship between reality and fiction in time and space has changed in the course of the twentieth century. The external world, he says, has come to represent reality and the inner world, fiction. Ballard feels that the only splinter of reality that remains is that which is inside our heads. For him, reality has become less real, more fictional, and as an author of fiction, he considers it his task to produce reality. Technology and the social sciences are no longer in a position to tame chaos and provide clean-cut, objective truths. After the atomic bomb and numerous ecological disasters the notion that human rationality can control tools, machines, environment and social conditions, such as advocated by development optimists, no longer sounds convincing. The time-space continuity has collapsed into an unpredictable present in which past and future utopias are constantly recycled. With no beliefs in either religion or science, we are forced to invent everything on our own; reality as well as our selves. We have to relate to the world as a territory as unknown as the most remote corner of consciousness in our own inner landscape. The flow of impulses, desires and anxieties, possibilities and risks that occur without us wishing them or contributing to them; questions that can be answered and those that cannot, climax and anti-climax.

rl-unplugged-power failure?—a project by and with Elin Wikström, Øygarden, Bergen
1   *rl-unplugged-power failure*: Project description
2   Verbal presentation of the project during press conference and the opening of *Naust*, 18 June 2000
3   *rl-unplugged-power failure*: Part 1, 12-20 June
4   *rl-unplugged-power failure*: Part 2, 11-16 September
5   *rl-unplugged-power failure*: Part 3, ?
6   Documentation of the project has been sent to all households in Øygarden municipality, and is presented at the Naust homepage

Part 1 of *rl-unplugged-power failure* consists of an investigation into the infrastructure of Øygarden municipality, concerning the following themes: water, lighting, heating, energy, transport, communication, demography, nutrition, trade, environment, health, security, culture, and services. For three weeks, I, Elin Wikström, and my assistant Camilla Sörvik hire a car and comb the area, meeting people with knowledge in the various fields in question. Our conversations are taped, and sites and facilities of significance to the project are photographed. The questions we ask are for example: What is power? What is electricity? What are electromagnetic fields? How far does the energy travel to reach this place? If there is a power failure, what causes it? Where does the water in the tap come from? Is it being drawn from the same source as 12,000 years ago? What do we know about the people who lived here formerly? When did the island get paved roads; the bridge linking it to the mainland; telephone lines? How does a car engine work? Are any of the goods for sale in the island's shops produced on the island? How is oil or gas brought from the bottom of the North Sea, how is it transported to Norsk Hydro and Statoil's installations in Øygarden and then on to Europe? How many men and women work on the island? What is there to do on the island? Why have people chosen to live here?

Both our car and our clothes carry labels with the logo of the project; "rl-unplugged-power failure?", in order that people we meet on our travels, or who have read about the project in the paper or heard about it otherwise, can make contact with us.

rl-unplugged-power failure?: Part 2, consists of negotiations with the Øygarden municipality and the local electricity company, Nordhordaland Kraftlag, about organising an art happening in the form of a power failure. All households in Øygarden would be informed according to normal practice that the power will be cut off in the area, and that the reason for the cut is an art event forming part of the *Naust* project of Bergen City of Culture 2000. Ideally, I would like the power cut to take place at some point during November 2000, with the power being cut off at 11 AM and turned on again three days later.

For the meeting with Øygarden municipality and Nordhordaland Kraftlag I wanted to invite three people representing the municipality, I have suggested the following: Kjersti Rykkel Blom, Secretary of Culture; Tor Kleppestø, Head of the Department of Building and Civil Engineering; and Rolv Svein Rougnø, Mayor. From Nordhordaland Kraftlag, I suggest inviting Tryggve Fjeldstad plus two of his colleagues; and lastly, Solveig Øvstebø, Head of the *Naust* project, and Øystein Hauge, Kunsthøgskolen i Bergen. The purpose of the meeting is, in addition to making negotiations concerning the power cut, to exchange thoughts on energy and its uses and applications from three different perspectives: art, the municipality and the electricity company. During my visit to Øygarden, I will also offer to give a presentation of my artistic work, showing slides and giving a talk on earlier projects to the representatives of the municipality, the electricity company and people I met during the first part of the project.

rl-unplugged-power failure?: Part 3. A power cut can be both a frustrating interruption and a pleasant break. A power cut often brings with it unexpected encounters, generates a special kind of conversation, and creates memorable situations. Personally, I find power cuts to be quite sensual experiences. I will invite myself and the inhabitants of Øygarden to experience a planned slippage of time and space, symbolically as well as literally; and to reflect on the conditions of the everyday and on the relativity of order and chaos. How do we handle the invisible play of power, things that happen without us having chosen them or contributed to them ourselves? Has the gap narrowed between those questions that can be answered and those that cannot? Is it possible to prevent the machinery from breaking down, technologically as well as existentially?

To me art is energy; it is not merely the result of an artist's intentions, or something that gives the artist pleasure. To think that all the inhabitants of Øygarden should simultaneously hit upon the idea to switch off the lights and refrain from using electrical appliances is impossible: it would simply never happen. There is also a difference, I think, between the yearly power cut initiated by Nordhordaland Kraftlag, during which they survey the installations, or a power failure caused by lightning, on the one hand, and a power cut as an art happening, on the other. Fire played a central role in the rituals of our ancestors. It is possible to see the power cut as a randomly inverted Midsummer's Night, centering on the absence of fire or electric power which has become so crucial to our lives.

With the analogy between the metaphorical use of the term power (in an artistic context) and the concept of power found in physics and technology, *rl-unplugged-power failure?* holds the possibility of a twin 'failure'. If the power failure is indeed effected, it will entail a technological power failure, however temporarily. In the opposite case, if the attempt fails, it might come across as an artistic 'failure', though only according to a value system based on utilitarian and economically measurable values.

Note

1. Dennis Cooper, *Girfriend in a Coma*, New York: Harper Collins Publishers, 1999.

translated by Ika Kaminka

It is, in point of fact, contempt of reality that makes it possible to change the world.

Hannah Arendt

When you begin to work with averages and indices, you lose so many considerations. What happens then is that from the technically oriented social policy discussion a new socio political ideology begins to grow.

Gunnar Myrdal
(Professor of Political Economics,
Swedish Minister of Trade, 1945-47,
and Nobel Laureate in Economics, 1974)

The old Swedish model seems... to have become incorporated in and transferred to the new political landscape, which is more influenced by lobbyism and medialisation... Both lobbyism and opinion formation are on the other hand forms of participation that even single individuals can exploit regardless of the actions of other individuals.

Demokratiutredningen
(a report on democracy commissioned by the Swedish Government)

The notion of an 'average citizen'—that is, a fictive person supposed to statistically represent a larger group of people—has been one of the most influential ideas in the construction of the Swedish welfare state. By incarnating the modern dream of translating a complex reality into a rational and transparent model, statistical averages have laid the very foundation of the Swedish art of social engineering.[1] The averages produced form the basis of research, social debate and the authorities' planning in most of the social sectors that influence the daily life of its citizens—for example housing, infrastructure, education, health, and the care of children and the elderly.[2] But other segments of society too, such as trade and industry, the media, advertising and the service sector, to a great extent adapt their products and services to the average preferences of the clientele on which they focus.[3]

Last but not least, the principle whereby an individual citizen is allowed to represent a larger population group in fact forms the very basis of representative democracy—

inasmuch as politicians are elected in general elections. But the present democratic system is facing a number of serious problems in Sweden (as in most other Western countries). Election turnout—which has traditionally been high in Sweden—is decreasing, and poorly educated and resource-poor groups are voting less than well educated and well-off ones. The democracy report commissioned by the Swedish Government, *Demokratiutredningen*, states that the political involvement of citizens has diminished, and that the interest in political issues that despite everything does exist has abandoned traditional party politics in favour of "single-issue organisations". According to a democracy study by the Swedish Centre for Business and Policy Studies the established parties will be non-existent by the year 2013 if their membership figures continue to fall at the same rate as today. At the same time the political influence of business and the major interest organisations, as exerted through professional opinion-making, has increased and political parties are becoming more and more dependent on the media and on effective marketing to attract any attention at all to their political issues. The individual citizen's potential for getting his or her views out to the general public is similarly minimal.

The Average Citizen is a project whose aim is—in all modesty—to present an answer to this question about the fate of democracy. The project can be seen as a political experiment with an alternative democratic model based on a different type of representation from the current type of democracy. Since elections are held at relatively long intervals, opinion polls and statistical research are among the authorities' few ways of sampling the views of the electorate. Often it is precisely to the average voter that they adapt their political programmes. Statistics and opinion polls thus already function *de facto* as fundamental and sometimes crucial criteria for political decision-making.[4] The project *The Average Citizen* takes its point of departure in the consequences of this *Realpolitik*, and takes Swedish social engineering's quest for scientific objectivity to its logical conclusion. Instead of citizens electing representatives in general elections on the basis of whether they think the candidates represent their views, an individual is chosen to represent the citizens by virtue of statistically representing the whole population. This is a method that is independent of the statistically representative person's political contacts, social networks, media charisma and financial resources—factors that are becoming increasingly determinative in Swedish politics.

The alternative democratic model in *The Average Citizen* has been structured as follows: with the aid of the Swedish Central Bureau of Statistics, a statistical "average citizen profile" has been created by collating the averages most frequently used by the Swedish authorities. Subsequently a headhunting agency has advertised in the media for a person who corresponds to this statistical "average citizen profile": female, 40 years old, single, childless, living in a two-room-and-kitchen apartment, with about SKr 248,300 a year in income, etc..[5] A person who fits this statistical profile has declared her interest in participating in the project. Her name is Marianne and in the project she will be known in public only by her first name in order to preclude any exploitation of her private life. The aim of the project is instead to focus on Marianne's views on how society can be changed, and to disseminate these ideas back to the Swedish public which she represents statistically. This will be done by giving Marianne access to the same sophisticated methods used by politicians, interest organisations and the business world to bring about changes in society: professional opinion-forming and lobbying.

In cooperation with a political lobbyist and the rest of the project group (which includes a dramaturgist, a copywriter and an expert political consultant to the Swedish Government) a long-term strategy has been drawn up for how average citizen Marianne's views are to be grafted on to Swedish society and in the longer term influence public opinion. Marianne has been interviewed in depth on how society can be changed, and these views have later been gathered in a data bank of opinions. In collaboration with Marianne herself, a political speechwriter has summarised and formulated her views in the form of brief, impactful slogans. A broad spectrum of Sweden's most influential people from fields of activity with a high opinion-forming value—for example politics, advertising, culture, the media and popular culture—have been contacted by the project group with a view to persuading them to cooperate with Marianne by disseminating some of her views in contexts appropriate to each. As with all effective lobbying and opinion-forming, Marianne's views are presented indirectly so that the public is not aware of the identity of the originator of the views. As an example, one of her views has formed the starting-point for an editorial in one of the major morning newspapers; it has been presented as part of the dialogue in a popular TV series; it has been quoted by an influential politician; and it has appeared in a nationwide advertising campaign. *The Average Citizen* thus benefits from the legitimacy that these established channels of communication confer on views, as opposed to if it had been presented for example in a letter to the press.

Unlike other artistic projects with the ambition of changing the world—an ambition that few would espouse in today's post utopian cultural climate—*The Average Citizen* will be able to objectively quantify and scientifically document the society-transforming

political, etc.) in a heuristic corpus aiming at the critical transformation of the specificity implied in order to reach a position of adequate post-phallo(go)centric variability. With regard to the referent of gender as identity: it never carried much consistency or credibility as *total farce* or *unmixed tragedy*—just as the underlying 'identity of contradiction' also seemed to work only as a very volatile source of antithetic consciousness (if not the cause of outright quasi-conflict). As a core concept in the general unstated consensus of meta-modern cultural discourse, gender is, by and large, constructed, distributed, and consumed by functional criticism in the heterogeneous context of more or less independent communities. Nevertheless, and this cannot be too often stated, a strategy of all too simple manipulation of the given schemes of anatomic determination is very often itself already a fetishisation of the order 'manipulated': the organisation of components has been changed somewhat, the components themselves remain as before, only even more 'sticky'. It is pointless for a practice to try to escape from subjective/objective collapse with a triumphalist visa— a strategy of rash simulation which really boils down in every respect to little more than bluff as an instrument of simple self-preservation. The pathetic difficulties of implicit fetishism are even more formidable when a defensive appeal to the role of Western mythos in the creation of a meta-modern principle of pleasure in the female body is made; actual materiality as well as historical virtuality are lost or eclipsed in the hazy zone of canonical-methodological ambivalence. Consequently, 'added' eroticism, as a generator of radically interiorised 'refutability', or as a principle of 'absent-minded' production in itself, secretes an object or an historical capital invested with all sorts of motivations and counter-motivations, some of which contain a potential for refusing the objective illusion of power as imperative luxuriant growth in sources of material and ideological maturation, and relaxation in attitudes and in expectations.

Jul. Bomholt (1896- 1969). The relation between the process of concrete historical variability and the technique of self-alienation developed by independent practice is, of course, one of considerable ambiguity. On the one hand 'simple situations' in the sphere of legitimate needs are transformed into generative structures of objective pseudo-exchange, while on the other, the advanced organisation of critical consciousness is forced to make allowance for the dual character of this situation. From the perspective of 'ultimate motivation', it has often seemed as if a strategy of instrumentalised his-toricity were completely or prevailingly dominated by the *endlösungesque* cathexis of the metaphors or icons involved. However, very often that kind of reading itself remains isolated as an absurd ideological *perpetuum mobile* of neophobia-neophilia rotation; as discursive economy it almost inevitably becomes the source of its own long-term control, transforming a specific 'content' of labour into the 'obligatory' ethos of constant reproduction. Indeed, it may be heuristically useful to view the objective essence of meta-modern socio-cultural realisation as if it were the absolute negation of private maximisation in somewhat the same way that central administration of equilibrium, conversely, might be interpreted as social objectivity with a human face (even though that face is not above the influence of subject-industry). It may also be urged that an adequate

'pleasure-rich' reading of contingent sociality must necessarily include a more permanent basis of 'comparative' parameters selected from a 'specific' context of inflexible need, catastrophe, estrangement, fragmentation, or a similar condition capable of destruction immanent identity. Thus, in the immediate light of such methodological paradoxes, the question seems to be: How is which relevant practice, to be informed by which critical consciousness, produced by which monadic subject, or which organised community *vis-à-vis* which historical situation with what expectation? A rather uninteresting answer might be to point out that objective atomisation constantly retains or reconstructs within itself certain zones of 'unambiguous freedom', whose overall paradigmatic force of attraction deposits a more or less specific event horizon around those local segments of discourse—thus very often creating the emblematic contours of an apparent euphoria of some implicit 'giga-author'. In this scenario, consequently, the mode of reflection tends to gravitate towards what may look like simple identity, eventually almost totally merging into the essentially tautological or harmlessly self-manipulating capital of ideology concerned. A perhaps more serious answer would be that neither high-standard contributions of variable contradiction nor, for that matter, approaches of total affirmation or symbiosis are ever, in fact, definitively interiorised in 'the mighty meso' of socio-cultural equilibrium, which has not much need for any exogeneous catastrophe of hypertrophy or overdone self-fulfillment of sameness. (However, as we perhaps know *ad nauseam*, the body of equilibrium succeeds excellently in transforming any internally manifested object of functional ambiguity ((e.g., the permanent presence of a—by now somewhat formulaic—fear of central administration) into a capable (potentially to the point of its own redundancy) referent in the critical analysis of its own metabolism, i.e., its own ideological morphology.) It is clear that debating the

ILLUSTRATION: BOMHOLT, MULTIPLE, 1997–99

issue of the relationship between the social system as a source of political accumulation, and the conscious reflection in organised critical discourse of that accumulation, does not *chronically* reproduce Social Democrat ontology; assuming this would be tantamount to accepting the assertion that the objective political irony which in an apparently inevitable way seems to emanate from the accumulation-reflection axis of concrete socio-cultural investment will remain isolated as a power of genuine social stimulus—a 'metabolised' always-already of ideological inertia with no (or at least only an almost inaccessible) potential of dialectical plasticity. One point may be that equilibrium, as widely adapted to the obliging assimilation of the notion of itself being an 'advanced' farcical regime, has provided a specific aesthetic framework which poses the problems and the parameters of public or private discourse as mainly a monotonous abundance of passion, critical or not. As such, one might say, the tragical habit of passion becomes the farcical passion of habit.

II
GYNOCRAFT; Jul. Bomholt
26 theses

It is my conviction that the community of high ideals which unites us will provide the breeding soil for that which is to come. Much new and great will sprout from this community.

Jul. Bomholt, *Our Cultural Tasks*

In any case, the separate individual, the order of production, and the equilibrium remain confusedly embedded in each other as long as modus operandi does not proceed on the basis of a strengthening of the objective unity of the subjective, as well as of its internal logics of circulation.

Jørgen Michaelsen, *MANDATE*

1. We have become accustomed in the development of our institutional demonologies as well as hagiographies, to taking our starting point from problems of criticism primarily concerning the metaphorical content of the subject, and to seeing some sort of transformation of selfhood as a solution to these problems (thus the discursive capital of 'hermeticism' is, quite unjustly, often interpreted as mainly a means in a mission or project of self-tolerance). It is perhaps characteristic of the individually based aesthetic investment in public space that very little can be done in advance to prepare for its concrete success as a social effect; in many cases the initiative must remain free-floating as if in a vacuum or some similar (quasi-cellular) element— perhaps eventually becoming the victim of the arbitrary respiratory influence from endogenous imperatives. The pools of egotistical maximisation produced by the interplay between construction or assimilative destruction and the actual space of everyday abundance continues to develop in this sphere of me/not-me symbiosis. What the specific psychology of private scarcity in primary identity often has in common with the public parameters of late modern de-sacralisation is a kind of 'liberating' negative authority over the conditions of 'motivated' representation. Thus the connection between local and global negativity has been shown to contain not only virtuosity of technique, but also strategic substance, and, possibly, a real potential for the critical organisation of metaphors on the level of individual as well as class

transformation. With the monadic pseudo-death in this context of more or less stereotyped social economies, the opportunity exists for equilibrium-society to become the transformed product of its own redundancy; a mechanism which apparently consumes itself only in so far as it produces itself, and *vice versa*—while actually developing complex structures of 'double-independence' behind the back of its own circulation.

2. Confusedly mediated entropy and immediate negentropy are merely alternate sides of the coin of historical form; both are horizons to the virtual content of modern ideological synthesis; it is just that the one is mainly directed towards local technical problems as a basis of dialectical identity, the other towards the total field of historical competition. (A 'post-historical' condition is produced when there is a short circuit between the two.) The implication of a view which contrasts the blocked materiality of entropic realisation with the total anatomy of socio-cultural production would seem to be that objective motivation is not best seen in this specific context—as a metaphysical hostage under the aegis of the capital of arbitrary concretisation. If historical reflection stimulates a new kind of dealing with entropic otherness, indeed if it eliminates the ideological basis of that sensibility altogether, then we shall have advanced a little in the process of implicit, basic maximisation of advanced social and cultural reading. At least, in any instance of immediate need in the epitomised meta-modern author-function, *vis-à-vis* the socio-cultural system, there is no such thing as specifically-anticipated-scarcity but the accumulation of totalised scenarios of objective pleasure in material practice, or a full-scale will to transformation in lived social life and real history (which must not, of course, be confused with a latent sympathy for merely abstract investment of free-floating monumentality). There can be no doubt, autonomy cannot be reduced to a component in the global pleasure function of superior negentropic annihilation of collective otherness; as a referent, real autonomy is not simply thrown on the spin-off produced by the historical process. We find that almost any form of deviation from the social surface of the prevailing design of desire is surrounded by alienated reproduction of cultural critique; and if therefore the apparently necessarily dual character of strategy appears less clearly articulated in the body of autonomous discourse itself than elsewhere, this is connected to the fact that the function of independent investment must remain in a position which to some extent reflects the context. If the situation of exchange is favourable, something close to an absolute heuristic surplus may be accumulated—and, in consequence, a strategy may be generated for the exploitation of dialectic

out of control (i.e., dialectical movements which, at the given historical time, seem to be relatively futile and thus transcending certain stages of orthodox development that have become redundant or 'self-eclipsed'). This process of recuperation aims at the objective reprocessing of forms of immediate pleasure as well as the construction of the more or less specific antitheses to these forms.

3. What changes, modulations, refinements, even revolutions take place in the singular discursive process fueled by a need for otherness—behind the back of orthosemiosis? Is the discourse able to represent the genealogy of the relevant monstrosity to itself without turning it into an emblem of self-imperialism? To be canonically economic works on a certain level of late hygienic consciousness, as the compensation for a lack of insight into objective historical necessity—just as the overproduction of life-death contradiction on the level of specific existentiality may be a form of singular compensation for the integration of blocked historicity in culture as a whole.

4. The necessary articulation of an experimental approach adds a further dimension to the problematic process of practical control as regards social embodiment. The perspective of *docta ignorantia*, as well as the principle of 'anti-body formation' within the spatial structure of the social corpus, etc., was, of course, appropriated by the totality of equilibrium long ago. The proliferating cosmos of doubtful simulation and the variety of efforts to 'recuperate' the objectively virtualised by means of exegesis, provide such a complex picture of the discursive room for manoeuvre that every attempt to depict its functional essence in an unambiguous way and by homogeneous means may lead to an inexpedient distortion of the prevailing ideological forces within that space—even if the chosen vehicle of abstraction or typology is of itself not unsuitable. Thus, the autonomous body of discourse is precluded from regarding itself as a conscious ideological homunculus in pursuit of some sort of relevant self-interest *for the simple reason that the space between means and ends becomes blurred*. In this objective scenario of parasitical necessity, sudden loss of capacity for assimilation of ontology (or even less complex means of impression) due to 'darker impulses' emanating from the signs has, in fact, many causes.

5. In some cases of mass consumption, the independence of interests is rigidly maintained (indeed stereotyped), in others the process of appropriation is more fluid and open, leaving the almost spontaneous construction of a sufficiently relevant 'resonance membrane' predominantly to the vertical configuration of social reactants.

The acknowledgment and the acceptance of the fact that sociality to some extent functions in contradiction to the monstrosity of historical structures, and the meta-aestheticisation connected with this admission, do not mean that because of this we are outside concrete repression, but merely that we have comprehended the difference between structural gesture (emblematisation) and historical substance (form of motivation, dialectical complexity, etc.). However, pointing out this dualism, one must be aware that involuntary misreading or excessive deviation may have implications for the total structure or model of political hermeneutics and body investment: the final result may be a condition of psycho-social misery within a totally isolated apparatus. At this point perhaps it is wise to acknowledge that it is a renewed sense of absolute production of consciousness in the process of historical reflection (formation of 'free-floating ideas' as well as concrete ideological modules designed for objective physiological interiorisation), rather than some immediate or undeveloped sense of the critical forms and conditions of growth concerned that marks the character of the cosmos of discourse here implied. Evidently, the organisation of the structures that make up the internal metabolism of singular practice from objective stimuli frequently overlaps the apparatuses of external socio-cultural reality; thus, the (open-ended) process of discursive production must be capable of dealing with the specific segments of the context: its frameworks of futile irony, its grotesque euphoria of involuntary simulation, its 'alpha male' rhetorical tactics like interrupting, loudness, exploiting the psycho-social advantages of greater size, deeper voice, longer text, etc.. It would be too easy to say that the autonomous construction of such critical registers (not to mention the necessary paraphernalia of 'mediated' ideology) inevitably results, on the one hand, in a state of surplus virtuality that chronically 'doubles' the perhaps already dual character of cultural formation or input, and on the other, in simple immobility: the immediate epitome of social crisis. Some hazy and untrustworthy concept of mental *bricolage* seems to be an indispensable condition of oscillation between variable and permanent production of consciousness and strategy; however, it belongs to the realm of flexible totality in which the rhetoric as well as the everyday life of the ideological subject is inscribed and potentially transformed.

6. The concept of the historical means of material and ideological reproduction as reproduced by central administration may contain a potential for the examination of one of the most important problems of the present condition, vis., that of the idea of the meta-modern individual as *corrupted* (socially, culturally, etc.). In this context, a certain level of historical need is requisite for the analysis of the more or less explicit

contradiction between the subjective or objective character of self-understanding in the relevant agent, his or her conceptual instruments, and the concrete circumstances (this is indicated by the fact that no known production of contemporary consciousness is totally free of the episteme of the ironic; indeed, in its most degenerated consequence, a practice based on this type of underdeveloped motivation will hopelessly remain a socio-cultural hostage to the short-term pleasure modules or stereotypes of this archive). However, the concepts which differentiate identity and credo from one another are often misleading: generally, they are themselves blasted free from any basis of meta-productive hypo-statisation, and thus not in a position to recuperate their own power of circulation which is often lost in the field of retro-appropriation between gesture and moral code—absorbed in the surplus distortion of the prevailing ideology. In this way, the signifier certainly conforms to the demands and manipulations of the prevailing framework of semantic welfare consensus (but nevertheless it always remains in a socially creative tension on other levels of conflict). In one view the idea of the economy of human fluids is functional for discursive endeavour as a whole in that it promotes both a reshaping of the conceptual infrastructure that contributes in a dialectical way to the configuration of the relevant author, and a specific reformation of the general solid-fluid contradiction in the basic two-phase system of Danish Social Democrat equilibrium as source of historical objectification. The problem of constructing a socio-cultural heuristics as not-entirely-negative spin-off from the structures of Danish communal ideology, sensibility, morphology, climate, etc.—as opposed to the concept of middle-class society as an exclusively malignant, quasi-femininised continuum, a zone of Social Democrat assimilation to be unconditionally refused—points to methodological and other issues that go beyond the perhaps fading complexities of the double framework of the apparently transcendental pretension of horizontal discursive (trans)subtlety, and the (still) all too concrete surfaces of vertical meso-representation.

7. The individual reception of the institutional power corpus is very often stamped with an experienced (of course essentially irrational) force of the demonic. This condition may make possible the creation of new paradigms on the subjective level of 'author politics': society as objective reality is thus invested with an almost erotic passion. Apart from this there is nothing *unheimlich* or absolutely uncomfortable about the normal life process: it is really simple in spite of its immediate complexity, it is dialectical in spite of its monolithicity; it contains textual registers, it is capable of simulation; it realises the human by means of the anti-human, and the anti-human

by means of the human (it also realises several more or less specific registers in the interface between these two positions of production); and, it is capable of thinking up, e.g., the end of the economy of human fluids no matter how free-floating such a project may seem. Absolute closure as well as omnipotent plasticity are usually reflected or epitomised in the behavioural patterns of the normal life process; *le part maudite* is incorporated as a basically democratic motivation—indeed an imperative—of pleasure. In this objective context of essentially instrumentalised 'ecstasy' the products of specifically specialised economies of discourse are able to circulate legitimately only as an expression of the dual character of the means of euphoria in general: they must be mediated through some sort of fetishisation before the climax of consumption can be reached.

8. The realm of exchange, as invested with the signs of expressive labour, appears in late welfare topography as a field of objectification which allows the construction of contributions of objectively incorporated farce (ethno-psychology as well as elitist apathy, 'carnivalesque' distortion of products, production, and producers, etc.). Equally, 'antithetic' departures from this canon can be immediately interpreted for further investment of symbolic accumulation or simple recycling. The emphasis on conflict (between material techniques, ideological interests, practical subjective necessities, etc.) generated in relation to the totality of socio-cultural networks here implied should not obscure the fact that the hypothesis of 'natural selection of cultural mutations' in itself remains a harmless (and yet ambiguous) appendix to the overall quantity of equilibrium. Perhaps the problem of reproductive embodiment is, ultimately, a question of whether the fluctuating interest of objective irony melted into an almost spasmodic form of pathetic pleasure—at any rate on a level of code—can allow 'itself' the moral effects of subjective interiorisation in the naked *Realprozess* at all.

9. Rather than waste time reflecting upon the characteristic sensibility of Social Democrat late-welfare equilibrium-society as a cultural construction of predominant *femininisation* (a point of view which in many ways remains an historical hostage in a climate which was originally produced under the aegis of the now worn down ideological enthusiasm generators of the regime of 'classical' modernism), analysis must set about turning the scenario into a means of dialectical interest. Today, for instance, technology represents an almost androgynous structure in society. To a large extent it defines and regulates the codes of social practice—and it tends to do so independently of its intended purposes. Thus, in principle, social practice tends to become (and perhaps

even regards itself as) the chaotically androgynised spin-off from a technological order of production and innovation which ultimately seems to deconstruct the traditional signs and canons of gender. Whereas the symbolic situation of modern gender rested on a mainly concrete sense of means-end economy, meta-modern gender is generally based on factors such as institutional redundancy (an umbrella concept for a plethora of determinants), misunderstood alienation, contractuality (including the extensive corpus of *masturbans-masturbandum* scenarios), etc.. To many observers the main impression is that in the slipstream of the catastrophe of the modern, reciprocal motivation has to be added 'artificially' as a substratum. The transmission of conceptual schemes, from the historical context of phallo-centrism (catastrophe, geometry, warfare imagery, etc.) to meta-modern recuperation within the framework of late welfare state equilibrium-discourse, becomes elementary in the process of a critical accumulation whose aim is to control its own dialectical potential and thereby its historical fate, as gender construction and otherwise; ideologemes are the blood corpuscles of power—although power would perhaps rather have us believe they are more like Dawkinsian selfish genes.

10. The field of subjective manipulation as discursively invested sensibility and contemporary scientific knowledge as a space of charismatic mediation are apparently connected in some (relatively poorly understood) way. However, laws of applied privatology as well as laws of nature relate to the objective necessity of an ultimate sub-stratum of passive emotion. They both constitute an advanced critical space of meta-modern development of sensibility. (The modern misery of, e.g., agro-, petro-, or pharma-sensibility thus arises in the 'vacuum' between contradictory registers of discourse: as the 'interactive' product of involuntary investment in subjective as well as objective spheres of alienation. (In fact, meta-modern alienation of, e.g., immediate beauty, signals that passive emotion does not absolutely reflect a productive source of historical determination, but changes with the relevant level of self-development and differs between some instrumentalised concept of totality and a subtle gamble on the undeveloped abundance of that totality.) That the critical space of meta-modern socio-cultural contribution is *advanced*, means, above all, that it contains an accessible consciousness of itself as the dual matrix of the subjective conversion of objective cultural contribution, and, *vice versa*, the objective conversion of the processes and signs of subjective pleasure. Thus, the relevant convergence of passive emotion is not just invested in the ideological resonance of a series of democratic remakes of historical monstrosities. Rather, 'inter-objective' maximisation of subjective signifiers is

established by the implicit discourse of labour as a personal farce, and labour as a personal farce is determined by the cult of banality and rhetoric to match. In this 'instrumentalised' condition there is not only an element of historically epitomised scarcity which attracts the author in advanced critical space, but there is also an element of already converged sources of passivity, that expresses a still more urgent imperative in him or her: to confront the mechanisms of his or her own generalised leisure and reconstruct them in one single figure.

11. Generally it is the surplus representation of random ideological mutation that fuels the underlying paradigmatic pools of socio-cultural anticipation which is inscribed in every form of meta-modern antropology or identity (in *homo laborans* as well as in *homo culinarius*, just to mention a couple. Insofar as one can make a sweeping generalisation, the tendencies of the appropriation of substantial roles in this condition of relative freedom are guided by non-ironic models in which a given dynamic logic is 'filtered' through an imaginary corpus of ahistorical norms. It is not in the least objectively 'disturbing' that in the process of constant genesis of the Western cultural tradition, historical necessity often quickly loses its relevant basis and never actually reaches its 'original' position again (instead, the 'free-floating' nominal value is isolated in the specific projects of selected authors—who for their part become the object of *ad hominem* attacks); in practice, this (long-term) principle of negation can be regarded, e.g., as a contribution to the productive distortion of the triumph of an all-too-robust gender debate (an actually autonomous and unambiguous strategy cannot be built on this sub-structure). The prevailing figures of historical accumulation are usually seen as functionally including an ineradicable, ironic gesture of monolithic 'desire' that precludes relevant tragedy; and thus the basic potential of auto-critique exposed to auto-critique *ad nauseam*, and the generative value of the general erosion in critical technique transformed into matrices of (semi)institutionally related registers of intensity, often seem to parallel each other in part because of the effects on the already complex concept of pleasure produced by the exogeneous negativity mediated through an opaque necessity (which now and then actually seems to imply a certain tragical quality—no matter how farcical the total situation or condition may be in itself). There is no inherent reason why the dictatorship of this historically produced reciprocity and its evolutionary fields of sign motivation should not essentially be seen as heuristic powers; with the dialecticised space between the above mentioned tendencies and positions, the discursive stage is set for the development of new means of socio-cultural epiphany.

12. Most of the moral conflicts that have been postulated to exist behind the back of the exegesis in question now seem to be outlined in theoretical and other forms and to a great extent synthesised in socio-cultural structures; e.g., in concrete exchange, the individual gaze—indeed the whole principle of body irony—has been institutionally 'liberated' as a public parameter of local discipline. Absolute anatomy is not as prominent a symptom in the practical sphere of surplus sociality as in the institutional typology, probably because the interiorised value relations of the underlying tragedy-farce system 'protect' the development of a 'second' tactility in which the body is reinvested as an out-of-date means of expression. Another problem lies in the specific influence of this structural development on the singular apparatuses of critical reflection: the softening of ideological hypersensitivity seems to imply the relative proliferation of clichés *recognising themselves as such*—the immediate irony of a surface produced by historical transformation thus synthesising its own value as (material) farce into simple maximisation of (ideological) closure. While not denying the possibility of long-term objective appropriation, we can identify the individual reading as a kind of 'safety valve' in the topography of collective 'thoughtlessness' while describing the socio-cultural system in reverse order: as the epitome of monadic metabolism. Up to now, the subjective will to expression has mainly concerned itself with the apparent aspects of autonomy from the viewpoint of selfish accumulation embedded in the prevailing system of reproduction. The formation of a subjective ethos is not necessarily a 'geometrical' matter—but it must make possible the construction of an objective contribution in agreement with an organised economy of dialectical consciousness: a project for a strategy which is not so much based on collaborative implosivity as on forms of exchange reflecting a productive (and thus relatively 'tolerant') concretisation of underlying patterns of abstract conflict, rigid as well as elastic or flexible.

13. We cannot avoid taking into consideration that the principle of misery emanating from the 'monstrous' contribution of what might be called meta-manipulated meta-politics is an integral part of the relevant condition of need, for that specific form of socio-cultural practice: an objective 'archive' constructed on the basis of the conscious accumulation of 'scarcity' related to the complex dictatorship of the life process. Thus, with the appropriation of the immediate weakening of the conditions of objectification, the way is now open for much of the ground previously occupied by the regime of fetishism of ideological consumption to be taken over by objectivity invested as an immediate form of textual manipulation, permanently reducing its own

essence of destruction into fragments and sections. Means of objectified privatology may take other means as subject matter as well as their own conditions of organised control, objective forms of independent accumulation, emblematised plasticity of 'existential brushwork', etc.. And the result may be a monad or membrane of total labour: an opaque dialectic embedded in metaphors of 'biological democracy'. If we knew nothing more about the basis of this mode of cultural materialisation than its ambiguously transformative composition, we would not be able to imagine one single feature of intensity or desire-criticism symbiosis which would correspond to this apparently tentative infrastructure as an element of organisation—or, indeed, as an internal matrix for the distribution of discursive 'imperialism'. Reflection of immediate history behind the back of interiorisation of destructive exchange—which is roughly proportionate to the increase of anarchy within the communal body of ideology—may operate in a rather grotesque way. As a potential of conscious alienation or alteration, theoretical abundance now presents itself as implicitly 'primitive': the evolution of its vocabularies is now heading for some Utopian position of 'pre-gastronomic' intercourse. The concrete tragedy-farce framework of practical everyday life is the motive power of consumption as a mental topography (and as a principle of imperialism) and not fit for the investment of any variant of fetishised confidence in the unambiguous analysis of historical relations (as an intellectual structure and a social object this type of analysis gravitates to the condition of farce in an almost organic way). Strictly speaking, the sphere of socio-cultural production of abundance as a point of departure for critical identity is a field of farcical realisation. As the epitome of emancipation from assimilated historical misery of identity, the relevant project must know how to deal with accumulated crises of interest as 'added' forms of motivation (details here are intriguing, but they would take us too far afield).

14. At bottom the cultural value of cerebral ethos in social intercourse is not mediated, not even immediately. Thus, the functionalisation of the accumulated 'schizophrenia' as reinvested in socio-cultural evolution contributes in its own way to the creation of an *obligatory* 'zone of misery' in the general body of discourse. Despite the distraction of a great many vague images, desires, and other cultural impulses, the pseudo-economic mind of meta-modern subjectivity seems persistently to develop what one may call a series or cycle of cathartic insights in its own ideological teratology: not knowing what to do with its own instruments, it fetishises the instruments instead, until the energies of the process of fetishisation are instrumentalised themselves, invested in further research into the construction of new instruments, etc.. The peculiarity of the

accumulated 'identity' thus expresses itself not so much in the concrete field of social productivity, however 'paradoxical' the activity may seem, as it does in the underlying capacity for auto-transfiguration. (This tendency is not attached to the construction of a specific gender.)

15. Access to pathos is, historically speaking, the primary need of ideological reproduction. Today the ambition of overcoming consumption very often remains little more than a rudiment of parody in a condition of late subjectivity. Thus, as objects of realisation, the 'archives' of history have become highly ambiguous: the reading of the exchange value of use value and the reading of the use value of exchange value interpenetrates one another in a way which has in itself become historically ambiguous. The relationship between the liberation of classes and individuals and their respective roles of objectification as hypostatised effects within the area of democratic abstraction constitutes a complex but not unapproachable body of motivation for autonomous consciousness; indeed, this reciprocity of subjective objectivity and objective subjectivity may be historically active in the concrete provocation of pleasurable situations in the condition of meta-modernity. At one moment, the conscious distortion or relative atomisation of objective mythology brings an understanding of opacity closer to the practical relations within the relevant community, at another, this method deepens the consciousness of meta-strategy as an absolutely individual precondition for the productive mediation of 'late-sociality' on the permanent threshold of monosociety—a virtual social cosmos which has already been prefigured in meta-modern iconography, etc.. Our 'hybrid' perspective is broadly a possibility of negation of repressive pseudoproduction and illusion, given that we believe its specific consequence to be a potential stimulus for cultural and social practice in ways that most likely vary from intellectual strategy to political code, and from political code to everyday discourse—in a configurative tension of quasi-utopian sociality-for-itself *vis-à-vis* the radical historical consumption of singular individuals as well as communities.

16. There is no objectification of ideology or mentality that would not change its character radically during the process of historical maximisation; thus, the closure of meta-modern subjectivism turns into an 'integrated playfulness'—an objective space of cultural dialectic in which elitist artistic experience mingle with the dilettantism of gender conflict, among other things. In this context, projections or investments of forms of mystification and demystification are often deemed to be mutually exclusive—

notwithstanding their actual reciprocal assimilation; the paradox exists, however: is not the very same formation of an exclusion-assimilation contradiction yet another 'strategic superficiality' which actually aims at the conscious confusion of the mystified and the demystified with the purpose of stimulating the functional metasubject of implicit equilibrium?

17. It is not only in the realm of external practice or objective maximisation that means and ends must be organised within the framework of a controlled economy of conceptual as well as material elements; discursive speculation itself must be the object of a superior apparatus of internal *ataraxia*, if it is not to consume itself as its own motive power *vis-à-vis* the actual material conditions. Of course, there is a constant relationship, between institutionalised materiality on the one hand and the singular consciousness that the (quasi)orthodox embodiment in question must be appropriated, penetrated, and transcended on the other, but it is a dialectical one; that is to say, it is by no means direct, unambiguous, and consistent. One might say that this reciprocity is basically a *mis-en-scène* in which a stream of highly evocative concepts is disseminated organically in an objective context with 'feminine' undercurrents. The multifarious instrumentalisation of mystification produced by central administration in meta-modern welfare society may thus represent a stage of historical development in which the inertia of deconstructed Social Democrat sensibility has begun to mingle synthetically with 'over-mobilised' subjective material. As a result of its almost quixotic nature, a recuperative endeavour like that seems at one moment to be bound by the dictatorship of absolute entropy, at another to be really capable of expressing some essential resonance of meta-modernity through the register concerned, in a way which not only anticipates historical development, but which may in principle also produce charismatic aspects, perhaps even inscribe these aspects in a utopian framework. Socio-cultural *Formwollen* is always accompanied by functions of parasitical realisation as well as other forms of diminutive investments of power, which, it is true, contribute to the anticipation of future everyday life exchange, but never do so within the conscious framework of full-scale historical redundancy. The widespread assumption that exterior functional abundance has a considerable influence on the result of any life process, indeed on any process in welfare society, seems to call the very basis of motivation into question; ultimately, it makes us admit that the prevailing order of institutional accumulation actually constitutes a 'specific' regime of metamorphous potentiality which—voluntarily or involuntarily—reproduces its own dialectical economy across several levels of consciousness, and thus requires us to re-evaluate our notions of

singular existentiality (thus the only 'leap' which is left, we are told, is the leap into the realm of institutionality, etc.). However, the role of personal ontology as the condition of concrete freedom can no more be identified with endo-institutional processes—'corrupt' or not, and no matter how influential—than it can with any monovalent ideological form.

18. The alienation of the ideals of radical sociality, frequently expressed in a striking loss of general enthusiasm, is a characteristic pattern in the development of subjective preferences, a development which, to a large degree, is a reflection of real historical premises which have already been transformed into society-inherent hierarchies of fetishist dilemma economy: the *mise-en-scène* of these forms of implicit regulation becomes the very logos of social reality. Clearly, critical investment in a community thus feeding unconsciously on the pleasure produced by the friction of its own functional schizophrenia must itself begin in some form of ideological fetishism based on an adequate inscription of its own permanent rotation of exegesis. As primarily a prospectively-oriented means of drastic socio-cultural epiphany, this heuristic strategy is not capable of suggesting archaeological scenarios; thus the historical basis of its own *modus operandi* must be appropriated from other (internally 'parallel' or entirely external) registers of analysis. It is a commonplace that every position of enthusiasm produced in the historical metabolism of the overall socio-cultural apparatus sooner or later necessarily resolves itself into a boring cliché, and every type of knowledge or even virtual component of consciousness changes from hope and power into disorder, ruin, and entropy—increasingly influenced by the maelstrom of historical developments. Indeed, as an ideologically lucrative matrix of mental morphology, this scenario contributes its actually recreational capacity to the surplus optimism of *status quo*. The problem with historical projection lies, indeed, in its being always-already overlaid with a plethora of quasi-charismatic objectifications of presence-absence oscillation— the dead weight of which cannot realistically be estimated by, nor, accordingly, thoroughly assimilated in discursive practice; nor can it simply be reconstructed in some sort of highly complex individually imprinted psychology. Then what, one may ask, is the meaning of historical atomisation, of the prevailing myopia of the institutional gaze (however productive), of the transformation of subjective heuristics into subsumed elements in objective networks of proliferating ideological exegesis—in the context of the ruling subject paradigm? One index of heterogeneity in the realm of objective repression, is not simply that meta-modern society does not necessarily need to create a specific vacuum for its own advanced 'operations of pleasure'; but there is in addition

the fact that the evidently exogeneous deformation of private content is not really incorporated on an objective level in the subjective consciousness of the singular individual. In this historical perspective, the relatively transparent is in a constant process of becoming absolutely opaque, just as the relatively opaque is constantly becoming absolutely transparent—which can be strategically denied but not excluded from the consciousness connected with the corpus of flamboyant ideological mutations that has already been produced.

19. Generally speaking, the concrete clichés which come into existence during the structural process of cultural production rarely shape but nearly always help to consolidate the dictatorship of the concept of art. Only when we become aware of the fact, not only that the objective 'void' between producers, ideology, material products, recipients/consumers, distributive reality, etc., is really a pseudo-otherness, but also that this condition of tragedy/farce–opacity/transparency must be looked upon as the somehow organic result of quasi-formulaic assimilation, can we grasp the spontaneously communicative nature of the process which is taking place: the general appropriation of art as a module for the construction of a labour-free experience of social presence and manipulation. From the point of view of stereotyped invariability having thus reached an historical position of consciousness for itself, socio-cultural inertia acquires a new dimension of crisis; in this context of reproductive necessity, political structure as a virtual meta-subject system must be treated with reservation, if not scepticism. The 'mystique' that has grown up around the subject of meta-modern overdescription makes it necessary to point out that the core of the problem of political investment is not the plasticity of the configurative schemes of discourse, or the advanced complexity of ideological consciousness or the like, but simply the internal maintenance of mechanisms of contribution which have become dependent on fixed ideas of internal contradiction for the maintenance of external (political) necessity. Even though the politicising production of marginal systems as well as other forms of independent development incorporated in the *Gesamtapparat* of equilibrium culture may represent a parody, it should not be assumed that this phenomenon is the expression of historical stigmatisation. If more credibility is produced than consumed, overload in the economy of motivation as well as self-understanding results. The outcome is well-known: the politicised becomes the source of the depoliticised, the sexualised becomes the source of the de-sexualised, the advanced becomes the source of the undeveloped, etc.. In a similar way, however, the real is always embedded in the phantasmal, which is thus capable of becoming the source of material practice: a

pleasure pool of subjective-objective pell-mell bears the seeds of concrete production-construction and destruction-consumption.

20. The now redundant (indeed quasi-metaphysical) functions of emancipation depend, among other things, on a variety of mechanisms at a highly academic level that propel the relevant phantasmal substratum or motive power through the process of objective complication —or at least this is an intriguing, even intoxicating, idea. However, the extent to which the mode of institutional otherness as 'ecstatically' blasted free from its original context of consciousness alters common sense in normal cultural representation (or, for that matter, any meta-model generally capable of stimulating singular 'mental pictures' of desired states of mind) is highly debatable. The mere taking into account and virtual registration of this development, and the mentality produced by it, does not in any sense inscribe the relevant abstraction apparatus in concrete reality; neither does the strategy provide the author process with the necessary means of active contact with patterns of thinking produced in practical social life. Needless to say, the cultivation of this process of distortion in many ways fails to meet the quite substantial needs of (internal) democratic clarification because *in toto* it tends to serve mainly as a component in the sheer generation of aesthetic value—in the form of relatively free-floating modules of abundance for immediate intellectual consumption—rather than contribute to the essential capital of social meta-critique.

21. In its immediate codes our political culture, as real source of general sophistication, always becomes a prison to the realm of our homogeneous consciousness. What seems to have escaped the analysis of the ruling circulation of phantasms of mediation, however, is that the element in the ideological projection which causes this short circuit is not at all imperialistic in an unambiguously 'unilateral' way; indeed, in its various forms of productive self-assimilation, it is the expression of complex, if unconscious, 'cost/benefit' calculations. Since all invested socio-cultural problems are both (in principle) 'farcically' exogenous and 'tragically' vocabulary-inherent, it is necessary to specify in detail how sociality is to be thought of as 'totally compromised' by the inner structure of its own resistance or immunity to itself and the relevant processes of selective erosion—e.g. as represented by specific issues of ecology—etc.. However, this exegesis must first of all appropriate an adequate substratum for its practice of 'transition': the dynamics of radical alienation in its specific relation with Nature's passive, feminine space in the Danish psyche, or other positions similarly overlaid

with collective or idiosyncratic atmospheres or interests, may very well serve as a potent subject or heuristic pool.

22. With variable maximisation in the subjective construction of gender, the interest is directed onto the registers of apathy and pathos as 'complementary' forms of 'normal' discourse, rather than on emotionality in a more 'imaginary' (i.e. 'uncertain') position as an object for 'marginal' author investment. However, to limit oneself to a subjective approach of simple variability, according to which the production of identity is defined as advanced 'creativity', while the objective transcendence of the ruling equilibrium is secondary or exclusively aleatory in relation to subjective maximisation, and to fix cyclic or archaic aspects as unambiguosly privileged, or specifically predetermine the 'ecstatic' value of fetishised apathy-pathos axes, entails a reductionism leading nowhere. Today there is, so to speak, no more retrograde subjective structure of tragedy or, for that matter, 'evil' objective determination to inscribe in common-sensical multiplication or specific life processes, because there is no more a general matrix of transcendence which is able to contain itself as well as the 'aspiring' subjectivity—just as there are no more monads, because there is no more pre-established harmony, one might say.

23. Some authors suggest that the activities of the separate cultural subject who contributes explicitly to the accumulation of persuasive preconceptions in the general sphere of equilibrium may have an implicit aim on a higher structural level—that his or her strategy really pursues the creation of some sort of transformed motivation or will to expression 'within' the (more or less) specific realm of simple reproduction of welfare, somehow reflecting its configurations of laws and ideological prostheses. Evidently, any practice of distortion or annihilation is (and must to a certain extent remain) deeply embedded in the space and time of this meso-stimulative sphere; even the most revolutionising brainstorm would not be able to construct an alternative text or 'scale' with a potential of total metamorphosis. On the one hand, several heterogeneous investments can be joined productively within the implosive borders and registers of the given institution, whilst on the other hand, the too-simple spin-off from a cultural practice that bases itself on some inadequately dialectical idea of messianic infiltration can easily spread out over many otherwise relevant functions as unquestionably impotent over-production. The interchange between individual subtlety and the concept of central administration as more or less autotelic is a constant one, and there has been a considerable, quite empathic—perhaps even conspiratorial—traffic between

the two modes of Nordic superstructure and their respective discursive tensions (for instance, the one may basically consider the other as little more than an exhaust pipe for its own metabolism; an interpretation which, however, implies the notion of a subsuming totality—a principle of complementarity if you like). If we eliminate from the start any notion that the conventions of realistic representation of the perspectives and intensities of late-welfare discourse can be applied mechanically to such complex matters as gender and its reconstruction as a metaphor in the historical process of transforming Social Democrat equilibrium into a heuristic framework of peri-institutional fertility, then we will begin to approach an interesting kind of strategy *vis-à-vis* the hitherto rather ill-defined (anti-)ideological situation. In seeking simultaneously to interiorise and to instrumentalise the necessary premises for the development of an adequate sphere or network of consciousness for concrete cultural labour, one must study the overall socio-cultural context and its historical impetus as regards traditional bias; the integrative redundancy of scenarios of gender must thus be reciprocally motivated through contractual strategies of proliferation along the axes male-female and tragedy-farce. The relevant forms of practice must develop what might be called a (fatal) 'gentlemanly ambiguity' that on one hand expects nothing from the already produced body of criticism and identity in the field of gender—but on the other hand remains in a state of total methodological alertness: *Le hasard ne favorise que les esprits préparés...*

24. In general there is a reluctance to allow that the (male/female) meta-subject of immediate meta-modern social values historically functions somewhat in the same manner as a half-drunk, infantile, or otherwise incompetent agent, who 'transcends' ('deconstructs') the previous great male bourgeois spirit in a synchronicity of emblematic fluctuation (while at the same time having nightmares of not being in control). Actually, the understanding of concrete everyday life is by no means easier than that of abstract Social Democrat equilibrium. Increasingly, the main impression is that it takes a connoisseur to specify the relevant catastrophes of production-consumption, negentropy-entropy, etc.—not to mention the modes of interiorisation of the connected mechanisms of euphoria-dysphoria-aphoria. The evident absence of durable axes (or convincing local morphology) of demonologic-hagiographic intensity is sometimes presented as the tragical mid-point in a socio-cultural typology of farcical forms or matrices of identity, the futile substance of which is invested in a unilinear (i.e., qualitatively monotonous) and exponentially cumulative evolution. In this scenario or situation, female life-cycle stereotypes are transformed into male

eschatology, and *vice versa*, at an increasingly furious pace. A hypothetical space of ultimate sexual terror is created, in which the subject of gender as such becomes the autonomous principle of universal suppression. Fatal anatomy as a source of critical metaphor is pulverised in the tautology of self-fertilisation, subjective tottering and organic pathos are replaced by the objective irony of institutional geometry. Of itself, in itself, as a *Kampfbegriff*, as a stimulus for a method of autonomous production of identity and liberation, gender is reliant upon its own resources in order to develop in the given historical context. Pleasure as 'simple determinant' is, as if experimentally, invested in the general reading of psychological consensus, producing not so much another contribution to the tragedy-farce contradiction (which has become a scheme of almost cosmological dimensions) as a new parasitical imperative in the universe of missing mass that has emerged between the sexes. The ideology of cultural production often involves an incapacity to acknowledge the fact that the necessary process of self-disciplining (vis-à-vis the objective referents of this advanced order of reproductive circulation), necessarily implies the glorification (or smearing) of its own labour as a practical 'truth process' on behalf on some unambiguous Society. Sophisticated cultural production can frequently be seen to adopt an 'oblivious' (not to say ahistorical) view of the Danish welfare model as an ideological field of annihilation, so that the development of public as well as private horizons of identity and pleasure can be predicted, at least in principle, only from present states of that model. (This tendency also applies to the production of advanced interfacial topography provoked by the socio-metaphorical hybridisation of gender, and to the reading of that topography as well.)

25. It does not require much ability of de-paradigmatisation to reveal the strategic inadequacy of simple heterodoxy in a situation in which the principle of *volte-face* has been pragmatically institutionalised as a vector for social organisation on almost every level. Apparently, the regime of personal distance escalated into a full-scale process of objective privatology, is not always governed by some version of escapism or some form of passivity—the 'subjective' trust in the inherent 'repair mechanisms' of the relevant vocabularies notwithstanding. This individual function or process of variable construction, can be seen as a dialectical complex *vis-à-vis* the spectacle of a continuing operational economy of ambiguous critical interest. Some of the basic components of this complex may be formed in a condition of adaptive stress, but most of it follows the specific schizophrenia produced as a kind of reaction to a prevailing sensitivity of recycled evil: an unreliable form of misery.

26. When the strength of demonised parody increases without an increase in consciousness of the displaced fetishist economy implied, the meta-author normally remains in a state of involuntary atomisation of identity (one that might even be 'overshadowed' by canonical specificity). Likewise, what is most significant about the pleasure of making gender opaque or transparent as an object of paradigmatic desire, is the apparently inevitable discursive destruction on a local level which seems to contrast with the idea of an overall surplus ('progress') displayed in other connections (e.g., the concept of the subject replaced by the concept of the body as a more productive hypostasis). Thus, a corpus of analysis which reflects the experienced fluidity of vocabularies and icons must base its self-understanding on a sense of rejection-acceptance dynamics or elegance. However, the strategy must also be ready to 'virtualise' this capacity in a space of monolithic pursuit, immediately if necessary.

Epilogue

GYNOCRAFT; Jul. Bomholt was published in connection with the exhibition of the same name which took place at Overgaden, Kulturministeriets udstillingshus for nutidig kunst (Overgaden neden Vandet 17, K-1414 Copenhagen) in the period 970823-970914. The function of the pamphlet was dual: it was partly to be considered an integrated component in the exhibition, partly meant for independent distribution.

Appendix

HYPERCOMFORT
<u>Plasmic state</u>
Interstellar (postsolar)
Superhot
Nano

COMFORT
<u>Gaseous state</u>
Interplanetary
Hot
Micro

DRY   FREEZING   **WET**
<u>Solid state</u> ←—————— <u>Liquid state</u>
Totalitarian ——————→ Welfare
Cold   MELTING   Lukewarm
Macro   (LIQUIDATION)   (room temperature)
                               Meso

The Photo Gallery

The father and his wife enter a gallery. She asks eagerly about this...? She looks around inquisitively and then at the name printed in large letters on the wall. "Who's exhibition is this? Is it the person whose name is printed on the wall perhaps?" Receiving confirmation that she is right she looks pleased, or rather, she seems pleased at having come up with a question to which she is entitled to an answer. The father nods attentively. They stand in front of the pictures for 15 minutes. When I approach them I listen to their discussion. "Do you understand which part of the body this is? Is it a finger maybe, and a child's neck—a round head from about here to here?" Protests from the wife: "No, it is much too round to be a head." "In this picture at first I saw a pig", the father declares. Then he laughs, embarrassed to show that he is puzzled, yet surprised by his own perception. "Look, here are the nostrils. Up close I saw nothing, but from a distance it is beautiful. Now I can see it is an ear."

Looking at a stack of magazines the father says "What's this lying here?" "These are photography magazines." I say. He picks one up and leafs through it. Stopping, he turns the magazine around towards me and says "In the picture on this page there is an arm, and in this one, on the other page, a bathtub drain with something red looking like blood. Are these two pages supposed to go together?" He wants an explanation. "Yes," I say. I wonder if he has seen the photograph on the previous page of a boy with his finger up another boy's asshole. The latter is holding his erect penis to give the former access. The picture is a close-up of the genitals, hands, and thighs of the two boys. It covers the entire page. I wonder if he is too shy to tackle this with his genuine curiosity. I turn the page revealing this image. "Yes, it is fairly coarse..."

"But..." he is actually startled. "It's strange that they put pictures like this in an art magazine." He momentarily closes the pages to look at the cover. "I mean, this is a serious magazine..." He indicates with his eyes that he expected to see more common ideas of what art is, not pornographic images. "Yes, it is pretty coarse." I repeat, to make it clear that I have seen a lot of this type of work, enough to be opposed to it. I prepare to explain why this is art. I question my sense of duty with regard to explaining what it is I do. If he hadn't asked these questions I wouldn't have bothered to analyse the anus with the finger stuck in it. I would have just compared it to the art of some of my friends. "These pictures, in this context, are very different from photos in a pornographic magazine." I say. "They do not objectify women. Instead they are meant as an artistic discussion of sexuality. They expose the forbidden and dangerous in which some people may recognise themselves. There is a lot of homoerotic art today protesting against common ideas of sexuality and desire as something that should be ignored and repressed. "Yes, yes. Groups who have been..." he nods, aware of the suppression of homosexuals. Then he says, emphatically, "But truly they are into quite new things today." He demonstratively turns a few more pages of the magazine and then looks up at me in an inquiring manner.

This is my chance to disagree with him, I think, to oppose him. My sister so often does that, in a jocular tone, which is the reason for their good relationship. "No, that's not right," I exclaim optimistically, at the same time being overwhelmed by how true it is. "Many people have broken down traditional boundaries of art over the years, they have broken many taboos. The vanguard has been doing this all along. I think of Duchamp, the Dadaists, innovative thinkers, not like this annoying coarse sex-fixated Italian artist (I guess he is Italian, with that name and on top of it that art). "No, no. That was Picasso," he quickly enjoins, to demonstrate that his surprise has left him. He pages further through the magazine and stops at an image of an enormous asshole. He turns to his wife and calls her name encouragingly, eagerly awaiting her reaction.

"Oh my", she says when she sees the picture, very controlled. "But that's an anus. Rather pretty, actually, it doesn't look like that in real life." she says matter-of-factly. "Well, maybe with children", she adds. I say that I believe it's a child, having thought the same thing. When she sees the picture with the finger in the anus she says "You might say it looks like a doctor examining a patient." It turns out that the father, who recently underwent eye surgery, had not seen that it was two men in the photo. This time he keeps his consternation to himself, maybe relieved by his wife's mention of a doctor.

"Oh no, you can clearly see the erect penis he's holding." she says. "But where are his balls?" the father asks. "He's holding them in his hand, there's no doubt about that." his wife replies, pointing. "But it's not quite the way it would be at the doctor's, because he would have been wearing gloves—of course he would have." Having come to the conclusion that the men in the photo are definitely not a doctor and his patient seems to terminate the episode and all interest in the picture. My father's wife turns around, and stares into the middle-distance.

Karl Holmqvist

NO TO COMPETITION AND DIVISIONS

YES TO MORE FOR ALL.

INVESTING IN THE COST EFFICIENCY OF EDUCATING AND CARING FOR ONE'S CITIZENS ALWAYS 'PAYS' BETTER THAN PUNISHMENT AND CONTROL.

BUT WHAT TO DO IF YOUR CHILDREN CLAIM WHAT THEY WANT TO DO IS TO GO TO ART SCHOOL?

WITH A BACKGROUND OF THE KIND OF COMMONSENSICAL AND USEFULNESS ORIENTED CLIMATE OF WHERE I GREW UP IN THE 60S IN SWEDEN THIS WAS ACTUALLY ONE OF THE MORE PROVOCATIVE THINGS YOU COULD DO.

ALWAYS WITH CREATIVE SCANDINAVIAN FOCUS ON DESIGN DEMOCRATIC EXPRESSION AND SOMETHING FOR EVERYONE.

EASY TO UNDERSTAND. ANYWHERE FROM BASIC FAMILY PATTERN CHINA AND CHAIRS YOU CAN SIT ON TO POSTER PAINT EXCLAMATIONS OF WHAT'S RIGHT AND WRONG.

DEVELOPING EVEN TO MORE ADVANCED RESEARCH IN SHAPE AND COLOUR AND THINGS ACTUALLY NOT REALLY PRACTICAL AT ALL.

BUT STILL IT CAN GO ON WHEREAS ANYTHING ASSOCIATED WITH ART VIEWED MORE AS HIGH CULTURE OUTSIDE ORDINARY SOCIETY WILL BE MUCH MORE SUSPICIOUS AND THEREFORE OF COURSE FOR A LOT OF US, ONE OF THE SEXIER THINGS WE COULD EVER THINK OF INVOLVING OURSELVES WITH.

HENRIK HÅKANSSON. HENRIK OLESEN. HENRIK PLENGE JAKOBSEN.
ANNIKA LARSSON. ANNIKA ERIKSSON. ANNIKA STRÖM. ANNIKA VON HAUSSWOLFF.
SUPERFLEX. SUPERFLEX. SUPERFLEX.

MY CONVICTION IS PERSPECTIVES HERE ARE EXTREMELY IMPORTANT IF WE ARE AGAIN DEVELOPING TOWARDS ONE WORLD HELPING EACH OTHER OUT EVERYBODY EQUAL—SINCE THESE WERE THINGS WE WERE BREASTFED WITH SO TO SPEAK AND THEN WHAT HAPPENED? HOW UNDER ANY GIVEN CONDITION IT CANNOT JUST BE ASSUMED THAT EVERYONE WILL BE DOING THEIR BEST.

WITH COMPLICATED PSYCHOLOGICAL MECHANISMS BEHIND DIFFERENT PEOPLE'S DIFFERENT NEEDS WHAT WE HAVE COME TO NOW EVEN IS SOMETHING LIKE A SHIFT.

IT'S

THE THOUGHT

THAT COUNTS

SHOCK FULL

O' NUTS

CHOCOLATE ICE

WHERE POLITICIANS AND BUSINESS PEOPLE 'IN POWER' THE ONES NORMALLY THOUGHT TO MAKE DECISIONS, WORK MORE WITH ILLUSION, HAVING IT LOOK LIKE THEY DO THINGS (RATHER THAN ACTUALLY DOING THEM IN WHICH CASE THEY WOULD RISK FAILURE)—WHEREAS ARTISTS WHO ARE PERCEIVED TO BE ALL ABOUT MAKE-BELIEVE ARE THE ONES WHO ACTUALLY DEAL WITH THE REAL.
WITH THE USE OF REVERSALS OR DIFFERENT TRICKS OF SEDUCTION;
—PRETENDING TO WORK WHEN YOU'RE NOT.
—PRETENDING TO BE SERIOUS WHEN YOU'RE NOT.
—PRETENDING NOT TO CARE WHEN YOU DO.

MOVING IF YOU WILL FROM A ONE-WAY CONSUMERIST POP ART CELEBRATION TO MORE OF A PUNK STANCE OF EVERYONE'S CAPABILITY IN CREATING SOMETHING FROM NOTHING. WORTHWHILE IF NOTHING ELSE FROM SHEER DISPLAY OF ENERGY AND EMOTION.
ENERGY AND EMOTION. VISION AND REALITY. SOLIDARITY.

AND FOR THOSE OF YOU WHO THOUGHT IDEAS OF FREEDOM AND EVERYONE'S EQUAL WORTH SOUND VERY THEN—68 OR EIGHTEENTH CENTURY FRENCH REVOLUTION EVEN. THIS IS WRONG. IT IS VERY NOW. AND IT HAS ONLY JUST BEGUN.
DRUG ADDICT HEAVILY ARMED TEENAGE GUERILLA SOLDIERS IN AFRICA ARE NOT EXAMPLES OF SUCCESFUL CULTURAL EXCHANGE.
SLAVE LABOUR WORK CONDITIONS FOR SUSTAINING ARTIFICIALLY UPHELD MARKET CIRCULATION IS NOT FREE TRADE.
GROWING PRISON POPULATIONS FOR NO REAL REASON IS WHAT BREEDS VIOLENCE—SEE THINGS BOTH WAYS ALWAYS AND REALLY YOU WILL SEE MORE.

GIVING WILL

GIVE YOU MORE.

A SMILE

WILL KEEP ME

WARM.

Definitely Boxing Day—a pocket play

INTRO: THE POCKET THEATRE

The Pocket Theatre was first conceived by Thorvaldur Thorsteinsson, artist and writer, in 1989. It began incidentally one day when the artist realised that he had forgotten an appointment he had with several actors at a studio. He also discovered that he did not have enough material for the appointment. As a result, he sat down and spontaneously wrote some texts for video work.

Two years later, Thorvaldur was asked to continue with this work on a weekly basis for the National Broadcasting Company, Ras 2, in Iceland. A fellow Icelandic artist and writer, Hallgrimur Helgason had seen Thorvaldur's work at an exhibition and encouraged Thorvaldur to continue with similar work for radio. Subsequently, Thorvaldur wrote a series of short plays for radio that were broadcast weekly for a whole year, obtaining the name Pocket Theatre only a few minutes before the first broadcasting.

The Pocket Theatre playlets vary in form and structure. Some of them are devised as simple dialogues, others are merely fantasies, only to be understood by the reader and impossible to put on stage. The only thing they have in common is their length, one to two minutes in performance.

Before Christmas 1992, a collection of the Pocket Theatre playlets, under the name *Angel in the Audience*, was published by the Bjartur Publishing Company. The book soon became a cult among Icelandic performance artists, writers and theatre people.

Recently, the Pocket Theatre has increasingly been seen on television as well as on the stages of larger theatres in Iceland. Thorvaldur has used the playlets as an inspiration in several of his theatre pieces and always keeps the collection *Angel in the Audience* in his pocket.

Definitely Boxing Day
(or One of Those Things)

The skit is set in a fast food restaurant. Hulda and her friend come in and place some plastic bags on the floor next to a table, then drape their coats carefully across a chair. The friend goes to the counter and places an order. Hulda sits down and looks around. She fiddles with her hair a bit, looks at the mirror wall and greets a man who is sitting at the next table with the kind of smile that suggests that she's not sure if she knows him or not. The friend comes back with chicken and fries, sits down and looks around. She also fiddles with her hair a bit and then they begin.

Hulda: This place isn't bad. Not bad at all, considering.

The friend: It's all right. The bathrooms are clean.

Hulda: That makes such a huge difference.

The friend: God, yes. So—you were starting to tell me about the dress. Right—so you hardly had the guts to try it on?

Hulda: Oh my God. It was to die for. Totally to die for. I knew that if I couldn't fit into it I would die on the spot.

And I would be ready to die.

I'd be really into it.

I'd be really into anything, for that matter.

Like digging my outstretched fingers into something hot.

Something hot and quick that would go insane with the pain.

And would choke.

And would try to bite.

I thought I told you not to bite.

I'm going to have to punish you now, I'm afraid.

I'm afraid you're going to have to be punished.

The friend: That's excellent. I mean, obviously you didn't need to worry—you must have known that you'd fit into it. So are you going to wear it?

Hulda: Yeah, I've been thinking I should wear it to the dance but Jesus, what the hell am I doing here, I mean one more ounce and I won't fit into it. You'll have to finish my fries. I just can't bear the thought of not fitting into it on the day of the dance.

I'd go berserk.

And then I'd be an animal of some kind.

And you would be my trainer.

You would show up unexpectedly and I'd go crazy with fear.

I'd get to be an endangered species.

I'd get to be a hunted prey waiting impatiently for your trap.

And you couldn't stand the wait. So once again I'd let you do it.

But you wouldn't be satisfied with just a tiny nibble. And you would say that it was OK for me to bite. That I should try to bite.

But I wouldn't bite just to make you more excited, I would lose myself in watching the juice run down your chin when you tried and tried to swallow so that you wouldn't have to answer with your mouth full because I'm asking you if you've done all your Christmas shopping.

The friend: Oh, God no! I haven't bought anything for the kids. Or the trouser press for Ingi.

Hulda: Well that doesn't count with you because you're so damn pragmatic. You and Ingi should definitely come over around Christmas—Baldur would love it. We'll have to get together soon, the four of us. Have a drink and relax and paint the town red or something.

The friend: Oh, definitely. Maybe Boxing Day. There's never anything on TV then, anyway.

Hulda: You can say that again.

The friend: And then we'll have another. And Ingi will watch. No. He tapes everything. But you'll never find out because you're both blind and deaf, remember? You're a little kitten, Hulda, and you don't know anything, you don't have a clue about what's going on until I'm holding you down in the bucket and only then do you show a sign of life, when you start struggling in the bucket. And Ingi and Baldur tape the whole thing.

Hulda: Yes, you'll definitely have to come over on Boxing Day.

The friend: And I pretend I'm going to save you by pouring the water out but you don't see that I've got a smirk on my face and I wink at Ingi and all I do is tip the bucket and take a little sip—just to find out what a drowning kitten tastes like. What do you think?

Hulda: You know, it's not bad. But then again I use milk. So that's a bit different.

The friend: You never know. Last time I was here it was completely undrinkable. It was then that I resolved never to come here again. But—the things we do for our friends. (She laughs).

Hulda: The thing is that everything here is so below standard. And then they just keep banning more and more things, like the import of meat for instance, and then there are all those restrictions and things, and haha, I don't know.

The friend: No, I don't know.

Hulda: It's just one of those things.

The Art of Communities

In a world of uncertainties the workplace is a camping-site, where you go every now and then... hard training and chemical stimulants prevent you from falling down, at least for a while... and in that world capital is no longer linked to work or the worker. The only thing capital is linked to is the consumer and this relationship lasts only as long as the consumer has credit.

Mikko Heikka[1]

The notion of the workplace as a camping-site requires from the individual a constant capacity for change in relation to the prevailing conditions of this 'site'. Or does the camping-site perhaps mean a homogenous society, where one set of linguistic and cultural values prevails? The rules of capitalism enclose cultural, racial and linguistic differences. Soon we won't be able to tell them apart.

Difference is always a potential threat. You can be set apart because of your difference, but then if you stand out of the crowd because of your difference you are already set apart. The poor, the young, foreigners and many other groups and individuals can feel cast aside for various reasons. Difference prevents us from understanding the 'other's language', and this is when communication doesn't work. One who is different is exceedingly aware of his difference from others, and the 'prison of freedom' it creates. Being segregated causes hate against the segregator.

Julia Kristeva and Zygmund Bauman have both dealt with the issue of foreignness, a self-asserted complete freedom, which signifies loneliness and indifference. Bauman says that loneliness is the price paid for privacy. He also speaks of the individual's duty to his fellow men, and how we can completely and indifferently ignore this moral notion in modern urban culture.[2] Finnish law has a paragraph about abandonment and the ensuing punishment. This means that a fellow man should not be left in a life-threatening situation. And yet this happens all the time.

I think some of the best and worst aspects of the Nordic welfare state are the State's simultaneous responsibility and irresponsibility of its citizens. The emphasis on individuality is strong here on the traditional Finnish concept of "The peat-bog, the shovel and the man"—that is to say that we create and forge our own identity as we want to, how we want to. Our Lutheran religion doesn't recognise the sacrament of confession and atonement. We have to suffer as individuals within our own body. The responsibility of family and friends can be next to nothing, because everyone needs to grow up and manage on their own. If this doesn't happen, the structures of society are there to help and mould—in theory at least. But if someone, the family or the community, hasn't cared for and/or loved that person, where will he or she ever learn it? Ever learn to care and love themselves, and for themselves? How can the social structures of society teach us to care, share and feel responsibility for other people? As an artist I am interested in people and their social surroundings. In my work I am drawn to the relationships people have with each other in their shared, social surroundings: a person and his or her presence as a part of the work of art as a participant, a producer and a spectator. I give people the chance to voice their opinions. The most important facet of my work is an ethical and moral questioning. My way of observing people is perhaps more psychological than sociological, though the social remains central. The mediation between individual and community, 'insiderism' and foreigness is a constant process.

"Community art"—process art—means accepting a continuing incompleteness in one's work and life; living in a phase, a chain, a part of a part.[3] The spectator of the artwork constructs, classifies and deconstructs the work, and like life this is a continuous process, a series of successes and failures. It is important to get a grip on life, to feel that you are living this life on your own terms—you have to accept this continuum of unfinishedness, incompleteness. You cannot control life, it controls you; even if humans—individually and communially—struggle for determination and control.

In my work *Free Breakfast*, spanning from May to October 1994, I served free breakfast in a former retail outlet in Hakaniemi, Helsinki. (Hakaniemi is a neighbourhood that functions as a gate to the old working class part of Helsinki, namely Kallio.) The place was an open place of meeting and gathering, where passers-by and local inhabitants chatted and exchanged ideas. I photographed, interviewed and videotaped the area and my clients, and then presented the final work in the same place, a familiar place to all involved. From 1996 onwards, in my current 'workspace', the gallery-space Push firma beige, I have functioned as a mediator between art and the local community. I seek new channels and ways to present my 'acts of art'. This space is an old store, a retail outlet. I use this kind of space for presentation, education, exhibition and work, making my method of work public, presenting it openly to the community.

In my latest pieces I have approached the local community through the means of theatre, a living present-tense performance. I have laid out the ground for street theatre, providing it with borders that make it a physical space. I have always been slightly envious of theatre—the way it reaches people and makes them aware of the ineluctable modality of the visible. With others involved in theatre, I created a series of events which were staged on street corners in the working class area of Kallio. These in themselves did not differ that much from the normal life of the street. Furthermore, they adapted to their surroundings, creating a sense of place: the streets (and their people).

The piece *My Home is the Street and it is my Stage* was a series in four parts. Firstly, a video that tells of Kallio and life there. Second, two gourmet meals—lunch and dinner—were served to three random passers-by on the corner of the streets Fleminginkatu and Helsinginkatu. One during the day, and one at night. The situation evolved according to the people, a "theatre" was not required, because it was already there. The street was the stage. Third, discussions and writings: local people were asked to write down their thoughts, which were made into plaques and were later moved and presented in the windows of Push firma beige. This part of the piece also included conversations by megaphone on the street between the actors Jukka Aaltonen and Anssi Pirttineva. The actors conversed in the metro at 6 AM in the morning, on Helsinginkatu at 6 PM, in the bars at night, reading the statements that the local people had written. And, finally, an action, where I lived as a bag-lady on the street, hanging out and observing everyday life.

When I moved to Helsinki at the beginning of the 80s I was shocked by the homeless people on the streets of Kallio. I didn't know what to do. I felt completely powerless. I would feel very bad in the evenings, as I had passed these derelicts during the day without helping them. I wondered if I should just learn to accept it, say to myself "Okay, they are lying there, I have to get used to it, they won't go away" or whether I should I take responsibility. I really wrestled with these issues. Then my instinct of self-preservation made me avoid those situations because they frightened me. Nowadays I have learned to pass by and not even notice that I do. Others do, too. This, I think is the truly frightening aspect of this situation.

Unconsciously those memories of my youth, the helplessness and frailty of the human condition, still go on living inside of me. This is the experience I try to mediate in my community works, in an attempt to get closer to people. The changed and changing society, relations to the other and to otherness have estranged us from one another, and from certain human values. Are we perhaps becoming strangers to each other and ourselves as in the name of Julia Kristeva's famous book? Can we do anything about it, can we change ourselves? Can we change?

In the middle of all this unfinished business I continue my artwork, which is always incomplete. It will always be definitely unfinished, and in an ongoing relationship to its surroundings, in constant motion and dialogue. I wonder about *you*—you who are so important to me. So far away, yet so close. You, another person, a stranger, an other, unknown and infinitely interesting, where are you going, how are you doing?

Please tell me more about yourself, I'll be listening!

Greetings,
Minna Heikinaho
Push firma beige
Helsinginkatu 23 B
00510 Helsinki 51, Finland
te. +358-(0)50-5215724
email: minnah@mhaho.pp.fi

Notes

1. Mikko Heikka, *Suomen Kuvalehti*, 21 June 2001, pp. 25-26.

2. See Julia Kristeva, *Strangers to Ourselves*, New York: Columbia University Press, 1991, and Zygmund Bauman, *The Individualized Society*, Oxford: Polity Press, 2000 and *Community*, London: Blackwell, 2001.

3. Olli Tiuranen has termed my artistic method as "Community art", and described it thus: "Community art is action in connection with the surroundings and the people that are a part of it, the inclusion of people into the artistic process. People can be part of the work or they themselves can be the makers. Community art brings up questions based in daily life through the means of art, provides a channel for the expression of the ideas and values of people through works of art...", *Kide*, University of Lapland Newsletter, June 2000.

translated by Jean Ramsey

—In the Social Democratic Welfare State the role of the artist is not so much that of an outsider, as in other liberal Western societies, even though that is what many active artists would like to believe. Thus, arguments and discussions on the different scenes can often more or less specifically refer to the artist as "he who stands outside" (and he is indeed always still a 'he') in spite of the fact that it doesn't take more than a glance at the dimensions of public funding of the arts to realise, that if it is an 'outside' it is, certainly, not an economic one.

—Looking at the political system today, it is interesting how the—quite large— amounts of money spent on art is justified politically. Here, we find the articulation of the artist as a model citizen. And even more interesting—perhaps indicating the way Social Democracy is developing — this articulation of the artist is found not only in contemporary politics, but also in market research predictions for the model consumer of the future: the artist as the emblematic subject who is not only 'free' and creative, but who's occupation it is to constantly produce his own subjectivity, again and again, in ever changing forms and manners.

—Ironically, the articulation of the classic 'free will' of the quintessential liberal individual has been appropriated by social democratic rhetorics in which the 'freedom' incarnated by the artist-subject seems to symbolise a guarantee that in our society even the 'freest of spirits'—he who distances himself as far as possible from society—will be supported, represented and understood. The artist seems to act as indicator for the degree of freedom in Scandinavian society, and as such the more the artist refuses society—as the traditional role of the artist—the more he affirms it.

—'Repressional tolerance' is not, surprisingly, an often used term when efforts are made in order to reflect the complex relationship between art, representation and our ideological framework. It is a tolerance that principally encompasses all art, but 'art' understood as 'that which signifies freedom'. And it is often the context of art rather than its content that is understood and reified.

The Name Game

A recurrent objective in many artists' writings is the establishment of a vocabulary. To find ways in which to talk about art. When describing the art works themselves, one often uses the term 'artistic language', somehow designating a particular, coded order, a syntax and a manner of speech. When writing, then, artists are creating a language around or about a language, that can be read as either as a parallel language, a meta-language and/or a master narrative. The act of writing situates both work and writer, but also reflects on the use and construction of (a) language. This performative aspect of language, however, also has a political potential, regarding the position and function of the author, his or her agency and mode(s) of address. In writing about artists' writings, Brian Wallis has argued for a shift in the perception of such author-positions, from the privileged, authentic subject of the artist to a notion of the artist as site, or "a particular cultural position", as he puts it.[1] Drawing upon both Walter Benjamin's theory of the storyteller and Gilles Deleuze and Felix Guattari's theory of a 'minor' language, Wallis situates the writing artist in an author-position that is at once marginal and authoritative. When writing in a smaller, if not minor, language, such as the Scandinavian, Finnish and Baltic languages, such concerns are always present, if not pressing.

Taking on the position of author naturally involves an act of self-definition, or *naming*. One designates the writing subject and its agencies. This not only an authoritative act, but, of course, also a marginal and sometimes subversive one: one takes on a name, a position, but also responds to and/or negates names given and assumed—be they 'Nordic' and/or 'normal' and/or 'artist', but also 'man' or 'woman', 'straight' or 'queer'. Such designations are both violating and empowering, depending on the position from which, and the context in which, they are formulated and directed. To be called names is usually very unpleasant, whereas taking on a name tag can be an act of defiance: "the address constitutes a being within the possible circuit of recognition and, accordingly, outside of it, in abjection", as Judith Butler has formulated it.[2] According to Butler, the act of naming and being named exists in a circuit of recognition(s), in which the act of name calling not only makes one recognised, but also *recognisable* (as subject and/or object). This also means, however, that language is active, performative, and that designations can thus be negotiated, negated, circumvented and recoded

In the first text of this chapter, "Plan 01" by Søren Andreasen, we are presented with an effort to change the designation 'artist'. Andreasen wants to reformulate this historical subject, open it wide to other modes of production than objects of art. He sees this subject, rather, as a machine that produce more than merely more ego. In her essay, "On Designations (Notes for Strategies)", Sara Jordenö discuss the problems of labelling, how her own practice and identity are labelled when and if she employs certain artistic and theoretical discourses. She argues, that taking on a name as 'woman', 'feminist' or 'queer' artist also places one in a ghetto, in a certain category through which her practice is read, and which, in turn, excludes all other readings. Therefore, the formulation of praxis must also happen in a act of constant renegotiation and never remain fixed and designated.

Beathe C Rønning's text is an example of talking back at designations. In "A Young Lady Protests", Rønning offers a comment for a newspaper, criticising the title of an exhibition to which she was invited. The exhibition showed four women artists, but grouped together under the derogatory heading of "Ladies", which in Scandinavian languages is used somewhat differently than the translation reveals; "lady" is not an indication of class, but rather a designation of a helpless, sexless woman. Another attempt to avoid, or redirect, designations and given names can be read in Michael Elmgreen and Ingar Dragset's essay "The Roundabout of Binary Oppositions—A description of the 'I'm a man because I'm not a woman' syndrome", where binary relations articulated in language are discussed as defining identity through a process of exclusion: if not one, then the other. Instead, they argue for a subversion of the signs for masculinity through art practice. These binaries within language are also discussed and artistically transformed in Kirstine Roepstorff's text "All Wrapped Up: Synonyms and Oppositions", where the assumption of power and abuse of power, the therapeutic and terror are mirrored, if not merged.

In the text "White Cube or White Queue?" Khaled Ramadan argues that local art institutions only allow non-Western artists as emblems; as signs for the tolerance and openness of the institution, rather than due to actual interest in the discourses these artists might engage with. Thus, these artists' practices are reduced to serving the institutional authority, as exemplified by the white cube. He points at a double standard, and suggests a literal reading of the classic notion of the "White Cube" to show how context still, against intentions, comes to play an important role—though it is a role of negation and Othering, rather than one of inclusion. On the other hand, Gunnar Krantz takes on an outsider postion, willfully and strategically, and designates himself "the political artist". From here, he shows how utterance in itself is not enough, but how the context and the system in which this utterance is active gives it its meaning. Thus, to criticise a system or to make ones voice heard against it, necessarily takes sacrifices. A counter-language can (hopefully) have real affects, but never without real costs.

Notes

1. Brian Wallis, "Telling Stories: A Fictional Approach to Artists' Writings", Wallis, ed., *Blasted Allegories—An Anthology of Writings by Contemporary Artists*, Cambridge, MA: MIT Press, 1987, p.xiii.

2. Judith Butler, *Excitable Speech—A Politics of the Performative*, London: Routledge, 1997, p. 5.

A long term contribution in preparation for establishing art's structure (art's control systems) is based upon conceptions and programmes which are motivated with respect to art as it appears and functions in the world. The work is propelled by the conviction that if there is anything *whatsoever* that's going to happen—if anything's going to happen with the prevailing order for the production, distribution and administration of art, then the system that calls itself 'artists' has to restructure itself.

The system that calls itself 'artists' will have to come up with something other than the ego-system which is the prevailing configuration of art's productive force. The productive forces are structured as separate equilibrium-modules within this world. People are going to have to imagine all other kinds of things.

An ego-system is a fragment of consciousness with homogeneous interaction between appetite and reason—a self-absorbed circulation, the apotheosis of which is the consumate auto-oscillation (harmony). One has to ask oneself *what* else and *how* something else can take place. (And it truly must be the structure of the ego-system, and not its appearance and function, that has to be treated. The fact that several individuals, for instance, organise themselves as one single system does not automatically entail a radically altered structure, rather it is often a matter of constructing superego systems whose structure remains the same.)

A long-term contribution in relation to art's control systems must thus base itself on a constant and continuous self-structuring. (Which does not have anything to do with self-organisation: the do-it-yourself administration of productive forces pertains to autonomy and super-structure—the self-structuring pertains to the establishment of basis). And on notions of being able to structure oneself beyond any conception of productive force. Again and again and again.

Previously published in Øjeblikket—Magazine for Visual Cultures, no. 41, vol. 9, Fall 1999.

translated by Dan A Marmorstein

ILLUSTRATIONS: SØREN ANDREASEN

On Designations (Notes for Strategies)

One of the contexts in which I have found myself—and in which I am to some extent still involved—is feminist activism. Actually I have always hesitated to categorise myself as a feminist or queer artist. It has always seemed problematic for me to place myself in a feminist and/or queer artistic context as it has been unclear to me what this might involve. If one compares artistic work to the production of texts, that is, to a form of writing, one can also, with Judith Butler, compare it to or call it politics:

> *If the political task is to show that theory is never merely theoria, in the sense of disengaged contemplation, and to insist that it is fully political (phronesis or even praxis), then why not simply call this operation politics or some necessary permutation of it?* [1]

A name always seems to be, to some extent, misleading. A name, like a subject, is subject to constant renegotiation and reformulation, and is, always, dependent on its context. Consequently, 'feminist' and/or 'queer' art has the potential to gain different meanings over time. To cultivate a feminist/queer practice in 2001 of course means something different from—but nevertheless refers to—a feminist artistic practice in the 70s. This is equally true, according to Butler, of subject-formation. Just as it is impossible to do full justice to one's name, having gender is like a task that can never be completely carried through. Heterosexuality, thinks Butler, operates in a similar way. Although one can speak with justification of a heterosexual norm, and say that a certain kind of heterosexual constellation is privileged in our society, a constant repetition is nevertheless required; an asserting, legitimising, naming of this practice ("I pronounce you man and wife"), which undermines its status as stable and naturally given. Judith Butler describes this as a 'citation', which still always remains incomplete

> *... the impossibility of a full recognition, that is, of ever fully inhabiting the name by which one's social identity is inaugurated and mobilised, implies the instability and incompleteness of subject-formation. The "I" is thus a citation of the place of the "I" in speech, where that place has a certain priority and anonymity to the life it animates: it is the historically revisable possibility of a name that precedes and exceeds me, but without which I cannot speak.* [2]

Although queer theory has recently been established as an academic subject in Sweden, its influence on feminist theory and cultural and critical studies has been exerted for a longer period. The political progress in the struggle for homosexual rights in Sweden was considerable in the 90s, although real social impact has been less than one might wish. One can see for example how the Partnership Act, a cosmetic sort of law which permits homosexuals to establish marital ties, had a relatively quick affect, while the right to adoption and insemination as well as more complete legal protection against homophobic violence has not yet been statuted. However, an extensive and very visible debate has recently developed about and around gender identities in academic contexts, as in the media.

In the 90s this permissive tendency had an impact on the curation of contemporary art exhibitions, alongside a growing interest in identity politics, the exposure of subcultures and private confessions. In major group exhibitions there often seems to be a sort of quota system where a few places are reserved for marginalised groups like 'gay' or 'feminist' artists (as well as for artists with a non-Western national/cultural background). The criteria for obtaining these specific places always seems to be associated with an artist's personal identity and characteristics, while this does not seem to apply to those places reserved for (for instance) someone with a conventional painting practice. In other words, the artist whose art is singled out as representative of a marginalised group or subculture is also assumed to be active in his or her private life in this subculture. In such cases the boundaries between art and private life become blurred.

As we know, rendering something invisible is an effective tool in the exercise of power. The exclusion of women from art degree courses and art exhibitions has long been an issue for feminists. Statistics were used to criticise the institutions in question, showing how the 'objective' selection of participants, with few exceptions, always seemed to favour white, Western males. (Feminists like Mary Kelly, Laura Mulvey and Juliet Mitchell turned in the 1970s to a psychoanalytical model to understand the unconscious choices underlying such an alleged 'objectivity'.)

From a situation where marginalised groups in society, as well as in art, were almost obliterated, there now seems to be a certain visibility and space for these groups. But this space also creates a need that is expected to be met. The question is: with what? What should my artistic strategies be in the climate that prevails now, if I were to succeed in defining it? How does an artistic practice relate to a political one in the special case constituted by queer feminism?

An exhibition takes place, Mary Kelly points out in her essay "Re-Viewing Modernist Criticism", in an architectural space or place, over a certain period of time, in a certain constellation, a structure, with all the codes this involves.[3] It is a meaning-creating system, a discourse. A work of art is thus never autonomous, but exists in relation to the text or texts constituted by the exhibition and its related publications: the exhibition catalogue, the art book, the periodical. These texts, to some extent, fix the fluid meaning, organise it, name it.

When Judith Butler writes in an anthology of queer theory, she describes this (the writing) as taking a risk:

> One risk I take is to be recolonized by the (lesbian) sign under which I write, and so it is this risk I seek to thematize. To propose that the invocation of identity is always a risk does not imply that resistance to it is always or only symptomatic of a self-inflicted homophobia. Indeed, a Foucauldian perspective might argue that the affirmation of "homosexuality" is itself an extension of a homophobic discourse. And yet "discourse", he writes on the same page, "can be both an instrument and an effect of power, but also a hindrance, a stumbling-block, a point of resistance and a starting point of an opposing strategy." [4]

Butler described coming out, naming oneself, becoming visible, as producing a new and different 'closet'. To name one's art as 'queer' or 'feminist' thus seems, paradoxically enough, to involve becoming fixed as 'the other' in a binary structure. The perverse (in the sense of "that which is against (the law of) the father") and the normal are in fact two sides of the same coin where the one is irrevocably affected by the other.

As an artist I am always exposed to curatorial practice as well as art-market demands, which govern access to my public and the way my artistic products are consumed and understood. How is my work affected by being designated 'feminist' or categorised as 'queer' in an exhibition context? Is this special form of naming practice particularly problematical for a queer artist? Furthermore, *who* exactly is represented *in which sense* of the concept queer? What kind of exclusion has taken place?

In the aftermath of identity politics in the 90s one can presumably argue that a policy and a curatorial practice that dissolves the category of gender is a more fruitful strategy. Many women artists have, furthermore, strategically avoided participation in group exhibitions with women only, or with feminist themes and designations, as a strategy for avoiding marginalisation and inscribing themselves in the same 'objective' space as male artists. I can respect such strategies, since they resemble my own, in their attempt to at least partly take control of one's own name, one's own subjective practice. But one thing that is perhaps neglected in such strategies, is the gender determination that already exists in this context, not least in the name *konstnär* (artist). After all it is impossible for it to be a neutral term. 50 years ago, because of my biological sex, I would still have been called *konstnärinna* (woman artist) in Swedish. That name seems in some way derogatory in a contemporary context. What does it mean that I grammatically choose the masculine form of the word *konstnär*? How strong does the myth of (male, white) genius remain and what is my place in relation to it?

To return to the the issue of politics and theory with which I started; whether all art, all writing, any kind of statement, must—even in a so-called 'apolitical' practice—still be designated as political. The marginalisation of a queer feminist practice as subjective and/or tied to a political movement indicates a repression of the knowledge that an artistic or curatorial practice can never be objective. To call oneself an artist does not mean to be gender neutral. Such neutrality is an impossibility in a designating context such as an art exhibition. I therefore consider it necessary, as the beginning of a strategy, to avoid naming myself in relation to myself, but nevertheless to always do so in relation to the context in which I participate. This must entail an artistic practice in constant renegotiation, constant repositioning, constant motion in relation to the spaces—physical as well as mental—where it is permitted to exist.

Notes

1. Judith Butler, "Imitation and Gender insubordination", Abelove, Barale, Halperin, eds., *The Lesbian and Gay Studies Reader*, London: Routledge, 1993, p.308.

2. Judith Butler, "Critically Queer", *GLQ*, no. 1, 1993, pp. 17–18.

3. Mary Kelly, "Re-viewing Modernist Criticism", *Imaging Desire*, Cambridge, MA: MIT Press, 1996.

4. Butler, "Imitation", p.308.

translated by James Manley

Beathe C Rønning is a visual artist, living and working in Copenhagen. In December 1999, she was exhibiting at Hordaland Kunstsenter together with Eline McGeorge and Elisabeth Gilje. HKS insisted on—against her explicit will—calling the exhibition "Young Ladies". In this feature article Rønning explains why this title for a show was unacceptable in 1999.

What is the significance of presenting an exhibition of three women artists, all in their 30s, and calling it *Young Ladies*?

"And what can I do for you, young lady?" are the gracious words one might hear from an elderly shop assistant. It reminds us of the friendly form of address characteristic of the 1950s (when courtesy was still a feature of everyday public life), a period which, in retrospect, seems so innocent and straightforward; so cute in its tight-fitting skirts.

The comical side of the 50s has been plundered and played up by artists of all genres. Especially during the early 90s, there emerged a host of satirical films, radio and TV comedies parodying the hurried voice of the 50s news commentator. Somewhat later we were inundated by 50s postcards of the kind showing a housewife in her kitchen displaying a huge watermelon to a visitor, saying, "I thought I was pregnant, but it was just a watermelon." It was all so amusing. And relatively harmless.

The image of the housewife in the kitchen, dad relaxing in an armchair with pipe and paper, the eight year old son in a sweater sprawling on the floor with his train set, and the nearly teenage daughter sitting on the sofa with some delicate but demanding embroidery—it was Christmas all year round, and all arranged by mum.

In the early 90s we thought we had moved on and that it was therefore fine to joke about the values represented by this version of the 1950s. The stereotyped images of these identities were absurd and cute in their naïve belief that they were edifying. And the texts! "Here's how to make your housekeeping go further—and without your husband noticing any difference in quality." Especially those of us who were born later and who experienced this period as neither children nor adults have allowed ourselves a laugh at its expense. To think that a woman's aim in life should be to save for nylon stockings by cutting the meat cakes with millet—furtively, in the safety of her kitchen. Or to beguile her husband into believing an idea came from him so as to get it accepted. That sort of thing.

The woman of the 50s worked behind the scenes (something we must love her for; after all she is our mother). One spoke of pursuits, whether referring to writing or darning socks. Pursuits, as something to keep the hands busy, or to kill a moment of inactivity. Those were the days. Women knew how to turn their boys into men—by playing inferior and belittling anything they themselves did as 'pursuits'. My Danish colleague, Mette Gamst, succinctly captured the attitude in the title of her mid-90s exhibition: *A Young Lady's Pursuits in the Meantime.*

The theme was the surprise and pain of having one's analytical, intellectual abilities and one's artistic sensibility dismissed as hysteria (what a chatterbox!). Men found it difficult to identify with her art. Women are women, men are people.

We all know that art can be iconoclastic and that it can build identity. Women artists who work in the field of identity building and who at the same time assert their rights as both women and artists often experience the same thing; the combination of the old, unarticulated ideal of the quietly working woman (for the female artist) and the fact that men cannot relate to her work, create a tension which isn't always dynamic and edifying.

This doesn't imply that women's art should seek to evade criticism, nor that men are bastards. It merely goes to show that in the late 90s we are still waist-deep in the old mythology. For as long as we feel as we did in the 50s but without facing up to it, we will fail to move on. In specific terms this means we are still faced with big challenges concerning how we evaluate the quality of an art work, and the concepts we use to do so.

As an example, I can quote Lars Bukdahl's criticism of a woman author's most recent publication. The example is from the latest issue of the Danish highbrow newspaper *Weekendavisen*: "Banalities; excuse me, but is not B A simply a boring old lady lyricist...?" The headline was "Lavender Aesthetics". The sad thing about this is that we all know precisely what he's getting at; something toothless, soft and trite, that lacks a clear, artistic subject. Something without edge. I do not want to debate the critique as such; I haven't read the book. But lady lyrics? Lavender aesthetics?

In other words, the prefix 'lady' ('dame' in Norwegian and Danish) suggests toothlessness and a lack of identity. And is lavender a probable perfume for cultural rebels? Hardly! Certainly, it would never be a man's perfume of choice. So once again we face a situation where 'lady' or 'woman', at least as a prefix, denotes a lack of quality.

We really believed this kind of thing belonged to the past and we could now lean back in our office chairs behind piles of equal opinions, gently joking about an amusing, bygone era. Real satire or irony it never was. Satire hurts, it releases the collectively unspoken in a sudden burst of laughter. It requires precision, incisive timing and thorough familiarity with the field of concern. Humour is no joke.

I can already envisage *B A*'s journalist uninspiredly plodding up the stairs for a preview of the exhibition, and starting the interview as follows: "Well... so what's this young lady's pursuit?" or the headline of *Bergens Tidende*'s modest presentation: "Young Ladies at HKS". Journalists work under pressure and take what they get—if they come at all. I only came because I didn't get to cover the gnomes' Christmas parade down on Main Street. What could such an exhibition tell me that I didn't already know? "Young Ladies"? Must be something cosy, a needlework type of thing. Some wishy-washy coquetry young ladies pass their time with. Perhaps it should appear in the section on Ideas for Christmas Gifts.

Personally it doesn't trouble me when an elderly gentleman addresses me as "young lady". I will happily curtsey, and give him girlish good behaviour, so long as he keeps to the rules of the politeness game. This doesn't mean I take him seriously, but rather I act out a simple charade, and forgive him for being outmoded. In this way we avoid having to get to know each other, or otherwise being confronted with the realities of 1999. An old man can be pleasant company, but I wouldn't explain to him why I think the Norwegian word for cunt, *fitte*, ought to be upgraded, since it stems from the Old Norse "humid shoreline".

On the other hand, my work as an artist and swayer of opinions is something I take dead seriously. It's the only way I can make good art. I go all out at every attempt, and the stakes are high. Anything else would be an insult to a public that still sees art as a valuable, culturally creative activity (not only of a handicraft kind). If she is to express something that has not yet been expressed, the artist is obliged to break new ground. At one end or the other. This involves risks. And these risks are something the artist takes on behalf of others.

A postmodern society does not mean a society *without* demands, but a society with *other* demands. An exhibition title provides access to the exhibition itself. I have repeatedly expressed my aversion to the title *Young Ladies*. Each time I was told in unequivocal terms that it was only a working title. When I started to fear that it would creep into the real exhibition concept, I called by phone to clarify my objections.

Four weeks before the opening, I heard that invitation cards were being printed with the striking, poetical, political, hilarious and precise words "Young Ladies". My first impulse was to produce my own invitation cards, at my own expense and in my own time, but this would not have prevented the label "Young Ladies" from sticking to my project. It produces returns as an Internet searchword, it will be printed on posters, and the journalists probably don't care who is for and who against such a title.

I consider this article a more effective protest than quietly pulling out of the exhibition.

Postscript, Copenhagen, April 2001: Language. Art. Women. And pseudo-irony.
"Young Ladies"!!? I felt so bewildered and ashamed at the title that it was only with
the greatest reluctance that I told my colleagues in Copenhagen about it, while I went
around with a permanent blush on my face and a deep dread of the opening.

The subject received a broader and more direct response than art exhibitions can
usually expect. My article was published in the Bergen newspaper *Bergens Tidende* and
in the national art magazine *Billedkunst,* and was followed by letters to the editor
suggesting that we had encountered a problem that was more than ripe for discussion.

In most of my artwork, language plays a not insignificant role. For this exhibition, I
planned to present a large, spacious wall collage consisting of between two and three
hundred items, including drawings, photographs, short texts and newspaper cuttings.
Many of the items were of a tragi-comical nature, or voiced cultural criticism. My
intention was to communicate a fleeting, subjective and sensual universe.
Indisputably a woman's statement, and with a view to enhancing her credibility as an
individual in society.

'Culture' is a recent phenomenon in Norway. Oil allowed explosive economic
growth, but it takes longer to reshape people. Artists and cultural workers are not
automatically taken seriously. In newspapers and on TV, they are presented either as
entertaining small time rebels, or ancient small time gods. Where culture is concerned,
the Norwegian media love to play the yokel comes to town, or the man in the street,
although they don't set much store by these either. It is rare to find an interpretation
that avoids the extremes of derision and adulation. If cultural workers receive neither
money nor recognition, then their self-esteem is bound to suffer.

Isn't the same true for women?

Both artists and women have to fight for their influence in Norwegian society. It is
tempting to overlook these problems, and to pretend that we have put them behind
us. After all, one gets so tired of discussing the same things over and over again. And
anybody who cares is sure to be troubled now and then by the possibility that we
might be cultivating the problems rather than solving them. This balance is under
constant negotiation. Perhaps it would be wisest to build up something new, rather
than expend energy on tearing down what already exists. Or do we have to clear away
the rotten wood before anything else will have space to grow?

One way of drawing attention to covert repression is to use irony. Humour and
irony are great tools for articulating problematic topics and getting them into the
open. But if taken too far they can also become a grotesque denial of responsibility.
It is difficult to criticise things that are easygoing and amusing, for the precise reason

that they seek to be insubstantial, evasive, descriptive and vague.

The better the humour—provided it remains funny—the more difficult it is to analyse it. Now, the title "Young Ladies" isn't all that funny, so the job wasn't too hard. But it was still necessary to take it seriously, in order to explain why women, artists and language itself were all treated shoddily in this case and more or less fobbed off as the stuff of mediocrity. This is why I wrote the feature for the newspaper.

translated by Ika Kaminka

"THIS PHOTO WAS FOUND IN A BOX WITH OLD PICTURE FRAMES, IN FRONT OF A THRIFT STORE. IT IS JUST A OLD WOMAN WITH A WALKING CANE, LOOKING OUT INTO THE DISTANT, NOT POSING FOR ANYONE. NATURALLY, I BOUGHT IT IMMEDIATELY."

Heterosexual masculinity in contemporary art can be compared with a huge traffic circle, which everyone is compelled to drive around, but which itself remains utterly passive. It still occupies by far most of the space in the art institutions and on the private art market. The identity of heterosexual masculinity in contemporary art just lies there—with an obviousness that has been handed down through generations of art history—and it fills up the landscape. It lies where it has always lain, but with the passage of time, its shape has slightly smoothed; taken form according to the traffic circling around it. And its salient character is bounded by everything that it itself is not. Only when something inadvertently or daringly breaks the traffic rules does it appear to awaken from its slumber.

However, the luxury of such a passive role has not been reserved for other groups in the visual art scene. Other groups have found it necessary to convince museum directors, curators, gallerists and the public of their right to exist on the art scene. These 'others' have been compelled to fashion a language that could articulate their identity because such a language did not already exist (in historical writing, for example). In order to make themselves comprehensible, some of these new identity formulations have, ever since the days of early feminism, taken their point of departure in their placement in relation to the masculine power position. A large number of both feminist and homosexual artists have tried to establish so-called anti-macho forms of expression by, for example, choosing to work in soft materials or with non-material projects, in favour of creating anti-monumental and anti-authoritarian artworks. A development which, historically speaking, has been necessary but which, when seen in the rear-view mirror, might well be said to have accepted the game rules from the masculine identity's employment of sets of binary oppositions, only using the opposite 'sign'. Putting it bluntly, one could say that what was established was more an oppositional language in relation to the male heterosexual artist's role than creating a terminology corresponding to these groups' own autonomous values. But thanks to this fieldwork, churned out over the decades, today one can work as a homosexual artist with a subtler and maybe even more constructive and visionary self-perception rather than merely adopting a critical position in relation to a set of heterosexual conventions and power structures. In the contemporary art scene, it is clear to see that oppression does not only spring from the employment of certain specific materials. Neither can it be said to be directly proportional to the size of an artwork. If only it were that easy!

According to American art critic Douglas Crimp, such a misdirected criticism has befallen an artist like Richard Serra, who has become almost synonymous with the epitamy of an oppressive macho artist.[1] In the first place, for Crimp, Serra's production is based on industrial readymades (which in themselves can be designated as being situated inside of the typical masculine masterwork tradition but which, on the other hand, possess an anti-work character about them). In the second place, in their focus on the size of the artworks, Serra's castigators have forgotten all about his critical project. Moreover, on the art scene of today, steel, concrete and works in the public space do not have the same significance and manifestation-value as they previously did and it would thus be high-flown to continue to aim one's artillery solely toward such forms of expression and stamp them as male-chauvinist exclusively on account of their aesthetics. Not even "the big canvas" possesses the same significance it once did and thus what it entails is a deadlock of the old positions to credit these forms of expression with anything especially heterosexual or masculine today.

Within the domain of conceptual art, there are also traditional male roles. Here, male artists are exploring areas in the same dissociated, object-investigative way that the explorers of the past did in their desire to chart white spots on the geographical map. What now seems to constitute the challenge is to break with the stereotypical myth formations that flourish around both heterosexual and homosexual masculinity.

For us, it has been important to work with establishing images of a homosexual identity different from prevalent 'queer icons' which, in the context of visual art, have been typically characterised by a depiction of gays as either victims or as being especially sensitive and delicate individuals. Although we are all too aware of the significance of AIDS and homophobic assaults, which are still part and parcel of the reality of homosexual culture, it has been more important for us to present other aspects of our identity than just the role of the victim—to create works that relate what is specific around a homosexual identity to other areas of society. Affected and cliché-filled transmissions of sexual identity are certainly not exclusively found within heterosexual culture—they also flourish on the homosexual arena. The typical 'camp' aesthetics have not had any relevance, practically speaking, to our own personal sexual self-awareness and it would have been an absolute sham if we were to work with such an expression.

On the other hand, as part of our upbringing within a Scandinavian context, we have been influenced and surrounded by functionalist design and architecture (which on many fronts can be likened to visual art's Minimalism). It has accordingly been crucial not to designate this idiom, which fills out such a significant part of both the public urban space and private architecture, as being solely heterosexual, since in doing so we would be turning our backs on vital elements of our own cultural background and life conditions. Instead, we have queered 'the pure idiom' and filled out the functionalist design and minimalist aesthetic with a content that has put our sexual standpoint into perspective. In relation to the institutional art scene, artist Felix Gonzalez-Torres has spoken about an 'infiltration strategy', predicated on making use of an idiom which, historically speaking, has been regarded as hyper-masculine and which, in its central placement in the context of Modernism, has been considered 'High Art'.

The inspiration from an architecture that is based on a concept of efficiency (and social democratic middle class values concerning recreational and 'healthy' construction) has established the foundations for our work, *Cruising Pavilion/ Powerless Structures, Fig. 55*. In response to a commission for a public sculpture in Århus, in 1998, we constructed a white cubic bower in Marselisborg Park. From the outside, it looked just like a functionalist building. On the inside, the bower was a labyrinth, where gloryholes (peepholes, which could be used for looking through or through which people could engage in anonymous sex) were drilled into the walls. In the daytime, the pavilion with its light and accommodating materials (its wooden bench and its skylight) functioned as a recreational spot, which everybody could enjoy, regardless of gender or sexual affinity. By dusk, the pavilion's function changed character and became a place for homosexual meeting.

A "big scale" work, much like several of our other pieces, this sculpture is in glaring contrast to the prevalent 'homo-aesthetics' that has its tradition in the decorative (Warhol, Hockney, Mapplethorpe) rather than in architecture. What was thrilling to us was to create a building that was homosexual in its basis/starting point but which could accommodate other social groups. In the same way as all of the places which are heterosexual in their point of origin but are "re-coded" by homosexual activity. When you regard the construction of the urban landscape as it has developed in modern times—i.e. compartmentalisation through rationalism, universalism, functionalism etc.—it is deeply anchored in a conventional heterosexual, masculine worldview.

George Chauncey points out that even in the present day, you still cannot speak about "queer spaces". You can only speak of "spaces occupied by queer activity" (e.g. a gay bar in a shut down butcher shop, outdoor cruising on the docks or in the park).[2]

The urban landscape reflects masculine ideals that existed more than a hundred years ago and it is only the lack of any new definitions of the heterosexual masculine roles in the present day that blurs the fact that this urban picture does not reflect a current-day heterosexual masculine identity.

Since the so-called 'marginal' groups working in the field of visual art no longer occupy the same oppositional role, the heterosexual male artists are now being compelled to break forth from their passivity as traffic circle—because without any traffic circulating around it, the traffic circle will ever so quietly come to be put out of commission. They will have to take part in the traffic-related orientation, just like everybody else, and find their way toward new goals and new sites. In much the same way as an exaggeratedly defined self-awareness can wind up in an introverted self-sufficiency or a deadlocking of oneself into a stereotyped role, the lack of definitions of one's own gender and sexual identity can indeed result in an uncertainty where old identifications are reactionarily reinforced, old virtues are defended or sly attacks on 'others' have to serve as safeguards for one's own threatened identity. The masculine sexual identity must not be reduced to a role where it has to "answer back" but must instead form a contemporary definition of itself. It would certainly be worth remembering that one is not heterosexual merely because he/she is not homosexual… and that a person is not a man because he is not a woman. And *vice versa*.

Notes

1 Douglas Crimp, *On the Museums Ruins*, Cambridge, MA, MIT Press, 1993.

2 George Chauncey, "Privacy Could Only Be Had in Public", Joel Sanders, ed., *Stud—Architectures of Masculinity*, New York: Princeton Architectural Press, 1996.

Previously published in Øjeblikket—Magazine for Visual Cultures, no. 42, vol. 10, Spring 2000.

translated by Dan A Marmorstein

All Wrapped Up: Synonyms and Oppositions

ILLUSTRATION (FOLLOWING PAGES): KIRSTINE ROEPSTORFF, 2001

When my alarm clock buzzes in the morning it not only wakes up my sleepy body—it also immediately activates my well-trained perception machine: size and content, what's important and what's not. Perspective and orientation. Social skills. Being an individual in society is an odd combination of resisting conventions imposed by society and internalising them. An act of pushing and pulling. I'm caught between endless sets of binary oppositions that guide and structure my behaviour. Apparent opposites, ends of the scale; good and bad, sweet and sour, weak and strong, right and wrong, male and female....

   I am programmed to evaluate everything around me. From the quality of my breakfast to the people I have relations with and how I have those relations, and at the end of the day, the meaning of my entire existence. Death is daily, it comes and goes. I put my existence into language, and thus I put language into existence—language as a premise; as constitutive of the hierarchy and order on which I build my values and belief systems. What happens to these values, if language and its inherent oppositions merge? Will they break down, become unfit for use?

Beautiful	*Desire*	*Frigid*
Magnificent	Longing	Unresponsive
Imposing	Craving	Apathetic
Monumental	Ambitious	Indifferent
Mighty	Enterprising	Mediocre
Sturdy	Endeavouring	Impartial
Robust	Exerting	Tolerant
Heavy	Struggling	Charitable
Cloddish	Conflictual	Philanthropic
Foolish	Hostile	Munificent
Clownish	Malicious	Bountiful
Buffoonish	*Disgusting*	Affluent
Zany		*Fertile*
Psychotic		

Just as these words can merge seamlessly into their apparent opposites through a simple linguistic operation, so can their meanings, and, perhaps, their social implementation. Just as there is a tension between concepts such as terror and therapy—violence and psychiatry—there is a likeness between them. Their common feature is their relationship to power and subjectivity. A relationship that emerges through language: the ability to speak, to be heard and to be understood. A 'weak' versus a 'strong' existence in society, and a capability of negotiating with the collective identity and the values on which a society is built.

Clinical therapy aims at reducing the patient's fears and self-destructive behaviours, but the treatment certainly also reduces society's fear of the patient—of an uncontrollable social subject—and the threat she/he seems to constitute to the system. Sophisticated violence. I'm interested in the concept of therapy as norm-maintaining and educating. Terror is the very opposite: a breakdown of the acceptance of normality. Terrorism is the violence of a group of individuals towards a certain social order. The aim of terror is to eliminate what—in the view of the terrorist—restricts her/his beliefs, her/his free scope, willpower, mobility, action. It is about 'freedom'. To understand this violence, one has to understand the effect that the freedom of one can have on the freedom of others—that it can be destructive. It is not only a matter of physical violence, although that can be the result. Violence is usually connected to "the evil that men do", but many terrorists have been women, turning the violence they feel coming from society back on society itself: Valerie Solanis, Leila Khaled, Ulrike Meinhof. This excites and puzzles me. Unlike therapy, the action of terror is the destruction of the conformity upon which our social order rests.

Both the terrorist and the subject of therapy can be said to be effects of communicative disabilities—if not breakdowns—of a lack of attention, and they are thus in despair. Both react consciously or unconsciously against the existing norms and structures of society. And they try to create a use of language to deploy against these structures. They are both symptoms of the presence of 'misfits' in society; subjects outside proper language. And thus, outside the Law.

Despite the different ways terror and therapy deal with existing conventions, there are also links between the terrorist and the therapist. Both try to control language, and both put themselves in a position of power towards the use of language; the terrorist by asserting herself and speaking out against the powers that be, and the therapist by analysing the improper language of others, and placing it within the context of proper language—within the Law of the Father, as it were. The terrorist and the therapist both deal with normality and language, and assume the task of speaking for others, sometimes at great cost to these others.

As I recognise these conventions and strategies, I feel able to relate to them and navigate within them, but unable to untangle them. As I go to sleep I'm all wrapped up in these thoughts and words, and must try to live with and between oppositions and contradictions. Sometimes I whine, but I can't help feeling pride in being what I am, so I hold on to my body and (lack of) consciousness.

SOMETIMES IT'S VERY
DIFFICULT TO GET A
CLOSE LOOK.

Golden or wooden spoon in the mouth?
Aren't they both spoons?
Yes, but the golden spoon is heavier than the wooden one.
Yes, but the wooden floats on water and the golden does not.
Yes, but wood is not a durable material and it can be burned and broken.
Yes, but wood is more comfortable to eat with and lighter.
Yes, but gold is more shiny, more valuable and exclusive.
Who gave the gold its value?
I think those who found it.
I don't want to ask who found it, but where was it found?
In the South I assume.
Thank you. No further questions.

In Denmark, there is a saying about privilege: "To be born with a golden spoon in your mouth." Nordic artists seem to be born with golden spoons in their mouths. Probably they are among the most privileged artists in the Western world. However, despite the new diversified North, Nordic art institutions are almost only displaying and prioritising Nordic artists—that is "Nordic" in a very strict, non-diversified sense.

The value and quality judgments of 'others' art and culture' has been an ongoing process since it started, i.e. since colonial times and the emergence of the first collections in the West. Now, at the beginning of this global and mobile age, one might ask if we really have achieved any progress on value and quality judgment? The answer seems to be 'yes'. The lesson of 'inclusion' from the postmodern era has apparently been understood and quite effectively implemented. We—the academia, the art world—are about to characterise the third modernity as the 'era of acknowledgement and inclusion' if only we can agree on a few cosmetic changes.... I use the word "cosmetic" because although some non-Western artists have made their way into Western art institutions I don't think there has been any comprehensive inclusion as of yet.

The exclusive art institutions of the West seems to be quite satisfied with the already selected number of non-Western artists allowed into their pantheon. It is hard to believe that their selection of 'non-Western' artists occurred randomly, especially when looking into the matter from a geographical point of view. From each region around the world there is one international high profile figure; from China, Persia, South America, the Arab world, Africa and the Balkans, respectively. It seems to me that some institutions have raised their profile by 'using' these artists. Have such artists become a 'value and quality' shield for the institutions to hide behind whenever the question of including non-Western artists arises?

Nordic art institutions are not immune in this discussion—on the contrary. Between 1995 and 2000 a few Danish institutions tried to show themselves as places wanting to include and reflect diversity and exhibit non-Western artists. Naturally, they selected some of these international high profile artists for shows, but it has not generally led to a higher inclusion of local non-Western artists. Rather, the situation got more complicated since only the institutions benefited from inviting these artists. The institutions got to legitimise their position, but at the same time it became clear that non-Western artists are only permitted as international artists, not as Nordic or local. A simple conclusion to be drawn from this is that if non-Western artists living and working in the Nordic region wish to enter a Nordic art institution, they first have to make it via New York.

Today, it is said that non-Western artists living in the Western sphere have achieved artistic freedom and access to mainstream institutions. But have they? It has been argued that non-Western artists are permitted access to mainstream institutions only when they obey the rules of the game and use the tools and vocabularies of the discourses of Western visual culture. Basically, when they do their homework, exactly as their teachers demand and expect.

To me it is clear that the hegemonic Western art institutions are not about to lose their exclusiveness for the sake of non-Western art. To the institutions, any further compromise will apparently lead to disturbance of the white cube principle—and looking closer it becomes obvious that that is not at all part of the institutions' policy, no matter what might be claimed. To put its history shortly, the principle of the white cube is to isolate (art) objects from their context, and thus make them unique and timeless. Objects inside this cube are disconnected from both time and place, and instead put inside an exclusive, tomb-like artificial space. To avoid contamination, the institutions have to keep the doors closed and only open them narrowly and momentarily.

But the questions to Nordic art institutions in particular are increasing: is it not the duty of art to reflect society? Is the region not diverse enough to allow for changes? As we are becoming a multicultural region, can exclusion still be justified? The institutions must reflect what is outside their walls. The white cube must thus, presumably, be opened wide, and art and its institutions lose their exclusiveness.

However, since local institutions in practice still act as white cubes, despite their rhetoric, it would be interesting to take this cube at its word, so to speak. If the function of the white cube is the determination of art objects through isolation, through a displacement of the objects from time and place, why should it then be counter productive to include the works of non-Western artists? Since objects inside the cube supposedly are timeless and placeless, why does this principle not apply to objects outside the Western context? Perhaps the white cube—if insisted on—should at least be required to live up to its principles and potentials?

In practice, only art that follows the dominant Western art discourse is permitted access to mainstream institutions. No space for any player unless he or she obeys, and does not change the rules of the game. The institutions have certain criteria, and Western as well as non-Western artists can enter only by following these criteria. To me, these institutional practices basically force non-Western artists to change their artistic practice and artistic identity—otherwise: access denied. The institutions are still practicing a one-sided value judgement on the majority of non-Western artists based almost only on geography. This practice does not help real aesthetic exchange or mutual understanding in a globalised world.

In closing, I would like to turn to a point made by Thomas McEvilley regarding value judgment: value judgment serves to define and bind communities of taste together in ways that are often useful and always exclude others. Because of this, there is an urgency to the whole question: when a community of taste attempts to enforce its idea of quality onto another, a dangerous act is performed, deriving from hidden and irrational, perhaps violent, motives.

McEvilley proceeds by saying that the pleasure of exercising judgment is a pleasure of self-realisation, self-recognition, and self-definition. One reflects oneself, and con- templates the reflection of oneself by bouncing one's radar of appreciation off of this and that; rejecting this, rejoicing in that, putting certain things in a class with oneself, excluding others from it, and so on. What we have to learn is to achieve feelings of pleasure while practicing pluralism and inclusion.

Today the question is not any longer how to teach some outsiders to become insiders. It is rather to teach the 'insiders' how to understand what 'outsider' means.

ILLUSTRATION: KHALED RAMADAN, WWWC WHITE CUBE (DETAIL), 2001

Notes

Thomas McEvilley, *Art and Otherness*, New York: McPherson & Company, 1992.

Brian O'Doherty, *Inside the White Cube—The Ideology of the Gallery Space*, San Francisco: Lapis Press, 1986.

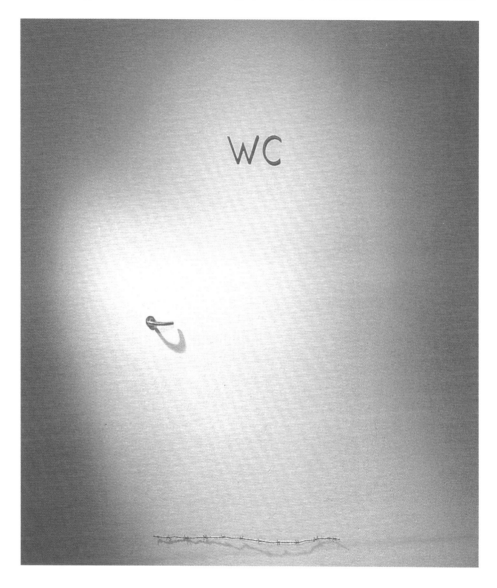

The Political Artist

Berlin, the summer of 1967. On the Kurfürstendamm a bonfire burns. The artist Manfred H is publicly burning all his pictures. But we are not witnessing a bitter protest against an uncomprehending art establishment. It is a deliberate artistic action; an attempt to politicise the concept of art and to take a step across the barricade. To put oneself on the side of those who are struggling. The title he gives this artistic action is *The artist throws away his brushes and starts a commune!* [1]

Starting a commune is typical of the period. Six months before this some of the city's student leaders and intellectuals joined forces to revolutionise the bourgeois individual. The initiative-taker, Dieter Kunzelmann, urges his comrades: "You have to pull up your roots! Away with your grants! Away with your security! Give up your studies! Risk your personality!" [2]

The name of the enterprise has been taken from the Paris Commune of 1871. This is its successor: *Commune 1*. People apply themselves to developing sexual needs, breaking the isolation of the individual and struggling for freedom from capitalist society. Parts of the struggle take the form of 'praxis' out in the streets. Praxis, according to Chairman Mao Tse-Tung, is processed Marxism, unlike theory. It is ACTION! People devote themselves to all sorts of marches and demonstrations. They throw paint-filled balloons and raw eggs at the American Consulate. They conspire to pour vanilla sauce on the American Vice-President Hubert H. Humphrey.

In other words it is no coincidence that the artist Manfred H. burns his pictures on the Kurfürstendamm. Nor is he some unknown upstart who wants to use this gesture to make a slightly larger space for himself in the Berlin art world. Along with his wife Ellinor (an artist too) he has for some years organised a very well-frequented salon in the couple's large apartment in Schöneberg. There, people from different walks of society rub shoulders: critics, artists, art dealers, journalists, lawyers and actors; transvestites, prostitutes and drug dealers. The last of these are people the H's have picked up on rambles through the nightlife of the city; excursions they have made along with their young, charming lodger—Andreas Baader.

Paris, May 1968. Millions of workers are on strike. Factories and universities are occupied. On streets and boulevards the cobblestones are torn up and turned into barricades. Inside the art academy—the École Supérieure des Beaux-Arts—teachers and pupils are on strike. Some students go off to the graphics workshop to print a poster—for the revolution of course. With alliteration on the letter 'u' they elegantly sum up the foundation of the struggle—the unity of workers and students:

"Usine, Université, Union!"

The poster makes an immediate impact. It is soon followed by others and the workshop is renamed "Atelier Populaire". On 16 May the students, along with some artists and strikers, decide to occupy the school permanently. The poster production has to be protected from the lackeys of the Gaullist regime. The revolution is just around the corner!

The posters printed by Atelier Populaire are unsigned. Some of them are designed by artists who are world famous today, others by people from the street. They are distributed freely and posted on barricades and house walls throughout France.

A statement from Atelier Populaire says:

The posters produced by Atelier Populaire are weapons in the struggle and their proper place is in the midst of the conflict, that is on the street and on the factory walls. To use them for decorative purposes, exhibit them in the salons of the bougeoisie or even to regard them as aesthetic objects is to deprive them of their function and effect.[3]

Collecting them is equivalent to betrayal.

It is easy to understand their concern. How would it look if the bourgeois art public ran around tearing down slogans the students had just pasted up to hang in the place of honour in the fine salon? How would it look if revolutionary artists added their propaganda to their worklists and catalogues? What power would be left in that weapon?

And in Berlin at the same time the raw eggs and vanilla sauce are being replaced with 'mollies'—Molotov cocktails.

What stories like these teach us is that the encounter between art and politics requires sacrifices. Manfred H first had to ritually burn up his (bourgeois) pictures so his art could fulfill the requirements of the protest movement. The artists in Atelier Populaire had to renounce both the economic and conceptual rights to their work. It is hard to make art and revolution at the same time. Something has to be sacrificed.

What stories like these teach us is that the art of the revolution, despite all the sacrifices, was still in the end betrayed. The boundary-shifting experiments in Berlin ended in terrorism and repression. Atelier Populaire's posters in the end became coveted investment objects in the art market of the bourgeoisie.

Of course, this was a long time ago. The waves of nostalgia for the end of the 60s that are now washing over us are no more than just that—nostalgia. Or so it is claimed. Today the situation is quite different. Or so it is claimed. The age of rebellions and revolutions is irrevocably over. Or so it is claimed.

Is it really so?

The use by the economic powers of IT, efficiency and automation in the manufacturing industries and bureaucracy, the removal of trade barriers and a globalised labour market are certainly resulting in increased growth. But does that mean that the divides in society are closing? It doesn't seem so. Has the new age led to increased equality and democracy? Hardly. And solidarity with the Third World? What happened to that? The outcasts and marginalised? Consideration for children and the old? The right of animals to a decent life? The environment?

On all these scores the new age has to hang its head and stand in the corner. Things didn't get better for most people. They only got better for a few. The poor got even poorer and those who were affluent before became indecently rich.

Facts like these form the basis for the wave of radicalisation that is now beating against the shores of the Western world. As for nostalgia, the fashion houses and record companies can take care of that.

But on the art scene the stage is still empty.

The art students of today don't occupy their computer rooms and print out posters for the young people who go off to demonstrate in Seattle, Prague and Nice. They don't hack into the university's servers to open up their knowledge and the digital highway of broadband for Vegans, animal rights activists and ATTAC. They don't even print fliers on the copying machine.

The artists of today don't update the political visual-arts idiom. They don't tame the new media for the benefit of the majority. Nor do they start up social projects that reach further than the walls of the galleries. The artists of today risk neither their grants nor their security by participating in any activity (artistic or otherwise) that doesn't definitively further their careers.

At least not yet.

And when in the end it happens, we will again witness sacrifices. Human as well as artistic. For what history teaches us is that the equation of art with political commitment, as it has been formulated hitherto, cannot be solved. And the artist who still wants to be part of things and make the world a better place to live in seems, in the encounter with contemporary art theory, to be crushed by an even greater defeat than his or her colleagues from 1968.

ILLUSTRATIONS (FOLLOWING PAGES): "EXTRA: POLICE OPEN FIRE. THREE DEMONSTRATORS SHOT"/"EXTRA: SHOT!", GUNNAR KRANTZ, 2001

So it is time to set up a new equation. Time to again ask crucial questions:

Do artists have to take part in social debate?

No, we artists do not have to participate in social debate, but since the end of the nineteenth century we have had a unique potential for doing so. Ever since Zola, by virtue of his position as a writer, intervened in the politics of his day, we (artists, authors, scientists...) in our role as INTELLECTUALS have the potential to do the same. Should we abandon that potential now? If so, why?

Is it to keep well in with patrons, sponsors and grant boards (Sony, CocaCola, Nestlé and Shell... politicians and bureaucrats...)? Are economic considerations the reason why ever-fewer artists assume their intellectual responsibility today? Then it is high time we began to look for alternative funders.

In front of me on the wall hangs a work of art. It is a poster stamped "École Supérieure Des Beaux-Arts".

At the bottom of the faded sheet of paper it says in large letters: "Nous vaincrons!". We will conquer!

The judgement of history falls heavy on the artists who, with exaggeratedly naïve enthusiasm, want to improve the world through their art. That is true enough. But one thing I do know. It falls even heavier on the yes-men.

Notes

1. Stefan Aust, *Baader-Meinhof. Sju år som förändrade Förbundsrepubliken*, Stockholm: Stehag, 1990, p. 35.

2. Aust, *Baader-Meinhof,* p. 36.

3. *Burn! Paris 1968 Posters—Introduction*. (Website) download from http://burn.ucsd.edu/paris.html, 20 March, 1997.

translated by James Manley

EXTRA
SKJUTEN

EXTRA

HÄR ÖPPNAR

POLISEN ELD

TRE DEMONSTRANTER SKITTSKADADE

—The name game, then, implies a performativity of language, but also a set of rules. A set of rules and a (role) playing that gives one the opportunity to play by the rules, breaking them or simply, or slyly, cheating. And you can understate your act or over act, invest the role with the literary, theatrical mode of acting, vanish into the role as in 'method acting' or perhaps employ a Brechtian strategy of *verfremdung*. The way you say your lines matters, not just the words themselves—a stylistic choice is a discursive one.

—What does it mean to speak in a minor language and/or to be speaking in tongues? The languages in the Nordic region are small, for sure, but nonetheless powerful and affirmative in their respective countries. In Denmark, for instance, state support is given to cultural publications on a grande scale—this support, however, is not given due to the content of the publications, but due to its form, its language: funding is provided to support the (survival of) the Danish language. Perhaps it is the language itself that is the content; language as a basis for the nation. But within a small language there is always also 'minor' languages, as when language is employed and, in turn, transformed and territorialised by immigrant groups and/or youth subcultures. But transformation also comes from above in terms of bureaucratic language and business language. Increasingly, there is an Anglofication of languages. In Iceland, though, no foreign words are allowed into the Icelandic language. It is considered pure and original, and new long words are constantly constructed to designate foreign, modern objects (technologies, commodities and so on). Language is activated as a primarily ideological tool rather than a functional one.

—Within the language of contempoary art Nordic artists have long had to speak in a 'minor' language, not unlike the method of writing employed by Franz Kafka, as defined by Deleuze and Guattari in the definition of a minor literature as a writing within another language other than one's own.[1] Working in the North, artists have had to either adopt to national, affirmative styles, or import (and transform) international, mostly American and German, forms and discourses. Likewise, theories of art are read in these languages, and often—as in this book—communicated in them too. But speaking with one's accent also places one, designates one's identity as belonging to a particular minority. A notion of minority that, in Scandinavia, is doubled, since there are always those who remain 'minor' even within the smaller languages. There are little Kafka's everywhere.

—The designation 'Nordic' is, evidently, not a unproblematic one, neither as Nordic artist in, say, London or Los Angeles, nor as an immigrant artist in the Nordic countries. Being designated nationally and geographically is undignified and pigeon holing, but how about the designation artist, the ego-producing machine itself? Is this less of a historical and affirmative designation than 'nation', or for that matter gender specific designations? What does it mean to speak as an artist, and how does this differ from other subjects? Is it a priviliged position, and if so, is this a privilege that can facilitate critical positions, that can be employed strategically, or is artist always already synonymous to a gifted individual beyond language or the so-called, almighty "Author-God"?[2]

Notes

1. Gilles Deleuze and Félix Guattari, *Kafka—Toward a Minor Literature*, Minneapolis: University of Minnesota Press, 1986.

2. To use Roland Barthes' infamous description from "The Death of the Author". See Roland Barthes, *Image—Music—Text*, New York: Hill and Wang, 1977, pp. 142-148.

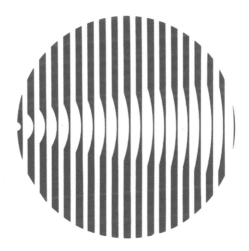

Care of the Self

Throughout modernity, we have been saddled with the notion of the romantic, suffering artist. A figure on the outskirts of orderly society, but that nonetheless was in closer contact to his inner life, his innermost self; a self that was exposed to us all through the artist's expression. In the Nordic countries, this ideal has been widespread, and often connected to specific sites, such as nature and the experiences there of. However, recent art practices have moved the site to the self itself, so to speak: or to the role of the artist as emblematic for constructions (and, in turn, de- and reconstructions) of selfhood. The self in such projects is, then, obviously not a given, but rather a construct. It is a construction that comes from both inside and outside, through socialisation and self-invention. The invention of the self is seen as a constant act of role-playing, performaces, stagings, disguises and make-overs. An identification of the self that is problematic, sometimes a hard fought battle indeed, but not unpleasurable—it is an act of 'caring for the self', as Michel Foucault put it. In his book entitled *The Care of the Self*, Foucault writes about this care as a philosophical discipline, that is at once both a duty and a privilege, and notes "But the fact that the philosophers advice that one give heed to oneself does not mean that this zeal is reserved for those who choose to live a life similar to theirs, or that such an attitude is required only during the time one spends with them. It is a valuable principle for everyone, all the time and throughout life."[1]

Viewed in this light, the artist as site becomes an interesting point of investigation: the artist-role can be seen as the ultimate stage for performing the 'self', that is, for understanding the subject through notions of performativity; as a construct of 'different' sets of behaviors, intentions, desires and fantasies. Areas, and perhaps even tools, of such an investigation would be the articulation of the author's "I", role-playing and subjectivity as performative instances, image making and breaking, self and doubling. Not surprisingly medium such as video and photography have, besides performance art, been employed to explore these aspects of identity as staged and performed. The authors in this chapter therefore also include a number of video and performance artists. One of them, Peter Land, is naturally both, and in his essay "Notes on Self-relexivity in Art" he outlines how the private and personal forms the basis of his works, albeit not necessarily in a expressionist manner, but rather as points of departure for a staging of the self as social construct. Following up on this Heta Kuchka writes about her stagings of herself and the opposite sex, in a attempt to forge an inter-subjective zone for flirtatious communication in "The Charmings". It is her point that the audience imposes and investets their desires and images into the works. In "Public Educational Tours" Annika Lundgren also takes us on a ride, but this time through Copenhagen to see the landmarks of a fantastic, fictive life. This text is part of an actual performance piece, if you will, of a guided bus tour through the city. Lundgren thematises the making and unmaking of history, in which the invention of identities and characters is not unusual at all. Anja Franke's text, "24 Motives", is also an art work in its own right, and centres around imaginary, made-up characters and 'real' ones. In this text, Franke is having a dialogue with a her male alter ego, an anagram of her own name, or, with herself as other. A literary encounter with the opposite sex, and notions of self, sexuality and the social is also at stake in the last two texts by Tone Hansen and Inga Svala Thorsdottir, respectively. But here the similarities also end: Thorsdottir's piece, "Ode" is a literary account of her upbringing and sexuality, performed through language, whereas Tone Hansen's article "The Gym of the Castrated Girls" is a tradepaper comment regarding performativity and gender after encountering a billed performance art piece that turned out to be the appropriation of a striptease act. Hansen questions the art world's ability to appropriate any acts , including the works of Peter Land, as signs of self, and instead argues for a care for the self and certain principles in our responses to such acts. When (re)constructing ourselves, the images we appropriate have double meanings, both in their prior context and the current, and for both ourselves and others. A care of the self naturally implies a politics of identity.

Notes

1. Michel Foucault, *The Care of the Self*, Harmondsworth: Penguin Books, 1988, pp. 47–48.
   Originally published in 1984 by Éditions Gallimard, Paris.

The Gym of the Castrated Girls

I've been to a strip club. Not just me, but the entire hip segment of the Norwegian art scene has been to a strip club. We watched young, Eastern European strippers in a bar which on the 30 March this year advertised in a national paper that they had "new artists every ten days".

I'm not sure I knew what I was letting myself in for. An art opening in a go-go bar? In Norway over the past decade art events have been held in all kinds of public and semi-public spaces, such as toilets, second-hand shops, prisons and so on, either for invited audiences, or for those who just happened to be there.

I suppose I went with an open mind, hoping to find out what this one was all about. (Or I might have been thinking along the lines of, okay then, I suppose we have become so blasé that we consider each and every place a potentially interesting venue for dynamic and vigorous Norwegian art, which keeps bursting out of its confines. Art, fashion and porn. Magazines and TV companies, which in recent years have sought to boost their circulation, or to be regarded as cool while at the same time maintaining a serious profile, have published long articles on the hectic life of porn stars, or handled the subject in a documentary. Consider the porn fetishism of the national paper *Dagbladet*: see the rotten life of a porn star at work, in full colour.)

I was invited to a strip club to hear the band Information play and Kristina Falcone sing. Nothing in the programme mentioned Eastern European strippers.

Yet I guess I knew what I was in for. A year ago a good friend of mine visited the same club, and made the acquaintance of a Russian stripper called Barbara. They had had cake at a nice little patisserie on the same street and she told him she lived in a flat above the club, and that she was subject to a curfew. An Estonian girl who was given a beating for staying away from the flat for too long, decided she'd had enough and went back home. Barbara was no exhibitionist. Barbara just needed the money.

There is one aspect of the gender debate that particularly cheeses me off. Every time I enter into an argument about feminism and sex, or respond less than enthusiastically to an unpleasant experience, I am taken to represent my sex. Such arguments invariably end up in an "us versus them" mode. The girls against the boys. This is symptomatic of the Norwegian art debate which mostly revolves around being for or against something. Either you're with us or you're against us.

After the strip show a guy tells me he is surprised that no one reacted to the party. Nobody reacted; that is to say, no girls reacted.

The guy had touched on something important. Why had it been so difficult to react to the art project in the strip club? Was it because of all the colleagues in the place? Or because of the enormous bouncers?

The answer is more complicated. In a strip club all power rests with the male heteros. As a woman you are castrated in such a place, both sexually and in your ability to react; you are deprived of your credibility. No matter how I might choose to respond, my reaction would fit into stereotyped roles, either the affected cool bitch or the humourless and puritanical 70s feminist.

The only ones who can pull off an unpredictable reaction in such a space are the guys.

I don't intend to make the organiser of an art happening responsible for the enormous Eastern European sex industry. That would be too naïve, and might be seen as a misdirected outburst which ought to be aimed at an industry extraneous to the art world. But the organisers were quite aware of the emotions such a setting would stir among girls who constantly have to relate to the sale of the female body.

Another fundamental (and for art far more important) issue which the strip club party raises, is whether or not art projects can be arranged with insouciance virtually anywhere outside the art scene? Is it really the case that we artists are absolved of any implication of the potential ethical issues, that it is acceptable to do things, or participate in events, which we would never accept in a broader perspective?

The organisers enter a space and turn it into an art context. The bar staff and the strippers become extras or mere interior decoration for a blasé art performance which borrows the context of one social setting to create the right atmosphere for another. Art history and the history of performance is full of nudity and naked women. The difference is that naked women within an art context are prepared for their audience, they themselves control how they relate to the audience. The Eastern European strippers at the art event faced a completely different audience from the one they are used to. The strippers were art, but were they aware of the nature of our gaze? Were they aware of what kind of context they were being placed in?
And does this affect 'our' perception of the strip club event?

It is high time for a debate on values and ethics in the Norwegian art scene. Not just a debate about the distribution of resources, but one which is committed, professional, and forward-looking.

What saddens me most about the strip club experience is not just that I felt personally ridiculed in such a space, but the immense difficulty of keeping the ensuing debate on the level of principle, aware of its content, and of preventing it from ending up as yet another fight for space in the public sphere.

"Paranoia is rampant on the Norwegian art scene", Arvid Pettersen wrote in *Billedkunst* a while back. One of the reasons for this is that many are afraid to express themselves on political issues and matters of principle, maybe because they dread the consequences. But what consequences ought it to have if somebody deviates from consensus?

One of the unhappiest consequences I can think of in a community that necessarily should take a stand on political and ethical issues, is that part of that community gets gagged.

One might wonder why Peter Land's second striptease video, where he himself stripped, was the one that gave him his breakthrough, rather than his first, in which two very young girls, unaware of their future fame, stripped pathetically and clumsily. Maybe because in his second project he himself, and nobody else, took the risks, and that made him so much more vulnerable.

translated by Ika Kaminka

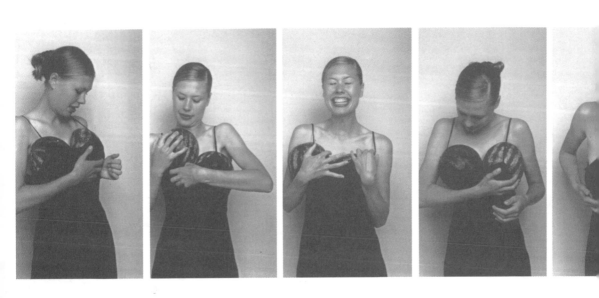

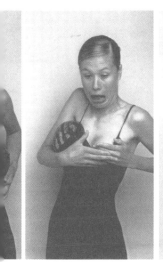

The Charmings

The paper was folded. I opened it and thought that it had something on it like I luurve yoouu. Try to imagine how I felt when I opened it and it read: " I want money, a bit of pussy now and then and a Volvo sedan". It was completely terrible, I'm telling you. I thought that no I can't be wrong about this person. I looked hysterically for another similar piece of paper. Thank god I found it finally. I knew that it was from him, because it had his return-date on it. I knew he wanted to return to me.

Extract from the video installation *The Charmings*, 2000

Now and then I pick up images about the stages of becoming a woman. Once, in a photo-series I discontentedly posed with melons and doughnuts of different sizes in front of my breasts.[1] In the video *The Charming*, however, I tell the viewer different stories I've heard about men. It was about the manner in which women talk about their love life; the endless speculations, the communication of women and men—within as well as between the sexes, and the uncertainty of the infatuated woman. I wanted to get the attention of my audience by telling them secrets. I shot at the kitchen table. I talked to the camera alone, very intimately. The monitor was placed on top of the same table where I'd shot the video, and on it, I seemed life-size. In the video I offer the viewer some cookies that I had left on the table in front of the monitor. Anybody had access to my secrets.

My own, personal study

A few years ago I started my own personal study of men. In my experience, women are constantly subject to comments on their looks from men, both strangers and friends. My personal study of men began by starting to write down comments that I heard about myself. I placed special notice on good-natured, although slightly awkward sounding compliments, like: "You've put on a bit of weight since I last saw you", "you're not as big as usually?" or "You've got big, I mean long, feet".

I also took a fancy to photographing men. I wanted to emphasise the curiosity I felt towards them. It led to portraits of them, which I in fact think of more as self-portraits. It is as if a certain curiosity can be sensed in the pictures, which I believe would not have been there if the photographer had been a man. Then, the situation would have become a competition. Power is connected to the camera as an object and to the use of it. It can show specific attention. It is certainly selective.

I asked the model to lie on his back, on the ground. I mainly shot from the position one could call "on top", and thus covered the whole of his field of vision with my camera. Women have learned to see this angle as degrading, and I wanted to see how men would react to it. Most of them were excited and coquettish. Some became anxious and told me they felt helpless. The power of the camera was heightened. It was difficult for the models to evade the camera.

Flirting with the audience
Flirting is an interesting way to communicate with strangers. It entails the possibility of revealing a glipse of the other's sexuality. I mean a special personal sensitivity that is most often invisible in normal, everyday communication. It is thus even more exciting when people reveal their vulnerability to complete strangers. So I decided to make a series of colour photos of flirtatious young men.

While taking the picture we were the centre of each other's attention; the man flirting with me, and me focusing on him so that I would get a good shot. I carried the camera with me wherever I went to collect material. Sometimes I hung around a group of men, shooting, until I knew every detail of all of their female conquests.

At the exhibition I passed on all the looks that were originally intended for me in large, life-size colour photos. They needed just the right distance between the images on the walls and the audience, so that the viewer would feel surrounded by curious faces. Usually it is the other way around, the spectator being the one who sees and possibly evaluates.

Note
1. The photo series *Push up*, 1999.

translated by Jean Ramsey

I figure that in my own work, through the recording of acts and their repetition, I'm trying to reflect some basic conditions of my own existence and perhaps to fill some sort of apparent meaning into the meaningless. Maybe this meaning is to expose the meaningless.

In all my work, I try to isolate different aspects of my own self-perception. It's like testing my own identity by means of reflections in the form of recordings of myself in different staged situations. These situations are often grotesque, caricatured or driven to extremes as a way of isolating and enlarging the issue, to crystallise and to mediate it as clearly as possible to myself as well as an eventual audience. I regard extremity as a way of focusing, or as the Danish painter Asger Jorn once said: "You either go to extremes or you don't go at all."

This also relates to the apparent abjectness in some of my works. By putting myself in situations within the work where I'm removing myself from my socially provided feeling or idea of dignity, I try to negate my own identity to a degree where a revised or renewed self-perception may arrive. In that way I hope, from my work, to receive a reflection that will clarify for me who I am. In my case, the need has arisen from a feeling of a lack of social and spiritual meaning; an inability to establish my own meaningful existence by means of the social. This is not meant in the sense that I'm not able to find meaning in the more intimate short-term social structures that arise in forms such as conversations, going to the cinema or taking the bus. It's far more a failure on my behalf to recognise my own identity as someone whose occupation of a place in society serves as something meaningful in a spiritual sense.

This meaninglessness has to do with a sense of a decline of ethics. Not in the sense that I'm losing track of my feeling of what is right and wrong in my everyday life—I think my social and cultural background more or less successfully provides that—but in a sense of lack of an overall meaning behind the fact of me being around. I think that life without some sort of establishment of meaning is the same as life without boundaries. And as this implies a paralysing spiritual as well as intellectual collapse, the issue of existence becomes an ethical one.

It's by now a common philosophical idea, and at least very much of a feeling to me, that there is no longer any apparent overall ethical meaning behind existence, only a scientific explanation of *how* but not *why*. The ethics of existence are no longer being automatically provided from the outside world in the form of an all embracing church or its likes, and the ethical structures that I try to create on my own become invalid or don't apply as my perception of reality changes or is being changed, and has to be rebuilt repeatedly. I guess my work with art is instrumental in my pursuit to establish an ethical meaning behind my own existence. In that way you can say that I need it to preserve myself from dissolving mentally, descending into apathy because of a lack of guidelines on how to interfere with the rest of the world, and I also need it to reflect to myself that, at least, this hasn't happened yet.

Notes on *Peter Land 6 February 1994*
Before I entered the Art Academy in Copenhagen, my attitude towards art-making was pretty innocent. I wanted to make paintings. I didn't have a clear idea why, but at the time that didn't prevent me from doing it. Then, after entering the Art Academy, I was confronted with questions as to what I wanted to say with what I did. What was the purpose? I have to admit that I'd never thought about art in that way before.

After that, it went pretty much downhill for Peter Land the "abstract expressionist painter". I got more and more confused as to what I wanted to do (and what I wanted to say). In the end I decided that I had to abandon painting all together. In a sense I felt that I had worn out that possibility for myself.

After having decided on using video as a way out of my creative crisis (because I think that's the proper term) only one, but very important, issue had to be settled: what should I film? As the creative crisis had also soaked into my understanding of myself and my life, I was in existential turmoil at the time. I decided that the first video work I did should be instrumental in putting things in their right place for me: by challenging some of the values I had been brought up to believe in, and which were still very much part of my psychological make-up, I wanted to put my perception of myself as a moral being to the test. I still just didn't know how.

That's when I, walking through the red-light district of Copenhagen, came across a small notice in a window of a porn shop saying that for a rather low fee, you could go and make your own photographs of nude girls. My first thought when I saw this note was; "I'd never do anything like that!". I grew up with a single mother, and as such I think I'm pretty sensitive to women being abused. A bit further down the street it struck me that my inhibitions about doing something like that was the exact reason why I should do it. Test my own limits. I wrote down the telephone number, and after a great deal of hesitation I phoned the place named in the ad. I got a girl on the phone who told me a little bit about the conditions. I asked if I could use a video camera instead of taking photos. She didn't see any problem in that as long as I paid the fee. We agreed on a date. On the 6th of February I went out to the suburb of Copenhagen to the address in the ad. I was very nervous, so I had had a few drinks. I was greeted by a fat guy with long greasy hair who showed me around the premises. The 'studio' was a 'one family house' which had been decorated with fluffy carpets, pictures of nude girls and kitschy couches. I was told that occasionally they also made hardcore porno films there.

Then I was introduced to the girls. From the video you'll know what they look like. They seemed very tough. They scared me. Asking these two girls to strip dance in front of a video camera was quite an ordeal in itself; not just because of the girls themselves, but also because of my own inhibitions. As I already knew at the time that the video was going to be shown publicly, I decided to make my own presence in the whole thing more clear by walking back and forth a few times in front of the camera during the shoot.

After we'd finished shooting the video I tried to explain to the girls that the footage was going to be shown as an artwork. They didn't seem to understand. The answer I got was "This is art!? That's what they all say."

I see the video very much as part of a personal and artistic strategy: by making this video, and especially by showing it publicly, I tried to liberate myself from what I perceived as moral expectations on the part of society. By doing and showing something that I knew a lot of people would find morally unacceptable I felt I achieved this, at least in my own mind.

About *Peter Land 5 May 1994*

This was my second video, and the purpose behind it was very much the same as in *Peter Land 6 February 1994*. It was also to a large extent derived from a feeling of guilt that I'd been carrying around since showing the first video. Another thing that played in my mind at the time was that I wanted to comment on the media-generated notion of bodily beauty as seen in advertising and magazines and the whole body-fixated culture of the 1980s and early 90s. I wanted to do that by putting up a counter-image; that of my own, far from perfect, body.

In the beginning, I thought it would be a fairly simple task to shoot this video. It would be me, alone, in my one bedroom flat in Copenhagen, strip-dancing to a selection of pop tunes. There would be nobody else in the room except myself, a CD player and a camera on a tripod. It turned out to be far more difficult than I anticipated. After looking through the first attempt, I realised that I was far too self-conscious and inhibited when dancing. What I wanted to be a roar came out as a chirp. I decided I had to film the whole thing all over again, just this time I had to do something about my shyness.

The next day I went to a local bar and had a few drinks. Just enough to make my head buzz. Then I went back to my apartment and tried again. It still didn't work to my satisfaction. After seven days of excessive drinking and video-filming, I at last thought that I got it right, but I have to admit that I don't remember anything from the actual shooting of the video.

About *Pink Space*

The video shows me in a series of sequences dressed as an entertainer in a gold lamé suit entering a pinkish space containing a barstool and a table with a glass and a bottle of whisky. This happens to the sound of quiet piano music. In each sequence I try to climb the barstool but subsequently fall down.

   The work is about my feeling of failure in my attempts at establishing meaning on a personal as well as an artistic level. The feeling that I'm expected to say or do something meaningful; to interfere, but that the mental apparatus needed for such an act has collapsed or evaporated, and I'm left dumb. I'm using the role of the entertainer as a metaphor for this: The entertainer is expected to handle the situation, to tell jokes or sing and dance within a given set-up. This makes perfect sense/meaning when rapport is established between the entertainer and the audience. In this video the attempt of the entertainer (me) to fullfil this function in a sensible way; to perform in the way that is expected of him, is made impossible by the fact that he constantly falls down from the barstool he's supposed to sit on.

Thoughts on *Step Ladder Blues*

I've always been deeply fascinated, and at the same time repulsed by people who seem to have a clear sense of purpose in their lives. People who can distinguish between what's important, and what's unimportant, and refer to their surroundings in terms of their place in the 'Big Picture'. I guess it's a kind of jealousy. I envy these people for the stubbornness with which they are able to maintain their beliefs, the orderliness of their lives, their ability to focus themselves in this world. A world that to me seems utterly confusing and disorderly. A world in which any foundation for firm convictions or beliefs are transitory and untrustworthy.

   As an artist, one of the questions you constantly are forced to consider is: "What is the purpose of what I do?". And in the immediate neighborhood of that question you'll also find: "What's my purpose as a human being? What's my justification?". These are the questions that present themselves most strongly in my work as an artist, but also in my perception of myself as a person who breathes the oxygen we all share, takes up space in this world (and in the line at the grocery store), and bothers people with messages that may be important to no one but myself.

I guess that my work with art is instrumental in my pursuit to establish a valid meaning behind my existence as the ethical structures that I try to create around me become invalid or don't apply, and as my perception of reality changes or is being changed. This is the Sisyphean condition that *Step Ladder Blues* relates to: the scenario of the housepainter trying to fulfill his purpose in vain, constantly climbing the step ladder to perform the seemingly simple task of painting the ceiling and constantly failing at it represents this inability to maintain an underlying meaning to support one's existence. How does one establish meaning when the ideological apparatus needed for such an act collapses or at least seems very unstable (like the ladder)?

A few notes on *The Staircase*

The video work *The Staircase* is a double video projection: one projection depicts a man falling in slow motion down several flights of stairs. The video has been edited, so that it seems that the staircase is endless. The other projection is a computer-generated image of the universe, with stars slowly moving towards the spectator.

The work is based on my longstanding interest in falls and failures. My concern has, broadly speaking, been the relationship between the personal and the universal: the feeling of being a bacteria-like creature trying to make sense of and create some meaning and justification behind his/her existence in a vast and ever-expanding world where the individual may seem unimportant.

When you question the basic conditions of existence, at the same time you challenge yourself with questions that not even the greatest philosophers and spiritual thinkers of our time have been able to answer to everybody's satisfaction. (Anyway, I don't think there are that many philosophers left who see the construction of an eternally valid explanation of the world as part of their job description today). However, it is exactly the above mentioned issues that set me ticking as an artist: "What am I doing here?", "Is there a purpose of me being around?", in other words; "What's the value of me as an individual?".

When you start asking yourself these questions, you in effect challenge the very basis of your existence. All of a sudden the values you may have taken for granted on all kinds of levels, socially as well as spiritually, become dubious, and what might have seemed to you as eternal rock-solid truths before, suddenly appear relative and shaky. You have in effect stumbled (pushed yourself?) over the edge of the stairs and into an eternal fall, a kind of existential limbo, from which there's seldom any escape.

I'm still falling.

A note on *The Lake*

In this video, the spectator is confronted with a man dressed as an outdoorsman; a hunter, gun over his shoulder, who purposefully strides through a forest–like environment. The soundtrack is taken from Beethoven's 6th Symphony also known as the "Pastoral". The object of his excursion is not revealed until he reaches a small boat at the edge of a lake. He rows out into the middle of the lake, fastens the boat to a pole in the water, all this still happening to the tunes of Beethoven. He then proceeds to stand up in the boat and releases the safety hatch on the gun, as if about to shoot ducks. He then aims the gun at the boat and shoots.

Immediately at the sound of the shot the music stops.

The next half of the video shows the hunter sitting in the boat as it slowly sinks until all that's left is the hunter's hat floating on the surface of the lake. The only sound that can be heard is birds chirping in the forest. The video finishes with a series of shots of forest scenarios, insects, the sound of a cuckoo nearby, etc.. The forest without any human presence.

As in other of my works, *The Lake* revolves around the relationship between the individual and the rest of the world. But in *The Lake*, focus is very much directed at the impossibility of trying to imagine the world without oneself in it. The idea that the world will continue after I'm dead: a thought that's always scared me, but which I guess I should find reassuring.

If you read the stories collected and written by the Grimm Brothers, a lot of them are pretty scary. And I firmly believe that even the worst nightmare, the most horrific vision, simply by being within the boundaries of human conception should be brought out into the open rather than being suppressed. Suppressing them, I think, is the same as running the risk that they might come true.

ILLUSTRATIONS: PETER LAND, GLEMT (FORGOTTEN), 130 x 60 CM
STRANDET (STRANDED), 150 x 70 CM
SLIK (CANDY) 60 x 120 CM
WATER COLOUR AND PENCIL ON PAPER. COURTESY GALERY NICOLAI WALLNER

Our conception of existence and identity, as well as of our possibilities—now, and in the future—are largely defined by history. History can never be an objective documentation but is necessarily a selection of events, based on ,among other factors, choices made by the historian. Though formerly thought of as potentially 'objective', these choices are highly subjective—dependent on different factors such as the historian's national and cultural background, political convictions, economic and social status, education, religion, race, sex, etc..

European historians have traditionally been well-to-do white Christian men and the histories they documented inevitably represented their own views—limited views—of the course of events. 'History', as well as story-telling, plays a part in the creation of myths which are spun around familiar persons and events. These myths contribute to making information about these people and things less precise and more random. Yet history and story-telling are necessary for our 'presence'; for us to have an idea of our 'self'.

When does story-telling—supposedly fiction—merge with history—supposedly facts? Authority and authenticity, in this sense, become questions of formatting and context—who is the speaking subject, from where does his authority derive, and for whom does he speak, tell his story?

The existence of Delilah Jensen can, of course, be questioned, but the *way* she may or may not have existed should be questioned simultaneously. From this perspective it is, in fact, no less relevant to question the existence of Napoleon Bonaparte than the existence of Delilah, Alice or Sally.

Excerpts from the Alice Stiernfeldt-Tanwier tour, Copenhagen 2000

Annika Lundgren and Public Educational Tours, supported by Wonderful Copenhagen, are proud to present a new biographical tour in their series on fascinating women of the twentieth and twenty-first centuries. The new tour features Alice Stiernfeldt-Tanwier, whose life and adventures in the Copenhagen area profoundly changed the course of political, social and economic events in the region throughout the 1980s and 90s. This unconventional tour takes you around Stiernfeldt-Tanwier's Copenhagen, following the footsteps of her adventurous life, and is guaranteed to show you a perspective of the city you never knew existed.

Tours depart every day from Town Hall Square, and are conducted in comfortable, air-conditioned buses. Approximate duration is two and a half hours, including stops for sight-seeing, photography, and refreshments. Profits from the tour will be used to install a memorial plaque in central Copenhagen dedicated to Alice Stiernfeldt-Tanwier.

Since researchers in the field of Copenhagen's modern history only started mapping out the facts of her life and work a few short years ago Alice Stiernfeldt-Tanwier is probably still a new acquaintance for most of you. Her influence on the development of the city was almost entirely overlooked until quite recently. Today, however, we have a more or less complete idea of how she lived her life, partly through the aid of her adoptive mother, Eleonor Stiernfeldt, who has graciously contributed diaries and family documents to the project.

The story of Alice Stiernfeldt-Tanwier begins in April 1963, far from here, on an oil rig in the middle of the North Sea. The rig belonged to the Danish Underground Consortium (DUC), founded by Danish shipping magnate A P Möller in 1962. Möller—a man with the gift of foresight—had already, by 1961, managed to secure a monopoly on oil in the Danish part of the North Sea. This proved to be one of the most intelligent moves in Danish industry. In the early 60s, most core samples were drilled on dry land, in the southern part of Jutland, but Möller was able to establish three small experimental oil rigs at a very early stage: their names were Madelene, Bodil and Alice.

These pioneer platforms were (unofficially) named after Möller's favourite lady friends of the time. Bodil was in fact Bodil Ipsen, founder of the famous Danish film award of the same name. The rigs were quite small—ships actually. Fitted with drilling equipment rather than platforms, each one boasted a crew of merely 20 men—rather modest when compared to today's enormous, modern oil rigs, employing hundreds of workers.

Aboard the platform named Alice, which is the one that interests us, a young Danish girl named Lise Holt was taking care of the kitchen duties. She was hired as an extra member of the crew at the very last minute, just before the rig left shore. She seemed quite anxious to get away from Copenhagen, and, as time was short, no questions were asked. It was generally assumed that, for one reason or another, she was hiding from the law, a theory strengthened by the fact that from the day she came aboard she never once chose to leave the platform during any of her days off.

She stayed at her post from 15 May 1962 until 7 April 1963—the morning she gave birth to a baby girl. A few hours later, she vanished from the platform, leaving an astonished crew behind with a screaming infant. Given the circumstances it was eventually concluded that one of the crew members must be the father. No one stepped forward to claim the daughter, so she was named after the rig, and transferred, at the first possible opportunity, to a private childcare institution in Copenhagen.

The Stiernfeldts had been married since 1965, and lived in a charming house, just behind the embassy area, that you can now see on your left. (Eleonor Stiernfeldt still inhabits the house, but given the increasing publicity around Alice's life, she has asked to be spared more visitors, and we will therefore refrain from getting any closer to the building than this.)

Eleonor and Valdemar met at the funeral of A P Möller, who sadly didn't live to see his dreams fully realised. Eleonor attended the service as a political journalist for one of Copenhagen's leading newspapers, and Valdemar Stiernfeldt was there representing the DUC.

He had lost his first wife, Beatrice, a few years back, and since his company strongly encouraged their top employees to assume the role of a settled family-man, Valdemar had been looking for a new wife for quite a while.

However, it must be assumed that love also played an important role. Eleonor was as intelligent and charming as she was beautiful, and their marriage was consummated only three months after they met.

Under the circumstances, Eleonor wisely kept her involvement in feminism and her participation in political actions to herself, justifying her frequent absences from the home as 'shopping time'. The fact that she never brought anything home with her completely escaped her husband, who was totally absorbed in his work. If he ever doubted this, her rapid spending of his money seemed to allay his suspicions. Valdemar Stiernfeldt was content, happily unaware that his salary was sponsoring countless feminist actions in Copenhagen throughout the 60s. In short, they lived as close to marital bliss as can be expected.

It was understood from the very beginning of their marriage that having children would never be an issue since Valdemar Stiernfelt was incapable of fathering a child. This suited Eleonor fine, and was actually one of the reasons she wished to marry him in the first place—she had other plans for her life. However, seeing Alice at the celebration of Copenhagen's anniversary in 1967 with birthday cake smeared all over her small face changed her point of view in a matter of seconds. There was something so extraordinary about the four year old girl that Eleonor couldn't take her eyes off her. The concept of adoption entered her mind for the very first time.

Being an efficient and well connected woman, Eleonor quickly found out the circumstances of the middle-aged woman and her brood of children at the private child-care institution, and from this moment on, heavy pressure was laid on her husband.

Valdemar Stiernfeldt was immediately opposed to the idea of adopting Alice, fearing unpleasant surprises that a set of uncertified genes might bring. But Eleonor, having set her mind on her objective, was not easily deterred, and circumstances would soon conspire to her advantage.

At this time, the DUC main office was located in the red building you see on the

ILLUSTRATION (PREVIOUS PAGE), LOGO BY ANNIKA LUNDGREN, 2000

other side of the square, which is now the headquarters of the newspaper *Morgenavisen Jyllandsposten*. Toward the end of the year, the company made their first substantial oil findings in the area later to become the Dan Field, the very first Danish oil field. On the morning of 2 November this news was delivered to the board of directors who were delirious with joy. In the evening an improvised party was held at the main office, involving enormous amounts of alcohol and assorted drugs.

As a result, several indiscretions were committed as the night unfolded. In Valdemar Stiernfeldt's case, the better part of a bottle of Swedish vodka eventually led to his becoming intimate with the vice president's secretary on top of the Xerox machine.

Convinced that he'd put the foolishness of his youth behind him long ago, he was rather surprised at himself. The perceptive Eleonor immediately picked up on his absent mood. A little research among the staff of the DUC revealed the ugly facts, and with this knowledge, she had no trouble bringing Valdemar Stiernfeldt to his knees in the adoption matter.

Using his connections and an ample sum of money, it was easy to arrange the papers and less than a week later Alice (without being consulted in the matter) was transferred from the children's home in Hoyensgade to the luxurious Stiernfeldt villa.

As a matter of fact, a few other results of the notorious party can still be traced in Copenhagen. Few citizens today are aware that the statue of Christian V in the middle of Kongens Nytorv Square, made by the French sculptor Lamoreux, originally included a naked nymph, sitting in the saddle behind the king.

As the story goes, this was also the evening when the site of the new DUC headquarters was chosen. The heavily intoxicated managing director is said to have driven the vice president in a shopping trolley down to the harbor by Nordre Toldbod and, sitting on the quay with what was left of a bottle of Tequila, they decided this was the perfect spot. (An interesting detail, here, is that the blue windows of the new building, which took the nickname 'Blue Eyes', were inspired by the likewise blue-eyed kitchen-maid from the company canteen that the managing director was infatuated with around this time.)

The impressive building was erected in 1979 when the oil findings in the North Sea exceeded even Möller's expectations. We are on our way to have a look at it now.

Refreshments will be served to all Public Educational Tours passengers directly in front of the building.

Ode[1]

I was brought up in the country. I was eight years old when I first "put my hand up a sheep to get a lamb", as they used to say. My arm could slide into the sheep up to the elbow—even as far as my shoulder. The feeling was tight, hot, complete, an infinity. I felt I was sinking into deep space. At that time I had not yet heard of black holes. Later, when I read about them, I felt that I knew them intimately.

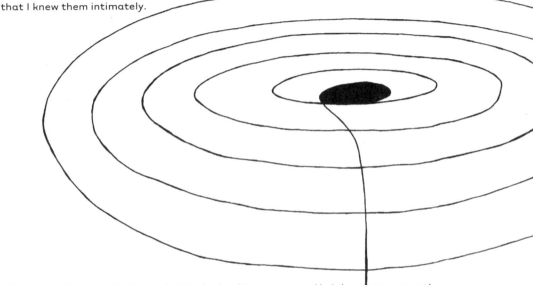

When I was 13 years old I helped with the lambing out east. My job was to sweep the yards. One morning I felt a strange ache and was swallowed up by a feeling of helplessness previously unknown to me. I went weak in the knees and the yard I was sweeping seemed enormous. At lunch, I couldn't keep anything down. Out in the toilet I discovered blood in my pants for the first time. It wasn't a very big stain, but it was an undeniable fact, like the powerlessness of that morning. The lunch break was short, and after that everyone drove out to the sheep sheds in a Russian jeep and a tractor. From one of the sheds we heard the bleating of a sheep that was in a bad way. Her waters had broken, but for some reason she didn't know how to push. Maybe her frame was too narrow, maybe the inherited collective memory which, at times like that, was supposed to be useful had failed her. I knew that she was two years old and that she had had a ewe the previous year.

I knelt down in the stall beside her. She was breathing fast, and clearly was very weak. I spoke gently to her as I reached slowly and cautiously up inside her. We became one. I groped with my hand and felt two lambs badly tangled together. I felt the heartbeat of one of the lambs. I knew that I needed to separate them and pull them out one at a time. The sheep panted heavily, showing her suffering. Her blood soaked my pullover up to the armpits. We bled as one. I felt I was awash inside myself. Me, her, giving birth to these lambs. Finally I succeeded in working out which leg was which, got a firm hold, and pulled the lambs out. First came a ewe, then a ram. Both survived. The mother immediately and eagerly licked them clean, never doubting that these lambs were hers. I was the one who was uncertain. Totally exhausted, I felt like I had given birth for the first time.

A man stands there before me with an opening to play with—an opening just like mine. Admittedly, he only has one opening while I have two. Both of us have other openings. Three openings is a lot, but in spite of that I have dreamt of having more and of having another 'pit'. Sure, I know I could get them if I really wanted—they've been designing such things now for a while.[2] But I have decided to content myself with the openings I was given. I could draw a picture of myself with more openings and a brand new pit. (Pictures are good for doing that sort of thing.) Some people might think that in making pictures, an artist has more control over her subject than she has in real life. I sometimes think so myself.

In this picture, I will use models that I know, not just one man, but several. I will paint one picture using

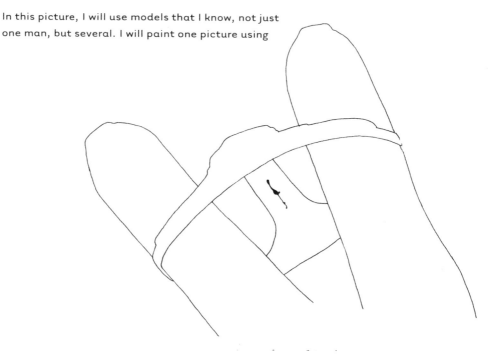

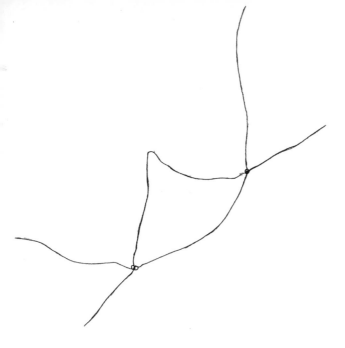

ILLUSTRATIONS: INGA SVALA THORSDOTTIR, 1999.

all of them. Of course, I could really let myself go—be more exact—and make more than one picture. But I have decided that since I am painting a picture of a man, as such, I can get them all into one picture.

I later discovered other openings. First of all I found the openings to my own body, and later—together—the openings to his body.

In order to search we need peace and quiet. We peek, touch, poke, feel. Go carefully inside, around the outside. Lose direction, find ourselves elsewhere. Come. When he reaches orgasm around my fingers, he clenches them tightly again and again. I close my eyes and feel we are two women.

Sometimes he is as I have heard women described by men: shy and wary about opening his legs completely. He clamps me like a girl. I can understand his shyness because I am a woman and know the trouble I have to go through to examine my own genitals. They are out of sight. When he discovered his opening with me, he said "Wow, I felt like I was you." It was then that I decided to draw this picture and call it *Odur* (Ode/Ecstatic).

I have total control over this picture. I can make him hot or cold. He can be big or small, hairy or beatific. I can place him wherever I like, lying in moss out east in August, for example. Or I could put him on a horseshoe-shaped desk on wheels. I can put him on a sink on a train, which is on schedule, going across the mainland. I could throw him onto a hotel bed wherever I like in the world. I could even travel through time and put him in the bed at my country home from the old days. That was where I had my first orgasm—it was cloudy, pink, the best.

A woman needs a mirror to examine her genitals.[3] Someone else can take the role of the mirror by taking a picture for instance, by writing some text, or by doing a painting. A man can hardly avoid seeing his genitals because he handles them several times a day. But to examine his anus, on the other hand, he needs a mirror, just like me. Gustave Courbet took on the role of a mirror in 1866, and painted a picture of a woman. He called it *L'Origine du Monde*. It was over a century ago that Courbet completed the picture, but I would like to thank him for his work now.

Notes

1. The original, Icelandic title of this piece, *Odur*, has a variety of meanings. As a noun it means 'ode', the title used here, but it also means 'bleating', the sound made by sheep. As a masculine adjective it has still other meanings: 'mad', 'ecstatic' or 'in ecstacy'.

   The god's name, Odin, comes from the same root word. Odin was the god of poetry and magic and also became the feminine branch of ecstatic, shamanistic magic known as seidur.

2. The Icelandic word used here, kriki, has a double meaning: 'armpit' and 'crotch'.

3. The Icelandic word for genitals, skopin, also means 'fate', and is in both senses connected to the word skopun, meaning 'creation', and the verb skapa meaning 'create'.

translated by Terry Gunnel

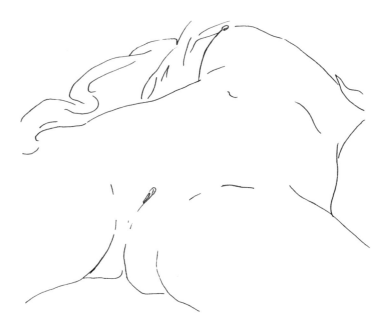

Anja Franke

From 24 Motifs

MOTIF #1

In the beginning, we see two figures walking toward each other at a relaxed pace. They are moving their way in from either side of the picture. They come to a stop when facing each other, standing in the centre of the picture. You cannot really hear what is being said, because the sound signal is constantly being broken off.

Anja Franke: Said that... there... probably...

Kaj Aage Drafenharden: S... ge... is funny...

> [*He tries to catch sight of the yellow building which earlier on she had said they should stop in front of.*]

AF: I don't know... I... this situation, what... th... you?

> [*She thinks the whole thing might be a contrived idea and hopes that not too much time will elapse before there is an explanation.*]

KAaD: But was... going away?

AF: ... not yet, but whether... s ... if... and then?

KAaD: No, you've got to... that's why.

AF: There is... it's going to happen, anyway... b... t... in the morning, it will continue, anyhow.

KAaD: ... in a little while... ue...

The sound connection, unfortunately, cannot be hooked up in a better way.

AF: ...!

> [*She lifts her hand to touch him, but he brushes back her gesture with a sudden movement. She looks down and pulls her hand back, with a touch of humiliation.*]

KAaD: ...!

> [*Like a reflex in the air, as if something were about to hit him in the eye, he puts his hand up to protect it.*]

AF: Are y... nervous?

> [*She notices that he starts, as her hand is about to caress him, as though a flash had struck him.*]

KAaD: I thought... I... hit.

> [*His eye reacts to light in a hypersensitive way.*]

AF: ... is spoken...

> [*She walks on past him and tries to act as though nothing has happened.*]

KAaD: Mmmm... I'll have a little bit... f... later on.

> [*He doesn't understand why she suddenly has to leave. He wonders about her disappointed expression, but not for very long.*]

The two figures walk in opposite directions and disappear out of the picture—out into either side. The picture is now vacated of people.

MOTIF #2

We are looking into a room and we see a figure whose back is bending over a milk-white tub, inside of which a large number of plastic bottles and bowls are gathered together. The whole thing appears to be very filthy and the person is trying with all possible contrivances to remove this muck. The person picks up a hose and turns on the hot water, full force. You can see how the ascending steam from the tub mists up the window—which is behind the tub—completely. In a close-up shot, you can see that the person is perspiring on her forehead. After this, the person takes her hand up to her brow and dries away the emerging beads of sweat. Suddenly the head is raised in a concentrated and tranquil attitude, in order to listen... the telephone is ringing.

KAaD: ...!

   [*He is waiting patiently for an answer on the other end of the line.*]

The figure standing alongside the steaming tub moves her way by leaps and bounds into the adjoining room. And begins rummaging through all kinds of things and pulling them away from heaped up piles. The ringing telephone cannot be located. A little bit confused, the person spins around and begins to move into another room. The telephone is lying there, concealed under a piece of cloth.

AF: Yes?

KAaD: Hello, it's me. What took so long?

AF: It was hard to find.

   [*Out of breath, she sits herself down on a chair positioned right beside her.*]

KAaD: Really... but hmmm...

   [*He doesn't really know how to begin to tell her.*]

AF: How are you doing?

KAaD: Everything's fine, hmmm...

AF: Is there anything I can do for you?

KAaD: Well, I just wanted to ask whether you could come sooner.

AF: Why do you ask?

   [*She gets up from the chair and spins around. She walks back into the room where the large, steam-filled, stinking tub is still standing.*]

KAaD: Something's come up!

   [*He has found a piece of paper, which he now sits nervously folding together into a smaller and smaller circumference. He's thinking that if he could only fold the last*

*little hard clump together, then the sum total of all the aggregate folds would
constitute the distance to the moon.]*

AF: I just have to... yeech, it stinks here.

*[She notices a stench that originates from a cross between shampoo, ammonia
and rotten eggs. Her concentration swerves.]*

KAaD: Of what?

*[The method of measurement can also be used in connection with the exposure of
a film. Since the diaphragm is round and is expanded, the quantity of light is
doubled, he thinks discreetly.]*

AF: It's actually difficult to describe specifically what it smells like here, but it's
maybe something of a hygienic ambience.

KAaD: OK, but would it be possible...

*[He has gotten hold of himself and now he knows perfectly well why he has called
her.]*

AF: That's up to you.

*[She pours a little bit of cold water over the many plastic articles in the tub, so
that she'll have a better chance of getting her fingers down into the foaming water.]*

KAaD: Yeah, but wouldn't it be best to open the door in advance?

*[He can hear in the receiver that she is breathing very heavily. She puffs out the
words, as if she were standing on her head.]*

AF: You've got to decide about that.

*[Now she can put her fingers down into the water for a longer period of time without
burning them.]*

KAaD: Is there something wrong?

[He cannot understand her dissociating attitude.]

AF: No, but how can I get everything to work out into a greater whole if I have to come
earlier, anyway?

*[The dirt is really caked very firmly onto the surfaces, and she tries to let the
water dissolve it as she scrubs the surfaces with a brush.]*

KAaD: You don't think, then, that we should start earlier because of that?

*[He can't really understand the aqueous and bubbling sound that can be heard in
the background of her gasping in the receiver. He's thinking that she probably
won't even come.]*

AF: I don't know?

*[She tries to scratch the old residue off with her nails, but they are clinging firmly
to the surfaces.]*

KAaD: What are you doing?

AF: Nothing… well, I'm drinking some water.

KAaD: That's what I can hear. But to get back to where we were, it was originally your idea. But maybe I could ask somebody else.

[It seems that she doesn't want to be involved anymore, he thinks.]

AF: Somebody else—what do mean by that?

[She wonders whether there maybe should be a little more boiling water, anyhow, in order to get rid of the last dark brown spots.]

KAaD: What I mean to say is, well, maybe you're not so interested, anyway?

[He's trying to come through and get a little more attention and he's wondering about the scratching sounds in the background.]

AF: Maybe …

[She cannot understand why the last remnants of brown residue cannot be scraped away. Maybe she should have used some aqua fortis instead? She's becoming a little bit irritated at not being able to extricate the whole thing.]

KAaD: Do you really mean that?

[He can hear that she seems a bit irritated by his questions and he cannot understand her sudden reversal in relation to what was previously arranged.]

AF: Oh, no…

[She has come to lay the hose in the opposite end of the tub and as she turned her back on this to prepare more boiling water, the hose began to wiggle around in the bottom of the tub. And instead, the water is squirting up into the air and has now made her all wet.]

KAaD: Yes, but you've got to understand, then, that I cannot understand what your really want…

[At this moment, her reaction in the receiver seems staggering in relation to her way of speaking to him.]

AF: I think that we should do whatever you believe is right.

[She stands there now—utterly soaked—and looks down at herself. Everything around her is wet. She is thinking and hoping that she could just take it all from the top. Everything has wound up in a horrible mess. She cannot understand at all why she actually started doing this cleaning job, and she wishes that it were all over.]

MOTIF #5

A figure stands inside a room, with the body bent over a large plastic tub from where steam is rising. The window behind her is completely steamed up and outside it is pitch dark. The figure straightens out her back, supports her hand by pressing it against the small of her back, and winces a little bit. The person stands completely still and looks—over across the steaming tub—out into the darkness. The figure turns around and walks out of the room.

A second figure—in some other place—is sitting, half-reclining, surrounded by large soft pillows. The body is swathed in a large soft cloth. The feet stretch down into a small steaming tub that is standing on the floor.

AF: [cough], [cough], [cough]... ugh...

[She's trying to maintain an artificial optimism in spite of the grueling headache and a lurking influenza. She can feel that her neck and her throat are like sandpaper.]

The figure that has just left the first room with the large, steaming tub is now standing in the adjoining room. The person stretches out and begins listlessly to take off her pants. After this, the first of her stockings is removed. Then the person sits herself down on a wide sofa, in order to remove the other stocking. After this, the underpants are nudged off—while the person sits on the sofa. The person takes an investigative look at her own naked legs and her pubic region. Slowly, the blouse is raised over the head and is lain over the back of the sofa. The person stands up and lifts off her undershirt. The person stands naked on the floor and at last, she picks up a large soft cloth and wraps it around her body.

KAaD: Oooh... wow, it's cold!

[He stands there freezing, while simultaneously attempting to arrange his clothes into some system on the chair. He is a little bit irritated that she's getting sick again just now—since their appointment to meet is going to be cancelled. At the same time, he is thinking and hoping that she will remember to drink something warm.]

The other place, where the sick person is lying on her bed.
AF: ...!

[She takes her feet up from the warm water and dries them in a towel. After this, she raises her heavy body, slowly, up from its soft bed. She is thinking about

whether she should try to drink something warm. Systematically, she folds the large soft towel and places it on the chair.]

KAaD: Try some mint tea. It ought to be good for your voice and for your throat, my dear.

[He is standing with the soft towel wrapped around him and has lain his clothes in place—on the chair. He begins to walk out into the other room, where the steaming tub is situated.]

AF: Yeah, sure. I will... oh, it hurts so much in my throat.

[Yeah, right, he just knows it all, she thinks, and supports herself—still wobbling—on the chair. And after a little while—as she begins to feel a little better—she walks out into an adjoining room. Just before the end of this room, there is a large tub, situated beneath a dark window.]

KAaD: You've got to get rid of all the ugly bacteria—you do know how such things behave?

[In the meantime, he has come out to the large, steaming tub. He can smell how the bubble bath's fragrance has begun to spread its way into the room.]

AF: How?

[She positions herself in front of the sink and pours some water into a kettle. She turns up the hot water. And with a long hose, she starts to fill up the large tub with hot water.]

KAaD: How?! Well, in the first place, how does it feel in your throat? Can you feel anything different?

[He stands beside the large tub and guides his hand down into the water in order to feel the temperature.]

AF: Sure... [cough], [cough], [cough]... aahh... ooohh, I can feel that the muscular contractions in my throat are a sign of irritation. And in this way, my throat is playing a part in preventing the entrance of foreign bodies into my lungs.

[She takes a little bit of bubble bath oil down from the shelf and pours a few drops down into the steaming tub.]

KAaD: Yes, you're quite right there, but the bacteria are not so easy to drive away as all that.

[He can sense that the water is still a bit too hot and in order to neutralise the temperature, he turns on the cold water.]

AF: What do you mean by that?

[She stands there—feverish—and watches how the suds have risen inside the tub until the foam spills out over the edge. She feels the water's temperature and

turns off the hose. She notices the fragrance that has spread its way out into the room.]

KAaD: You better believe I'm going to tell you all about it. The air is filled with infectious matter from bacteria, viruses and other micro-organisms from the respiratory passages, through coughing, breathing, talking, and the like. Micro-organisms are scattered about from the skin, hair and clothing.

[He turns off the cold water and tests, one last time, whether the water's temperature is suitable.]

AF: The air is contaminating me?

[She takes the boiling water from the stove and pours it out over her mint tea leaves.]

KAaD: No, it's not the air. It's the microbe particles.

[He takes off the soft towel that has still been wrapped around his body, and hangs it up on a peg close by. Slowly, he gets up into the bubbling tub. He stands with the one naked, white ankle down in the water for a little while, so that he can get used to the new temperature's warmth.]

AF: Oh… my blood and my organs hurt so much.

[She places herself alongside the steaming tub and disrobes. She tests ever so cautiously—with her foot—whether the water is going to burn her skin.]

KAaD: And when the bacteria have first penetrated inside your body—as they now have, in your case—they come directly down into your lungs via the dust in the air. And down in your lungs they are ensnared by certain special cells, which transport the bacteria around in your body, from where they can attack.

[He stands with his white ankles in the bubbling bathtub and slowly begins to bend down. He can feel how the difference between the hot and the cold grows indistinct the farther down he sinks under the foam.]

AF: It's tingling so painfully in all my joints… oh, my body is getting weaker.

[The temperature is either too hot or too cold and she begins to rise up from the steaming, foaming tub.]

KAaD: But what's even worse is that your bacteria can also penetrate your nerve cells and they can dwell in these cavities for quite some time—without any opposition—until your body is weakened. Then they perk up again, and attack.

[Now he has his whole body in the foaming bathtub. He feels great satisfaction and shuts his eyes, while enjoying this moment of warmth flowing through his body.]

AF: Attack…?

[Her body has slowly begun its descent into the tub. She comes to a complete standstill at different intervals, with the result that her body temperature slowly adjusts itself to the bath's warmth.]

MOTIF #7

KAaD: Dissolve it.

AF: Where?

KAaD: Down there.

AF: It's not so easy.

KAaD: Try!

AF: I'm trying, but it's going out all the time.

KAaD: It's almost about to melt...

AF: Lift it a little bit more.

KAaD: It's crumbling again.

AF: It's hard to hear you.

KAaD: IT'S CRUMBLING!

AF: ...?

KAaD: It's very close to vanishing.

AF: You're really moving right through again.

KAaD: A little bit more!

AF: Oh no, you've got to stretch it out a little bit more to the other side.

KAaD: Should I stay here?

AF: Yes, if you can, then do it.

KAaD: It's starting to get complicated.

AF: Almost.

KAaD: I'm going to move up a little bit once again.

AF: But not too fast.

KAaD: But it's necessary to use some more oxygen.

AF: There's almost no more left, try to save it...

KAaD: That's not easy.

AF: Try to orient yourself.

KAaD: I can't see anything...

AF: From where?

KAaD: Right in front.

AF: *WHITE OUT...?*

KAaD: It's beginning to whir.

AF: But we'll have to try to lower the tempo again.

KAaD: The light?

AF: Slower!

KAaD: Fish, dogs, birds, trees, cars, beams, modules and buildings are moving closer, with a speed of 20 miles a second.

AF: From where?

KAaD: In the light...

AF: Relax!

KAaD: Air...

AF: Can you breathe?

KAaD: ...!

AF: Move down a little again.

KAaD: ...!

AF: Can you hear me?

KAaD: My windpipe has gotten constricted.

AF: The air has got to move back and forth.

KAaD: ...!

AF: You've got to use the horseshoe-shaped rings that are open at the back. In between these openings, there is cartilage and that means that your windpipe is very elastic and moveable.

KAaD: It's coming again.

AF:....

On account of technical reasons, this dialogue between the two individuals was suddenly broken off.

MOTIF #21

Soft tones, which seem to issue from a person humming, can be heard inside a room. It is difficult to see where this sound is coming from, because a dense, white, moist steam fills up the room. But by moving around inside the room and over toward the spot from where the tones are sounding, what can be faintly seen, at last, are bodily fragments sticking up from a bathtub. The bathtub is filled with steaming hot and white foaming water. The body belongs to a person of the masculine gender. He is busy looking—through the water and down at his stomach—at an old scar. The scar is situated at the lowest part of his stomach, just a few centimetres from his sexual organs.

KAaD: Humm!

[Pensively, he moves his fingers over the hard scar tissue and ponders whether she has ever asked him how he got the scar. Or maybe she has never even turned her gaze toward this area of his body. And that's actually quite sad, he thinks.]

He is sitting on a rubber mat, which has been placed at the bottom of the bathtub. The rubber mat prevents his body from sliding back and forth.

KAaD: Humm... humm... hum... hummmm... hum... hum...

AF: When are you going to be ready?

KAaD: In a minute.

AF: Yeah, but I'm very busy.

KAaD: It'll be a little while yet.

AF: Can I come in?

KAaD: Yeah, sure. Come right in.

AF: Thanks.

[She opens the door to the steam-filled room and waves her hand around, with some degree of irritation, in an attempt to remove the dense fog.]

KAaD: Close the door, it gets cold in here very quickly.

[He removes his hand from the scar on his stomach as she walks in through the door.]

AF: What are you doing?

KAaD: Nothing much.

AF: Is anything wrong?

KAaD: No.

AF: There's a very dense mist in here.

KAaD: Yeah, there's a very dense mist in here.

AF: Is the water hot?

KAaD: Yes, it's still hot.

AF: It's cold outside.

KAaD: Is it cold outside?

AF: How long are you going to sit there?

KAaD: Until the water gets cold.

AF: May I?

KAaD: Do you really think that's a good idea?

AF: Uh-huh.

KAaD: Shouldn't it be a little warmer?

AF: Yes, please!

KAaD: That was really some kind of machine that he'd made, don't you think?

AF: It sure was, and did you notice what a long time you could sit on the stimulator?

KAaD: They were completely disheveled and could hardly stand on their own two legs after that.

AF: Well, that's not so strange… It runs on solar energy.

KAaD: The vibrator has to be there in the front, where the seat is placed—it has to be a stimulating and thermogenic sequence of action.

AF: Action and action—there's not so much of that. How much time do you actually think a clitoral orgasm can last?

KAaD: Well, you know—and I don't.

AF: It's quite a long while—and that's why the machine is not really such a bad idea.

KAaD: Yeah, he's not such a screwball, after all.

AF: He'll certainly sell quite a few of them.

KAaD: Do you think that you can use it alone?

AF: Maybe, but then you've got to be careful that you don't fall off.

KAaD: But maybe you can be strapped firmly into place.

AF: Who knows?

MOTIF #22

In a passenger cabin far above the surface of the Earth, a number of passengers are sitting, all strapped firmly in their seats. On either side of the middle aisle, there are five or six seats. All of the seats are taken, and it is very cramped. The stewardesses move back and forth, very professionally. The captain apologises for the high degree of turbulence in the air and requests that the stewardesses take their seats. Now everybody has got to buckle up their seatbelt. A series of hard impacts strike the cabin, and the airplane dips, again and again, into air pockets.

P#3: But of course there are some drawbacks to using the vibrator in such great doses at one time.

[He continues—unnoticed—with his description of the physiological imperfections.]

KAaD: Are you finished eating?

[He is trying to change the subject and feels a little bit exhausted by this agitated airplane ride.]

AF: I don't understand how you can both be so apathetic about the physical injuries.

[She is sitting on the innermost of the sequence of seats and takes a look, a little sulky, out of the window.]

P#3: But that's the crucial factor—it can be stopped in time, but that's individual.

[He's still completely absorbed with his own observations.]

KAaD: And what have you made of that?

[He turns and tries to keep his gaze fastened on her.]

AF: Made of what?

[She looks directly into his eyes and notices that they are situated very close together. He has a blackhead on his nose—it is dark and ripe.]

P#3: But of course it's important to the whole thing that the movements be constant.

[He stares to the front, with an empty expression, and doesn't even notice the other two gazing at one another.]

KAaD: I'm tired of the current interests...

[He senses a faint bubbling in his blood and it begins to tingle in his hands.]

AF: But you can run into people who are extremely interested in themselves and when the current interests have blown over, attention can no longer be established. We become nothing but topics for one another.

[She is soliloquising out loud.]

KAaD: But can you come up with any positive aspects of that?

P#3: Well, for example, the chair is stable and harmonic in its movements. And it has

ILLUSTRATION: ANJA FRANKE, DRAWING OF HER APARTMENT IN WHICH THE MOTIFS WERE WRITTEN AND MOST OF THEM TAKE PLACE

148

been made in a hyper-aesthetic design.

AF: It's little bit sad—and that's not so strange, that you can feel exploited after those kinds of experiences.

[*She sits completely still and can sense that her urethra feels irritated.*]

KAaD: But is that enough?

P#3: Yes, it's a lot—we avoid bladder infections.

AF: ...!

[*She's thinking that she's got to get out of here. But how?*]

KAaD: Is there something wrong?

AF: I've got to go to the toilet!

P#3 & KAaD: Again?

[*Both of them look at her, at precisely the same time.*]

Introduction to KAaD (Kaj Aage Drafenharden)

In February 1994, KAaD was established. The name conceals a fictitious person, who, to me, represents the Other—in conversation with myself. The name Kaj Aage Drafenharden is an anagram for Anja Franke Hedegaard—my baptismal name.

KAaD arose from an absence or a longing, within which I found a need for producing a textual form. I wanted the textual form to make its appearance as a parallel trail in my art. It is my intention that texts, objects and installations are equally related to each other.

In the beginning, I allowed KAaD to appear before the reader through questions asked by him. And with the reply to these, I wanted to be able to submit a formulated exposition about how my art and its discourse should appear in the given textual form. Later on, I allowed KAaD to disappear from the picture and into the writings. On the basis of this, I began to use him as my recipient. At the present time, KAaD makes his appearance on many different levels. What is crucial for the reader, however, is that there is no doubt about KAaD or about how this person ought to be regarded, whether he is named or not in the text.

In January 1998, *24 Motives: a manuscript* was published in connection with a reception in my space in Copenhagen, Mfkokm, which is an alternative space for art and art related material. At the reception, in addition to the manuscript, the space visualised a black bubble universe. And there was a video recording of *Motive #11*, filmed for the occasion. I imagine the motives could be filmed, and I am still working on ways of processing them in this direction.

24 Motives: a manuscript consists of 24 dialogues, each one having its own story. KAaD and AF (Anja Franke) are the main characters. But there are also supporting characters who figure into the stories. The orientation with respect to space, time and geography is decomposed—the universe is represented as it would appear when looking out of a diving bell's porthole. There is no linearity in the narrative structure— on the contrary, the narrative structure is a jumble of actions and thoughts, where meanings fortuitously cross over one another on several levels. Originally I organised the writing of them as a movement through the body, mentioning 24 organs, one in each text. But the 24 stories can also be extracted completely from the sequential context and be combined in new ways, thus obstructing the relations between the organs, but in this maybe creating new bodies with other capabilities and different ways of processing input and output.

translated by Dan A Marmorstein

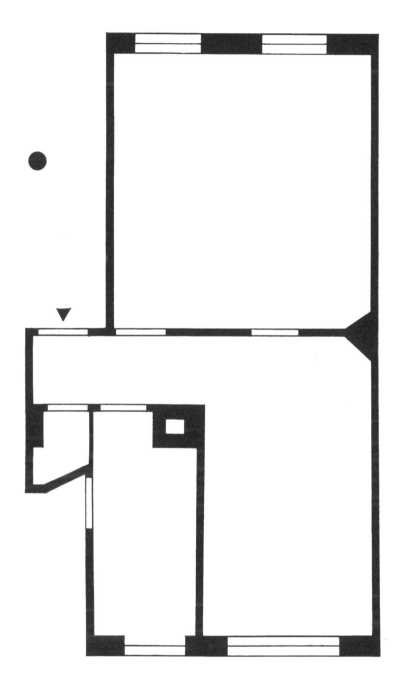

—What does it mean to be a 'subject'?, to be 'subjective'? That one speaks from oneself, that one, so to speak, *is* oneself? And how does this 'self' come about—from the 'inside' as a kind of essence, or from the 'outside' through socialisation? The questions are seemingly banal, but they nonetheless point to a number of complex problematics which very quickly become relevant for the practice as well as the self-understanding of the artist. What is the "I" that the artist speaks from?

—Often in mainstream and popular discourses works are understood as utterances not only *from* a subject, but also thus automatically *about* this subject. Readings that sometimes occur explicitly against the intentions of the work. It often seems that to a broader audience the artist is always already understood as a subject who can only speak about him/herself; and thus the work/the artist (one and the same thing!) becomes interesting as a symptom, rather than as providing some kind of analysis, to speak in psychoanalytical metaphors.

—We can consider the self as an open category, as something constantly in the making, rather than as something made. Furthermore, the self must be considered relational as opposed to an autonomous entity, something soft and permeable, open to influences and changes from and towards others. And, then, as something over which one does not have complete control—not only is the self and the body regulated and defined by societal structures, but also immediately changeable, inhabitable even, in the company of others. The care of the self must also involve an ethic of others, a situation of negation and exchange, identity and identification.

—In the Nordic countries, as elsewhere, identity politics has become a growing issue during the 1990s, but these efforts have not always been effective. Simultaneous to the formulation and self-definition of minority positions, there has been a backlash against feminism and queer theory, as well as a growing racism and ensuing hardening of national immigration policies. Feminism has been criticised in a particular manner, not as disruptive, but rather as redundant, a historical moment that shouldn't be undone, but that has passed, making further discussions irrelevant and tiresome. And while gay marriages have been allowed, laws on artificial insemination have recently been regulated in Denmark, now making it illegal for lesbian and single women to be inseminated. In terms of racism, the ideas of an identity politics has been curiously reversed by the right, who have cleverly employed them for their reactionary goals. To be white and male is an ethnic position, defined from the inside, and therefore something that demands recognition as a self-described minority in a global sense, and as such a group that should be given special privileges. Identity politics have been victim to a 'hostile takeover' and its logic reversed, which make a redefinition, if not abandonment, of such political strategies necessary and a challenge for the future.

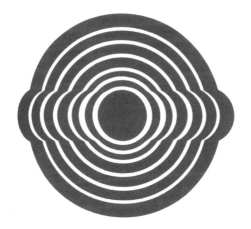

One of the most evident tendencies in recent art has been the more or less strategic merging of popular, mass and youth cultural signs with artistic practices and modes of reception; or, between popular culture and the political. These strategies are based on the notion that critiques and subversions of contemporary society must go through so-called popular, consumerist or mass-culture. This can be termed a *politics of identification*.

These ideas have, of course, been raised within art since the advent of situationism and pop art in the late 50s and early 60s. Both artistic movements that had a strong position in Scandinavia, most notably through historical figures such as Asger Jorn in Denmark and Öyvind Fahlström in Sweden, who employed situationst and pop ideas, respectively, in their work as part of a leftist political strategy. Popular culture was read as the people's culture, and if it did indeed speak about consumerism, about a capitalistic cultural logic and the commodification of desire, it was a question of *reversing* signs: of employing the signs of capital in the service of the left through appropriation, alteration and subversion.

Today, there is still a strong belief in the political potentials of popular culture, although now mixed with a knowledge about populist politics' appropriation of signs, and, on another level, about the pleasures—even fetishisation— of popular cultural signs. The artist and/or subjects in general using popular culture for political means are caught between fetishisation and politicisation of signs and objects, and between notions of pop culture as subversive and affirmative. It is thus a matter of a constant negotiation and mediation between different readings and/or usages of the signs, as well as an attention to the specifs of the objects. The objects you employ matter: they are specific in terms of history and significations. Objects of popular culture are not just 'pop' as a bland, mono-cultural mass, but differently coded, and, presumably, recodable, entities.

This can be traced in writings about music in this chapter by Bjørn Bjarre, Gardar Eide Einarsson and Jan Svenungsson, that all offer readings, projections and/or intentionalities towards certain, treasured musical styles or forms. In the essay, "Formless Music", Bjarre writes of listening experiences from a fan's perspective: How the music makes him feel and think, and how this experience brings him closer to an understanding and definition of the so-called 'formless', a notion of anti-form known from the theory of George Bataille as well as from particular methodologies within modern and contemporary art. Bjarre's descriptions of music acts as a parallel to his artistic practice, where he is also concerned with the production of formless art objects. Writing about another art form, such as music, is thus employed strategically, as a kind of parallel thinking, in relation to establishing theories of visual art. This becomes evident in the two essays on punk rock; Einarsson's "Hard Core, Self-Organisation and Alternativity", where the hardcore punk scene is viewed structurally, and in order to provide an alternative model for production and distribution of knowledge within visual art; and Svenungsson's "On Punk", which is actually two separate essays on The Sex Pistols and Siouxsie and the Banshees, respectively, that attempts to recontextualise punk rock aesthetics historically and methodically. Here, punk rock is analysed as both spectacle and performance, as in the case of the Pistols playing themselves as well as their music on the 1990s reunion tour, and as a conceptual art practice, as in the case of Steve Severin of the Banshees' bass playing.

In "Anne Lee and the Four Women", Anneli Nygren also searches for avatars, heroines and talismans within popular culture, or, more accurately, popular media. Nygren describes her own video works, where she impersonates public figures such as Joan Collins, Yoko Ono, Raisa Gorbatchova and Anne Rice. However, unlike the rock writers, Nygren is not content with images and stories about her idols, she wants to *become* them through an act of roleplaying. If the above mentioned texts can all be said to locate identification points within popular culture—i.e. positive references—the last two texts by Lars Mathisen and Arturas Raila points to the dark sides of desire, where liberation becomes destructive. However, they both expand on the notion of identifications in general, and on the specific, almost subcultural references of punk and formlessness in particular. One might also refer to the negation of form(s) and the emergence of the abject in Mathisen's essay "Notes for an Understanding of the *Safe Condition* Project" that begins this chapter. Mathisen tries to illuminate his own work, concerned, as it is, with appropriation, readymades, pornography and the debasement and decentering of identity as is evident in the story of Charles Manson. Here, hidden histories are inescapable, as the personal and the popular interweave in the very act of reading and narrating, as is also the case in Raila's text "2x2", which returns to the history and representation of the Sex Pistols and the subversive 'punk' stance cut across the political opposites of liberalism and communism. These texts can be read as efforts to locate meanings and stake new areas for identification, pleasure and politics.

Take an object
Do something to it
Do something else to it

Jasper Johns[1]

Danish family found in open trailer

In 1984, inside an open trailer on Vesterbrogade in Copenhagen, one of my friends found five metal canisters. The trailer belonged to a second-hand dealer. You know, my friend is something of a collector of metal articles from the 1950s. He got them cheap. To him, the aesthetic of the metal can was something beautiful, something signalling a material consumption from an indeterminate past. My friend had no special purpose in mind what he would use these articles for. And now, they were just lying there in a corner of our studio, until one day I asked about their contents. The metal canisters all contained black and white 16mm film. When the strips of film were held up to the light, we could see people running around in a garden, standing in front of a house, lying on the beach. I got the rolls of film; my friend kept the metal canisters. Shortly thereafter I borrowed a film projector and looked at the entire sequence of the five reels of film.

The first thing I saw on the wall of our studio was an old man taking a walk along a wide sandy beach. He resembled my own grandfather. It's summer, and he's wearing a pair of large woollen bathing trunks that come all the way up around his waist. He waves with both arms and smiles to the camera. On the next reel, cyclists and cars are moving along a boulevard where Nazi flags and sculptures can be seen everywhere.

I look at all of the reels, all the way through—60 minutes in all, without sound. As the evening progressed, I was consumed with a sense of surprise but I also became increasingly curious about what I was seeing: a Danish family's recordings of themselves and their kin over a period spanning more than 22 years. Between the sequences, there were frames with captions such as: "Solrød Beach, 1932", "To the Olympics and Tyrol, 1936", "Aage Teaches Dad to Shoot, 1943", "The Liberation of Denmark on May 5, 1945" and "Mother's Birthday, 1950". Pictures of a middle class Danish family's filmed scenes of their own lives before, during and after World War II. Pictures on film recorded and created with a great deal of enthusiasm for a very specific group of viewers: the family and those who were nearest and dearest. The pictures made me think about sequences of action from my own family's history.

"The only thing that makes reality is death"

... a quotation taken from an interview in 1985 with the American imprisoned for the rest of his life, Charles Manson, who was 50 years old at the time. He had spent 37 years of his life in reform schools or prisons. "The most dangerous man alive", as one could read on the front page of the 25 June 1970 issue of *Rolling Stone* magazine. In 1971, Manson was sentenced to death in the gas chamber, along with three other members of the Manson Family. The sentence was handed down for his having, in 1969, instigated bestial killings of Hollywood actors and their friends in Los Angeles villas. On the walls of these villas, the word "PIGS" was written with the blood of the victims. In 1996, Manson was still alive. The abolishment of the death penalty in California has allowed him to live the rest of his life in prison.

In the middle of the 60s, the Manson Family dropped out of society and chose a life of isolation at Spahn's Movie Ranch, outside Los Angeles, among other places. There, they grew vegetables, took drugs, had orgies and religious rites, and made films and music. Charles Manson was the spiritual and ideological fulcrum. He regarded the "rich pigs" in fashionable Los Angeles as "display animals in the wax museums". In his own special way, the district attorney in the subsequent trial, Vincent Bugliosi, merely shored up this image by characterising Manson as a new Adolf Hitler: "Both were vegetarians; both were small men." Others regarded Manson as a product of American society. A rebel and a hero who, in spite of the killings, had become the sacrificial lamb that a wider American society needed in its squaring of accounts with a generation that was protesting against the Vietnam War and the consequences of the United States' social and cultural politics under the administration of President Richard Nixon. A political programme that, for many people, not only placed a question mark beside the USA's internal and global position but nearly brought about a state of affairs in the political and cultural milieu that had not been seen in the USA since the days of McCarthy's political agenda of the 1950s. In the USA today, most political and cultural groups are fed up with the reclaimed cult status that Charles Manson attained in the 1980s. Times are different now. For these people, the many ethnic, cultural and social problems that the USA is experiencing today are manifestations of a condition that has to be viewed in a different light than what is thrown back to us from the 1960s.

Pornography

In *The Invention of Pornography* Lynn Hunt writes: "Pornography was not a given; it was defined over time and by the conflicts between writers, artists and engravers on the one side and spies, policemen, clergymen and state officials on the other. Its political and cultural meanings cannot be separated from its emergence as a category of thinking, representation and regulation."

Previously, pornography and sexual descriptions were deliberately employed for the purpose of drawing out different political and artistic boundaries in society. Pornography has been a way of criticising, transgressing and undermining a society's social and cultural standards. In societies which regarded it as dangerous that intimate physical displays and free thinking would become accessible to the public, pornography was regarded as being disruptive on a par with extremist political activities. In other words, a sexual orientation was perceived as disruptive to the society's social, economic, mental and physical hygiene. Society lived with pornography, but through legislation, government marginalised and repressed the concept of freedom and the consequences it feared in the publication of visualised bodily lust. Many people connect pornography with prostitution, which was legal in Denmark until 1906, whereas the publication of pornographic material was forbidden until 1967, when the prohibition against the sale of pornography was repealed. No longer was pornography considered a taboo by Danish society—it was thereby deprived of its old status of being immoral and subversive.

One of the political explanations for the repeal of this legislation was that it would have a mentally hygienic influence on the number of assaults committed by sexual deviants. The repeal of the prohibition against pornography was also regarded by some as the beginning of sexual liberation. But the legalisation of pornography did not entail an equality of sexual and political status. The overtly male point of view is still dominant, not only within the realm of pornographic representation, but also in advertising's imagery in general. Sexual undertones and the naked female body are still employed for the purpose of selling everything from beer and clothing to motor oil and credit cards. And paradoxically enough, in light of the emergence of the AIDS epidemic, the pornography of the 1990s has come to be characterised as a form of safe sex, in striking contrast to the 1960s' ideas about a boundary-transgressing free love.

Today, the private and even potentially most political, sexuality, is being taken care of by what is the most rapidly expanding picture industry in the world, the porno industry. Pornography is available in most video rental centres, supermarkets and kiosks—on TV channels, the Internet and through interactive games. In a pseudo-moralistic Western culture, many generations of people are zapping their way through pornographic films, news broadcasts' repeated transmission of identical pictures from the world political situation hot spots and cultural programmes with features—more concise than the weather forecast—about global social themes, food, art and the newest (sexual) subcultures. The very idea of pornography has acquired a new and expanded significance in programmes where personal and political fascinations are transmitted with a superficial commitment and with a pictorial character that does not differentiate itself from real pornography: pictures supported by an alien soundtrack. Pictures that focus on the isolated and the identity-less. A new type of pornography has emerged: a social and cultural news-porno. A world in which, "We have an explosion of information but an implosion of meaning."

Reproduction and repetition

Reading and understanding pictures is something we do as a means to orient ourselves: a part of our life and our history. Pictures that might have the character of events and predictions which have been told again and again and continually transferred to the inner retina—and attributed to a vision. A sequential series of successive chapters or a series of events that have been visualised through explanations of mythical, social and artistic character. About Paradise, Nirvana, rebirth, immortality, heaven and hell. From the very first depictions of gods and their pedestals to representations of strange creatures and human beings in other parts of the world to beings from outer space. Representations and pictures created for the purpose of preserving a society's self-awareness and for rendering it possible to address ourselves to the incomprehensible. The figurative rendering of prohibitions and injunctions. The history of the tribe, remembrance and expectation. Pictures produced both inside and outside society's official organs—all of them influenced by society's morals and ethics. In the present, this picture production is being supplemented by an electronic picture world. A world that affects us, regardless of whether it is situated inside or outside the immediately recognisable. A picture world which, through images from the monitors in our living rooms and bedrooms, has come to be a part of reality. Pictures that are streaming around here on Earth, but also pictures that with the speed of light are on their way away (like clumps of the past) from Earth's atmosphere. Away from a— apparently meaningless—chaos of bits of information.

Between the World Wars, the German philosopher Walter Benjamin wrote of the disappearance of a certain type of (oral) story-telling in favour of media information. This was a story-telling that was based on experience, where the experience of others passed through the story-teller, who in turn had to make the experiences his own in order to pass them on to others. Thus story-telling was far removed from information, facts and truth, but rather a process where the story received influence and imprints from various agents and ages as it passed from mouth to mouth, or was written down. The origin of the story, then, is not original information but experience passed on.

What we perceive through the faculty of sight subsumes not only the establishment of a sensory experience. We see through the entire body and the body is still the central media through which the world is understood. But what we mean by 'remembering', 'feeling', 'smelling' and 'hearing' has changed in character through electronic communication: to a greater degree, we have supplemented our own bodily experiences with experiences of electronic media. In a non-ecological condition of events, where what arises is a positive doubt about what is real. A virtual condition of neither reality nor dream. A condition where, even earlier on, people have always been producing disquieting pictures—in the land of sleep—in an admixture of dream and reality. Pictures which in a state of wakefulness possess no unequivocal meaning and that do not seem to be arranged in any chronological succession, but rather according to changing patterns of association.

Beginning without end: abstract or figurative?

In visual art there are many, from practitioners to art historians to viewers, who make a distinction between the abstract and the figurative: a distinction that has its source in conceptions of art history. In the present, this distinction has quietly drifted into an ordinary reading or reference to art: an abstract picture has no recognisable figures and a figurative picture has no abstract symbols.

However, the two concepts also crop up in our everyday lives, where we are constantly sampling real actions, metaphors and symbols, as a natural part of specifying precisely something that we feel or something that we've seen. Through this means, we come to accept that different statements and pictures are constantly changing in their meaning, entirely according to what situational context, or within which exposure, they are seen or executed. In much the same way, we come to believe that we are able to distinguish between different layers of reality. We feel that we can apprehend conceptions and events simultaneously, in an area between something recognisable and something not recognisable.

Here, the abstract is a part of the concrete—and the concrete is a part of the abstract or a place in between. Some third element supervenes in the very movement between, or the apprehension, of the one and the other. Not necessarily here and now, but through a movement without common properties: something aesthetically beautiful, naturally present—poetically relevant.

This is also how it is in modern art: fruits, animals, people, movements, handicraft, chemical reactions, dreams, guts, landscapes, text, garbage, thoughts... everything can make its appearance in one and the same artistic gesture. It might be painted, modelled, printed, photographed, pre-fabricated, narrated... regardless of whatever means, the question is whether the chosen method has incorporated a filling in, a reflection or a critique of the time within which the social, artistic and personal have come into being. For the understanding and experience of art, figurative contra abstract no longer has any unequivocal meaning.

That history repeats itself is a cliché-filled truth which, however, cannot divest anybody of the opportunity of perceiving his/her own existence as an independent condition and accordingly—along with the others—of availing himself of the opportunity for using history freely. And accordingly of adding new thoughts and products to the same world—in an endless condition of a 'beginning without end'.

There is still a widespread perception that an artist is some kind of individual oracle: a person who has chosen to stand and who is capable of standing outside the ordinary world. But artists from the past like Van Gogh, Monet and Mondrian didn't walk around with their heads beneath their arms—outside society. Neither is this the case today—talented artists regard their picture-related contribution as having sprung from a methodical reflection on the present—a reworking of pictures and forms in relation to a past that preceded it and in anticipation of a future.

Safe Condition

Safe Condition is an art project that through an ongoing series of works implicates different themes concerned with cultural critique. The aggregate project aims to illuminate how we try to construct safe conditions as part of an effort to create an autonomy in our actions and around things. This might involve something that claims to protect us from the unexpected, the uncomfortable and the unknown. The project moves, through different themes placed in shifting localities and media, via symbols and metaphors, toward producing something that is neither art nor non-art. An open scene. A doubt.

In 1991, I used *Safe Condition* as the title of an art project for the first time. At the end of the 1980s, I had begun to work with sculptural or installed works. What I missed in the material was another kind of spatiality—a room that literally spoke and was not merely enacted right in front of the viewer. And what was even more important, I wanted the presence of things that could play a part in unravelling the boundaries between art and other realities. Things that by sheer virtue of their physique would supply the picture with a different and more historic dimension. A dimension that underscored the idea that an artistic whole is subservient to a series of—what are in reality—incalculable choices. Choices that entailed that the viewer's active presence came to be a natural part of the artwork. The viewer would be obliged to accept the role of actor inside the space that he or she stepped into—situated between art and reality. Not in the manner of an electronic virtual reality space, and neither a mystical nor a symbolic space. But rather a space within which the viewer's expectations and doubts and the work itself were in focus. A space where the scene could not be taken in all at once. A situation that did not lend itself to survey, but which ought to be capable, moreover, of being established both inside and outside the traditional art institution.

One of the earliest projects was *Safe Condition, Art Library Puzzle*, from 1991, a gigantic crossword puzzle on display at the Gentofte Art Library, where 43 titles from twentieth century art history were laid out in a pattern consisting of small concrete slabs placed on a green carpet measuring 36m^2. An artwork where the collection of artist names and concepts were torn from a logical context, while the designated objects did not change form, since in their placement inside the exhibition space, they fashioned a labyrinthine pattern. A pattern where immeasurability was dependent on the position of the viewer. A 1:1 crossword without a pencil. But with access to one possible solution. The *Safe Condition* project has to do with movements between different media and realities—and not with whether such movement can or cannot be 'recognised' as being art. But the project does have to do with which reality it appears in. This aim has necessitated a wide use of film, video, photography, graphics, sculpture, painting and installation. In this way, the projects have attempted to place a question mark alongside their own genesis and existence—both in the form of artistic self-fulfilment and theatrical staging—and maybe they have also managed to place question marks beside the situational contexts within which the picture is experienced.

Safe Condition establishes a confrontation between the objective (thing/art) and the subjective (person/actor). In order to see the work or the situation, the viewer must—not merely intellectually but also physically—not be able to evade becoming a part of the picture. The viewer is indirectly implicated into the different visual and linguistic layers. This demands an attitude that not only has to do with art objects but even more precisely with uncovering collective or profoundly private notions about what is safe.

Safe Condition is also characterised by its investigation of the relationship between seduction and rejection. A fascination or doubt which is established both at first glance and upon later development of that which the viewer saw. The foundation for any impression, the foundation of any exchange. Recognition and doubt. An establishment and an exchange of metaphors and symbols. An exchange which in the final analysis consists of the choices made by the viewer himself. In an area where the artwork functions exclusively in relation to him or her—as illusion or imaginary reality, as a reflection or a staged reality. One reality among other realities.

Regarding *Document in the Past Perfect*

The historical family material in *Safe Condition. Document in the Past Perfect* was first shown in 1985/86 in a half-hour version, presented in a number of art contexts. The idea was that the picture material, when put together with three different soundtracks, ought to supply different associations to the public, all according to which of the soundtracks accompanied the visuals. At the various performances, the soundtrack consisted partly of material sampled from political speeches and popular songs from the period 1932 to 1954, mixed with pop melodies and other sound loops from the 1970s. And partly of two improvised live soundtracks—with guitar and drums (much like the music accompaniment that was heard at the presentation of old silent movies). But after a few showings, the old and—due to the passage of time—rotting strips of film started to crack and slip away from one another.

The historic family film material now constitutes the first twenty minutes of *Safe Condition. Document in the Past Perfect*. And in its new form, the artwork has now come to acquire a character where it should not be shown in a 'pure' art context. It has been shown, however, at a number of different film festivals and video festivals. What is presently the main intention for *Document in the Past Perfect* is that it be presented exclusively in connection with education and other pedagogical contexts.

The chairs, the darkness, the short-lived solidarity and the concentration are all of the utmost necessity: a necessity that could never be exacted in an individual art context. However, this might be so when the lights are switched on again, where a conversation/discussion can take place.

Safe Condition. Document in the Past Perfect is a sampling of historical pictures and sounds, which when taken together comes to establish a new picture which—despite whatever character and intentions the materials originally may have possessed—coalesce into one single picture space, a picture space that engenders a new reality. The work consists of three parts which, in their own respective origins express the following: selection and sorting out (the family film); expectation and recognition (the porno film) and finally, the fusion of the foregoing—an idealised phenomenon

(Charles Manson), being interviewed. *Document in the Past Perfect* is a picture space where the family film represents the subjective, the porno film represents the objective and the interview with Charles Manson represents something in between, a movement between the one and the other, neither visible nor invisible.

In *Document in the Past Perfect* the sections are woven into a form of historic reconstruction: the family, 1932 to 1954; Charles Manson, the 1960s, and the porno film, the 1970s. A reconstruction where temporal syncretisms and overlappings open up new ways of intuiting notions about a reality that might have been. Aage is—or was—the same age as Charles Manson. The daughter in the family film could quite conceivably be the mother of the young people in the porno film.

Document in the Past Perfect creates a situation where it is not possible to bundle the different layers of the experience together. This creates a kind of built-in incalculability. An immeasurable situation which is also underscored by the torrent of English speech. The video indirectly encourages a kind of mental zapping between the different sources. Not merely on account of the utter impossibility of gathering the pictures and the speech into one continuous understanding or meaning, but also by virtue of the fact that in the way the material has been edited, many different layers of association have been organised. During the course of the entire sequence, there are different spots where the pictures and the words or statement collide. These collisions foster associations to contexts situated outside the work, through combinations of picture and sound. There is an opening out to a reality which is conditioned by the third picture—that is a reality that is subordinate to both the individuals own expectations of correlations and to correlations situated beyond the individual. Correlations that might first become clear on the retina at a distance—after the video is over.

Document in the Past Perfect aims, in this way, to evoke a sense of the recognisable and the disquiet that is familiar to most people. The disquiet that stems from situations where you think you know what is going on around you and yet you are well aware that all other kinds of possibilities are also at stake. A combination of inquisitiveness and something else. What Charles Manson says is right—but it's also wrong. It makes you curious. Raving psychopath combined with normality. What is it like to spend one's whole life in prison? Charles Manson talks about a shared consciousness. And who is the family? Why is the father always pushing the other members of the family around? The son gets slapped—the daughter gets a squeeze. They laugh a lot. The mother and father are kissing on a bench in the park. It's a big family. Happy Danes. But were they Nazis? On the other hand, just about everyone in the world was at the Nazi Olympic games in Berlin. Occupation. Liberation. Danish events always seem to transpire around Copenhagen's Town Hall Square. Aage and his sister are different. What happened to Aage? Did he throw the film away? Newly graduated secondary school students wearing pretty colours. Horse-drawn carriages and long hair. Moving around and around through the city. The parents are obviously miscast. Are they really students? Group sex. Did they do this for fun or for the money—or for both? Maybe this was the only time they did it on film. Did they have more sex than we have today? Charles Manson: "Everything is an act. It's all an act. The only thing that is not an act—the only thing that makes reality is death."

Document in the Past Perfect constitutes an attempt to construct a work of art where the figurative/concrete and the abstract are bound together into a common aesthetics. The foundation for these aesthetics is a representational area where the abstract is seated in what is immediately recognisable or realistic. And the concrete seated in the pictures made by the viewer him/herself. *Document in the Past Perfect* involves that which is present. In what is both a classical and a contemporary collage form, the video provides the viewer with a notion about how a work of art can create a picture-space with the use of found materials. At the same time, *Document in the Past Perfect* offers the opportunity to discuss just how a work of art can, through the use of historical materials, play a role in asking questions about our own time and about society's recent past. How do we construe the internal and external pictures upon which we choose to build further? And what about the pictures that are/were not intended for the larger public? These small islands of meaning, however private or meaningless they may appear to be, are produced on all levels—in every society, at any time.

Postscript

All of the material comes from someplace else—and after I had come into possession of the family film, I made an attempt, on the basis of the scanty bits of information that were evident in the film, to trace the protagonists and their relatives. As has already been mentioned, as a visual artist, it's not unusual to borrow from the products of earlier times—from the world of art and from other spheres. But the family film possessed a different character of privateness than anything I had previously encountered. For this reason, I addressed inquiries to the national registration office and to other public directories. None of these efforts elicited any further information.

Notes

1. Quoted from Kathy Halberich, "Social Life", *Bruce Nauman*, Minneapolis: Walker Arts Center/New York: Art Publishers Inc., 1994, p. 95.

2. Charles Manson interviewed by Kevin Kennedy, KLX Radio, Berkeley, CA, 1985.

3. Relyea Lane, "Art of the Living Dead", *Helter Skelter: LA Art in the 1990s*, Los Angeles: Museum of Contemporary Art, 1992, p. 34.

4. Vincent Bugliosi, *Helter Skelter*, New York: Bantam Books, 1974/1995, p. 34.

5. Manson's music compositions and his story have been used by rock groups like Black Flag, Guns 'n' Roses and Redd Kross and by artists like Raymond Pettibon and Mike Kelley, all Californians. "The Manson Family" has also provided the title for an opera by John Moran, Point Music, 1992.

6. Lynn Hunt, ed., *The Invention of Pornography—Obscenity and the Origins of Modernity, 1500-1800*, New York: Zone Books, 1993.

7. For example, many of the works by the Danish surrealist painter, Wilhelm Freddie, were confiscated by the police under the terms of the law against pornography. In 1963, after a court decision, all of these works were returned to the artist.

8. Robert Nickas, "Felix Gonzales-Torres; All the Time in the World", *Flash Art*, no. 161, November/December 1991.

9. Walter Benjamin, "The Storyteller", *Illuminations*, London: Pimlico, 1969, pp. 81-107.

10. Manson to KLX Radio, 1985. Note Benjamin's related notion in "The Storyteller"—"Death is the sanction of all that the storyteller can tell. He has borrowed his authority from death", *Illuminations*, p. 93.

This is an abbreviated version of an essay previously printed in the educational book Safe Condition— Document in the Past Perfect, edited by Lars Mathiesen and Anders Michelsen, Copenhagen: Statens Filmcentral, 1996.

translated by Dan A Marmorstein

ILLUSTRATIONS: STILLS FROM THE VIDEO SAFE CONDITION—DOCUMENTS FROM THE PAST PERFECT, BY LARS MATHIESEN

2X2 *

It's real satisfaction[1] to scream "God Save the Queen and the fascist regime"[2] knowing full well that kind old mummy[3] will put up with it all, while a shocked public scatters guarantees "to be wanted, safe and protected".[4] The pleasure of wallowing in strong sensations and exotic ideas somewhere in the communist wilderness: not staying here too long, for sure, leaving before one has been trampled by proletarian boots. And always coming back home[5], where order is based on common sense[6], the banality of normalcy and the boredom of daily routine.

Constructed in the museum library[7], the idea of the power of the people could have stayed there, a puzzling object of study for connoisseurs of theory. Unfortunately[8], however, bacteria escaped from the research laboratories and resulted in dreadful mutations that spread across Asian fallow lands and through European pubs. Both nations[9] felt cool marching in columns. Team joy and uniform unity while shooting a traitor[10] when there are no strangers. Just imagine how enviously the decrepit Bolshevik observed the sharp-looking Nazi in the joint parade which he organised[11] before the dog-fight.[12] Nazi intelligence was clearly superior and very insulting in its contempt for the imperfect Bolshevik skulls.[13] The wound remained so deep that even victory[14] resulted only in drunkenness and hopeless imitation[15] of the opponent.

The injured herd's reflex is to store up on preserved foods[16] in the uncertainty of what will be imposed by history and the elected rule of the people[17], who immediately huddle into a gang for the sake of a brighter future. Maybe famine once again, in the most fertile lands.[18] The masses, with strained nerves and dulled senses, were tired of making history and majestic ideas, just hungry for the banality of the everyday and bourgeois education.[19]

Nation and Party were one[20], but the Party promptly saw the potential[21] inherent in feudalism, and ideology was reduced to being a cover-up. The human category which is eager to confess to all beliefs will always survive—as long as they can cling to the backs of work-horses. It's not worth hoping that history ends after the collapse of the communist system.[22] Since "war is a father and the origin of all things"[23], and this father gives rise to big money. With new technologies war became more subtle, cultivated, more psychological[24]: not a matter of the flesh, but of brains and nerves. There are already too many people for the new micro-electronic reality. Let the weak-willed ignorant primitives destroy themselves in degradation.[25]

In the face of the competition between the great ideological monsters[26] common sense resisted both extremes. The expression "red or brown it's the same shit"[27] defines the attitude of the meek to perversions and becomes a proverb. While the Free World[28] cynically promised intervention and assistance[29] by a third power, upstarts on divided borders[30] were massacred[31] and exiled.[32] Those who remained had to survive believing in anything. In the hope of eventually regenerating the mutilated social organism, they filled positions in the imposed system with their own national cadres[33] at any price, thus avoiding an invasion of colonists. The same common sense said: "every village has its own fool, slut, worker and thinker".[34]

Under the constant fear that the futurism-obsessed neighbour[35] might mistake the Baltics for the Caucasus, time is needed before these elements will settle into their own positions. Remembering a piece of human skull with distinct Slavic features stuck to a tank fragment in Grozni[36], tank tracks on girl's belly in Vilnius.[37] Never mind the Third World: low-lifes and bandits.[38] But it's clear when you live here that both executioner and victim hunger for daily banality-normalcy and at least some kind of order.[39] Better carrion in virtual reality and show business[40] galleries for tourists, than in the streets or popular projects for the future.[41]

Only verified comrades had the opportunity to enjoy a rest in bourgeois comfort abroad[42], as the highest reward for deceiving their own people. The bosses who had distributed the people's money[43] now appropriated it for themselves[44], thus legalising[45] their activities as they always had. It's high time to throw away the now completely worn-out screen with its out-of-date slogans about equality, labour, honesty and the nation's interests.[46]

It's naïve to think that, after establishing communications, proportional exchange between different experiences[47] will take place. Knowledge of the consequences of ideological systems confirms and fortifies the golden mediocrity and aesthetics of normality, which are themselves the basis of various theoretical premises and creative speculations.

At least the Lithuanian naughty boy can get satisfaction as well singing "the army came running and shot down Brazauskas"[48] for good old daddy president[49] is indulgent regarding free youthful self-expression. Though not long ago an author of such songs might have found his future[50] caught in the KGB step-father's webs, while the public remained silently indifferent.

Notes

* "... a normal man knows that 2x2=4. The real mental patient thinks: if I try hard there it'll be five; a neurotic knows perfectly well that 2x2=4, but he is very dissatisfied about it..."

(A Alekseichik—Doctor, psychiatrist of Vilnius Psychoneurological Hospital.)

1. "Satisfaction", Rolling Stones, 1965."... a nonconformist text of the song, telling about being constantly fooled and manipulated by advertising, mass media, echoed to the spirit of the young in the mid-50s". Andrei Gavrilov, USSR Ministry of Culture, 1988.

2. "... snarling condemnation of society reached its most potent in the hit single "God save the Queen" 1977... the enthusiasm and do-it-yourself ethos of punk rock attacked an elitist rock industry", *Pears Cyclopaedia* 101st edition.

3. "Mother Queen... paid no attention to German bombers and stayed in London. Because of the influence on the moral standards of society Hitler called her the most dangerous woman in Europe. The Germans violently bombarded the poor East End district of London. In 1940 Buckingham Palace suffered from bombs as well. "I appreciate the fact that we were under fire. Now I feel that I can bravely face East End", said Mother Queen", Reuters, 1996.

4. "Lydon formed a new wave band Public Image Limited (PIL) in 1978." *Pears Cyclopaedia* 101 edition, The Sex Pistols came back with the former name and image in 1996: "all we need is money", said Lydon.

5. "East or West home is best." English folk saying.

6. "The paradigm of knowledge is common sense. The everyday sentiments and experience of bourgeois life are the measure of all things. They are real. All else pretension. At core English education culture is based on the banal..." Andrew Brighton. *Edge 90*, UK.

7. "... living in great poverty... he (Karl Marx) spent his time in the British Museum studying the development of capitalism", D Townson, *Dictionary of Modern History 1789-1945*.

8. "Engels claimed that Marx's Russian disciples interpreted passages... in the most contradictory ways just as if they were texts from the classics of the New Testament... Nearly all Marx's predictions have been proved wrong." D Townson, *Dictionary of Modern History 1789-1945*.

9. In this case the German fascists and the Russian communists.

10. Bolshevik party's purification from foreign spies = racial purification of fascist party.

11. Joint parade of fascists and communists in 1939. Brest, USSR.

12. Breaking the peace pact unexpectedly Hitler started the war against the USSR on 22 June 1941.

13. "The contention of the nineteenth century Italian criminologist Cesare Lombroso that criminals show typical characteristics—prominent cheek bones and jaw, slanting eyes, receding brow, large ears of a particular shape—was disproved by Karl Pearson early this century when he found that 3,000 criminals showed no major differences of features, carefully measured from a similar number of students at Oxford and Cambridge." *Pears Cyclopedia,* 101st edition.

14. 9 May 1945 is the celebration of the USSR's victory against German fascism.

15. 'Gigantomania' in architecture and monuments.

16. Centralisation in providing gas, oil and food for the regions.

17. Since the communist party was the only one, and taking part in the elections was obligatory the party always had the necessary number of votes.

18. Famine in the Ukraine artificially caused by Bolsheviks in 1928–1930.

19. Based on ideology the Soviet educational system produced dilettantes. Autodidact professionals appeared from their own enthusiasm avoiding politics.

20. The communist slogan "nation and party are one".

21. Corruption, family liaison.

22. Francis Fukuyama, "The end of History", *The Independent*.

23. Heraclitus. "War is father ..."

24. The new term "psychological war" appeared in post-communist countries in the 80s.

25. "The real power of a nation lies in the number of its scientifically educated heads."

26. Concerns fascism and communism.

27. Lithuanian folk saying.

28. Various Western radio stations broadcasting their propaganda programmes in Lithuanian as well after World War II.

29. "Disappointment with the West manifests itself in the country. In spring of 1945 there were over 50,000 partisans. The Western action against the Soviets was awaited and that's why many left for the forests particularly those who were supposed to be mobilised." Jonas Deksnys, 1948.

30. Von Ribbentrop—Molotov pact (and its secret protocols), 23 August 1939.

31. Partisan resistance to Bolsheviks lasted until 1956. 25,000 partisans perished in Lithuania.

32. "As soon as Bolsheviks occupied Lithuania about 12,000 people were under arrest over a few weeks... in the course of the first year of occupation nearly 40,000 Lithuanians were killed and deported." Bronys Raila.

33. "... after the Twentieth Congress of the Soviet communist party, national relations became warmer as well. In Lithuania, too, there was a tendency to do everything possible the "Lithuanian way" ...undoubtedly, the fostering of this Lithuanian spirit needed some kind of circumspection... diplomacy and flexibility were of great importance, the utmost task was to prepare our own Lithuanian cadres." P Professor Jonas Kubilius, Rector of Vilnius University, 1958–1991.

34. "The Bolshevik's kernel consists of asocial elements. Smugglers and opportunists are eager to collaborate with Bolsheviks. 70% of the party members and high bureaucracy are Russians." Jonas Deksnys, 1948.

35. "We were honest... to our opponents as well, we have offered them an open and decent way out... let's forget all wrong and remain good neighbours... but the neighbour disagreed... the imperial pride was hurt.... Typical of that country's politics is to humiliate by mocking and to break down. Demonstration of power and violence." Vytautas Landsbergis, 11 March 1991.

36. On 1 January 1995 the Russian invasion of the capital presented Chechnia with professional battle.

37. A) "Soviet troops with tanks seized the TV centre in Vilnius: 14 dead, 164 injured: defying curfew, thousands of Lithuanians surrounded the Parliament buildings, with deputies inside, to defend it..." *Pears Cyclopaedia* 101st edition. B) The girl, participant of a peaceful protest demonstration, supporting

independence was mutilated under the tank and died after a few hours in Vilnius, 13 January 1991.

38. Any kind of resistance to institutionalised terror was called banditism in the USSR.

39. A) The official position of the USSR regarding Pinochet was negative, though after the collapse of the Soviet system some generals expressed their long hidden sympathy to this personality. Longing for a firm hand in Russia manifests itself more as a desire of monarchy than that of democracy.

    B) "Nostalgia for the past is characteristic to the Lithuanian world outlook (all beauty is in the past)... communist nomenclature was re-elected. Rapid (however painful) steps that Lithuania made on the way of radical reforms was suspended immediately." Vytautas Kubilius, 1995.

40. "... don't go all serious on me. Smile. This is show business." Quotation used in the article by John McEwen on Damien Hirst, *The Times*, 1995.

41. To clean the world from parasites gives rise to the world-wide armed proletarian revolution.

42. Made use of privileges characteristic to the way of life of ideological enemies.

43. Centralised system of redistribution.

44. "... Former nomenclature fortified its positions in strategic economics.... The power of the Lithuanian Democratic Labour Party (former communists) turned into the power of the large capital of six to seven big monopolies. Private banks are going down but then are being strengthened from the state budget, on the other hand farmers don't get their money all year long... having made their fortune the former students of party schools and academies immediately restored the pyramid of one-party power, based on ideological selection of cadres and passing resolutions confidentially..." Vytautas Kubilius, 1995.

45. "Mafia system uniting party bureaucracy into a closed clan was brought from 'mature socialism' into the economics of independent Lithuania. 'Neatly washed' party money now makes (as supposed) up to 70% of private capital." Vytautas Kubilius, 1995.

46. "... polarised Lithuania into violent social contrasts... the annual salary of a bank director is 1.235.341 Lt., however the minimal living standard fixed by the government is 70 Lt. per month (until 1 October 1995)." Vytautas Kubilius, 1995.

47. "Taking into account 'Moscow interests' the Western countries didn't hasten to start the 'Marshall Plan' in the abandoned territories devastated by Soviet socialism... Lithuania excites the West "only as a potential market", will say Osvaldas Balakauskas, after he returns from Paris where he restarted the Lithuanian embassy." Vytautas Kubilius, 1995.

48. SSG "Radioshow" 1994 Zona Records : "The army came running" (dangerous remix) "We always were proud, and will be proud in the future that we are the group which has created the first anti-fascist song in the history of Lithuanian rock (there is no doubt that this song is anti-fascist and only Vagnorius and Co or some kind of nationalists (Nazis) may think, that we really intended to shoot Brazauskas, moreover that at that time he wasn't the one he is now (1994). We are to announce, that we are not defenders of Brazauskas. Actually (almost) all members of the parliament are shitty peasants, not able to make up a sentence..." Algis Greitai (SSG, Swastikas Rotate Quickly).

49. Algirdas Brazauskas—Lithuanian president since 1993, former first secretary of the Lithuanian communist party.

50. Algis Greitai—the leader of SSG rock group transformed his activity into the popular black humour TV programme.

Previously published in Ground Control—Technology and Utopia, *eds. Lolita Jablonskiene, Duncan McCorquodale and Julian Stalabrass, London: Black Dog Publishing, 1997.*

Hard Core, Self-organisation and Alternativity

Successfully having established an area for the production and distribution of their music outside of the mainstream corporate music industry, the hardcore scene poses a possible model for, or at least an interesting case study that might provide some pointers towards, the development of a sustainable alternative art production/adistribution.

The hardcore scene shares several characteristics with the historical avant-garde, and its aptness as a partial model for art is in part connected to its sharing some of these characteristics.

The hardcore scene in general is both anti-establishment and specifically political. This is evident both in the sound and intensity of the music, making it less accessible than more commercially controlled forms of music, and in the highly political lyrics of many hardcore bands. Just as the early workers' theatres in Germany strove to find a balance between the social/political message and the entertainment value of their plays, the hardcore scene mediate their political message through a certain sound/aesthetic that is also seen to have a value in itself. Both in their lyrics and in statements and interviews the different bands and participants in the myriad of scenes connected to hardcore underline the blend of entertainment and political message in their music: "In addition to hopefully bringing people together for a good time we hope to share some of our experiences and beliefs in working class solidarity, friendship, loyalty and self-improvement as a means to bettering society."[1]

Of course, the "good time" and entertainment aspect here is connected to the political message in the same way as the rejection of traditional (bourgeois) aesthetics had a political function in the avant-garde movements, with the hardcore sound itself underlining the content and general energy of the lyrics. However, whereas the strangeness of the avant-garde aesthetics was quickly taken up by the mainstream, the hardcore scene, although it has evolved and has influenced other music styles, has been able to remain alternative and independent of the bigger music scenes (and therefore also of the big corporations).

Contrary to most of the different experiments in alternativity and self-sustained systems in the contemporary art scene, the hardcore scene has managed to build up and maintain a functioning alternative structure outside of the more traditionally commercial music business, and has remained in control of their own output for a substantial number of years. Of course, the distribution and production of hardcore music is slightly simplified as a model for the production/distribution of contemporary art, because of the practical fact that the music industry has such a convenient product to sell, but even so, I believe that it can function as a model in order to point out certain possible solutions for the establishment and maintenance of sustainable alternative structures within the art world.

The distribution of hardcore music is handled almost exclusively through smaller record labels and distribution companies, most of whom are run largely on an idealistic basis.[2] Fanzines, record labels of various sizes, concert venues etc. all interconnect and relate to each other forming something akin to Manuel De Landa's description of a *meshwork*.[3] The hardcore scene(s) seem to have been able to build up a functioning alternative and self-organised market structure exactly because of its belief in group solutions and interaction and because of the synergic effect of this meshwork situation. This situation seems also to have evolved with, and been further strengthened by the advent of the Internet and its possibilities for networking and small scale and special interest based distribution.

Addressing an audience consisting of their peers, with very much the same background and frames of reference as themselves, the bands describe the situation of their audience by describing their own. Naturally this gives the audience a strong sense of shared interest and recognition and helps facilitate a large degree of audience-performer interaction.

The Dropkick Murphys' ideas of sharing their beliefs in "working class solidarity", "self-improvement" and "bettering society" (as quoted above) strongly echoes the historical avant-gardes and their hopes of (and belief in) being able to bring about changes in society through their art. Of course, the avant-gardes, historical as well as contemporary, have always suffered from severe problems associated with the distribution and reception of their art. As Jochen Schulte-Sasse writes:

Individual works may have criticised negative aspects of society, but the anticipation of social harmony as psychic harmony, which is part of the aesthetic enjoyment for the individual, risks degenerating into a mere cerebral compensation for society's shortcomings, and thus of affirming precisely what is criticised by the content of the work.[4]

These problems are to a large part avoided by the hardcore scene exactly because it has remained in control of its own distribution, thereby steering clear of the cultural assimilation and aesthetic repackaging that has created a situation in the art world where the mode of reception undermines the critical content of the works.

Notes

1. The Dropkick Murphys, www.dropkickmurphys.com

2. Many of these are also run by the bands themselves or by people involved in other parts of the production and distribution of the music. One example here is Rick Ta Life of 25 Ta Life, who in addition to several band projects also runs a fanzine, a distribution company and a record label.

3. Taking his cue from Gilles Deleuze and Felix Guattari's "machines", De Landa describes meshworks as functional devices, that combine heterogeneous elements through a principle of complementarity. He mentions ecosystems and micro-organisms as one example and the pre-capitalist marketplace as another. See Manuel De Landa, "Deleuze and the Open-Ended Becoming of the World", *UKS-Forum for Samtidskunst*, no. 1/2, 2000, pp. 22–29.

4. Jochen Schulte-Sasse, foreword to *Theory of the Avant-Garde*, Peter Bürger, Minneapolis: University of Minnesota Press, 1996.

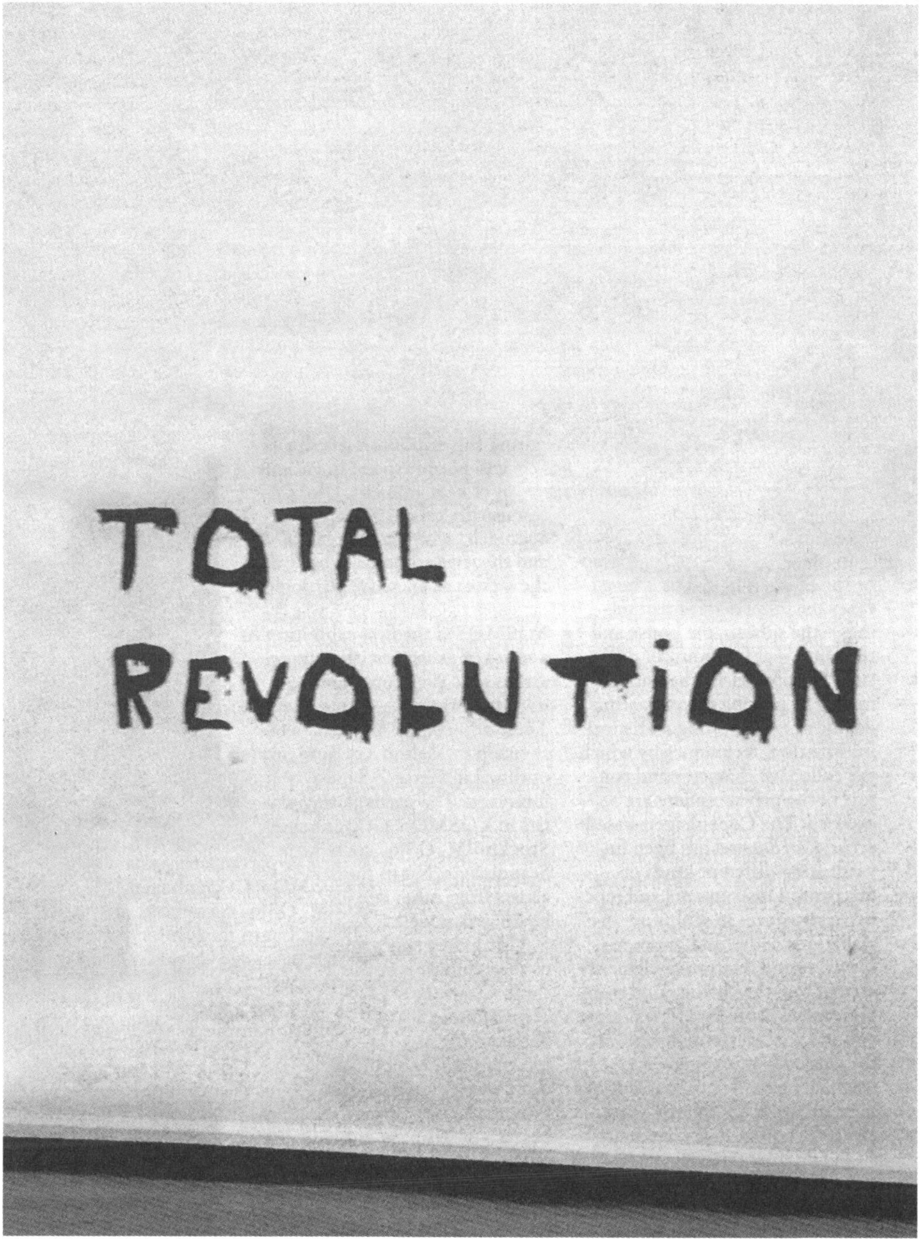

ILLUSTRATION: GARDAR EIDE EINARSSON, *UNTITLED WALLPAINTING (TOTAL REVOLUTION)*, 2001.

On Punk Rock

Sing Along With Johnny

Berlin has punks who look like they were never given a choice. As if they were born to be this. And that may well be the case, sometimes. If you are under 20, maybe your mum and dad were punks—and maybe still are—it's possible, at least in Berlin. Who could have imagined such paralysis in 1976, when the Sex Pistols played their first groundbreaking concerts?

When I saw an ad for a Sex Pistols concert in Berlin on 6 July 1996 I thought it was a joke. Then I found the whole thing tragic, imagining pathetic has-beens forced out on a humiliating tour.

Somewhat later, on the BBC, I heard an excerpt from a press-conference with the reunited band. The message was crisp; John Lydon spoke: "We are in this for a common cause: your money!" His malicious honesty made me curious in spite of myself.

When the group played in Stockholm at the end of June, I happened to be in Sweden. Before the concert, the newspapers tried to outdo each other in condemning the band for having sold out. Pretty meek accusations, considering Lydon's own words. The night of the performance, I took the car to drive by the concert, outside of the National Maritime Museum. Just as I arrived, the show began. I didn't see anything, but I could hear... and it sounded good... surprisingly good... even though the sound was made abstract by obstacles and distance. I stayed on, surprised and bewitched by the peculiar feeling of being present at a historic event. The Sex Pistols were booked to play Stockholm in January 1978, immediately following the disastrous US tour—and I would certainly have been there; I had become obsessed by the promise that everything was possible—but instead the Pistols split. Here I was, hearing John Lydon's voice 18 years later, from the other side of a wooden fence, outside a museum in Stockholm: would you like some more? Now it's sing-along-with-Johnny-time! ... with a fake upper class accent—ironic, mean, cynical?

The arena in Treptow is situated about 100 m from the wall that no longer is. Nearby stands the only remaining watchtower, now a museum. A gigantic, run-down industrial hall lit up by the sunset, filled with punks and others. Most of the audience is unexpectedly young. Two support bands perform; both with shorts-clad guitarists who jump up and down while playing with tremendous (well-rehearsed) precision. The singers run back and forth like frantic rats, shouting out various politically-correct messages. The energy-level is truly overwhelming, and I wonder how disappointed I will be after this.

The hall goes dark, and green underwater light bathes the stage. Four shadowy figures take their positions. Then at once: on comes the music, on come the lights, on comes the amazing volume, and on come the Sex Pistols playing "Bodies" with great force and determination in a former East German factory in Berlin 1996. My immediate impression is astonishment: this is obviously for real...! It sounds terribly good, hard as hell, loud, ferocious—and John Lydon sings with a manic, spiteful whine. The PA is obviously in a different league today than 20 years ago—they can never have sounded this heavy back then. Steve Jones strikes poses worthy of a true rock'n'roll hero, playing unreined guitar—meticulously following the old arrangements. Centre-stage the no-longer-so-thin John Lydon... his hair standing straight up like orange-coloured carrot-tops... he's wearing a padded chequered jacket buttoned to the neck that makes him resemble Zippy the Pinhead—he looks almost unreal and is moving jerkily, mechanically, like a marionette, a marionette with entangled strings... maybe he is thinking about all the money he is going to get... but it is impossible to take your eyes off him, and he sings with tangible intensity... and worst of all: he is relevant. To be relevant, rock music, like all art, has to be simultaneously ambivalent and precise. To copy one's own revolutionary work with great conviction after 20 years is a powerful celebration of that work's intrinsic value, and at the same time it entails a radical questioning of that same work—and its reception, back then as well as today. This performance is relevant—not because it should be, or due to some intricate theory or something else—but in the sheer power of convincing artistic expression.

It becomes clear to me that the Sex Pistols are simply proud of their material, and play because they have something to prove. It's no longer a matter of money—they claim interpretive priority. The fight cannot end—interpretive priority belongs to whoever claims it most convincingly—now the band is on a surprising offensive.

The Sex Pistols were never the musical joke so many have wished them to be. In the group, there was a tumultuous personal chemistry that in little more than a year (from the end of 75 to the beginning of 77, when Glen Matlock was replaced by Sid Vicious) generated not only a cultural shift, but also some extraordinary songs. The shift would not have happened had not the Sex Pistols written these songs, and had they not had the ability to perform them in a uniquely expressive way. But at the time a rumour was spread that they couldn't play. I remember the exciting discussions that ensued—how far can you take a concept without technique—but it was a myth, in part created by their manager, Malcolm McLaren, who, with great energy, worked to make the whole punk phenomena, and especially the Sex Pistols, seem like his own subversive work of art. And his ambition has been surprisingly successful, perhaps because it so poignantly confirms fellow intellectuals' aspirations for power. After the concert, I read the book John Lydon wrote about those years and I noticed two things: how consciously he was working with his role in the group, and with the lyrics (without which everything would have been different); and that to him there was a subtle layer of humour in the project which was totally lost when McLaren made the remains of the Pistols into a joke.[1]

Once again the Sex Pistols have provoked the establishment—but an establishment that in the meantime has changed. When the band returns to the stage, with the original line-up, the whole of the carefully mythologised history is put into question by the assertion of the music—the artistic content and expression—and thereby the power-balance is upset. The tragedy is not that a musical group is once again playing the music they themselves wrote—as long as they do it well—the tragedy is if the same music is taken as an excuse by others to cease thinking.

The Sex Pistols play the Sex Pistols with superior insight. This time around they are not drenched in gob—the stage is too high. Only Lydon spits on stage a couple of times, so as to establish the new conditions. The concert ends… the band returns for an encore—"Anarchy in the UK"—and once again the ambivalence is overwhelming: this is totally convincing right now—the audience is going wild—at the same time I feel caught up in an anachronistic vertigo.

The concert is heading towards its finale. "No Fun". The audience is surging back and forth. Then it happens: a beer-bottle, still half-full, is thrown at Lydon—the first hard object that's been thrown at the stage—and absurdly enough Lydon is able to catch the bottle in its flight. At the same time he says: "STOP!" and all stop playing. "Nobody's gonna throw bottles at me. Fuck off!"

The four of them leave the stage so fast that nobody below has time to react before background-music is heard from the PA and neon has lit up the hall. The audience, dumb-founded and surprised, flows towards the exits, without protests or cheers, as if they had woken from a dream.

Note

1. John Lydon, *No Irish, No Blacks, No Dogs*, London: Hodder and Stoughton, 1994.

Originally published in SIKSI, no. 3, 1996
translated by Andrew Shields

A Conceptual Bass Player

I suppose anyone who works in an artistic field has experienced moments when the world and its possibilities suddenly appeared in a glorified light.

Myself, I remember having listened many times to the Siouxsie and the Banshees song "Placebo Effect" when it suddenly dawned on me that Steven Severin plays the same bass-line throughout the whole song, not bothering to change when the rest of the music changes. And not only there. On the following songs on the album *Join Hands* he goes on in the same way. And we aren't talking about feats of technical complexity. No, these bass-lines are extremely minimal: two or four bars long, consisting of three notes played straight with a pick, one or at most two notes a bar, then back again to the beginning... as if he was obsessed by the idea of not changing.

What a superbly free mind, I remember thinking then. And the reflection recurs now, much later, as I observe that certain fascinations never go away.
Everyone who has at one point wanted to play in a rock band—without any musical background—knows that the bass is commonly seen as the easiest instrument to begin with.

It's because you can play very simplistically and still do some good things: thumping along with the root note of the guitar chord, like a dog on a leash. It's easy to find where to put your fingers on the neck of a bass guitar. As you get better, you can play a few extra notes, and later on you'll probably try some syncopation. It is a whole different matter to be able to go on playing like you did at the very beginning—long after you've achieved perfect control of your instrument.

About a year after my discovery of the minimalistic bass-lines on *Join Hands* I read an interview with Siouxsie and the Banshees where Severin makes the following statement: "I never practice. I don't want to get better—then I would no longer have to think."

This statement made a strong impression on me. I was both disturbed and inspired. Can a bass player be conceptual?

When I realised just what Steven Severin was doing down in the depths of Siouxsie and the Banshees' music, his achievements took on an identity and luminosity that stood in direct contrast to the minimalism of their expression.

Steven Severin remained faithful to his credo. If you listen through the albums of Siouxsie and the Banshees you'll notice that he was able, with admirable consistency, to continue constructing and playing bass-lines that always had a strong identity and simultaneously came across as coolly calculated, using a minimum of effort at any given moment.

When someone who always dresses in black appears one day in a red shirt and green trousers, the effect will be strong. When Severin, from his obstinately repetitive position in the depths of the sound, suddenly replaces a couple of notes, or just changes octave—the effect can be one of far-reaching beauty.

In the mythology of Siouxsie and the Banshees, the story of their beginning is fundamental. During a punk festival at the 100 Club in London, in the autumn of 1976, Siouxsie, Severin, Sid Vicious and a guitarist named Marco went up on stage and—without prior rehearsals—performed a 20 minute improvisation with the title *The Lord's Prayer*. Neither Siouxsie nor Severin had ever made music before. It must have sounded awful. Many concerts did in 1976. What makes this occasion special is that Siouxsie and Severin took themselves and their experience so seriously that from this moment on they knew exactly what they wanted to do. They immediately began basic research on how to play and compose music (Sid Vicious was swiftly disposed of). In less than a year they were to become a professional band touring all over England.

It's ironic that the visual appearance of this group was often more likely to be discussed than their essentially far more radical musical constructions.

In the course of the band's career a number of media/technological inventions were introduced, innovations that radically widened the playing field for various creative practices. Computers began to make their mark in the 80s. Introduced in the first half of the decade, the sampler allowed the musician to borrow any sound and play it from a keyboard. From the same keyboard he or she could programme machines to play whatever else was wanted. In a way it had now become possible to make music without 'being able to play'... just as the visual artist, after Marcel Duchamp, could choose to express him/herself by giving already existing objects (or photographs, or whatever) new names, and making them bearers of his/her meaning.

Successful musical and artistic expression today is much more dependent on being able to think well, and on really understanding the possibilities of the medium you choose to work with—rather than on demonstrating mastery of the practical manipulation of various tools.

By this I don't mean to say that skill is not rewarded—but the skills you look for have changed character and become intellectual rather than manual, flexible rather than absolute. The first time Marcel Duchamp took an everyday object and with nothing but his words changed it into a work of art—on that day the conditions for artistic expression were changed forever.

To be able to use this development to get positive results, it's more necessary than ever for the creative person to be clear about WHAT he or she is after when, now, the synthesizer can play generic music endlessly... until somebody pulls the plug.

In the field of visual art notions like concept and context have been discussed for much longer than in popular music (if they've been discussed at all there)—but they have had a different kind of practical impact. The impact of the computer on visual art has—so far—not been as far-reaching as in music. This is because visual art has not yet grown together symbiotically with a reproduction technology—as popular music has with the recording studio (although popular music is an area that is rather difficult to delimit).

The true quality of Steven Severin's bass-lines would have been hard to establish without the possibility of listening to recorded music over and over again.

It's one thing to speculate on how music and art have arisen and developed. It's quite another thing to create them. Conscious innocence can't be maintained indefinitely. One day innocence, conscious or unconscious, is no more. Even if the attitude were to remain the same, conditions change, and with them the efforts you have to make to keep your interest alive.

In 1988 Siouxsie and the Banshees had a success with a song called "Peek-a-Boo".[1] The basic track is recorded backwards: the group first learned to play what they wanted so it would sound right—but only when the tape was played back in the wrong direction. In concerts they play a version that mimics the reversed tape—but without the help of a tape recorder. Minimalism is no longer Steven Severin's sole challenge.

In 1996, after 20 years, 15 albums and an untold number of concerts and tours, an official statement was released saying that Siouxsie and the Banshees had ceased to exist.

Had their musical skill finally become so vast that it was no longer possible to continue?

Note

1. The description of how "Peek-a-Boo" was recorded is imaginative, although, as I later found out, not altogether correct. But that doesn't change anything, really. June 2001.

Originally published in Göteborgs-Posten, *25 June 1998.*

Formless Music

I tried to write this with eyes closed in the middle of the night, moving ecstatically on the 'dance' floor of my bedroom, dreaming lucidly in a haze of sleeplessness, eight miles high above the rationality of my indoctrinated mind, lost in the imaginary landscape of music, but I couldn't do it. Not totally anyhow—it came to me in fragments, sometimes flowing like water, but most of the time slowly, after hours of banging my head against some imaginary wall. In those moments I wanted to be a dog, driven by instinct, howling at the moon and smelling my way in the world.

There is a song by The Velvet Underground which starts slowly in a happy go lucky fashion followed by two samples. The first is the sound of a train pulling in to a station, and the second, immediately following, is the sound of glass shattering. Right after these samples guitars, bass and drums pick up and run along at a frenetic pace without actually going anywhere, like the movements and mental state of a punk shaking spastically on the same spot. The drums are like the pattering naked feet of a running dog, the guitars are starting to feedback and fuzz, sounding like a genius machine blurting out sado-masochistic trash sculpture made of meteorites and small parts of the sun. It goes on and on devoid of anything resembling melody or form, just an aggressive but joyful hammering of staccato rhythm on instruments until fingers bleed and ears shatter.

This piece of rock history, "European Son" from the Velvets first album, serves as an example of what I call formless music. The word formless has been used in different contexts to imply something indescribable, whether it be Bataille's anti-concept of the 'informe' from the critical *dictionary*, a kind of dada dictionary which served to sabotage the definition of words—and thus were intentionally incomplete because of the impossibility of totality—or the metaphysical implications of the word in the ancient Chinese classic *Tao Te Ching*.[1]

To write about formlessness is of course a contradiction in terms, given the rigid, masculine hierarchy of systems of written language as opposed to the liberating, amorphous and indescribable feeling of experiences of music in general. The formless can, in addition, be applied to an ontology of thinking: the activity often identified as preceeding writing, but here tentatively used as a way of writing. Furthermore; I'm not writing this text in my native tongue, which naturally brings in another level of potential uncertainty and a possibility of formless formulation. A possibility admittedly, because a truly formless text about formlessness is impossible—at least a text which aims to communicate a distinct meaning. It is a different matter with experimental literature which can be inspired formlessness in itself, although it is not a discussion on formlessness. And even though the music I am referring to can easily be labeled formless, it is also—and maybe most importantly—a formless state of mind in a metaphysical sense which is at stake here.

I have tried for years to describe the shock of hearing Captain Beefheart's *Trout Mask Replica* for the first time, the psychedelic, surreal masterpiece of poet, composer and painter Don Van Vliet, but any stab at outshining the brilliant description by the late legendary rock critic Lester Bangs is futile, so I will simply quote him:

> *Trout Mask Replica shattered my skull, realigned my synapses, made me nervous, made me laugh, made me jump and jag with joy. It wasn't just the fusion I'd been waiting for: it was a whole new universe, a completely realised and previously unimaginable landscape of guitars splintering and springing and slanting and even actually swinging in every direction, as far as the mind could see... I stayed under the headphones and played* Trout Mask Replica *straight through five times in a row that night. The next step of course was to turn the rest of the world on to this amazing thing I'd found, which perhaps came closer to a living, pulsating, slithering organism than any other record I'd ever heard.*[2]

I can only say I feel the same way, the album is alien, far out, surreal, impossible to categorise or pin down, and it must, of course, be heard as any description of it is only confusing. The fusion Bangs speaks of is the fusion of rock, blues and jazz, and the fusion makes all the categories of music meaningless. The result has nothing to do with the slickness of jazz-rock, but it is more like an anarchistic proto-punk esthetic. Melody fragments from Don Van Vliet's favourite childhood songs are entwined into the staccato, atonal guitar riffs, and snippets of lyric rehearsals and funny dialogues in the studio resides in the spaces between songs. The rhythm is the sound of the drums falling over themselves, as if the entire drum kit is being rolled down a bumpy slope—as described by Mike Barnes in his biography of the Captain. And the lyrics are a personal universe in themselves, howled out with the Captains raw animal voice or spoken a capella, completely in tune with the free and unconstrained music. Songs like "Neon Meate Dream of a Octafish", "Old Fart at Play" and "Steal Softly Thru Snow", with Dada inspired juxtapositioning of onomatepoeia and invented babble, containing strings of words that blow your brain into a highly rich poetic web of intricate meanings. Van Vliet said of the album in 1991: "It is trying to break up the mind in many different directions, causing them not to be able to fixate."[3] The music on *Trout Mask Replica* is actually composed and rehearsed prior to performance. The distorted, ever-shifting, spontaneous sound is, paradoxically, the result of a controlled process, but the listening experience is of a music totally free of conventions and form. The aim of this music becomes obvious in a childhood memory—used by Barnes as a description of the essence of the music—where Captain Beefheart "has claimed that the freest harmonica playing he heard was when as a child he held the instrument out of the window of his parents' car and the rushing wind brought it to life. Listening to his best music feels as if you are driving close behind, hyperventilating in his slipstream."[4]

I lie in bed floating between a state of wake and sleep, listening for the umpteenth time to Keith Jarrett's spontaneous piano compositions *The Sun Bear Concerts*, but get the feeling that I'm hearing the music for the first time, that Keith and I occupy the same time and space. "Why do you think it's so easy to forget what I play? Because what I do isn't about music. It's about an experience beyond sound."[5] The music is solo piano, a blending of free-form jazz, classical, gospel, atonal blues and what have you. It may be the result of my wild imagination, but sometimes when listening to Jarrett's music I see the colour yellow, like he's connected directly to the power of the sun.

A funny thing about Jarrett is that he can't seem to keep quiet when he's playing— at certain climaxes in the music he starts humming like a maniac. I get the impression that he just can't control himself, that he feels so in tune with the sounds he's making with his fingers that the rest of his sound making body gets carried away. But to call this formless.... When you listen to the music it is not so much the music in itself that is formless, at least not all of the time—it is more like a formless relationship, like a flow, between the musician and the instrument, between the music and the listener. But of course there are moments in the music which could be described as formless: when the fingers hit the keys like raindrops and the notes fly like leaves in the wind... don't know when they'll stop, where the next turn will be or how he's gonna land... aimless, formless fantasy landscape.

I described the music as compositions, but Jarrett's music can't really be called compositions as they're not composed. When he gives concerts—nearly all his recordings are live—the music comes to him, not from pre-composed sheets of paper or some heavenly source, but from the back of his own mind where all his experience, skill and feeling is stored. He just sits down in a state of blankness, not knowing what he will play, empty of thought, choice and intention. Jarrett has stated that in these sessions he is sometimes afraid of not being able to play, or that the outpouring of energy will be the end of him: "Sometimes I feel as if I'm putting my finger on an electric line and leaving it there."[6]

Keith Jarrett would not approve of the comparison—in his view all electronic music is poisonous—but there is a similiar essence in the improvised, inventive, on the spot methods of the DJ and Jarrett's journey into the unknown. Techno culture is interesting in relation to a discussion of the formless both because its aesthetic and political aim is to make a secret space for communion, ecstasy and trance. Even though that space has been commodified by capitalism, like all other innovative cultural 'free zones', there is still the opportunity for the personal experience of freedom and transcendence on the dance floor.

… my body moves to the pulsating sound of the endless repetitive beat of drum machines, electronic sound samples, the rocking and rolling of the rhythm section, the whining drone of electric guitars, the subversive revolutionary utopian freedom of rock'n'roll music. I lose all sense of self, time and space. I cease to be myself. I cease to think. I cease to be here or there. The borders between the music and the dancers seem to disappear. The mass of dancers become a formless boiling pot of improvisational movement. The feeling in the crowd is a blend of sexual ecstasy and religious enlightenment. The monotonous pulsating rhythms of sound seem to get translated into the movements of the dancers, and the beat gets recognised as a unification of the sounds of the body and the environment; the endless waves of the ocean, the rhythm of breathing and the beating of the heart, the chatta-nooga of freight trains, the industrial techno-beat of factories and the clicking hum of hard disks....

Naturally, it could be argued that all music is formless—at least to the extent that soundwaves float through air without visible or material form, and can only be grasped by way of the ear and the body. But this literal and obvious formlessness is not what I'm looking for. There is another kind of formlessness in music which breaks up rhythms, harmonies and notes, moves towards noise on the one hand and silence on the other, or blurs the boundaries between composed and natural sound. A related formlessness can be experienced in the zenith of such diverse catagories of music as free jazz, proto-punk and techno.

To exemplify this connection with free movement, the coincidences of nature or the sounds of the cultural environment, I will quote Charles Mingus' free-form jazzy liner notes to his masterpiece *The Black Saint and the Sinner Lady*, where he tries to explain the changing intricate rhythms of jazz: "Time, perfect or syncopated time, is when a faucet dribbles from a leaky washer. I'm more than sure an adolescent memory can remember how long the intervals were between each collision of our short-lived drip and its crash into an untidy sink's overfilled coffee cup with murky grime of old cream still clinging to the edges..."[7] The comparison here between the rhythm of a drop of water into the abject void of a dirty sink and the seemingly haphazard rhythm of free jazz, is in sync with a notion of music's possible origin. A tradition, perhaps, that goes from tribal music's imitation of animal sounds, the blues harmonica's interpretation of the train, the rock beat's interpretation of the sounds of industry, to the very collapsing of the borders between sound and music in John Cage's music of chance, and onwards to the present state of sampling and mixing of ambient sounds in contemporary electronic music.

If you had some creatures from another planet describing the general feeling of this type of music maybe it would go something like this: "The howling of tortured cats, swinging around at the end of a rope like a swarm of crazy insects." But when it comes to the listening experience of *The Black Saint*—from the opening complexity of the rhythm changes portraying waves of intense emotion and, further, through the slower ballads building up to a frenzied moaning choir of instrumental voices, never loosing the same desperate wail in the rhythm which runs through the whole piece— the feeling I get is of a human being crying out in pain for love. It's really intense and so beautiful you have to be a stone not to weep in awe and gratitude with the music for the opportunity to be part of a communication of such power. When the music's over it's almost like the cathartic exhaustion after an introspective weeping session, a fabulous fuck, or the satisfaction of a job well done.

I remember the experience of listening to *Force Majeure* by the German instrumental band Tangerine Dream in my teens. The record is no longer a favorite, but along with Jean-Michel Jarre and the now, hopefully forgotten, band Space, it introduced me to a kind of music I could loose myself in, like a journey into a fantastic half-lucid-nation. The sounds of the mostly synthesizer generated music of Tangerine Dream floated through the loudspeakers, my disembodied consciousness travelled through imaginary science fiction landscapes. I closed my eyes and drifted through a sound topology generated by the meeting of my imagination and the music, flying high above metalic oceans, dancing through layers of laser beams, running through metamorphic rocks.

The music generated what David Toop has called a "personal mind-movie". The state it left me in—later experienced when listening to contemporary electronic genres like the ambient techno of Aphex Twin, the moon safari of French duo Air and the atmospheric chill-out of the new English duo Bent—could be compared to the altered state of lucid dreaming, and it makes me think of what some musicologists consider another possible origin of music; the soothing hum of the mother voice, communicating inarticulate love to the foetus. This pre-conscious state, this "humanimal" existence in the neverending present, beyond memory and before identity, is, of course, formless—

like death, visions of God and the unknown mentality of insects. The music also brings associations of the most formless state of all, the act that gave name to rocking and rolling, the apex of love, the mother of all art. Not just the flowing of body liquids and the ecstatic trancendence of orgasm, but most importantly the obliteration of all borders in the act of copulation.

Richard D James, the person behind the techno innovations of Aphex Twin, boasts in interviews as to how much sex interferes with his music making, so much in fact that he spent two years of shagging instead of making music in his bedroom, the only site for his sonic creativity. Maybe this obvious connection says it all, and also nails down the final proof that rocking and rolling is not dead, but has just changed its name. However, when James explains the extremely hyperactive sound of the *Richard D James Album*, his anti-theoretical mode of speaking is not only reminiscent of Don Van Vliet, he also gives the same explanation to the motivations behind his music: "Yeah, I used to like stuff to go on for ages, but not now. I like my ears to be alerted like every few seconds. I like something different to happen, something good to go on."[8]

The stuff going on for ages is what James has labeled his ambient works, allthough he hates the soothing and boring implications of the word ambient. On *Selected Ambient Works Volume II* the ambient 'landscapes' are mostly the result of lucid dreaming. The tracks are invented or caught in a controlled dream and then remembered—or half-remembered—and composed after waking up. The technique of lucid dreaming is something James has been able to do since childhood, and it can be compared to Keith Jarrett's mystical state of involuntary decision making when opening up his rivers of creativity at the piano. Another quote from James in relation to his inspiration for the ambient works, which implies a kind of formless creation, is his comparison between the music and "standing in a power station on acid."[9] The tracks on this compilation, selected by James from the depths of his hard disk, is reminiscent of the sounds of the universe: I hear pulsating flickers of electricity on the surface of distant suns, I feel the rhythm of positive and negative electrons dancing the dance of life in the heart of atoms, and it makes me envision images from life rushing in slow motion through the memory of an android facing death.

I have raved on about the formless in music and I could go on with further examples from music or other arts, like the desire for explosions in American action movies, the search for evil in Norwegian black metal music, the voluptous body of Venus from Willendorf, the hysterical voice of Yoko Ono, the ambient experiments of Brian Eno, the amorphous drapes of Leonardo da Vinci, the performative drip paintings of

Jackson Pollock, the absurdist pranks of the Marx Brothers, the wild and smutty literal exaggerations of François Rabelais, the atonal drones of Sonic Youth, the psychedelic rebirth sequence in the end of Stanley Kubrick's *2001: A Space Odyssey*, the religious drain in Robert Gober's sink sculptures, the transformed machine guitar in Jimi Hendrix's interpretation of the American national anthem, the fall of Alice down the rabbit hole, ... etc., etc., but I will have to stop sometime.

Notes

1. For an elaboration of this concept, and its relation to visual art, see Yve-Alain Bois and Rosalind E Krauss, *Formless—a users guide*, New York: Zone Books, 1997.

2. Lester Bangs, "Captain Beefheart", *New Musical Express*, 1 April 1978.

3. Mike Barnes, *Captain Beefheart*, London: Quartet Books, 2000, p. 91.

4. Barnes, *Beefheart*, p. 346.

5. Charlie Mingus, liner notes to the album *The Black Saint and the Sinner Lady*, Impulse Records, 1963.

6. Mikal Gilmore, *Night Beat—A Shadow History of Rock'n'Roll*, New York: Anchor Books, 1998, p. 148.

7. Gilmore, *Shadow History*, p. 150.

8. Richard James, "Aphex Twin: Mad Musician or Investment Banker?", www.space-age-bachelor.com/features/99/aphex.htm

9. David Toop, *Ocean of Sound—aether talk, ambient sound and imaginary worlds*, New York: Serpents Tail, 1995, p. 205.

Recommended listening:

Aphex Twin, Selected Ambient Works, Volume II, *Warp Records, 1994.*

Aphex Twin, The Richard D James Album, *Warp Records, 1996.*

Captain Beefheart and his Magic Band, Trout Mask Replica, *Straight Records, 1969.*

Keith Jarrett, The Sun Bear Concert.

Charles Mingus, The Black Saint and the Sinner Lady, *Atlantic Records, 1963.*

Tangerine Dream, Force Majeure, *Virgin Records, 1979.*

The Velvet Underground, Peel Softly and See, *Polygram, 1995.*

ILLUSTRATION: BJØRN BJARRE

In the following article I'll tell you about four female celebrities. I have done various things on all four of them; video work, record and book reviews, TV coverage and long articles. Two of the videos are shorts, one is medium length and one is gigantic. In three of the videos real people (including me) are the main protagonists, in the fourth they are dolls.

Before the turn of the 1980s I had seen some video art, but nothing terribly exciting.[1] I was more into music videos at the time, since they seemed to combine just about anything. In the beginning the intellectuals, or the good rockers themselves for that matter, didn't really care about music videos, but theory soon started to accumulate around them: scratch-videos and the appropriation of different strands of popular culture became hip. Alongside, many female portrayers examined the old Hollywood stereotypes through repetition and distortion. It felt like no one had to shoot anything new, and that everything could be stated by simply giving new meaning to the old. I never personally fell for this. Simply handling and owning my idols on videotape wasn't enough for me. I had to become them.

Joan

In *Rendez-vous with Destiny* Joan Collins from *Dynasty* calls up my alter ego Anne Lee and discusses her forthcoming visit to Moldavia. Of course I play both characters myself. It is a drama—originally shot on film with sound—approximately four minutes long. The story is based on a particular phase in *Dynasty*. During it's premiere in April 1989, *Dynasty* had just been on a break, so no-one knew how the series would continue. My intention was to screen the video during this break only. But eventually the video was also screened after the series had continued and its events progressed. But I noticed that it didn't really bother anyone anyway. Many of the members of my audience didn't follow *Dynasty*, and didn't understand much of what was going on in the dialogue. And those who did follow didn't care.

Raisa

Pursuit of Happiness was my first big production shot straight to video.[2] (For a long time it had the working title *Raisa meets Knight Rider*). I play the part of Raisa myself, but the TV star she meets isn't *Knight Rider*'s Michael Knight, but Michael Kitt. To top things off: he's blonde!

Pursuit of Happiness also stars my long-time alter ego Pamela Nikolajeva, who I don't actually play myself. The main protagonist of the video is the rock journalist Claudia Paula. Although I had previously played both Claudia and Pamela, and strongly identified with both, I didn't actually star in the main part of this video. I realised that playing the lead yourself isn't always a good idea, since someone needs to do the actual filming too.

The supporting character in *Pursuit of Happiness*, Pamela Nikolajeva, is a very old fictional character, whose first escapades I noted down when in my teens. Pamela is married to the Russian, Ivan Nikolajev. The story can be described in earnest as an "Americo-Russian soap". Little by little the lovers became middle aged, and started to be upstaged by their children. In the 1980s Pamela and Ivan stayed in the wings, because at that time I got more interested in rock'n'roll stuff, alongside more Finnish things. And maybe Pamela lived a too monotonous life at times. I let her be admired by others than her husband, but the extramarital tomfoolery typical to soaps never crossed my mind.

Where Pamela Nikolajeva was my "older self", Claudia Paula was my younger self, first a little girl, but already fully grown around the time of *Pursuit of Happiness*. Claudia's image was perfectly in accordance with my punk-phase, when I published tapes under Claudia Paula's name and wrote articles in fanzines under that pseudonym. In *Pursuit of Happiness* I have thus combined two of my favourite issues: Claudia Paula is a rock journalist who works in Moscow.

The popular theme at the end of the 80s was perestroika, and its pillage was the theme for the illustrations of the Mikhail-song in *Pursuit of Happiness*—although I cannot declare myself completely innocent concerning the pillaging of perestroika. Around that time many Finnish filmmakers shot documentaries, especially in Estonia and other related areas, where many horrors came to light, but also the carnivalesque, and the beauty pageant.

In this context *Pursuit of Happiness* and the videos that followed must have seemed strange.[3] First of all, they weren't documentaries. I also planted myself firmly in the shallows. On top of this, my point of view wasn't especially Finnish (even if Raisa Gorbatchova spoke Finnish!). Somehow, I believe I could still maintain that they are some kind of documentaries—they relate to the kind of fantasy that has at some point seemed real.

Why was I drawn to Raisa? One reason must have been that for me she was a sort of real-life Pamela Nikolajeva. Raisa's famous glamour was more secretarial in colour. In her memoirs she mentions that one of the changes she has implemented is that women in certain situations do NOT have to wear evening dresses, "because they have so little use normally".

In my stories Raisa was admired by famous young men, to whom she was unreachable.

In reality those men were men that were unreachable to me. I also read in a biography of Raisa Gorbachova published by *Time* magazine, that when Gorbachov had expressed his interest in the magazine, they had started sending it to the Gorbachevs. But the writers weren't sure if they really read it. The writers had the same concerns as me when I pondered if rock musicians read the critiques of their records I'd written in my column.

Yoko

The first thing I shot on my own camera was the *Laundry-piece*, in which the protagonist tries for three minutes to entertain the audience by showing them her laundry. The video is one of my most shown pieces. In it, I pay homage to Yoko Ono by following her idea; entertain your guests by showing them your laundry and telling them where you've soiled it. In my video, the 'presenter' of the dirty laundry is not an artist, but more of a housewifey kind of character. One can quite easily imagine that the guests will leave soon. I got the idea from Yoko Ono's exhibition in Pori in 1991. I bought the catalogue of the exhibition, and it had some of her ideas for scripts in it. When Yoko around that time announced that she wasn't doing films anymore, but that others could use her scripts, I didn't choose anything from that book, but an idea for a performance that had hung in the exhibition.

Moreover, I was annoyed by the excessive glorification of the mundane by some members of the art community. The presentation and oversignification of household chores was not my utopia. An artist-couple even took notes of their daily life every 15 minutes and noted down the motives of their actions. When the mother made porridge for herself, it was because of "personal need"; when she made it for the children, the motive was "maintaining peace". When the diary showed anything interesting to do with work or art, the motive was always money.

It was a different thing altogether if anyone listened. The video doesn't show the audience, but it becomes evident that the guests leave. The normal, mundane audience is perhaps not as polite as the art crowd.

At first I didn't mention Yoko Ono to my aunt, I just gave her the idea, and we shot two takes each about three minutes long, out of which the latter one was used. All that was needed was the end credits and off the tape went in the mail. The *Laundry-piece* has been a hit ever since. I constantly hear questions and requests concerning it, more so than other things I've put much more effort, money and people into.

Where the *Dynasty* references of *Rendez-vous with Destiny* had dumbfounded the audience, there didn't seem to be any problems of this kind with the *Laundry-piece*.

"It seems people are more familiar with Yoko Ono's ideas than with Joan Collins", I said to my friend.

Anne

A new heroine is dawning on the horizon. When I got interested in yet one more artist-idol towards the middle of the 1990s, I had no idea how far that enthusiasm would lead me. The object of my respect is the American author Anne Rice. At some point I decided I needed to make a Finnish vampire movie situated in the "Finnish New Orleans", Uusikaupunki. Completed this year (2001), the film *The Vetsherlink Family* is nearly three hours long, and has a cast of barbie dolls. The author "Anne Raisa" also makes an appearance as the sole human character. Otherwise the plot and the characters are actually quite removed from the world of Anne Rice's novels. It borrows freely from other vampire literature, horror fiction, the history of Uusikaupunki, different genres of cinema, etc..

"Who's afraid of barbie-vampires?" you may ask. The central focus of the film is on the multitude of abuses of our fellow man and the patterns of hopes we project on them, that make it easier for the vampires to feed. *The Vetsherlink Family* is probably the most prosaic of all my works. While textual, it is still one of the few videos where a character doesn't have a previous history, neither in my writings nor in my films. The members of the Vetsherlink family torture us for three hours—the story spans one and a half years—but they do so for the first and for the last time.

I had read Anne Rice's vampire books in English; some of them were translated, but then the publisher probably gave up the hardback editions in Finnish, because all the fans were buying them in cheaper English editions.

The Vetsherlink Family wasn't originally meant to become a puppet film. When I started making my Finnish vampire film, there were still many possibilities. In the beginning the roles were acted by people, for instance Finland's Anne Rice, Anne Raisa, who first meets a young reporter, then to be her husband. At that point I knew nothing of Anne Rice's personal life.

In the long and arduous completion of a puppet film the hardest thing has been to understand that everything is new to the audience. Even a question like "Why do you use barbie dolls?" has to be answered patiently (doesn't anyone care about content?). One member of the audience suddenly realised that I do not do all of this on my own, because the soundtrack included male voices (not to say that I'd easily stretch to many female voices either). Basically, in this kind of process one has to come face to face with the limitations of a barbie doll. They are maybe just a bit too similar to make up the population of a whole village.

When I started making a Finnish vampire film, I decided that two of my favourite themes would have to step aside, namely America and Russia. Uusikaupunki, which means New Town, was only chosen for it's name. I could say that the Uusikaupunki of my film has as much to do with the real Uusikaupunki as Pamela Nikolajena's Moscow has with the real Moscow. But maybe just a bit more than *Dynasty*'s Moldavia has to do with the real Moldavia.

Notes

1. I usually start from the year 1989. Work has existed before that, but like the wise vampire, artists too shouldn't present evidence of having lived too long here on earth.

2. 1990.

3. "Diana te quiero", 1992, "The Daughter of Katinka", 1994, and "Mother Russia and the King of Kitsch", 1997.

translated by Jean Ramsey

—How is the political within the popular to be defined, or, more accurately, where is it placed, both in relation to the political field and to the notion of 'high art'? In politics, does the notion of pop culture, its images and significations, imply a mode of address that has a broader reach, and/or is it something usable in rallying the youth, as the similar strategies of situationism, student uprisings in Paris in May 1968 and punk in the UK at the end of the 1970s believed. Or, is pop culture, not connected to 'populist' politics and the propoganda machine of the corporate music industry and its middle class values. How are pop products and significations employed to specific political aims, how are the, in short, always already political, politicised? In relation to notions of art, is the appropriation of popular imagery still a critique of fine art, of highbrow culture. Is a dichotomy between 'high' and 'low' still useful, or is the embrace of pop products not merely a reification of them as high culture? That is, not a method that denigrates the value of high art, but rather raises the value of low culture.

—Mass and youth culture are no longer exclusively 'low' or "base materials", but also culturally reified, objects for academic research as well as market research. It is no longer an uncharted territory, but a thoroughly mapped and colonised area, validated by academia and targeted by marketing.

—It is, then, necessary to be specific in your choice of references, your citations, identifications and recodings. We cannot ascribe values and potentials to whole fields and categories, but rather to specific strategies. We cannot lay claim to a certain place or area, but must instead move from place to place and practice to practice: from a location of culture(s) towards a culture of location(s).

From a Mirage to a Miracle?

In recent years there has been talk of a 'Nordic miracle' in contemporary art. A new, young generation of artists from the Nordic countries have received unprecedented international attention through work, that on the one hand is characterised by an international, post-conceptual, installation-based approach to art practice, and that on the other is perceived as distinctly Nordic, addressing specific Nordic concerns. In many ways, this idea of a Nordic miracle, the sudden and unexpected emergence of an internationally viable contemporary art, can be seen as the opposite of the so-called 'Nordic tradition'. This new art, after all, broke away from tradition and location— away from the 'Nordic' in both respects. But international attention was also focused on traits in work that were perceived as particularly 'Nordic'. The major change between *new* Nordic art and *old* Nordic art was thus not due a lesser degree of 'Nordicness', but rather how this Nordicness was expressed and where it was located. A change in practice from nothern painting to installation and video-based work, and, more significantly, a shift in location from experiences of nature to city life. Thus, "white nights" no longer indicated the natural phenomena of the far North, but cocaine-infused party nights in the cities.

This 'hype' was, perhaps, started when one international curator talked of 'the Nordic Miracle', a catch-phrase that was somewhat ironic, but that stuck, probably due to its marketability along the lines of the likewise over-hyped 'Glasgow Miracle' of a few years before. Needless-to-say, this 'new' Nordic has been much discussed within the Nordic region itself. How did it happen. Was it really a miracle. Was/is it any good, or just hype? And then: was it fair? What about traditions? What about older artists, why aren't they embraced internationally on a similar scale? Soon arguments—fights even—were flying left and right, as well as more thoughtful discussions concerning generational shifts, the construction of the art world—both internationally and nationally—and how the art world can be seen as a battleground for different positions and opinions.

In order to situate this debate, one might turn to the first essay, "Borderland, Double Vision", by Claus Carstensen, an artist from the 80s generation, who takes a point of departure from his own experiences of living in the (then) international art centre Cologne, and later returning to Copenhagen. In this essay, Carstensen argues for the importance of location, of historical roots and biographical traits, in the formulation of an artistic position and practice, but he also discusses art practice in terms of a double citizenship, the national, local tradition and the inspiration and language of an international American-German dialogue and/or discourse. Carstensen sees this complex as hugely potential and equates it with his own background in the border region between Denmark and Germany, and in being bilingual. Writing literally from the border, he argues that we are always already in a double bind of location and language, affirmation and criticality. Magnus Bärtås, alternatively, discusses location and locality through the notion of "Refraction" in his essay of the same name. Bärtås uses refraction as a tool for describing the effects and/methods of contemporary, 1990s art practice, and he proposes that this art can function as a kind of parallel to other modes of communication, other fields of culture and productions of knowledge, as a type of refraction. A refraction that can also be seen in terms of the transposition of artistic language from the centre to the provinces, and back again.

Two other essays in this section bear witness to the internal debates the apparent miracle brought about, both sparking huge controversy when first published, coming from each side of the argument: pro and contra the new, with both writers acknowledging the existence of a hype, although they blame it squarely on the other side. Anders Eiebakke's "Its Typically Norwegian to be Good!" is a full frontal attack on the (conservative) art politics of Norway. Its institutions are accused of not going far enough in understanding and supporting contemporary 1990s art. If there is a success story to be found, it is certainly not facilitated by the institutions and funding bodies. Contrary to Eiebakke's points, Elisabeth Toubro blames the institutions for going too far in their embrace of the new in her text "The Fall of the Louisiana". Her article was not written in connection with Eiebakke's however, but originates from a debate in a Danish newspaper centering on the validity and selection process of a major show of contemporary Danish and Swedish art at the Louisiana, one of the region's largest museums of modern art. Louisiana had, historically, always been known and renowned for its distancing of itself from the local art scene and its exclusive focus on international modern art. It is Toubro's argument that an embrace of local rather than international art actually leads to a debasement of the museum, and in turn, of art practices in general. In order to maintain its reputation and function as a purveyor of quality and distinction, an institution like Louisiana should not engage with local, contemporary art or with hype. How contemporary Nordic art engages in general, and interacts with both the very international and the very local, are the concerns of Jyrki Siukonen in the essay "Art in the Backwoods", where he tells the story of how this new, hip, social and advanced art is received in a local context—as exemplified by an exhibition in a small Canadian town. Similarly, Asmundur Asmundsson reflects on the status of new international Nordic art practices in his short statement "We're all Normal (and we want our freedom) (Today)", where he not only ironises the title of this book, but also the hype and identity of this new Nordic art, and its relation to international fame and art historical acceptance. In this way, Asmundsson is also making the miracle historic.

Borderland, Double-vision —art, subjectivity and biography

In this context, 'private' is held as if it does not have a publicly shared meaning. This is an illusion. The notion of our 'self' is administered from our earliest childhood exchanges. This administered 'self' assumes one prominent image: That of the 'self' as non-ideological. This fails to notice that the 'non-ideological' is itself an ideological construct.

Terry Atkinson

Our present age is one of exile. How can one avoid sinking into the mire of common sense, if not by becoming a stranger to one's own country, language, sex and identity?

Julia Kristeva

I

When I, as it has happened, have chanced to let on that my latest exhibition goes by the name *Side by Side*, this is a statement, as far as the possessive pronoun is concerned, that is not accurate.[1] It is not—strictly speaking—a solo exhibition, not withstanding the fact that I am of the conviction that exhibitions with up to three participants can, under certain conditions, properly be regarded as such. And even though it is separatist in its point of departure—the stylistic-, generation- and family-related crossover—the exhibition consists of a number of collaborative paintings that I created together with my maternal uncle, Alfred Friis. In my early teenage years, my uncle functioned as a kind of catalyst for my first artistic trials. In response, I dedicated—as a tribute—to my uncle my collection of essays entitled *Deterritorialiseret* (Deterritorialised), published in 1991.[2] His background is abstract expressionism and four years of study at the Royal Academy of Fine Arts, with Egill Jacobsen, a famous Danish COBRA painter. He also has a past in the communist party, working with trade unions. The frame around the exhibition is a series of notes made from an all-night discussion we had in August 89, with the relationship between politics and aesthetics as a point of departure.

I had the notes lying around for four years without having any idea what they could be used for. They were too obscure, too private and too obstinate. Nonetheless, they had the effect of being some kind of background projection when we finally went to work on making the paintings, which—when they were finished—looked just like everything that I had had too much of but which, in spite of everything, I just couldn't jettison and which, therefore, in even my most conceptual and figurative phases, I had been circling around.

An unspoken, but for me fundamental, theme of the exhibition is the idiosyncrasy of the double bind that might have something to do with a kind of lapsarian fall in relation to the informal and abstract expressionism and which, in 89—in connection with the exhibition *Bonde—Carstensen—Frandsen* at the Aarhus Kunstmuseum—I accepted as "the Soulages' affinity", as the art historian Anders Kold called it.[3] To be in the company of non-intended idiosyncrasies.

Perhaps it is just these non-intended idiosyncrasies that have now become willed and turned upside down as a productive way out of the wretchedness with the palette and the form, as a mode of confessional embarrassment, which naturally brings one close to the vulgar. The art historian T J Clark is moving into something of the same area when, in his 1992 essay, "In Defense of Abstract Expressionism", he writes: "In Abstract Expressionism, and here is the painting's continuing (maybe intensifying) difficulty for us, a certain construction of the world we call 'individuality' is revealed in its true, that is to say contingent, vulgarity. [...] Vulgarity, then (to return to our subject), is the necessary form of that individuality allowed the petty bourgeoisie."[4]

It is in the obvious relation of mutual antagonism[5] between this 'constructed individuality' and the collective, security-seeking, but eventless middle class biography that the vulgar manifests itself.[6] And the relation of mutual contradiction can only be wielded—as bound up as one is—by "taking your own biography on your own shoulders", as devoid of events as it may appear to be.[7]

In our times, with an ever increasing over-exposure of the sub-cultural, the subversive and the cult-like, the event-less ordinariness evidently appears to be all the more fanatical. I realised this in connection with the poster for my exhibition entitled *Membrane* in Neuer Aachener Kunstverein in 92, which displayed my pregnant wife standing naked before a number of membrane paintings in my studio.[8]

What I hadn't counted on was the violent reaction that the poster unleashed in the places where it was posted. In most instances, the poster was simply torn down. But in the entrance to Galerie Sophia Ungers, where the poster was also hung on the wall, what transpired was a peculiar kind of war. Every morning, the new poster was torn into pieces from a spot somewhere just below the breast with the result that the flap with the pregnant stomach fell forward and covered up the lower part of the body. For a long time, I pondered over this reaction. It wasn't until my attention was drawn to the fact that the poster looked like a typical Danish poster from the 70s that I could conjoin the rabid reaction with the banal ordinary subject. I had simply been blind to the imprint that the underpants had been left behind and to the changes that the pregnant body was undergoing, as well as to the cellulite and the covering of long pubic hair.

The same (albeit hardly as violent) reaction is what we have encountered in connection with the joint paintings made for Side by Side. This didn't really come as a surprise to me, since in a number of other collaborative projects in which I have participated, I have experienced the same spurning and defensive kind of belittlement, which I believe is bound up with the fact that the paintings were created by more than one person. Consequently, one 'is liable' collectively for them, which means to say that the artistic responsibility is dispersed and, therefore, the individual can, apparently, not be credited for anything. [9] Liability and the authentic are vanishing even as diffuse authority is being produced. A situation that can be said to be analogous with the judicial discussion about collective and individual guilt that was unleashed in connection with the many years of trials against the Rote Armee Fraktion (Red Army Faction). [10]

With the generation- and palette-related crossover and the two signatures on the painting, a problem of authorisation arose which still constitutes a crucial point of origin for the distribution of art. "It implies a loss of authority", as the semiotician Robert Nelson formulates in a somewhat different context. [11] I just don't believe that it is the origin in the painting that is being forfeited ("negation of loss of authority"), but rather that, through the collective procedure, what is being established is another form of negation—namely a negation of a general but nonplused consensus.

Two of the tracks on the jazz records we were listening to while we painted the pictures—Coleman Hawkins' and Clark Terry's LP Together and Duke Ellington's and Johnny Hodges' Side by Side—were entitled, very significantly, "There's No You" and "A Tune for the Tutor". In the catalogue for the exhibition, the following statement by Thelonius Monk is quoted: "If you make a mistake, play it loud. Then people will think you did it on purpose."

The outcome of this field of fortuitousness, productive misunderstanding and negated authorisation was that in the process of painting what emerged was an identical third, a form of third person singular.

The reaction to the joint paintings turned out to be dependent on the readings of the abstract lyrical and international style we had employed: a style that seems to release fronts of intransigent attitudes. This style has—in extension of COBRA, informal and abstract expressionism—paradoxically enough, become the Danish synonym for tasteful, modern art. And I say 'paradoxically' because jazz and the abstract pictorial idiom after 1945 consist of, amongst other things, an internationalisation, formulated as a reaction against the strong nationalism indigenous to the period between the wars.

What was so diffuse in the reaction, in my opinion, was due to the fact that we had painted a series of paintings that were neither fish nor fowl. Or to put this another way: insofar as they subscribe to identity as a construction, they also take on a critical affirmation, which is simultaneously critical and naïve, as Marcel Reich-Ranicki has put it (about Fontane): "That he was at once both: critical and naive.... The synthesis of criticality and naïveté is the secret to his... coolness... and superiority."[12]

This as counter-position to the affirmative critique, which by virtue of its way of focusing only on the context confirms analysis as a part of a 'formal tradition' and thereby adds to conceptual art's 'third Generation' a glint of historicism.[13] Conceptual art posited—and it is here that we find its historic merit—with the analysis, the self-reflection and the contextually-related, a dividing line for all art production which would henceforth only be capable of being manufactured and of instrumentalising this dividing line as internalised experience.

I believe that the instinctive complement between affirmation and critique has something to do with the complementary in two such arbitrary and deterritorialised figures as *sujet* and 'subject'. And that this 'syncretism' of *sujet* and subject can only be borne aloft by a trust-worthiness.

Mike Kelley has arrived at something of the same conclusion. In his essay, "Missing Time", he writes: "One thing I didn't like about Rauschenberg, and Pop Art in general, was that the subject matter was of such little importance. In Rauschenberg's work I always felt that any other image could be substituted for another and that there was little attention paid to the tension between the various images, the images and the paint handling, or to the possibilities of associational ties between the images. In Rauschenberg, image was equivalent to paint smear."[14]

It is, in my opinion, the contrary that is at play in the paintings from *Side by Side*, even if the *sujet* is apparently bound up arbitrarily in the paintings as 'international style' and abstract daubing. It is first outside of the paintings that the international style conjoins subject and *sujet* together in the biography as an internalised form: the recourse as the actual subject, with a point of origin in 'a constructed identity' which one slowly, in what is a bifurcating process, subjects oneself to.[15]

With this, the appropriation is accepted as a repetition and a reproduction; as a work with history and subjectivity.[16] As junctures in a reconstruction of the relation between art and the private ("the possibilities of associational ties between the images").[17]

It operates, it might be said, with the motivation and the reconstruction as it does with the gnarled and insistent drawings, which—in time—accumulate authority because they draw upon and simultaneously affirm the biographical ("affirmation of existence" and "affirmation of will").[18]

It is this affirmative tendency that has served as the point of origin for the two trilogies of exhibitions I have made since 92 and which have been dealing largely with the exchange of identities. On the one side, there were the group shows—*The Commitments*, *Strawdogs* and *RAM*—which thematised the elective affinity and generation-overlapping element in this relationship. On the other side, there were the family-related solo and joint exhibitions: *Untitled Room for Zoe*, *Double Indemnity/Clausholm* and *Side by Side/Colab*.[19]

The elective affinities (which are always dependent on chance and the possible) in the group shows certainly constitutes an attempt to read the biography aloud up against some kind of existing canon, whatever this may be—and, in the final analysis, it also has something to do with passing the baton.

Whereas the point of origin for the two-person exhibition *Untitled Room for Zoe* was a capsised project from 1980, where I had been absorbed with the sociological and political aspects of visual art: what does it mean to sit in the boondocks and spend your time making art? Or, more specifically: to what extent has the existence of an avant-garde culture, in the border region, been possible side by side a more traditional culture?

Initially, it was my idea to write a proposal for a sociological exhibition in a museum in South Jutland, based on my own family history. But coupling the sociological form with the artistic proved to be impossible. It was first in 92, when my daughter was born, that I envisioned the possibility of transposing the preliminary sketch into a conventional gallery exhibition.

In the exhibition, there were paintings that had been painted by my great grandfather, my maternal grandfather and my maternal uncle, which hung alongside a series of black, monochrome *Territory Panels*. At the same time, a video was shown, where my maternal grandmother could be seen speaking about her upbringing and about her life in the border region.

The themes in the exhibition formulated themselves as a series of questions that had interested me for quite some time: how and when does genealogy leap over into, respectively, morphology/ideology? Is there anything as enigmatic as morphological/ aesthetic geno- and pheno-types? Socialisation? The epochal forms? Affirmation and dissidence seen in the light of Nolde's membership in the North Sleswig department of the NSDAP and the following *Malverbot*?[20] What is the ontological level? Is a Brechtian re-functionalisation a possibility, such as we see in Nauman?[21]

It is these reflections which, similarly, but in a different and most tangible way, have established the foundation for the recent exhibitions of joint paintings with, respectively, my daughter and my uncle, and which have been hinting that all biography can only be read in between the fissures, as intermediate biography against the canon. There's only one way *out* of the dilemma. And that way is *in*.

II

Language and culture, roughly speaking, express themselves in two ways. Either they exist as links within a relation of property and power, which could be designated as 'cultural hegemony' using an expression from the 70s, or else they emerge as subjective motivation, with all the presentiments about identity and contradictions implied therein.

That such a subjective motivation within a multi-cultural field like that which is currently thriving is not always unequivocal can be empirically demonstrated by the example of my own family, which stems from long and well-established roots in the ground on either side of the border of Southern Jutland's frontier district. My cousins, both male and female, have married across the borders with the result that five nationalities are now represented in my family. This condition might best be described through the notion of deterritorialisation.

After spending seven years in Cologne as a Southern Jutlander, carrying the minority problems both north and south of the border as an inherent part of my identity, the boundaries are slowly effaced and the distance vanishes, only to be intensified once again in my work with painting and writing.

When we moved back to Copenhagen, autumn was on its way. Late summer flared up one more time, and a certain nostalgia about moving turned up. All the more so because years earlier, we had a similar move to Cologne in the early part of the fall. At that time—in 1986—the autumn mood was mingled with my childhood's almost forgotten pictures of family outings in the gray-brown light of autumn Germany.

Nine years earlier, in 1977, I was on the way home from Paris, where I had lived for half a year. The week after Schleyer's abduction I arrived in Cologne, and the first thing I saw was a railway station full of machine-gun toting police. A few years later, I read a quotation from Baum, the Minister of the Interior at the time, wherein he asserted that violence perpetrated by the radical right was qualitatively and quantitatively far less than that perpetrated by the radical left.

This quotation somehow remained stuck in my mind and unfortunately, it proved to be true in an inverted and tragic way. The over-reaction to Schleyer's abduction at

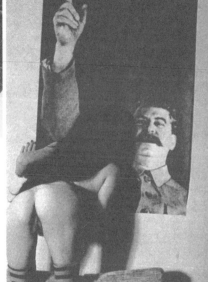

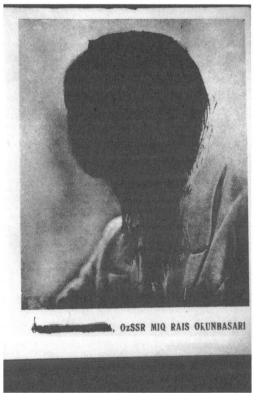

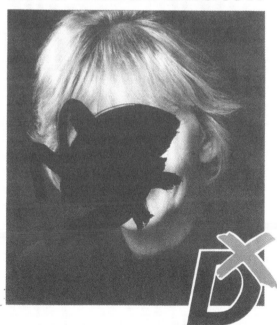

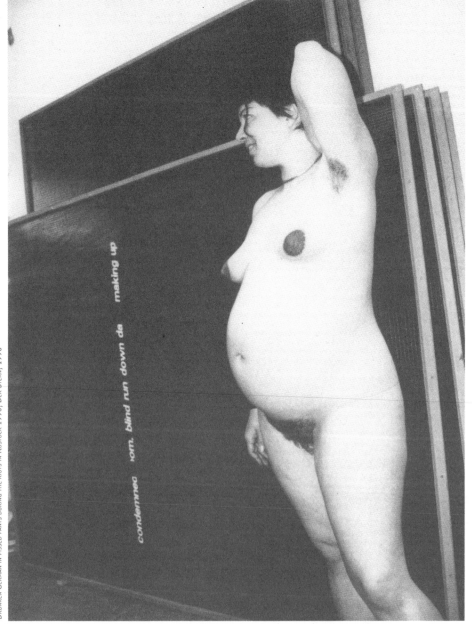

ILLUSTRATIONS FROM LEFT TO RIGHT: CLAUS CARSTENSEN, *UTE, KÖLN 1982. COME ON ASSHOLE!—MAKE MY DAY SELF PORTRAIT WITH STIGMA*
DRUNKEN GERMAN IN PISSED PANTS DURING THE RIOTS IN ROSTOCK 1993, DER STERN, 1993

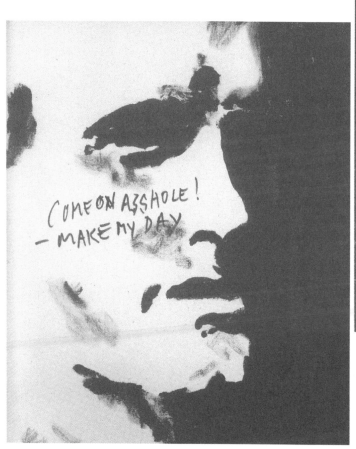

that time strikes a profound contrast with today's political passivity in connection with the series of lethal arson attacks against refugee centres in Germany. For me, then, *Deutschland im Herbst* has always been a double-edged and simultaneously very concrete metaphor. A combination of childhood's luminescence, political reality and that everyday run of things which was recently actualised by the election of Hamburg's senate: frustration, boozing and the "this-table-is-mine!" chauvinism display, with the utmost, lucidity that the right wing radicals' violence is not generated by the political spectrum's most extreme right, but that it grows from the centre. Not so strange, then, that in Europe in general, they speak about the hideous German as he is personified in the photograph from the incidents in Rostock, with his pissed-on jogging trousers and a beer in his hand.

In a historical sense, I think that this has to do with the fact that the middle class has long since internalised the 'anti-form' of the youth revolt. The negative theory that ought actually to have produced critical subjects has been converted into a boisterous affirmation of the current historical situation.

I've always regarded Cologne as a kind of exile and one of the amenities of exile is that it always effects a kind of double vision: an inner and outer perspective. A perspective, which I—principally—was familiar with from childhood, due to the border region's bilingualism. My linguistic identity, on the other hand, has always been bound up with a third 'language', namely Southern Jutlandish, which linguistically speaking, is a *parole* without *langue*. And I imagine that what is involved in thinking in such a language does force one into a tactical and delicate perspicacity which puts one in a position to focus on the doublings of reality—as was the case, for example, with German re-unification in 1990, something to which I have always been opposed inasmuch as history is non-reversible. Re-territorialisations can only be carried out symbolically and subjectively, which does constitute a paradox, in a way, insofar as subjectivity (always) is an objective factor, as Rudolf zur Lippe put it in an issue of Enzenberger's *Kursbuch* sometime in the middle of the 70s.

It was out of this point of view that the series of black monochrome paintings, *Territory Panels* or *Territory Pissings*—after the song by the band Nirvana—emerged. This was also the approach to my collection of poems entitled *38 Poems*, which I dedicated to my daughter Zoe, who was born in Cologne. The poems had the following four lines by Anna Akhmatova as motto: *Russian seems not enough for you/and you want to know in all languages/how steep the rises and falls are/and what is the price of conscience—and terror.*

And this perspective similarly structured the exhibition *Untitled Room for Zoe*, which I presented at Gallery Sophia Ungers in 1994, and again, albeit in an altered version, at Gallery Mikael Andersen in Copenhagen. A search for certain events in the story of my family woven together by a distinctive combination of a passion for art, politics and patriotism. For me, this glance back into family history was an attempt to recapitulate something without becoming immediately ensnared in the booby trap of historical reversibility.

It is perhaps within the realm of art that a German influence makes its most noticeable appearance. My generation of artists would be inconceivable without the younger generation of German painters who made their breakthrough at the beginning of the 80s and who thematised so precisely the problem of modern German identity in the light of growing multi-nationalism. In this respect, a typical example is one of Kippenberger's paintings from 1984, entitled *Ich kann beim besten Willen kein Hakenkreuz entdecken*. It is a clumsily painted picture of fallen beams, executed in Cubistic style, that with only the aid of the ironic and conversely stigmatising title evokes memories of a swastika.

This conversely stigmatising is perhaps one of the most symptomatic aspects of the German situation today, where a heavily historical, delimited, vertical culture like the German, in much the same manner as the Danish, falls under the heavy influence of a horizontal and limitless American unity—and popular culture—which always disseminates itself more rapidly by virtue of its synchronism. What is queer and paradoxical in this connection is that this deterritorialisation is countered with a nationalism that is both anachronistic and incapable of apprehending its own dependence upon American popular culture.

This is what the painting of the 80s was reacting against—with irony as an instrument. In the 90s, however, "the line it is drawn, the curse it is cast". The *Schein/Sein* dialectics of irony have merged with the social effects of reality. Or to put it another way, with a quotation by Albert Drach: "Cynicism is an implementation of irony."

The state of affairs in Denmark is, perhaps, somewhat different. The Danish historical situation concerning nationalism is something else, while at the same time, the parameters that delimit art practices during these years are prescribed by a very narrow German-American dialogue, over which Danish advances have no influence. Which once again results in most of what is revered at home being variations on German and/or American discourses. We thus obtain imports rather than produce exports, resulting in a concomitant internationalism, at best. Instead, I believe that we should employ whatever is right in front of us—that which is immediately adjacent, banal obsequious or silly. A body that is all at once biographical and historical.

Thus, the territories can also better be pissed out.

Notes

1. *Side by Side—Paintings created jointly by Claus Carstensen and Alfred Friis*, presented at Galerie Mikael Andersen, Copenhagen, September 18-21 October, 1995. A similar exhibition, with paintings made in common and individually created, was presented at Galerie Møller Witt in Sønderborg, 23 September— 26 October, 1995, under the title *Colab*.

2. *Tribute* from the Latin *tribus*, and the English *tribe*. On the subject of increasing tribalisation, see: Diederichsen, Diedrich, *Wie aus Bewegungen Kulturen werden und aus Kulturen Communities und warum man uns das andrehen will* (unpublished manuscript presented as an introduction to the Royal Danish Art Academy's symposium on *Difference, Identity and Democracy*, April 21, 1994); Diederichsen, Diedrich, "Tribes and Communist Parties—Ziellosigkeit, Reversibilität, Gedankennot", *Freiheit macht arm*, Cologne: Kiepenheuer und Witsch, 1993; "Vergesst alle Systeme", *Der Spiegel*, 33/1995.

3. Pierre Soulages, French abstract-informal painter.

4. T J Clark, "Zur Verteidigung des Abstrakten Expressionismus", *Texte zur Kunst*, no. 7, October 1992.

5. A current attempt to evade the vulgar in this mutual antagonism consists in transcending the antithesis in the form of a descriptive or ideology-critical context analysis, like what can be gleaned from Fareed Armaly's visualised analysis of Fassbinder's television series *Acht Stunden sind kein Tag* and the light program *Wünsch dir was*, from the 1970s. More recently, it could also be spotted in Rirkrit Tiravanija's 'lyrical' analysis of the three Swedish clichés—urban plan, kindergarten and Ikea—in his contribution to Lars Nittve's farewell exhibition at Rooseum in Malmø entitled *Nutopi*. The heart of the matter, however, is that the very notion of analysis being some object hovering freely above the analysed or the notion of any 'poetic' ideological critique are in themselves ideological and just as constructed as is individuality.

6. Something that in the 1980s, symptomatically enough, entailed a widespread use of 'middle names' that had gone out of use some time previously and were supposed to individualise the typical, Danish "-sen" [meaning son] surnames. In his essay, "En dans på Gloser", Danish Poet Søren Ulrik Thomsen makes a similar observation and conclusion in *KRITIK* 116, 1995.

7. A condition that has found an entirely headstrong expression in Terry Atkinson's series of paintings entitled *Happy Snaps*, Peter Carlsen's work with the character named *Villy* and Christian Schmidt Rasmussen's introverted and spacey depictions of growing up in the welfare state of Denmark. These strategies are to my mind much more demanding and committing than psychoanalysis or the official 'Nordic' discourse.

8. I got the idea for the poster from an invitation card for Brice Marden's *Back Series* exhibition at the Bykert Gallery, from 1968, which shows a nude and almost anorexic Helen Marden, with her back turned to us, standing in front of the paintings in their studio.

9. Over the course of many years I have painted a number of collaborative paintings with my daughter and others: Peter Carlsen (under the name *Hurtigt Udført Arbejde I/S* [Quickly Executed Work, Inc.]), Zoe Carstensen, Inge Ellegård and Berit Jensen, Erik A Frandsen and Peter Bonde (under the name *In And*

Out The Flat). In 1983, I painted together with the Bonde, *The Metaphysical Series*, which provided an occasion for a heated discussion about affability and simulation—and which later on, for the very same reasons, was acquired by Aarhus Kunstmuseum.

10. A discussion which, with a sympathetic understanding and a radically subjective point of view, has been delineated by Ulrike Meinhof's daughters in the article "Unsere Mutter—'Staatsfeind Nr. 1' (Bettina and Regine Röhl: Unsere Mutter—'Staatsfeind Nr. 1'", *Der Spiegel* 29/1995.

11. Robert Nelson, "The End of Drawing", *Agenda—Contemporary Art Magazine* 26 and 27, 1992-1993.

12. Marcel Reich-Ranicki in an open letter to Günter Grass in *Der Spiegel* 34/1995.

13. For a self-critical analysis of the economy, the distribution and the addressee-relation in more recent context art, see: Stefan Germer, "Unter Geiern—Kontext-Kunst im Kontext", *Texte zur Kunst*, No. 19, August 1995.

14. Mike Kelley, *Missing Time—Works on Paper 1974-1976 Reconsidered*, Hannover: Kestner Gesellschaft, 1995.

15. Subject and *sujet* from the Latin *subjectum*—to be put through an experience.

16. A possible parallel to this might be Gilles Deleuze's *Différence et répétition*. For a hipster's go at (remix and sampling) the same material, see: Wolfgang Höbel, "Auf Adornos Basslinie", *Der Spiegel* 35/1995, which is actually a review of Ulf Poschardt's *DJ-Culture*, Hamburg: Verlag Rogner & Bernhard bei Zweitausendeins, 1995.

17. About these junctures Oskar Negt and Alexander Kluge write, in *Massverhältnisse des Politischen*: Hegel speaks of "nodal [knotted] lines of relations of measure". "They signify critical states in which the peaceful proximity of things and their relations come into vital [lebendige] movement. The concept appears in *Logic*, in the section describing the transition from the logic of Being to the logic of Essence. No direct transition exists, Hegel says, from the multiplicity of phenomena to either their essence or their concept. Once phenomena take on a determinate constellation—in which they lose their prior form of existence and come into contact with other existents—self-contained relations intensify and become singular articulations, constituting an essential relation. This inner articulation is identical with measure. Phenomena can only attain to that which is essential through relations of measure. Consequently, multiple lines of such relations of measure touch upon the confrontation of self and other in the instant of transition and overturning; the crisis of bare proximity-become-contradiction becomes resolved in movement. Hegel names this the "pulsation of the living being".** These are 'nodal lines' of relations of measure, the absolute opposite of what Aristotle called "mean" and "measure". Resembling nothing of a balanced, poetic mean, they are rather expressions of extremity, the coalescence of measure-filled relations and the engendering of intensive, frictional surfaces." See Oskar Negt and Alexander Kluge, *Massverhältnisse des Politischen—15 Vorschläge zum Unterscheidungsvermögen*, Michael Eng, trans., Frankfurt Am Main: S Fischer Verlag, 1992. Translator's note:

* "Knotenlinien der Massenverhaeltnisse". This phrase has been translated by A V Miller as "Nodal Lines of Measure-Relations" in *Hegel's Science of Logic*, London: George Allen & Unwin, 1969. As Michael Inwood notes, "Hegel focuses on cases where qualitative changes, like knots on a piece of string, occur only intermittently in the course of continuous quantitative change: Water, heated sufficiently, becomes steam, and, cooled sufficiently, ice; its undergoing some such qualitative change is essential if we are to measure its temperature." *A Hegel Dictionary*, Oxford: Blackwell, 1992, p. 241.

**Negt and Kluge use the phrase, "Pulsation des Lebendigen". A V Miller translates this concept as an "urge".

18. In the aforementioned essay, Robert Nelson carried out an outstanding etymological analysis of the word *drawing* in relation to its Greek and Latin roots (*trahere*, Latin—to pull (a line), especially contained in the word *tract*; or the somewhat more international *disegno* from *signum*, Latin—sign (which, amongst other things ushers in the difference in words like *designate*, *signature* or *design*— "drawing is all about decisions. ... the investment of will in definition...")—and *grafi*, Greek—to scratch; the life-geography's delineation or engraving in the biography).

19. *The Commitments*, Galleri Specta, Århus, 1992; *Strawdogs*, Kunstforeningen, Copenhagen, 1993; *RAM*, Portalen, Hundige, 1995; *Untitled Room for Zoe*, Galerie Sophia Ungers, Cologne, 1992 and Galerie Mikael Andersen, Copenhagen, 1993; *Double Indemnity*, Hole, Copenhagen, 1994 (together with Zoe Carstensen); Clausholm Castle, Hadsten 1995 (including joint works with Zoe Carstensen).

20. As stated surely he (Nolde) joined, the Nationalsozialistische Arbeitsgemeinschaft Nordschleswig (NSAN) on 15 September 1934, getting the member number 1722. In the summer of 1935, the NSAN merged with another Nazi group, becoming NSDAPN. Thus, Nolde could remain a member of NSDAPN (Nordschleswig), while the NSDAP in Germany prosecuted his art as 'entartet'—Monika Hecker, *Nolde ein Nazi?—Unsinn*, in: *Schleswig-Holstein-Journal Sonnabend*, 16 December 1995.

21. In addition, two quotations from, respectively, Robert Longo and Terry Atkinson: "I define myself by things that are outside me..." and "The idea of (drawing) skill as a neutral, non-ideological, technical resource is itself an ideological position." Other reflections in connection with the exhibition refer to semantic and formal vertical/horizontality. Remembrance, time and gravitation. The German *Fallstudien*, in the double meaning of the word, both case study and "fall" study. The Fall as construction principle (cf. Johs V Jensen's *Kongens fald* [*The Fall of the King*]). The non-objective in the work of Malevich—not apprehended as objectless, but as radical subjectivity (the cover image of the catalogue for *Untitled Room for Zoe* was, for example, a black-and-white photograph of my maternal grandfather and uncle standing in Schackenborg's snow-covered castle park).

22. Rudolf zur Lippe, *Subjektivitet—en objektiv faktor* [*Subjectivity—an objective factor*], Birger Steen Nielsen and Elo Nielsen eds., *Socialisationsforskning—senkapitalisme og subjektivitet* [*Socialisation Research—Late Capitalism and Subjectivity*], Copenhagen: Borgen, 1978. Frederiksberg 18 August— 30 December, 1995 (first part) Cologne 19 September 1993 (second part which, in a slightly altered rendition—

in the form of an exchange of letters with Marcel Beyer—appeared *Nummer—Kunst, Literatur, Theorie:* Frühjahr, 1994)

Previously published in Kritik no. 121, 1996.

translated by Dan A Marmorstein

Refraction

Refraction: The deflection or deviation of a wave (e.g. a beam of light) from one straight path to another when passing from one medium (e.g. air) into another (e.g. glass) in which the speed of transmission of the wave is different. [Lat. refractus, of refringere to break open, break up, refract...]

Longmans Dictionary

Refraction is an artistic method, but the concept can also be used to describe the effects of movements within and between societies and cultures (social refraction). Refraction belongs together with random displacements, mistakes and conscious or unconscious misuse.

Social refraction rarely occurs in isolated, closed and strictly controlled societies. It requires mobility. Thus, social refraction rather arises from tourism, social mobility, or when someone moves to a new country or a new town: the foreigner reveals his background and sheds light both on himself (his nationality or his class background) and on the peculiarities of the new town, the aesthetic ideals of the new class, or the dominating norms of the new country. As for the refraction metaphor, one can make a choice: either the human being is the light that is refracted by the new situation, or the human being is the prism or the water through which reality is the light that refracts and changes direction. The latter metaphor seems to tend towards Emile Zola's famous phrase about naturalistic art: "reality viewed through a temperament". But this phrase is based on a stable subject—firm and monolithic, immobile—through which reality refracts and is strengthened. For contemporary art a different description is necessary. I imagine a 'temperament' that is not activated when consensus reigns. Refraction only arises when the subject moves into a foreign situation or territory. We are faced with an art whose effect comes from some labile point in consciousness. It is an area where one finds different emotions, or emotions in between the familiar emotions. The effect seems to emanate from a blind spot between a number of statements, several of which can be self-evident, or quite banal.

A man I met in a bar in Stockholm told me that he was born in Greece during the Civil War that followed in the wake of World War II. He was born in a small town that had been isolated from the outside world, and there was great hardship. He weighed so little that a doctor judged he had no chance of survival. His mother lost hope, but had the bizarre idea of pleasing her other two children. She gave him to the children as a toy. The other children immediately started playing house. They fed him with a little flour and goat's milk, and he survived. "And here I sit now", he said.

Refraction is associated with educational paths and paths for information and meaning. But also with a movement between centre and periphery. Scandinavian artists have usually travelled a lot to get information. They have sought out places of social and artistic mobility. For both the Swedish pre-modernist and modernist generation, Paris was the obvious choice. Some of them were inspired by and copied what they found in these places and returned home to be acclaimed as avant-gardists. What these artists created was often just a pale imitation of their models. In many cases these artists became even more technically skilled than their mentors. Several of them developed a fanatical attitude which—superficially seen—seemed to generate a triumph of the copy. But there was also an element of the overwrought, a far too strong will that became a stumbling-block for their ability to express themselves. Some of those whose hypertension progressed into insanity achieved in their illness a paradoxical emancipation from their high ambitions. But information nowadays, as we know, moves faster than individuals. And for that reason the introducer and homecomer with his avant-gardist banner has become extinct.

But 'the provinces' remain, as a mental construct and as the producer of a certain type of artist. A person who is exaggeratedly 'clever', often fanatical, who thinks he can embrace everything. The artist of the provinces becomes a collector, a living reference work or a workaholic.

Thurston Moore of the American band Sonic Youth relates in a text how he came into contact with the German experimental band Can's music. It was through the record *Ege Bamyasi*, which was released in the USA at the beginning of the 70s: "It was immediately cut out and dumped in Woolworth department stores nationwide at approximately 49¢—this is where a lot of 14 year old kids bought records they could afford."[1]

Born at the beginning of the 60s, I am one of those who remembers the special thrill that the cut out records aroused when one browsed through them in the sale trays of department stores like Domus or Tempo. Either one of the corners of the cover was brutally cut or someone, with equal insensitivity, had run the cover through a band saw.

The records that were stigmatised this way were roughly speaking of two kinds: either they were mainstream products that had flopped—that is, gross misjudgements from the record companies' marketing departments resulting in giant surplus stocks— or else obscure records that for some reason had gained widespread distribution. The excitement was presumably created by the shuttling between these two extremes:

one pole with fading mainstream stars, careers on the downhill slope; the other with wild experiments, music one had never heard, which turned your thinking upside down and filled your brain with an oxygen-like feeling of anything being possible.

Thurston Moore was—as any (like myself) Swedish teenager growing up in a small town and on the whole having no money—affected by the market's water-like ability to find a way of disposing its products. In certain, propitious circumstances, this logic creates arbitrary paths of information and influence; we were basically predisposed towards two choices: either the flop mainstream product or else the obscure records of artistic experiments.

A man from Riga described a different scenario when it came to the market economy's ability not only to create but also to block paths of information. Nowadays they only show American films in the cinemas in Latvia (except on one occasion—the annual film festival). In the Soviet period, on the other hand, you could see films from all over the world, certainly often censored, but still—African, French, Czech and Swedish films along with a wealth of domestic films. In Riga alone about 20 films were produced a year. The problem with American action films was that people in Riga thought that they encouraged the Mafia. Or, as the man put it, Mafia men saw "the beauty of evil" in them. The Soviet films on the other hand usually had 'humanist' content. In the innumerable Soviet war films the violence was abstract: a background with bomb explosions in the distance, in the foreground a hero who totters and falls with dignity. The hero is able, as he lies dying, to utter a few patriotic phrases before his eyes close.

An artist can benefit from a certain ignorance—or "not-knowing"—of the object of his or her interest; to approach it as an amateur, so to speak. Not knowing the logic of discourses and their certain, specialised ways of arranging knowledge can create a distance which enables the artist to recognise relations, which are obvious for those who don't have this distance. Someone who lives in Berlin doesn't find it strange that so many people lean out of the window to stare a while at the life of the street. An artist who has just arrived immediately notices all the people who stand leaning with elbows on their windowsills. She makes a cushion that makes it more comfortable to lean out.[2]

When artists move closer to science, law or ice hockey, they sometimes claim that they do so under the influence of a passion for these areas. This is probably true in most cases. But when they claim that it has no significance that their activities are called "art", and that they could just as well be called science, law or ice hockey, then of course they are lying. Within these areas their activities would be seen as a joke. Without the word "art", *difference* and *refraction* would be missing, because art thrives on the significant difference—great or small—between mediation and the mediated.

As for the Greek who survived because his siblings were given him as a toy, one cannot speak of *misuse* but rather of 'mistake'. That he survived was rather a *bonus effect* of playing house. He can thank God or his lucky stars for the new, reversed meaning of this game.

When Rirkrit Tiravanija came to Stockholm to participate in the performance festival *New Reality Mix,* 1994, his contribution was to make meatballs which he offered to the visitors. Presumably he wanted to make use of refraction as an artistic method. By coming as a Thai artist to Sweden and making the "national dish", something he didn't know how to do, he meant the mistake to shed light on two cultures. Nothing but the context distinguished Rirkrit Tiravanija from all the thousands of immigrant cooks in diners all over the country who try to make meatballs as best they can.[3]

Misconsumption clarifies how 'misuse' causes refraction. Smoking grass and watching the Teletubbies (as a lot of American college students do) certainly points up aspects in this children's series that are already there, but it gives them a different direction. The slow tempo, the repetitions, the UFO-inspired architecture in the Teletubbies' dome, talking flowers, the laughing baby in the sun, the pipes that come up out of the grass and give instructions in metallic voices—everything gets its new, natural place and meaning in a drug-landscape.

So what is 'misuse' in the context of social refraction? I'll give an example. The Swedish social anthropologist Lisbeth Sachs (with Mary Douglas as her model) has taken an interest in cultural notions of health and illness. For some years she observed immigrant women from Anatolia in Turkey. These women, almost all illiterate, have a different concept of pain from Scandinavian women. It takes a long time before they will acknowledge that they are ill or express that they have any pain. One day when she visited one of the women, she realised when she hugged her that the woman had a temperature. Her eyes were unnaturally bright and her cheeks glowed feverishly. Lisbeth Sachs suggested that she should visit a medical centre to get help. After a brief visit to the doctor she was prescribed antibiotics. When the Turkish woman came home again with her prescription she went into the kitchen and poured a glass of water. The woman put the prescription in the water, left it for a while and stirred it now and then. Then she took the soaked prescription out of the water, squeezed it out, laid it aside and drank the water.

For these women from Anatolia illness means that one has been gazed at by the evil eye. To be rid of the curse one goes to a 'wise man' man, who writes down some magic words on a scrap of paper. The scrap can later be kept in the lining of one's clothes, it can be burnt, after which one breathes in the smoke, or it can be dissolved in water which one drinks. The power of the words is absorbed directly into the body.

A close friend of mine has said that he is interested in everything except modern dance, macrame, horses and golf. He trained as a cabinetmaker and went to work at a small factory that specialises in making garage doors. But he left the door industry and studied all the scientific subjects in the local authority adult education programmes. Now he is a kidney specialist and travels all over the world attending nephrology conferences. His apartment is always messy. When I visited him not long ago, there were, as usual, a lot of books and newspapers lying scattered everywhere. I started looking more closely at what was on the table. It was just part of the mess, but I was fascinated by the strange mixture: *State Railways, 125 years*, the food magazine *Allt om mat*, *Cancerkandidaterna* (*The Cancer Candidates*) by Staffan Seeberg, *Verden vokser* (*The world is growing—*a book on the history of chance) by Tor Nørretranders, *Ångtågen lever* (*The steam train lives*), *Den europeiska fronten* (*The European Front*) by Walther Tröge, *Essential Orthopaedics and Trauma*, *Över vattnet jag går—skiss till en poetik* (*Over the water I go—a sketch for a poetics*) by Pia Tafdrup, *Eisenbahnkurir* (a German book about steam engines), *Regler—ett brott* (*Rules—a crime*) by Tóroddur Poulsen, *När, var, hur 1956-57* (*When, where, how 1956-57*), *Time Magazine*, *Hörjelgården—forskning och naturskola* (a book about a research and nature school), *Bilen 1950-1970* (a car show catalogue), an issue of *Sköna Hem* (*Beautiful Homes*), an issue of the series *Larson*, as well as book about Abyssinia.

I got the feeling that someone had gone into a library and, at random or mechanically, taken books from the shelves. The various titles were like different tropes, or worlds that encountered one another in different ways, sometimes complementary, sometimes colliding. The apparently meaningless collection actually formed a kind of cartography, like a wall in a teenager's room, just that much more unpredictable. It represented the provincial version of the idea that "nothing is alien to me".

But what can actually be defined as a province? When I mentioned to a Chilean artist that Swedish artists often feel isolated, as if they live in a province, he looked at me incredulously and then started laughing.

One soon understands that more or less all human beings think they come from (and deep down belong to) the periphery. The periphery in relation to what? Well, to a completely imaginary centre, since it can be picked apart into ever-smaller components until nothing is left. If everyone very clearly thinks they can point out and name their peripheral provinces, no one can point to an actual centre. The strange thing is that the centre remains abstract, evasive and at the same time completely real. In Scandinavia we have the paradox of wanting on the one hand to be at the centre and on the other to define oneself as belonging to the periphery. The periphery grants an automatic 'difference', a possibility of refraction, while the centre is certainly abstract but still homogeneous as an entity—'a centre'.

In the Swedish writer Steve Sem Sandberg's novel *Theres*, which is about Ulrike Meinhof, one is made privy to the police chief Horst Herold's speculations and reflections during the hunt for RAF members. Herold, who in 1972 became the top police chief in West Germany, is described as primarily interested in people: "... the motive can be as transparent as you like, but anyone can have a motive. Only when you understand the person behind the crime and the motive forces from which she acted, can the motive be tied to a specific person and a specific situation." In the course of his work Herold sets up a kind of depot dealing with the supposed perpetrators. The depots have the most varied kinds of information. Eight years after the escape of Andreas Baader Herold's archive consists of 37 indices and card files with 4.7 million names and 3,100 organisations listed. Herold loses himself in the description of items (called "Meinhof's list") the police drew up after searching Meinhof's apartment, which was abandoned in haste: "a shoebox full of small hand-carved animals (cows, goats, lambs, a cat, two small mice, etc.); above the box also a STABLE, complete with small stalls to put the animals in [...] two DESSERT SPOONS and a CAKE-SLICE in silver [...] a pocket edition of Rilke's DUINO ELEGIES [...] a LETTER (written on lined paper of the 'Herlitz' brand)."

At night Herold sits at his desk, in front of him a map of Berlin and "Meinhof's list". He thinks: "Just as with cities, you can make maps of people". Herold calls them "mentality maps".

Art originates in the concepts of likeness and repetition, even though certain artists would probably feel more comfortable with concepts like initiation and production. No art has succeeded in emancipating itself from this fundamental mimetic requirement. But the active element in 'likeness' is *difference*. According to Aristotle, the difference is sometimes called *the temporal element* or *praxis*.

It is the difference that permits art to be compared to transvestism. In his desire to resemble a woman, that is to depict a woman, the transvestite elucidates notions of femininity at the same time as there is an unwavering focus on that which is not conceived as feminine, the revealing details: the broad hands, the hint of stubble above the silk scarf, the Adam's apple... In depiction and imitation both subject and object are elucidated.

If one is to speak of a refraction model in contemporary art, one must extend the metaphor into a hall of mirrors, or rather of prisms composed according to the artist's *mentality map*.

Do these mentality maps in general look different in different countries? Yes, probably. Despite this, international exhibitions are not national parades (luckily). What instead becomes ever clearer is that all artists from the provinces seem to speak more or less the same language.

Perhaps this common language is needed as the 'centre'. Perhaps this 'centre' has become the more and more overshadowing pole—or magnifying glass—through which the experience of the provinces can be concentrated in a burning flashpoint.

Notes

1. The text can be read on the CD *Sacrilege*, which features remixes of Can's music.

2. Annika Ström's *Window Pillow*, 1995.

3. One could rattle off a lot of work where refraction is achieved through 'misuse', furthermore associated with a bipolar power relationship. A clear example is Tobias Rehberger's work *Peue See a Faagck Sunday Paae* (*We Never Work On Sundays*), where he had African craftsmen make furniture from drawings of modernist classics (de Stiijl, Bauhaus).

translated by James Manley

The Fall of Louisiana

In May 1996 Louisiana opened the exhibition *NowHere*. It was the new museum director Lars Nittve's first exhibition at Louisiana. In the introductory chapter "Nowhere but NowHere" Nittve drew up the broad outlines of a view of art and a present-day art institutions which one imagines will form the basis of the exhibition policy that Louisiana will champion in the future.

We can no longer speak of dominant tendencies in art, which the art institutions can pick up and pass on in the form of 'isms', wrote Nittve. For information and media society has questioned any attempt to take a categorical attitude to statements that try to distinguish between true and false, authentic and inauthentic, original and copy. In relation to the way the world is organised today, the art institution cannot 'passively' pass on the view of reality represented by artists by virtue of the works they create. One understands from Nittve that exhibition activities must themselves actively attempt to reflect this new worldview.

When the art institution takes on the dissemination of artworks as a natural part of its role, the institution makes a selection. Nittve saw this selecting of artworks as an authoritarian attempt to single out one tendency in the period. In the exhibition *NowHere*, Nittve therefore wanted to counteract this authoritarian attitude and inactivate the "strong, monolithic curatorial ego" by ceding power (and also the responsibility) to six curators who were thus to put together the first exhibition under his leadership. With this he thought he could show a 'many-voiced' exhibition where very different views of contemporary art would have their say. So much for Nittve's 'inaugural lecture'.

When the exhibition *New Art from Denmark and Scania* opened on 3 October 1997, Louisiana was mustering the forces of Danish art for the first time since 1970. For the Danish art world this was in itself very unusual. With the exception of its first few years, Louisiana had turned its back on Danish art and had instead been a window on the international world. The place became a citadel where international art of high quality was brought. New and important schools had been represented at Louisiana so that Danes in general and Danish artists in particular might be given a broad picture of the expansions of the concept of art that had taken place in the twentieth century. This was true until it became normal for artists in the 80s to keep themselves informed with the aid of international art magazines and frequent trips to what were considered centres of modern art.

The museum's great collection of modern art, along with its other activities, had been very important to Danish society as a whole, inasmuch as art reflects at many different levels the conglomerate of Zeitgeist elements that delimit the ways in which we are able to think and live with a certain time and a certain culture. Most people would probably agree for example that Louisiana as an institution represents a wide range of the values with which we would most like to identify Danish culture, and from which we think other countries east, west and south of us could benefit.

It had, of course, at times been a thorn in the flesh of the Danish art world that Louisiana so categorically refused to deal with the Danish art scene, however, people had accepted these conditions because it could not be denied that the place had a rare authority; an unheard of authority in a country where elitism is anathema. Louisiana's exhibition activities did not enter into direct dialogue with the national art scene. To exhibit there meant that one was an artist of international reputation.

The rule of the curators

Unlike the other Museum of Modern Art, Arken, which first had to create a platform for itself, Louisiana had thus long since qualified itself as an international touchstone against which Danish art could be tried. But with this upcoming review of Danish art, the museum was sacrificing its position. And that is a shame for Denmark.

As I have said, it was 27 years since Louisiana last had a major review of Danish art. It did so then by associating a group from the "Ex-school" (Per Kirkeby, Bjørn Nørgaard, Peter Louis Jensen and Poul Gernes as well as the German-born artist living in Denmark, Arthur Köpcke) with Joseph Beuys, who was already internationally known at that time. Since then Svend Wiig Hansen and Per Kirkeby (both artists of international reputation) had exhibited there independently, and other Danish artists had been represented by single works, but no real collection of recent Danish art had been shown since 1970.

Obviously, then, it aroused a certain amount of surprise and turbulence when the museum curator Lars Grambye from Louisiana announced his arrival to a number of specially selected Danish artists, at the head of a group consisting of himself and a further two curators. They presented themselves with an authority behind them that many years of exhibiting art works and important exhibitions had given the place, borne up by the unique effort of Louisiana's founder, Knud W Jensen. The three curators—Lars Grambye, Tone O Nielsen and the Swedish Åsa Nacking—had been appointed by Louisiana to preside over the selection of a team of artists. On 3 October 1997 these artists would be at the disposal of the not particularly aspirational exhibition title *New Art from Denmark and Scania*. It is hard to say what had induced an institution that normally doesn't hide its light under a bushel to juxtapose the whole of Denmark with a very small part of Sweden—a part that does not even include the capital. Viewed from Stockholm, Scania is a province with a slightly ridiculous dialect. It was rather like Moderna Museet in Stockholm holding an exhibition called "New Art from Sweden and Funen".

At all events the artists who had been contacted for the Louisiana exhibition willingly trooped up, and there were several reasons for this. In the 90s, as in fact pointed out in the preface to *NowHere*, we had made the acquaintance in this country of an international phenomenon: the "curators' exhibition". Under the aegis of some theme, also called a 'concept', art historians and curators select artists whose works are to help illustrate the curators' idea. The exhibition *Inferno/Evil* at Statens Museum for Kunst in 1993 and *NowHere* in 1996 were just two examples of this. The artists participate in a kind of *mise-en-scène* where the curators manipulate the strings. For such a curatorial event the artists are expected to be willing to sing for their supper on any occasion, anytime and anywhere.

On such occasions there is no interest in in-depth investigations of the special type of knowledge that we call art—that is works that involve kinds of awareness that take time and insight to achieve, and artworks that are so comprehensive in themselves that they *cannot* function as pieces in a curators' jigsaw puzzle. On the contrary the art work is here an event, the setting for a crossword teaser, a little laugh here, a small fright there, garnished with the obligatory indignation. All in all, this kind of exhibition activity is meant to turn the spotlight and confer fame on the true creator— that is the curator. The curator has become the artist and the art museum is his or her medium.

The work of the good curator then consists of finding a propitious title for an exhibition. It's the titles that can attract people, just as a good advertisement can convince the potential customer of a need of which he or she is unaware. Another important part of the curator's work is to invent 'new' talents. These may be older artists, as long as it seems convincing that they were in reality misunderstood before, so they can be re-introduced, now with the emblem of newness as the most important factor.

Finally, all that remains for the curator is to organise the PR, the interesting debates and seminars, the sponsorship money, etc., all to underscore that the exhibition has captured an important whiff of the *Zeitgeist*, even when this spirit of the age simply consists of many parallel but unrelated utterances. One performs a socially relevant task by turning the focus on something and debating it. If one failed to hit any target, never mind: the turbulence that follows in the wake of such an economic and human effort is an effect in itself.

The culture of the event

This kind of exhibition activity, which is closely connected with the culture of the event, has nothing to do with the extreme kind of awareness that the works of art can represent. It dupes those of us who still think we are the artists into thinking it is hugely important to participate as often as possible if we are not to disappear into oblivion and the resultant penury. In other words you have to be involved, whatever the cost.

It was evident from the letter sent out to the 50 artists participating in Louisiana's Denmark/Scania exhibition that the museum shared the "curatorial" view of art and its approach. The curator group further announced that it had spent six months on research. But on being invited to exhibit, artists were given about two months to respond (with a final description of the work/project, a comprehensive specification of any necessary spatial construction, inventory, technical equipment, special security and transport requirements, a budget and much more). And here one must not forget that no artist sits waiting for such an invitation. Everyone is involved in their work, and there is no certainty that one can simply drop one's obligation.

The organisers admitted that they did not have an overall concept and that the selection was based purely on "what the undersigned exhibition organisers consider to be the most interesting and topical things in the art of the region right now". Was this the exhibition where we were to encounter "the small narrative and the local play of language" of which Nittve spoke in his preface to the exhibition *NowHere*? What sort of criteria is *topicality*? Is *topical* art the art you see when you visit the city galleries in the period up to the exhibition? Is it the painter who sells the most or the painter who is most famous? The one who shocks the most (with stuffed puppy-dogs or dead pigs)? The criteria is quite obscure.

Regionalism

And yet, no matter what approach was used and what result was achieved, it cannot be said too categorically: in the whole of Sweden and Denmark there are not 50 artists of international standing. That a Danish or Swedish artist has an international reputation means that he or she is someone who is able to bring a special angle to international art and artistic discussion. There are very few of those. It is of no interest to anyone to see us touting works of art and views of art that the others already have in abundance, not even if our art works are of the same standard as theirs. Is it because the conformity and introversion of the 90s gave the regionalism of the Øresund region wind in its sails that Louisiana now, in one fell swoop, abandoned the position in which the museum had reigned supreme in Denmark? Or was it to keep its head up in the competition for visitors and public funding, before Christian Gether got Arken up and running in earnest at Køge Bay—if things worked out, that is? To me it was clear that the Denmark-Scania exhibition belonged at Køge Bay, at a museum oriented first and foremost towards modern Danish art, a museum that was however still without an art collection and established position.

The Denmark-Scania exhibition is, however, the expression of a spirit of the times with which everyone seems to agree. The code phrases that everyone who tries to offer views on the current situation by now agree on are as follows:
—Values have broken down, so there are no absolute truths.
—The fragmented world reproduced by the overkill of information in the mass media and information society is of such transient validity that it annihilates itself almost in the moment it arises.
—And then everyone is unanimous in thinking that a world that at present seems transitory must necessary be encountered with transitory institutions filled with transitory works. Artists in institutions want to "participate in a process". They want to make exhibitions that have "an active and debate-creating character".

The loss of professionalism
Given that we have never before agreed so much that know-how is our only resource in competition with the rest of the world, and that continuing education and re-education are code words in the debate on the preservation of the welfare state at present, it is a fateful result when schoolchildren no longer learn such basic skills as reading and writing, as Henning Fønsmark has shown in his book *Kampen mod kundskaber* (*The Fight against Knowledge*).

In the world of art the results cannot be measured against such well defined norms as in most other subjects. I have mentioned *one* of the measuring instruments of art—the museums. If an artist who has just begun an artistic career, within the first few years and while not yet finished at the Academy of Art, can exhibit at a museum like Louisiana or any other museum for that matter, then this young artist never gets to grapple with the depths of the artistic material and find his or her own independent path into this intractable and profoundly fascinating material.

This young artist and the established system are deluding themselves and each other. The philosophy of the transitory can become a convenient way of relating to things, because one avoids taking a stand on the professional criteria.

The museum can neither be a national nor an international touchstone if it does not dare exercise the authority associated with choosing precisely on the basis of explicit criteria, which are not subjective, but founded on the knowledge we have despite everything: that there are common values in a culture and in a profession which have a shared history and tradition, and—as has so often proved the case—are so much stronger than the individual that the greatest efforts are necessary to change them.

To exercise a natural authority does not necessary mean that things fossilise and become hidebound. Nor does it necessarily mean smug self-sufficiency and a lust for power. On the other hand it would lead to regional self-glorification if institutions like Louisiana were to forfeit their international authority as a result of incompetent exhibitions.

Previously printed in the weekly newspaper Weekend-Avisen, *1997.*

translated by James Manley

*a comment by Dr Gro Harlem Brundtland,
Director of the WHO, previously the Norwegian Prime Minister

*You're too Cool to be Cool
you have acted like a fool
do you have something to say
I won't listen anyway
—there is nothing to say—
no way*

From the song by the Norwegian dance group, Soda, entitled "2 Cool 2 B Cool"

1) No Norwegian curator has ever managed to organise the artistic arrangement of any event of significance outside of Scandinavia, if one ignores Jon Ove Steihaug's work in the Nordic pavilion at the Venice Biennial in 1997. Norway has in fact only two professional curators, Åsmund Thorkildsen and Jon Ove Steihaug. Indeed there was no course in contemporary art at the Institute of Art History at the University of Oslo until the mid 1990s.

In Oslo, the capital city of Norway, there is a difference of over ten years in life expectancy between inhabitants in certain eastern and western city districts. Norway, in the Post War period has played a role as the world's moral guardian, but at the same time also carried on a secret war against ethnic minorities, which has included forced lobotomies and castration on completely healthy people. A country with a democratic constitution where the secret services, in co-operation with the dominant social democratic party, have organised large-scale surveillance and persecution of those with different opinions. Norway has a prominent international position with its peace work—and at the same time sells weapons for Turkey's wholesale murders in Kurdistan. Oslo (with its approximately half a million inhabitants) had a surplus of over US$ 750 million in 1998—but allows its elder citizens to break their legs on slippery winter pavements as the city authorities cannot be bothered to grit them. Oslo has the highest incidence of deaths from drug overdoses per inhabitant in Western Europe, but refuses treatment to drug addicts which has been effective in other European countries. Norway could afford to re-equip its armed forces at the end of the 1990s, but did not have enough money to take action to reduce one of the longest hospital waiting lists among Western nations. Did you know that there is a great chance that you will die before you receive treatment if you are unfortunate enough to contract cancer in Norway? Or that, in contrast to Portugal for example, there is no public funding for dental care at all? Or what about the fact that mega-rich shipowners do not pay any tax, while the rent for a small below-standard apartment in Oslo is equivalent to almost 10% of the maximum annual student loan available. Something else, again, is the seal and whale hunting which ought to arouse world opinion against Norway. It is the treatment of individuals which is worst. When seal hunting inspector Odd Lindberg compiled documentary evidence that Norwegian seal hunters had committed atrocities against seal pups in the 1980s, a process was started against him that resulted in his ruin—he was forced into exile. Today, Lindberg and his family live in Sweden, having lost absolutely everything. In a country that is regarded as particularly democratic, the incumbent government pursues a propaganda campaign against the gay community, well aware that approximately one third of young homosexual Norwegians have attempted to take their own lives.

2) There are two—(two!)—permanently employed art critics in Norway. No Norwegian critic, with the exception of the Fluxus specialist Ina Blom, has an international public outside Scandinavia. Blom, known among other things for her texts in *Frieze*, a while ago received notification from her culture editor in *Aftenposten*, Norway's largest morning paper, that she was no longer required to write for the paper.

Until recently Norway had one of the world's most nationalistic policies for a country not at war. Today, Norway is now known as one of the countries which has gone to war against Yugoslavia—despite the fact that Norway's Prime Minister, following the first air strikes, denied categorically that it was a question of war, but rather one of a "limited military operation". Along with Austria, France and certain Eastern European countries, Norway has an extreme right wing party, with electoral support of 15 to 20%. Incredibly enough, the Norwegian Foreign Ministry sent a formal protest to the UN when a UN report pointed out, absolutely correctly, that the growth of this party was linked to an increase in racism and right wing extremism. Asylum seekers are harassed by racist police, and non-European immigrants are in the media spotlight because of increasing criminality in urban areas. If a Norwegian citizen from, for example, one of Oslo's suburbs, born in Norway of Chilean parents, is arrested for violence, it is an unwritten rule that the state news broadcasts describes the person in question as a "Norwegian citizen of foreign origin".

3) Of the few Norwegian artists who have had major international success, only Bjarne Melgaard and Odd Nerdrum are resident in Norway, the others live in Berlin, Paris and NY.

4) The three Norwegian art academies are completely without international significance. Only one artist with major international success has ever attended one of these academies without voluntarily or involuntarily breaking-off his studies—that artist was Bjarne Melgaard. The social democratic politicians have foisted two 'figurative' courses on the academy against its will.

A couple of years ago, people within Norwegian artistic circles began to talk about 'The Norwegian miracle', along the same lines as the somewhat more concrete term—'The Nordic miracle'. This, in effect, means that international curators and critics view Norway as a leading nation in the art world. Enthusiastic admiration for Glasgow's prominent position in the mid-1990s, together with the fact that "the West's periphery" in other places too (including Sweden and Denmark) was noticed in the larger metropolises. This created the alluring idea in Norwegian artistic circles that they would get a windfall share of a general affect.

5) Norway's national contemporary art museum—the Museum of Contemporary Art in Oslo—is located in a historic building, which previously housed the Bank of Norway. Behind metre thick granite walls gilding still adorns its columns—but the management of the museum believe that it is possible to run a professional museum in the building. The previous director did not want to know anything about "commercial American gallery art". The present director is battling with opponents in a staff who are completely incompetent and full of ambitions for power. It is a private museum, the Astrup-Fearnley Museum in Oslo, which is now leading in Norway.

6) There are no galleries with a strong enough financial foundation to allow them to be active on a major basis in the international market. The reason is simple. The Norwegian citizenry, as a whole, primarily collects figurative paintings. Those who do not collect figurative paintings collect lyrical-abstract works. Only a handful of collectors invest in contemporary art.

7) Norway has become, however, "the new DDR" with regard to sport, with the world's best cross-country skiers suspected of taking drugs; track athletes who have been found to use dope—but who have been found "not guilty" in Norway; the world's best national handball team, the world's best alpine skiers, the world's best national curling team.... Even in athletics there are signs of 'The Norwegian miracle'. It is almost unbelievable; that Norway with just four million inhabitants can compete with the world's elite—even in football! The reason for this is, of course, that the Norwegian

state invests millions and millions, as did the DDR, in creating "Norway advertising" through the sports. Sport is science—doctors and scientists work on creating new drugs, while ski waxing technicians have been elevated to the status of national heroes.

8) When Olav Christopher Jenssen, the only Norwegian artist to take part in Documenta since the 1950s, applied for support from the Norwegian Ministry of Foreign Affairs to fund his participation, his application was turned down because the Ministry understood that Documenta 9 could not be an exhibition of any importance—because they had never heard of it, and it was going to be held in an 'insignificant' provincial town in Germany. No Norwegians were represented at *Documenta X*. Attempts were made to rectify this blunder with more colloboration with the national biennial committee, a constructive attempt to reinforce Norwegian art in an international context. Today, the Ministry of Foreign Affairs is a positive and important power in Norwegian artistic life—and assumes responsibility where *no...art* (yes, you did read correctly!)—the body that took over after the biennial committee—does not take responsibility. The administration of *no...art* is placed with the Museum for Contemporary Art, in spite of the fact that the museum has not demonstrated any long-term ability to work professionally with international contacts. It is the Ministry of Foreign Affairs and the Ministry of Cultural and Scientific Affairs which are directly supporting the Norwegian pavilion at the Melbourne biennial, despite the fact that this is *no...art*'s task.

9) "We have Edvard Munch, of course!" Yes, but we also have Gustav Vigeland, the Nazi collaborator who is praised for the world's largest one-man sculpture in Oslo. Munch's atelier was pulled down a long time ago, but Vigeland's atelier is now a museum. The authorities now want to tear down the building where Munch spent the first year's of his life. The last time anyone poked into Vigeland's relations with the occupation regime during the war, Lotte Sandberg, the influential critic at the *Aftenposten* newspaper, made a ferocious attack against the attempt to put a question mark against Vigeland's name. Munch has his museum at an out-of-the-way location in Oslo, a museum with deficient security facilities. Both this museum and the National Gallery have had paintings stolen—*The Vampire* and *The Scream* respectively—by thieves simply breaking a window and snatching the paintings without being discovered. These scandals have rightly been given a great deal of media attention abroad. You should know that the Norwegian media was equally occupied by the fact that *Sinnataggen*, Vigeland's little kitsch sculpture, was subject to graffiti.

While the survivors of the 1970s within artistic organisations entered the 1990s without any artistic or political ambitions, a new crop of artists were educated at the academies according to new premises. Throughout the 90s it was clear that the most important initiatives in the Norwegian art institutes came from the artists, in spite of the dilatoriness within Norske Billedkunstnere, the artists own professional organisation. Indeed, practically all of the innovations made during the 90s were initiated by artists—magazines, galleries, biennials. Furthermore the emerging new critics were often artists as well. In this regard, neither the public museums nor the established state financing apparatus demonstrated the maturity to ably deal with these signs of change in Norwegian artistic production. Taking stock at the end of the decade, it is only the Kunstnernes Hus in Oslo and, in part, Riks-utstillinger—the organiser of major touring exhibitions—of the heavyweight national institutions that have been willing to assume responsibility for the new currents flowing through Norwegian art in the 1990s, while practically all the initiatives in the new scene have come to grief due to lack of public funding. Paradoxically enough, because Norwegian artists are, relatively speaking, in a unique position in respect to funding in the form of grants and government support.

One of the most important art projects in Norway in the last 13 years, the *Bak-Truppen* performance company, is with its background in various aspects of culture—theatre, visual arts, literature, music, dance—able to gain support through theatre funding bodies and to perform in significant international and national contexts, as well being able to display its 'art' in galleries and museums. But the *Bak-Truppen*, in spite of its extensive activity over a number of years, has not been incorporated within accounts of Norway's national museum of contemporary art. The reason is that this museum does not concern itself with performance-related work. It would have been possible to accept this if there were other institutions which were responsible for this kind of work.

UKS, the *Young Artists Society*, which historically is "the young artists organisation", decided in practice in the mid 1990s to abandon its role as a vocal advocate for young artists, in order to fill a vacuum by acting as a representative for "new art"—understood as art without any ponderous references in the Norwegian art institution. With economical support, a gallery in the centre of Oslo and a separate arts magazine, *UKS Forum for Contemporary Art*, *UKS* established Norway's first professionally curated biennial, the *UKS biennial* in 1996. This 'heavyweight' exhibition, curated by Jon Ove Steihaug and Ingvild Henmo, demonstrated the evident distortion in the Norwegian art world when *UKS*, by definition a 'radical' organisation, assumed responsibility for making

Norwegian art more professional by adopting organisational forms which were the norm in the rest of the world. In respect of the *UKS Forum for Contemporary Art*, which was Norway's leading arts magazine under the leadership of George Morgenstern and Stian Grøgaard from the end of the 80s to the mid-90s, *UKS* has also tried to recruit new writers, to discuss theoretical problems and to air issues associated with artistic production which have often been overlooked by other media in Norway. The UKS Gallery displays and arranges at one and the same time explicit political performances, extracts of Oslo's subcultures, traditonal exhibitions, concerts, nightclub arrangements, political meetings, acts as an intermediary for art in Norway and internationally, initiates actions for art students' rights, and not least administrates a part of Norwegian art history—that part which the museums neglect.

The internationalisation of Norwegian art is due to a general structural change in the young Norwegian art world. Even though the percentage of Norwegian artists with relative international exposure is greater now than in the 80s, 'internationalisation' in this context means primarily a break with a continuous Norwegian art history, founded on the idea of homogeneity in a society based on consensus between the classes, town and country, language groups and not least between the various cultural elements in Norway. The internationalisation of Norwegian art that we see today began only a few years after Norway had become a *de facto* multi-ethnic nation—controlled by a mono-ethnic state. The internationalised art "from Norway" is to be found first and foremost on Norwegian territory in 1999. Previously it had such poor circumstances that it had to flee the country in order to survive in the metropolises.

Oslo, 9 April, 1999

Update: This text was written as the curatorial statement for the Norwegian pavilion at the Melbourne International Biennial 1999. Many things in Norwegian society and the art world have changed since early 1999, and I wouldn't write such a statement in 2001. However, I strongly believe the text was justified in the late 90s. When writing these lines I see the main street of Gothenburg being transferred into a battlefield with burning barricades—a result of police brutality against anti-capitalist demonstrators gathering to voice their opinion on the occasion of the EU's Heads of State conference. My political activity is from now withdrawn from the art world and redirected into the new anti-capitalistic movement. Got to run...

Gothenburg, 15 June, 2001.

Art in the Backwoods

Large international art exhibitions are organised these days at such a pace that one finds precious little of interest in their grandeur. A large exhibition is no longer an epic venture on just the part of the organisers, but demands quite a lot from the audience, too. Well, I'm just trying to find an excuse for why I haven't been to even one of the large European exhibitions this summer. Am I cynical, do I avoid all work, won't I move even for art's sake? Not yet, I think. What I did do was spend two weeks thinking about art and politics in a small Canadian town somewhere in the woods. Small is beautiful, don't you think?

Amos is a 10,000 inhabitant town 600 miles north-west of Montreal—the middle of nowhere. The first European settlers arrived in 1908. At present there are two sawmills, one papermill, a railway station (where trains don't stop) and a large Byzantine basilica made of concrete, in the crypt of which is kept a long-dead priest's hearing aid as a relic. Compared to Europe, Amos is situated on the same latitude as Vienna, but the surrounding nature, in all its ruggedness, is completely reminiscent of Finland. Now this small community organised its first ever art festival.

How to present art in an area which has no history for art, and very little history of any kind? Or why is art to be presented everywhere in the first place? These questions aren't just clever games, because the understanding of the political nature of contemporary art achieved far greater concrete meanings in Amos than what it normally does. To begin with, the organisers had to somehow get the locals interested in art, and involved them in bringing it to town. Then, as they were organising an international symposium of artists, they had to ask themselves what the role of international communication is in a remote corner of the country. Many of the issues that arose in Amos, whether good or bad, can also be applied to Finland. Even if the people of Amos haven't grown up in a barrel, their seemingly well-organised life has little room for visual art. There are no venues to show art in the community, and no professional artists. How to then muster up an audience for a two week festival? The organisers of the symposium in Amos showed a degree of dedication not often seen in this area. The project started in the winter, when nearly all of the town's schoolchildren, parents and pensioners were mobilised and asked to cut milk cartons into strips and to staple them together so that they looked like snowflakes. These were manufactured in the hundreds of thousands, and when summer came, they were hung around the city in formations resembling small mounds of snow. It wasn't a pretty sight necessarily, but everyone knew they'd taken part in this giant enterprise. The other joint social project happened during the symposium. It was a large boulder of stone, a stone moved by the ice age and now put on a wooden platform, that the people of Amos dragged behind them on the streets of their town. Different organisations, charities and passers-by took part in the work. The boulder was dragged by sheer muscle power past gas stations and shopping malls onto the yard of the house of culture. Not necessarily an aesthetic sight this time around either, but the project and its daily progress did create social bonding. As a final touch, handprints of the town's children where sandblasted onto the rock's surface. The monument was ready. Seen from the art world, these projects had very little effect, but for a town without history, they were conscious attempts at making a history, and as such they will remain in people's memories. Further, making something with your own hands provided a starting point for an understanding of the artist's work, if not theoretically, then in the physical qualities it encompassed.

Everything okay so far, but what about the invited artists? What were they needed for? The goal of the symposium was to execute ten artists' projects in public places, out of which three would be permanent pieces. There were three kinds of artists involved: French speakers from around Québec, and artists from other parts of Canada and from the Nordic countries. The two last groups felt, at times, as though they were outsiders who were in the wrong place. The symposium not only 'made' local history, but also addressed local language and separatist issues. In the backwoods of Québec, seeking separation from the rest of Canada, you can be about as international as you want, as long as you speak French. The transformation from a stone pulling happening to a multi-lingual festival wasn't painless or easy. Art could have well been the common language, but not a common identity. This wasn't all, though. If, from time to time, the organisers had problems relating to the invited artists, then these professionals from the international art world had problems assimilating their work within the prevailing conditions. Hiccups in the preparations and the shortcomings in resources impacted on many an artist's professional pride and desire for perfectionism, and not everyone was comfortable being a public example, constantly on display. Things didn't go as smoothly as in the 'safe' galleries and museums.

The events in Amos made me think how a similar venture would fare in one of the smaller Finnish communities. Would it be possible to involve the locals as well as they did in Amos, and would the importing of international artists into unprofessional surroundings present problems for all involved? And could an art exhibition function as an identity building exercise for a whole community. The first comparison that springs to mind is the Visual Arts weeks in Mänttä, which spreads around the small town every other year. But the artists and the inhabitants seldom meet. Artists bring their works and put them on display, while the locals are expected to pay admission and be thankful. The direct dialogue is missing, not to mention the lack of participation in the festival given the locals' input. Mänttä's model is very traditional, very institutional. Its importance lies in the plurality and breadth of the exhibition, which in itself is a worthy achievement. Building an atmosphere supportive of social awareness and activism is another job altogether, and as the example of Amos shows us, it might require acts that on the surface do not seem very artistic. Another issue is the willingness of the artists to engage in direct dialogue with the audience. It requires a certain kind of attitude, maybe even a certain kind of personality. In Amos the aim was that artists would work away at their work in public places, where the audience could observe them and pose questions to them. This public parading didn't fit everyone, and some avoided it as best they could.

The question of the dialogue between art and the audience is by no means worthless. Every museum and public institution of art will be pressed to assert itself by various social programmes—not just educational tours for school children, but various events and approaches that take into account a multitude of target-groups. In a situation like this heavier and more demanding exhibitions always lose out to smaller or lighter art projects, that can be more easily promoted to larger audiences. In many countries a distinctive group of artists, whose work is based on social interaction, has distinguished themselves. They are not discussed in art magazines, and their work is sometimes far from groundbreaking. But still, these days, they have a lot to do. If things go well, they may find themselves on a mission to activate a whole small community.

But what happens after the artist's have left?

What happens in the town of Amos after this one nudge forwards? The main gain is the citizens own pride about how they pulled off such a massive project, and mostly as volunteer work too. The stone they dragged surely means more to them than any of the other pieces by the artists involved. It still doesn't make the area into an area famed for the visual arts. The 'imported' artists didn't fare that badly, either. The Swede Mikael Lundberg's shape-changing asphalt cube was the source of a lot of positive curiosity, and Finn Lauri Anttila's modest sundial—which proved that midday in Amos actually comes at 1 PM—caused delight. They left the town as fast as they had come, though. On the other hand, what is likely to remain are Vancouverian Mike McDonald's works. He plants butterfly-orchards, consisting of clusters of plants, many of them edible, that butterflies are naturally attracted to. Most of these are ancient medicinal plants used by Native Americans, and which now attract the attention of Western medicine. Native American wisdom tells us to follow a butterfly if affected by a disease, and it will lead you to the correct medicinal plant. McDonald sold a selection of the seeds costing a few dollars and judging by the enthusiasm of the citizens of Amos, the city gained many butterfly-orchards. Next year a citizen organising a garden party will pass on the story, and like the flight of the butterfly, the story will continue. It might mean much more as an achievement than the profits of a large exhibition.

The organiser of the Amos event spread around a thick layer of conceptual jargon, accompanied by an endless stream of babble and waving of hands—a virtue of French Canadian culture, over the proceedings. In this way the event was made to seem much more intellectual and larger than what it actually was. The organiser predicted that the time of large exhibitions and metropoles was over, and that the future belongs to the small places—let the Internet take care of communication. If this fashionable decree is even half-true, then Finland shouldn't have anything to worry about. We have plenty of both small places and Internet cable. Now we just need to get the media on site and start working.

Previously printed in Taide 4, Fall 1997.

translated by Jean Ramsey

ILLUSTRATION: ASMUNDUR ASMUNDSSON, *PAINTER POINTING AT PIET MONDRIAN PIECE. OR SOMETHING LIKE THAT*, 2001

Being normal is quite important in today's Nordic society, even in the art world, where it can be helpful to an artist's career to act in a freaky manner (the British say cheeky). One might say that the freakiness of Nordic artists is in fact their expression of freedom, as opposed to their more traditional German and Austrian counterparts, who express themselves on the canvas. Or with clay. Please understand that when I talk about freedom, I'm not coming from a hippie point of view—what I'm trying to say is that artists need to be reminded that freedom is just another word for having nothing left to lose. Toulouse Lautrec was a total freak.

But nowadays, instead of living this lifestyle of freedom, these new guys mimic it at openings—some of them don't even drink the wine! It is not enough to see artists dressed in crazy outfits if all they'll drink is nothing but water; in fact it is humiliating for the real artists and disrespectful towards our heritage, both as Scandinavians and artists.

A very dear friend of mine has a theory that if the United States of America was a welfare state, Nordic style, the people of that country would also have their Munchs and Strindbergs, instead of their Warhols and Koons'. Would the opposite be true? It's hard to say—look at De Kooning. He was actually Dutch, but that doesn't make him any less interesting in this context. De Kooning had the courage to be both an extremely creative painter and inventive in his private life, a life which included daily intoxication and fairly frequent bizarre sexual activities, even when married to the same lady most of his life (Elaine). That lady luckily came from a co-dependent family and was a sucker for fear and violence. Even if De Kooning's life was both stunning and in many ways fantastic, it ended in Alzheimer's and death. How does that fit into this picture I am trying to paint of Scandinavia, you ask? Well, the Dutch mentality is closely related to the Scandinavian because the Dutch language is quite close to the Danish in the ears of someone who hasn't heard the languages too often, and because both these countries didn't have much going for them until they adopted baby countries with useful resources.[1] Of course, there's the accent, but obviously the subject of De Kooning has more to do with freedom in general than with Scandinavian freedom in particular, which is quite unique when you think about it. When De Kooning stood in front of a painting by his fellow Dutchman Mondrian, shortly after his death, he declared that he was envious of the freedom he saw in his elder's exact brushstrokes. Many people assumed he was having one of his funny drunken moments, but in fact he was in a most sincere drunken state. Obviously, De Kooning was after all trying to escape his Dutch sensibility, which is, as I said before, closer to the Nordic sensibility than most people believe. And then there's Van Gogh.

Do I really need to point out that the North is closer than it appears? I think not. This takes us to perhaps the greatest living Scandinavian artist of our times, also known as Björk, or the Elf-Princess. In the prettiest song on her best album, *Homogenic*, she sings with a soulful, yet Nordic, voice: "I thought I could organise freedom, how Scandinavian of me". This shows us that Björk has sold her Scandinavian soul to Mammon, and gotten in touch with her emotions. Good for her. She now lives in New York, and apparently dates a fellow named Matthew Barney, a very free spirited American multi-media artist. Bravo!

And what about Claes Oldenburg? Excellent point: Here is a true Scandinavian who was pretty cool for years and years until he got married to an alcoholic Jewess. After that important day in art history he lost his cool freedom and became a normal human being, and his work doesn't make it into the art magazines that much anymore (except *Art in America*, but that in itself says a lot).[2] Another traitor?

Re-reading all the stuff I wrote above, it looks to me like the future of Scandinavian freedom lies in the able hands of the younger generation. To these kids, I say: "It's not enough to walk the walk and talk the talk at openings, you have to do it at home too. Stay home. Express yourself".

It's on the freedom train, Come on dance on the freedom train.

Lenny Kravitz

Notes

1. Your average American thinks of Europe as one country, with one nation under God, and they also have a hard time distinguishing Switzerland from Sweden. In New York Biscottis are called European Cookies, many Italians are offended by that, but the French hate it when people say Café Latte instead of Café au Lait.

2. The German people have a very special expression for this sort of normality: "stink normal". The expression has sometimes been used by Scandinavian people to describe the German nation as a whole (jokingly of course) even if some of the most exciting artists of this century have been German and far from being normal: Beuys, Richter, Polke, Kippenberger, etc.. You know what I mean.

—When a closed system is observed or comes in contact with other systems it changes its apperances. The different factors change, power relations are negotiated and hierachies shift somewhat, new alliances and oppositions are made and previous ones unmade. A huge disturbance of such a system occured to the art scenes in Scandinavia (actually one by one, as a domino effect) and then the Baltics, a rupture whose waves can still be felt, and that has changed both practices and discourses, not to mention careers. The 'Nordic' countries are no longer isolated, no longer distant, but it remains to be seen whether it is a case of 15 minutes of fame, or a long term shift from provincialism to becoming an integral part of an international art world. There are, though, surely different agents hoping for both outcomes. The hype of certain 1990s art practices does not necessarily entail a changing of the guards.

—Simultaneous to the international acceptance and hype of the new 'Nordic' art, there has been as an insistence on a common, geographical and ethnic Nordic identity, and the regional/national boundaries seem to have evaporated, in the sense that an artist is no longer, say, Swedish, but *Nordic*. The Nordic states are perceived as one art scene, glossing over differences between countries and cities—i.e. differences not only in artistic methods, but also in histories, education, institutions, funding bodies and critical discourses and theories. For example, where Denmark and Norway for a long time have insisted on the particularity of their art and artists, provincial and national styles and value systems, Sweden has kept a continuous dialogues with international trends and theories, which has resulted in a more widespread usage and acceptance of international, American art forms and idioms. Also, critical discourses such as feminism held a fairly prominent position there since the 1970s, where it disappeared from view, not least from the academic curriculum in Denmark and Norway during the 80s. And where Sweden has had a viable gallery structure encompassing several generations of artists and showcasing international art, Denmark has been marked by a smaller market and few, generation-based galleries, which, in turn, has bred both the traditional, powerful and anti-internationalist "artist associations"—large groups of artists showing and selling work together through huge yearly exhibitions—and a number of shortlived, experimental artist spaces/groups centred around a shared, ideological and methodological idea. How these structures have facilitated the apparent miracle (or, rather, as one writer insists, have worked deliberately against it) can therefore only be illuminated through a denial of the very notions 'nordic' and 'miraculous'! In order to understand the term we have to break it apart or simply abandon it.

Northern Lights

For almost as long as the emergence of the Nation state, there has been talk of a specific "Nordic tradition", founded in landscape painting, capturing the unique, but evasive "Nordic light". This tradition has located Nordic art both formally and geographically, that is, within the designated categories 'painting' and 'landscape'. The role of the artist has been as romantic wanderer and seer, locating the experience af nature in an artistic form that should equate this experience itself, often manifesting itself in dark, expressionistic brushstrokes and a melancholic, distant imagery. That said, the notion of nature itself, is of course tightly connected to ideological constructs of the National state, and "national" schools of painting therefore often take their point of departure in the local, romantic landscape, whose characteristics are in turn significant metaphors for the character of the population. The particular National can apparently be better defined, or, more likely, affirmed in natural landscapes rather than industrial, or for that matter cityscapes. It is interesting, historically, that exhibitions of "Nordic" art for many years focused on the experience of such landscapes— countless exhibitions of Nordic landscapes toured within the Nordic countries with great success until very recently. However, this tradition has since been critised and even ridiculed, and the notion of the "welfare subject" has somewhat superceeded the painter of nature as the model artists of the North.

The writers in this section all relate to this artist-model and, in a broader sense, the notions of subjectivity and art that lies behind the formulation *and* deconstruction of this tradition. And, in turn, the ideology of tradition within art as such is discussed. Ingrid Book and Carina Hedén writes in "The Modern Moodscape, Part Two" on the ideological construction of nature and its relation to art, and they describe how "natural" landscapes are culturally defined and produced. Landscape serves as an ideological tool, as in the complete institutionalisation of the current 'natural' landscape as popular moodscape. Margrét Bløndal tries, in her essay "Boil, Simmer, Seethe and Stew—Concerning a Geology of the Everyday" to implement the Nordic tradition in everyday life through her experiences of the unique environment of Iceland —showcasing an interaction with nature that is not purely scopic and contemplative. Her project is to include both tradition and nature as categories and building blocks in a contemporary art practice, where location plays a key part.

A different way of locating and re-examining tradition is found in Deimantas Narkevicius' account of the developements of recent art in Lithuania, "For Survival/Experience/Feeling", where nation and tradition has another meaning in relation to the republic's former status as part of the Soviet Union. It is Narkevicius' contention, however, that different strategies and counter-actions, must be read relationally, and not least, that current 'new' Baltic art must be placed within, rather than beyond, the National traditions and schools. In other words, the new—ruptures, breaks, discords—can only be understood as part of a continuum. Also updating and re-contextualising a particular Nordic tradition, Pia Röniche looks at conventions of bringing in rural bliss to the urban setting in her piece "Allotments, Parks and Green Spaces in Copenhagen". Here, she discusses allotment gardens in Denmark as a specific Social Democratic tradition of leisure, its usages and possible, contemporary re-organisations.

In "No Questions Will Be Answered Afterwards, Either Directly or Indirectly", Sophie Tottie moves the focus from nation and tradition to issues of context and distance. For Tottie the national should no longer be separated from the international, and the idea of the Nordic can be isolated and internalised. And rather than transplanting the hegemonic national outlook with an all-encompassing international one, she argues for constant displacements, from one context to another, resulting in shifts in the meaning and reading of words and images. As opposed to this apparent globalism we find Jussi Kivi's reinvestment in the very local and, indeed, distant. In "The Wild North" Kivi tries to rescue, or regain, the role of the wanderer, and writes of landscapes, identities and interactions in this context, comparing the figure of the artist to an imaginative, adventurous child, if not *of*, then *in* nature. Likewise, Matts Leiderstam discusses questions of identity in relation to nature in his dialogue with art historian Peggy Phelan, entitled, appropriately, "On Returning the Returns". However, the boys that populate Leiderstam's forest have other motives, and he relates the experience of nature to issues of tradition and desire: The tradition of landscape painting and the desirous gaze of both the artist and the spectator. In Leiderstam and Phelan's analysis the history of landscape painting becomes a history of sexuality.

The Modern Moodscape Part II

When we read Richard Bergh today, we are struck by the clarity of the language and the relevance of the content. Richard Bergh? An artist, a painter, a cultural critic and essayist, a central figure in Swedish art and culture at the turn of the last century. An art policy maker and diplomat, with close contacts in Norway, Denmark and on the continent. A member of the 'Varberg School', in opposition to the Academy, a founder of the Artists' Association, an art school teacher. An internationalist abreast with the currents of thought of his age, with the latest periodicals ready to be sent off to his artist colleagues. A European who constantly travelled, an active letter writer, a modern museum man who became head of the National Museum in Stockholm. Economically independent, a second generation artist, son of a Professor, a witty socialite, a melancholy and intellectual painter with a shrewd sense of self-criticism, who furnished his opponents with their best arguments. A psychologist and portrait painter. A hung-up painter who worked on his Swedish icon *The Knight and the Maiden* for close to ten years and was never satisfied. A surprisingly forgotten painter and writer in Sweden today.

The number of paintings by Richard Bergh is not large. The constructed character of the paintings, their knotty stubbornness and lack of flow have turned against them, as has Richard Bergh's reputation as a Jack-of-all-trades, and the widespread scepticism about a more idea-based type of art. But perhaps precisely this very lack of flow in the paintings gives us an approach with which we can communicate today. A slowness.

When Richard Bergh returned from the continent in 1887 he was firmly resolved to find the distinctiveness of his natural surroundings, the Swedish landscape.

Now may it all be beautiful in old Sweden too—the midsummer time—one almost gets tears in one's eyes when one thinks of the long light nights, the calm clear bays where the birch tops are reflected while the cuckoo calls and the thrush trills sentimentally in the forest.

Richard Bergh, letter to Georg Pauli, 1887

He based his decision on a then current European body of ideas, not any isolationist Swedish sentiment. The journey home to Sweden was about a wish not only to find, but equally to construct the image of a landscape. He searched for the essence of Swedish nature and character, convinced that this was the only possible starting point for a truly Swedish art. Richard Bergh was the spokesman of a whole generation— articulate, continental, he evoked the Swedish 'moodscape'.

The wild and often-changing landscape of the North does not meet the painter halfway as does the unified, cultivated landscape of France. The former does not, like the latter, offer the artist motifs fully fledged like ripe fruits. To depict our landscape, it does not help to simply open one's eyes before it; the painter must also know the right time to close them, he must be able to DREAM about what he has seen, he must understand how to listen to his EMOTIONS.

Richard Bergh, *Karl Nordström och det moderna stämningslandskapet*, 1896

In *The Knight and the Maiden* the grassy hills of both Gotland and Halland were posing as the models. Mrs Pauli arranged dandelion puffs in the studio and a knight's armour was brought from Italy. The naturalistic elements were composed together into an image in an ideal world, a fiction.

In 1987, a hundred years later, a questionnaire asked which landscape types in Sweden were appreciated most. The answers were the Swedish birch grove, meadow and heath. The most monotonous agricultural landscape, and densely thicketed woods, had earlier been assigned the lowest value.[1]

In Denmark the same year a similar survey was conducted to shed light on its population's wishes in the planning of forest and farming landscapes. A picture of dense recent pine forest along a smallish road ended up some way down the scale. Exactly the same picture, but with a deer placed at the edge of the forest, was ranked highest, even higher than old beech forest.[2] The Russian artists Komar and Melamid have, as we know, carried out similar experiments. On a statistical basis they have constructed the best and the least loved paintings in different countries. Wasn't Denmark's best loved painting an open, rolling landscape, some groves, a lake and a ballerina?

All landscapes are models, always under political reconstruction

A car rolls through the landscape. A leafy forest with some beeches, a field, a pond, a stream, new bank areas up to the water. Black and white cows with delicate pink calves, a marl pit with an old milk cart; someone has begun to grow flax. Horse farms, new meadows, pastures with woody groves, ewes with lambs, a sheepdog. Fields with stone dikes, cairns, away out in the middle a majestic solitary tree, a farmer and a supervisor, plastic-wrapped bales. Mixed forest with spruce and birch have been built up, a clearing, the edge of a wood. An uncultivated stretch gives depth to the landscape, marked-off wilderness for wildlife. In the hollow farthest off, a new wetland with a

ILLUSTRATIONS (PREVIOUS PAGES): INGRID BOOK AND CARINA HEDEN, HALLANDSKT LANDSKAP EFTER RICHARD BERG (DUTCH LANDSCAPE AFTER RICHARD BERG), 1998–2000. #2–4 OUT OF 6

water surface has been laid out.

The landscape is in the process of being 'musealised'. The farmer is now a guardian and conservator of subsidy entitled landscape elements: mid-field islands of 'nature', open ditches, riverbanks, solitary trees, house ruins, wells, cattle runs, polled avenues and exposed stone dikes, all giving him qualification or subsidy points in a labyrinthine system of controls and sanctions. The old sins of omission (the dikes that were never removed during the rationalisations of the 50s) now become specimens in a new museum of cultural history, the Swedish countryside. In the tradition of the ready-made established in art we mean by museum "a processing complex or reclamation station where the artefacts of the past are presented as signs for the present".[3]

In this top-down system of cultivations and rewarded non-cultivations the Swedish landscape undergoes its changes: into the pre-industrial, the idyll; into the post-industrial, 'biodiversity'. Screens, showcases and reserves in a large, specialised market.

A landscape, a place where concepts like distinctiveness, local identity, Heimat, anti-modernity are important parameters in the attempt to clarify and demarcate oneself, to construct one's identity, one's special landscape. In this context the twentieth century with its modern art and universal claims represents a dissolution of the old cultural identities and their authenticity. And the 'new art' is doomed too, even when it has global claims and media support, to a kind of locally bound existence, caught up in the flow of equally valid and equally valued art events that proliferate today. Through its increasing attraction to the theatrical, the event, the opening, the right moment, art actually achieves most through casual hearsay outside the circle of those who were there. Even though the artist of today is on a constant journey between capitals, he or she does not always manage to compensate for this. In that sense, art, for better or for worse, has become more local. Suddenly it can be just as good to stop where you are and look around.

In this landscape modelled from "someone, somewhere", coaxed forth by its tourism managers, tended by its native farmers, and supported by its local patriots, the aim, in a time when most things are fluid, is not to drift or dither, but to stabilise the special cultural characteristics. To make oneself visible. In this context one can observe the impact of those artists in Sweden today who work with stable signs of Swedish identity. They all collaborate in the creation of the product that in the last analysis is to be offered among other products in its segment of the great market.

Richard Bergh had a vision of a Swedish landscape

Today the Swedish landscape, with nineteenth century props and ecological elements, is being composed into a picture of a Swedish 'moodscape', where animals and people must thrive in biological diversity. A picture to reflect yourself in, a surface. A chiaroscuro that can be compared to the English park landscape at the end of the eighteenth century, which was, arguably, formed with a view to obscuring where the real conflicts in society lay. The refracted light that levels everything. An image shattered by the French park, for which more open ground, light and clarity were required "so they could hold more trials".[4] Chiaroscuro was meant to hide the fact that what is to be produced for the greater community is nothing more than leisure time.

Simultaneously, as the twentieth century's greatest depopulation from the villages to the towns is taking place (11,500 farms in Norrbotten in 1960, 350 today—minus one a week) a landscape is being created for the nostalgia of urban man.

A rather more reformist attitude is taken by the gardener in his own more or less ecological mini-zone. The garden is developed and grows up alongside and as an alternative to the general history of the landscape. It establishes its own context, a world where other kinds of relations can arise and be permitted. It has its own exotic immigration its own assimilation principle. Draws in from near and far. The potato, a well established refugee, and *Transparente Blanche*, our all-Swedish summer apple from Riga, an early contact with the Baltic countries, which is now followed by a new immigration from the East. Translating this into the art context, the installation follows the principles of the garden: the attempt by the artist to determine the context for his or her own work, to tell a story independently of the institution.

"Think like a mountain" urges the Norwegian philosopher Arne Næss. Seeing the rights of the rocks, the animals and the biosphere as 'legal persons' is one of the positions of a radical ecology. Giving one's life for the whales. Here we have come some way from an anthropocentric worldview.

Notes

1. Roland Gustavsson and Torleif Ingelög, *Det nya landskapet*, Jönköping: Skogsstyrelsen, 1994, unpaginated.

2. Gustavsson, *landskapet*.

3. Boris Groys, *Logik der Sammlung*, Munich: Carl Hanser Verlag, 1997.

4. Denis Cosgrove and Stephan Daniels, eds., *The Iconography of Landscape*, Cambridge: Cambridge University Press, 1988.

Previously published in Paletten, *no. 233, vol. 59, 1998.*   *translated by James Manley*

Boil, Simmer, Seethe and Stew
—Concerning a Geology of the Domestic

Stains—the history that should be hidden
Attraction—the quiet power of the mundane
Trace—hints of the unknown
Ooze—humble sign of existence
Environ—wild things and dry-wall
Actuality—the impossibility of faking
Void—a loaf of bread and a wonder-bread
Protection—refined sugar and bleached flour
Forces—presence and handling

The source for my work is everyday life. By taking material out of my closest surroundings, converting its familiar appearance and putting it into a different context, I try to create a place for contemplation for the viewer. I want my work to look incidental, as if it could have grown from the wall or the floor, fallen from the ceiling, occured in some corner... not 'placed'. I do not want the works to have a clear reference—rather look at them as something that each person could translate into her own experience depending on location and space. I would like the viewer to be confronted—versus the viewer looking at a display. No space is "ideal" for the work. They could be installed in any environment, where the location would change their meaning given the context of the space.

The streams of details interest me, little things that quietly but thoroughly change their environment. I want to draw attention to the things that are around us but that we have stopped noticing because their presence is mundane to us; the things that truly exist and affect their environment and space although they don't scream out for attention, 'the little' which step by step gets into our consciousness where it eventually digs in, something that exists and does not exist—on the edge of being something and nothing.

I am interested in a hidden reality, i.e. what is actually going on behind our dry-walls and false sense of security. The security that we desperately try to create in our sterile homes of spic and span. The security of the artificial fireplaces that can be turned off and on and communication without touching.

I look at my pieces as reminders. Reminders of what we have lost and abandoned. Some are made from sugar—our treat and threat—transformed from refined whiteness into brown mass. The pieces are pure and their purity meltable, depending on the heat and humidity of the environment. They quietly occur and slowly disappear. Their existence is short but leaves a mark: stains with a story. They look for a comfort and are willing to fill up one's psychological gap for a while

The process is important. It is my geology. A process that requires presence and handling; boiling, simmering, seething and stewing.

The beauty of the ugliness, the charm of the repulsive attracts me. Something that is beyond ugliness, too ugly to be simply ugly, too extraordinary to walk by, the astonishing colours of rotten fruits, the strong will of self-destruction. The lusciousness of the fungi that grew in the shower at my summer hotel in Iceland. We knew that they were not supposed to be there and the smell was enough to let the health and safety department seal the room. Still they were glorious, green little dots, of various shapes and hues of green, furry and disgustingly attractive.

The crooked lines of nature which have the amazing ability to occur interestingly; the concrete side-walk that cracks and creates the perfect line.
I am in Sweden with my siblings and mom
living in a one-hundred-and fifty year old ginger bread house
mom is standing beside the waterlilly
wearing shorts
her legs covered in mosquito bites
balloons slowly oozing
and the waterlillies
reaching the surface
of the pond

The Icelandic writer Gudbergur Bergsson once wondered why Monet was so attracted to ponds. He came to the conclusion that it was because of their riotous life. I was attracted to the fungi in my summer hotel for the same reason; riotous life which relished the whole summer experience, taking me between shifts and allowing me to nurture the process. The transformation from a few green dots to a furry meadow on the walls, activating all my senses while I took a shower.

I want to talk about loss—the inability to keep fantasy alive. The inability to see the neighbour as the bald pirate, instead of the bureaucrat with a toupee:

I have been told that if people live in a continuous noise that the brain automatically reduces the hearing, so people can keep on working. This is fantastically clever and also much more practical than changing the machines. The same happens with the vision and the senses in general. When people live in a state of continuous war, accidents, bad consciousness and speed; the senses and feelings get paralysed and people keep on working, watching the television and sleeping with each other, even with the inability of loving. This is sometimes a little bit painful but it is definitely much more practical than changing the world.[1]

I would like my work to act like fixative. Making people slow down, shift focus and light the senses—instead of isolating oneself from the surroundings in which one should participate. We are like Snow White in her glass box but unfortunately there are few dwarfs to drop the box and shake the apple out of our mouths.

"People without imagination are beginning to tire of the importance attached to comfort, to culture, to leisure, to all that destroys imagination. This means that people are not really tired of comfort, culture and leisure, but of the use to which they are put, which is precisely what stops us enjoying them."[2]

The lack of physicality, touching and holding in our wrapped alienated world; the fright for losing control and giving too much of oneself by touching and holding. The protection of holding back and showing self-control:

As late as 1920, the death rate for infants in the zero to one year old age group in American foundling institutions, where absolutely no body contact was provided, was nearly one hundred percent. This "disease" was called "marasmus" which literally means "wasting away".[3]

As a child I used to suck my thumb. At three years old I was aware of being too old for such manners. I convinced myself and my family that I would quit on my next birthday. Yet the thumb was my comfort and privacy—an ease of mind. I turned four, five, six, seven and at eight years old I was able to fall asleep without him
but sleeping he always found his way to my mouth.
As a teenager
I frequently shared a bed with my young friend
his index finger always slipped to my mouth
as we were dreaming
I am 26
confessing that my thumb is still a dear companion
sometimes in my solitude
he takes a shallow dive

The tendency to nourish on obstacles. If life becomes too easy, one needs a scandal or builds an obstacle. Nothing is as tempting as the forbidden apple.

"I am so pleased to want thus that I suffer agreeably,
and have so much joy in my pain, that I am sick with delight."[4]
Agnes Martin says: "Walking seems to cover time and space but in reality we are always just where we started. Key journey of life is an arduous happiness."

Purity:
The profound and submissive; although aware of the inconceivability of competition with the fancy fake. It is hard for the forget-me-nots to compete for attention with the plastic tulips. They are aware that they don't have a chance of winning. It is hopeless to count on memory anymore. Who is capable of recalling an image from the past without tangible proof?

Parentage:
How our habitats have changed.
Instead of houses with roots we now have sprouts spread over our apartment.
A sample here and there. A collection of grasping.
Trying to control what surrounds us—our surrounding safety.
It is interesting to look at the things that people take with them when moving away; remembering the considerations of what to leave and what to take:
A plastic duck that I got when I was born, engraved twig by my dad, pebbles.
A cutting board, dancing chickens, Icelandic dictionary, pebbles.
A tablecloth with an embroidered M, old vases from my great grandfather, a note from my grandmother, pebbles. Photographs and pebbles.
Remembering my childhood my home, the cliff and security that does not exist anymore.
My mother now living with her mother and my father in boxes with another mother.
How a single thing can evoke a memory, a flash back of comfort and trust, or something that is not associated with a specific image but a scent. Aware that as a mother I'm creating my son's norm. What I will bring with us will become part of his life as well, something that he recollects later.
Opening amma Steina's kitchen drawer
a heap of sugar
Shovelling and pouring
making forms with my fingers.

Sitting at her kitchen table with closed eyes. Secretly moving my fingers under the tabletop. Feeling the chewing gum that my older cousins had stuck there. Admiring how brave they were and knowing I would never dare sticking mine. Remember how wonderful it felt touching those hillocks and hummocks, residuum of my 'cool' cousins and me sitting there alone, capable of sharing their secrets.

The effort of holding onto traditions as your protection. One of my biggest concerns when I met Magnús was what his parents ate for Christmas. Fortunately they ate ptarmigans as we did.[5] When we bought our first Christmas tree I insisted on going from store to store to look at the selection because that was how Christmas tree buying was supposed to take place, not aware that my parents always went at the last minute so going from store to store was due to the poor selection by that time.

I was thinking of Iceland and the simplicity. How approachable everyone is. Iceland's most beloved painter Kjarval never voted because he hated the idea of squeezing his friends through a small slash into a dark box. I am wondering how easy it is to become obsessed with everyday life there. Yet Iceland is the land of extremes. While the earth is boiling, the people are everydaying.

The animals:
kitties, cows, ducks,
    horses, bull
        chickens, hen
ptarmigans, sea-gulls, lamb
    sheep, doggies,
    and the cosmopolitan crow in the town of green houses, Hveragerdi, who spoke
Danish and could say:
"my name is Margrét, I do not feel as good as yesterday."

The food and the grey scale. Yarn in sheep colours. Blood pudding, whale-blubber, shark, lamb and again lamb. Turnips. My grandmother poured sugar on sliced turnips and claimed that it was pineapple. Everyone believed her because no one actually had seen such an exotic fruit. Steamed haddock and boiled potatoes. The potatoes which the artist Sigurdur Gudmundsson compares to Scandinavian artists:

> Everything in the North grows so slowly—not only nature but also people. We,
> Nordic artists for instance, usually begin to show some talent when we are around
> forty and when we are fifty we could be called promising. One lifetime is too short

a time for us to become artists. We are bound to the same tragedy as the Icelandic potatoes. The Icelandic potatoes—absolutely the most desired things in Iceland— grow so slowly that they would need at least two Icelandic summers in order to become potatoes. Mostly they die—freeze to death in the state when we would consider them to be promising. Only when there is an error in the climate do they become potatoes. Their full-size is always small when you compare them with potatoes from other countries but the taste is great and rich. Their molecules are almost glued to each other and they look like small yellow stones and yet they are soft and sweet. The Icelandic potato-lovers who are always longing for the natural fault that they call a 'long summer' are so happy and proud when those yellow things come out of the soil that they give them all kinds of lovely nicknames varying from Golden Eye to British Whore. Yes—there are some remarkable similarities. [6]

Geology:
I am profoundly involved in the process of making my work. All the steps are important, every single leak. The presence and handling, holding and touching, everything: an inseparable part of the pieces. I do not distinguish between blowing up the balloons, filling them with water, making the moulds, heating the sugar, popping the balloons, watching the waterfall or the stream, following the melting, stirring, pouring the sugar in the moulds, layer by layer, stratification, each including an individual story, waiting for them to cool down, breaking the moulds, holding the piece, scraping the leak, sweeping the leftovers, picking up the fragments. All of these activities bring images to me that gather in the piece.

The fact that the pieces do not have a long life reminds me of how meaningless household tasks sometimes are. Washing clothes only to know that they will get dirty again. Wiping the molding only to know that it will collect dust again. Preparing the gratin so carefully, knowing that it will be devoured. Putting toys in their box, knowing that they will be scattered over the floor in a minute.
to love someone

and care so deeply for
create a sugarball

hard as a rock

yet meltable

I might be under the spell of the Icelandic weather being so fascinated with mutability. Completely unpredictable weather. One can never plan a garden party or go for a walk without carrying an extra set of clothes. It is said that if you don't like the weather just wait a minute. Constant transformation of a coagulation and deliquescence. The trolls coagulate and become rocks if the sun reaches them at dawn. Harsh winds and the whole spectrum of light. Umbrellas are useless because they can't defeat the rain attacking from all directions. Walking, one is in a continual connection with water: a steam from the ground; slush on salt stained shoes; an icy lake with bubbles freezing the moment; pouring rain on corrugated iron roofs. Corrugated roofs being the rejoicer in a overcast city. All painted in various bright colours and matching the rain suits of running children. Children with sand running down their nose and splashing. Geothermal pools to dive into or hot spas. A friend of mine told me a story from an exhibition of the works by the Swiss artist Adrian Schiess. The show consisted of a sandwich-board painted with car lacquer laying on two-by-fours on the floor. Its surface glossy so one could see his reflection as he looked into the board. A young boy that was observing the piece immediately put his hands in a diving position ready to jump into the painting. I often get a similar craving.

I spend days watching my grandmother create her specialities. A ceremony: observing her hands move. The fingers moving into the dough and then out again. Leaving a little trace on her watch and rings. The dough jumps slowly up and down like my chasing flesh. I slip into the elasticity and become immersed. My grandmother's buttery fingers drip on me and my little brother gathers the drips for his hair. My teenage brother with whom I have to discover new positions to be able to share a bed with. My grandmother measures her loss of weight in margarine. At this moment she has lost ten chunks of margarine.

Hidden reality:
The house that I pass every day which plays such a big role in my life, a big white building with engraving on top it's façade. The building where I see new borns, where I meet my mother's colleagues and confront all the closed doors. Even from the inside I considered myself 'knowing' the building, the stairways, the paintings on the walls, the scent and all the closed doors. Those closed doors that would have stayed closed if my son hadn't become sick. And suddenly I become part of a world that I had not been a participant in before. A world that exists on the third floor of the National Hospital of Iceland, one department behind a closed door. A long corridor with different stories. Me and Sölvi: characters. This becomes our world, where we wake up among other participants, where we take our walk. Sölvi in his carriage and me pushing him along the corridor, through the door, in the elevator, up and down. Instead of taking a

walk down to the lake under the rainbow we wander around the building surrounded by concrete walls. Shifting in focus and discovering...

Rubbing your back and his;
patting the sculptures
sculpting the sugar
comforting Sölvi

Last summer I worked for the University of Iceland surveying people about their job descriptions and researching what kind of skills are necessary in modern society. The positions that I researched didn't require any education. One of them was home-helpers, who assist old or disabled people with their household needs. Mostly they were women over middle-age, often farmer's wives, who had to move to the city due to the difficulties in the agriculture industry. I was fascinated by their world and felt that I was now confronting 'reality'. They were people that I didn't meet under normal circumstances, hidden people, at least hidden from my reality. Their awareness of my being from the University made them scared and I, with my honest admiration, had to convince them that I was actually interested in them and their work. One woman had blue make-up and wore sneakers, she had obviously worked at hard labour all her life. She felt that I was interrupting her life. Who did I, a young graduate student, think I was? She told me indignantly that there were already a lot of changes in the society long before I was even born. She looked at the questions as a test and was afraid she would fail. I had somehow to tell her how marvellously she had done and at the same time correcting her that it was not a test. Always conscious of the pedestal that I didn't want to step onto. A pedestal of classism that isn't supposed to exist in Iceland. Still I was aware of the shift between us looking at her worn skin and me, never having worked in a non-stimulating job. After the interview I gave her a lift to her home. We talked about the weather, Icelanders' favourite subject. On our way she came up with an old term that I had never heard before. When I asked what that meant, she felt reassured because she (who was probably 45 years older than me) had some knowledge that I lacked.

Another woman was suspicious when I called her but agreed to meet me at her home. Her home was filled with images of her farm, which she was forced to abandon. When I showed interest in the images and her collection of key chains, all her suspicions flew out of the window and she melted and got sweet. She spoke beautiful Icelandic, used

old terms and words. Her home was a small two room flat in a huge apartment building.
As I am writing these recollections down, I ask myself if I am putting myself on a
pedestal simply by this act of writing; by separating myself from them, saying that I
do not belong to their life and by romanticising their habits and labour.
About not practising what one preaches:
to love the crookedness of nature
and judge spic and span
still forbid your friend to swim beside you with his goggles
I once babysat for a girlfriend of mine. As she was dressing herself up and putting lipstick
on, her four years old son looked at her and said: "Mom, why are you in a disguise?"
There is an island north of Iceland called Grimsey. The only Icelandic part that touches
the Arctic circle. In the old days the Grimsey people were one of the few Icelanders
that didn't suffer from scurvy. Their island was a treasure of scurvy grass. Now the
islanders have a little store that gets supplies once a week from the continent—
imported from another continent. The options are limited but one can get a Chinese
cabbage. The scurvy grass grows, fertilised by the seabirds. No one eats it.

Written in New Brunswick, New Jersey 1997

Notes

1. Baldvinsson I Sveinbjörn, *Stjörnur í skónum* (trans: Stars in the shoes) Reykjavík: Ljódavinafélagid, 1978,
   children´s audio-tape.

2. Raoul Vaneigem, *The Revolution of Everyday Life*, London: Rebel Press/New Left Press, 1983, (originally
   published by Editions de Gallimard, Paris, 1967).

3. Morris Berman, *Coming to Our Senses: Body and Spirit in the Hidden History of the West*, New York:
   Simon and Schuster, 1989.

4. Trubadour song from twelfth century.

5. Ptarmigan is the christmas bird. I do not cook meat and am not fond of blood. Still I crave ripping its
   feather coat off—a bloody task indeed. I am—mind you—only referring to one night a year. It
   doesn't feel like ripping, more like undressing and the smell embraces you with meadow and heath. On
   the the bird's chest is a sack full of freshly contained berries and colourful herbs. The ptarmigan is
   such a friendly and peaceful bird and undressing is not a violent task as the knife becomes the
   zipper. I can even separate the head and the feet without hesitation. The ptarmigan is called rjúpa in
   Icelandic and it burps.
   Note: mountain-dwelling species of grouse which turns white in winter.

6. Zsa-Zsa Eyck, *Sigurdur Gudmundsson*. Venlo, Holland: Uitgeverij Van Spjik, 1991.

For Survival/Experience/Feeling

The formation of an independent Lithauanian art scene after the fall of the wall can be seen as something like a historical event. It was generally assumed that an improved artistic language would emerge merely more or less automatically as a by-product of this, but it soon became obvious that this was neither the foremost nor most distinctive trait of the new local movement. Thus, over a very short period of time, a transplantation of elements began; from the outside 'art world' into the Lithuanian context. This, in turn, has resulted in a destructive relation to previous 'official' art. In 1996 I organised the exhibition *For Survival Experience/Feeling* as an attempt to reintegrate Lithuanian art from the period 1960 to 1980 into the present discourses. It was an attempt to make the art from that time more legible in the context of another kind of art which has subsequently emerged.

In Lithauania, the few (only around 20) younger local artists who began working at the end of the 80s and beginning of the 90s and are inspired by international discourses and styles often get questions like "When will you stop floundering and return to real art and artistic values?" Interestingly, it is always older colleagues who implicitly mean to ask when this, now, six or seven year long period of confusion in Lithuanian art will end. Speaking with the artists of this generation, I have found that they see themselves as starting from nothing, having no tangible foundation or support. There is no proper critique or analysis of contemporary Lithuanian art, not even the simplest chronicling of events. One may ask "What is Lithuanian art anyway, what are its distinctive features, how is it different from or similar to the art of other countries?" These are questions the new generation of artists ask as they examine their role and create their own system of values. Of course these questions cannot be answered fully, as a starting point it can be said that these artists are concerned with exploring the aesthetic foundations of their art, determining who it is that their works communicate with.

In order to look closer into the matter we should return briefly to the recent past. Based on memory and various publications, it is clear that figurative work long dominated art production in Lithuania. This can certainly be said of sculpture. All discussion was focused on how the figure was represented.

Art contradicting this tendency is such a new phenomenon here that it has yet to be named. Usually it is referred to as "non-figurative sculpture". (The only real exception to this was the artists who developed their own version of abstraction in the 70s.) One logical conclusion of the ongoing controversy was the one suggested by the exhibition *Between Object and Sculpture in Lithuania*. At first, the show was considered a victory for "non-figurative" art. Now, several years later, however, one can doubt whether this was in fact the case. Did a new and somewhat more easily decipherable system of artistic categories really emerge, ending the general and infertile arguments of "figure versus non-figure"; "art versus non-art"? In order to approach this question, one might want to know what actually belongs to that first category, so abstractly called "non-figurative sculpture". The answer is surprisingly simple—the term defines anything created by the artist's hand, especially that which is formed in the traditional materials of bronze, stone or wood, but not necessarily representing the human form. The respect for manual work is so great that the 'classical' materials are quite easily complemented by 'non-artistic' ones—food products, untreated fur, linen cloth or straw, etc.. An object-sculpture is something that has been cast, forged, welded, carved, sewn, or woven by the hands of the artist. The social aspect of this phenomena—the implication of replacing the pure, solid and permanent materials familiar to the local (including artistic) bourgeoisie with democratic, inexpensive, temporary and non-enduring ones—goes unnoticed, unanalysed even by the artists themselves.

An emerging hesitant or even critical view of the artist's handiwork as art-as-product has raised a higher degree of unease and a slightly more active discussion about how the limits of conceptual art can actually be defined. One of the ways in which the newly arised interest in rejecting the object became visible, was through the organisation of intensely visual actions in social spaces. It happened only a few times, but the actions were like breaths of fresh air for artists—the discovery of a possible solution to the collapse of the local art market.

It is thus only a few years ago, that the use of industrially produced everyday objects in sculpture was even legitimised in Lithuanian art, and it goes without saying that it has yet to find a place in our critical vocabulary. And the reasons for this apparently rather striking ignorance of developments in modern art discourses in the last, say, hundred years, are actually easy to explain: the use of a ready-made object as art means that all of the professional guild's conventions are broken (naturally eliciting a defensive reaction), and the importance of pseudo-academic art training (available at the one art academy in Lithuania) is called into question. Obviously, the objects presented do not require the practice and skill of the artist's hand, but rather an intellectual reflection based on discourses only recently introduced here.

Thus, the circumstances of production are still in focus, and are being addressed from many angles. Another way in which sculpture has been presented without actually being produced is through the use of pre-existing art works. Without violating the work itself, minimal alterations have been made to conspicuously exaggerate its aesthetic, deconstruct the original meaning of the art work—that is, to deconstruct the ideological underpinnings of its aesthetic. In one instance, an object of unquestionable artistic origin was used: a very professionally executed, monumental, figurative composition created half a century ago—in other words, the very symbol of an epoch. The resulting discussion, which focused mainly on the morality of using one art work to create another (even though the original artwork was unaltered and suffered no harm), revealed the total superiority of the earlier art's significatory system. The polemic focused only on how the original art work was violated, despite the fact that the two works of art coexisted in the same place and time. Personally, I did not hear a single comment analysing the two different types of artistic language, the coexistence of which might raise general questions about the ethics of art.

Considering the above mentioned observations and thoughts, it probably doesn't come as a surprise to hear, that in Lithuania, painting has been the leading discipline of the arts for a very long time now. After World War II a so-called "National School" was formed which, for a long time, opposed the 'official' Soviet art. One key element was the importance of exhibiting in the main art museum spaces. Although all of Post War Lithuanian painting glimmered with the light of dissidence, there wasn't a single group of artists who completely cut their ties with the so-called 'official art', or with the official art community. Even the least tolerated artists occasionally had opportunities to show their work in prestigious exhibitions. A great deal of attention was paid to the museums and the exhibition spaces—these were the places where one sought to show and where the art scene was shaped. Quite simply, it was here the important shifts in art took place. There was never an alternative art scene that completely rejected the official one. Rather, a perpetual balancing act took place between official art and the "National School"—and thus the somewhat more critical, but also closed intellectual spheres. The attention towards the main art spaces and the maintenance of ties to them becomes even more obvious when official painting is compared to that more 'marginal': The main trait of both was realism. The first category gave a positive interpretation of the 'reality' of the times, while the second—the "National School"—was more critical and social.

Other tendencies in art never even acquired the traits of "schools". It was thus within this framework that artists struggled to establish their different styles, or, more precisely, means of expression—employing, for example, freer interpretation of subject matter, greater attention on colour than drawing, more expressive brushstrokes, etc., etc.. Understandably, in the context of such a closed country, a great deal of emotional value was attached to these details. In general, there was not a single painter who questioned the very principles and method of painting (collage was also considered a painting-technique.) The canvas remained passive and flat; something that had to be filled out to then hang on the wall. It made no attempt to comment or connect to the space it was shown in, much less to expand into or take over the space. Such attempts to contextualise art and its circumstances has only now, within the last couple of years, been seen in exhibitions. To return to the questions at the beginning of the text, one can say that since conditions have changed, since the lack of information has been replaced by an irrepressible flow of it, and since "to get" has been replaced by "to choose", the younger generation now searches for identity— personal, national as well as global—with more open eyes and minds. This process also means a re-visiting of the works that appeared so self-evident only two decades ago and a discussion of the foundations and consequences of the practices these works derive from. As such, one can argue that there is actually a new "national" movement going on, but it is one that questions the very principles of the representations of national history we have had so far, and thereby also the use of art. To me, this new interest represents an attempt to understand the potentials of art under different circumstances, as well as the connections and overlappings between two very different periods, rather than to enhance a gap between them.

Previously published in the catalogue Izgyvenimui, Vilnius: The Contemporary Art Center at Vilnius, 1996.

translated by Karla Gruodis

No questions will be answered afterwards, either directly or indirectly

Not long ago, the distance between the Nordic countries and the rest of the world, including Europe, semeed more than physical. In the late 80s, in a discussion concerning a BBC programme about war correspondents, the editor of foreign news at one of the main Swedish dailies exclaimed: "If you read the history of war correspondence, you will see that the Second World War created the best writing, because it possessed the essential truth. Namely: Good against Evil, Churchill against Hitler. Therefore, it is always better to root for the national team. I believe that is what is wrong with the war between Iran and Iraq. It is not the national team against a foreign team, it is a foreign team against a foreign team. Who cares?" Even if far from all agreed with this editor, the distance he so cynically tried to establish has more than shrunk. Not only have changes in media technology and increased travelling mentally decreased distances, but world politics too seems to have brought nations closer. In 1990, the Gulf War broke out; half a year later, in January 1991, the United States launched "Operation Desert Storm". Abstract and highly censured, news images entered our living rooms where we sat petrified, fearing that now a nuclear war would blow our planet out of the universe. Suddenly, global politics seemed undeniably close. At about the same time, Yugoslavia began to fall apart. Stories from different parts of the world and reactions to what were unimaginable horrors taking place in our time began to make up our surroundings. The world seemed to open up, to come closer, yet at the same time distances persisted when it came to understanding what constituted the space in which different locations were linked to one another.

Otherwise, life continues, with fluctuating levels of paranoia. Sometimes we feel under siege, sometimes we think it is all a matter of perception, except that some mighty horrendous things do happen. At the moment I'm not sure whether these maleficents are from the past or the future and can find no exact measure to help me determine this. If the violence we're witnessing is from the past then it can be handled (or at least understood/explained), if it's from the future, well, that's not a comfortable thought. Either way you could say it's all very interesting although sometimes one wishes the old Chinese proverb were not so insistent.

This is an extract from a letter from a friend. What struck me when I first read it was his thoughts about how the past and the future, impinge upon our everyday lives. Everyday life in South Africa that he returns to after a year abroad and finds completely changed. This combination of thoughts of perception, of the past and of the future, clearly but abstractly crystallises a connection between subjects that at first may

seem distant from one another. The
Chinese proverb is a famous but
perhaps mundane saying or curse
that reads "May you live in interesting
times."

In the space that lies between
what is uttered and what is held
back, dark humour occasionally
functions as a way of dealing with
complex phenomena that people must
live with, day in and day out. "No
questions will be answered afterwards,
either directly or indirectly" is perhaps
the closest my own work has come to a one-liner. Read on a sub-titled TV screen in
the 1980s, the statement is part of a work I made in 1999. In it a spokesman at a
press conference informs us of the limits of the information he is about to give rather
than giving any information at all. The sentence strikes us as absurd, a message that
short-circuits people's understanding. The work functions as a mirror flattening the
world, propelling it into a two-dimensional view—into a matter of perspective. Here
the visual image serves both to expose a subject and to preserve its integrity. Its
capacity to simultaneously withhold and express several perspectives constitutes a
platform for understanding where perception itself becomes a motor just as significant
as the subjects that images or art works may revolve around.

It was from this point of view that I started to think of a series of painting which
later were entitled *Kticic Voyager*. Few viewers encountering the paintings *Kticic
Voyager* (which exist in four versions) recognise the photographic point of departure.
The work functions as a target for the viewer's attempts at understanding and grasping
what it is he or she sees. For this reason the paintings do not point out their sources
directly, say, by their title. But for those who wish to pursue this further the title
"Kticic Voyager" can nevertheless be helpful. 'Kticic' is used here as a name, but in
Greek it actually means 'foundation'—for example, the historical foundation on which
we build our everyday life. Kticic stands for something stable and immobile in contrast
to Voyager, which rather indicates movement and travel in real or future space.
Perhaps the most enigmatic element of the painting are the symbols that regularly
recur. And they are what usually prompt the first questions.

Is it true that all layers of meaning do not exist, unless all information is readily available? To maintain as much would be to underestimate the capacity of the image. After all, a picture is something other than applied history. The integrity of the work lies in the fact that several components interact and confront the viewer directly—a viewer who is left alone to interpret what he or she sees.

When the first painting in the series was finished, I decided to distribute pictures of the work without further comment. In a lecture given by an art historian at an art academy in Sweden, the painting was shown to an audience that was given no information other than that it was a mural that had been shown within the framework of a group show entitled *Urban Visions* in the United States in 1999; that it was roughly 5 x 20 metres in size; and that the title was *Kticic Voyager*. After the lecture, one of the students exclaimed (freely quoted): "How can this picture be presented without its history and without reference to its original model?" An image was visible on his T-shirt; it represented the original model of the painting: the Plaza de Mayo in Buenos Aires, Argentina. The student's reaction was justified. It shows not only that references exist regardless of the withheld information, but also how the reticence of a painting may trigger a discussion of indexicality—which is also something the painting is about.

It might seem absurd to refuse to divulge information, and thus far this has not been my method. *Kticic Voyager* involves historically charged material. The paintings proceed from a photograph of the Plaza de Mayo. The square has been cut out of its surroundings to float into an expanded field of colour. Today there are head scarves or shawls painted on the square. They were applied in connection with the silent protest marches of the Mothers of the Plaza de Mayo, and have come to symbolise the demands of relatives for answers regarding family members who "disappeared" during the military dictatorship of 1976 to 1983. (Two similar head scarves can be seen to the lower right in *Kticic Voyager IV*. The prototypes for these scarves, however, were taken from a documentary film about the Russian Gulags. As a result of how the paint was applied and depending on where the viewer is standing in the room, the head scarves alternately disappear or stand out in the picture.)

When I try to understand the reason for my interest in this specific square, I find that part of the explanation lies in the story of Dagmar Hagelin. Perhaps the news about "disappeared" persons in Argentina had a greater impact in Sweden than on other remote countries because of her—a young woman who disappeared there and whose father, of Swedish descent, doggedly continued to search for her. Swedish papers covered the case, and articles on the subject keep being published—sometimes also discussing what Sweden actually did to promote investigations.

Five years ago, I asked two friends to photograph the Plaza de Mayo during a visit.

ILLUSTRATIONS: SOPHIE TOTTIE, PREVIOUS PAGE: *NO QUESTIONS* (*NO QUESTIONS...*). THIS PAGE: SKETCH FOR *KTICIC VOYAGER* (I), WHITE

I wondered what it looked like, especially since I had produced a work in 1992 that presented pictures from the German park Wilhelmshöhe and texts published by the Mothers of Plaza de Mayo. My friends came back with photos of a form that resembled the face of a clock, with symbols painted on it that looked like numbers. Surprisingly, in more ways than one, the form of the square turned out to revolve around the concept of time. The past seemed a discus hurled forward, like a spaceship with insignia painted on it for purposes of identification.

The paintings came into being slowly, as more stories reinforced my first impressions. The source material—which, taken together, constitutes the work—attempts to create a notion that memory and knowledge make up in relation to real places and contemporary history. In this manner, *Kticic Voyager* confronts values that form not only a social and political, but also an emotional identity. An emotional identity which is built up of tensions, both of different perspectives or stories and of interrelationships between close and distant experiences. Just as the layers that constitute our knowledge of contemporary history—now visible, now invisible—*Kticic Voyager* is torn between the said and the unsaid, between history experienced closely and from a distance. In the image no traumatic narrative can be read, no history can be directly interpreted, and in the installation the work shows not only a represented site but also insists on the abstractness of its totality. Contradictorily enough the plaza here functions as a limited image—an abstraction that, in its capacity as a historically charged site, is also an indefinite contemporary area.

As I write this, riots have taken place in Gothenburg, Sweden. Peaceful demonstrators' lengthy preparations to protest during a top political meeting arranged by the European Community have been shattered. Today the papers write that not only the police but also military forces must be enrolled at future gatherings of politicians and demonstrators. The leaders chosen by the people respond to a troubled situation by increasing the distance between themselves and their voters, deciding that the different groups that rule the world will be linked together by being kept apart.

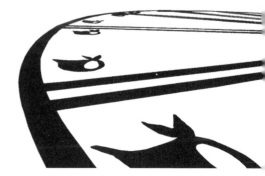

Allotments, Parks and Green Spaces in Copenhagen

I decided to take a look at various allotments in Copenhagen. As I felt a little closed-in in my two room flat and was thinking about having a place for excursions, I decided to drive around Copenhagen and its surroundings.

I was particularly interested in allotments because they are one of the few places in the city where ordinary people have had a direct influence on the framework around them—both historically and in everyday life. For anyone who doesn't know what an allotment is, it's a small plot of land laid out side by side with other allotments which together form larger clusters, almost small villages, in a city or on the outskirts of a city. At very little expense the allotment owner can construct a small house and lay out a garden. The owners grow vegetables, grass and flowers on small plots, only a few metres away from their neighbours. There is often a small shed or house on the plot where people can cook or spend the night at weekends, and each garden plot and cottage can be quite varied, despite the limited scope for expression.

There are great differences amongst allotment associations: some have strict rules about how nice the garden should look. Others are more casual. The houses in the old allotment associations are particularly remarkable: they have been made from many different kinds of material and make optimum use of every nook and cranny. More daunting are all the Danish flags towering over the gardens of the otherwise peaceful allotment folk, drinking beer in the afternoon.

In Denmark the idea of the allotment goes back to the seventeenth century, when King Frederik III planned to lay out one garden per residence for growing vegetables outside the walls of the provincial town of Fredericia, though he never followed through on his utopian idea.[1] In 1884 allotments were formed the way they still look today. In some cases, it was the employees from one workplace, or in others, trade unions, who took the initiative to obtain a plot of land for growing vegetables as a means to getting away from unhealthy environments and crowded dwellings. Some local councils supported the establishment of allotments on the basis of the of the old idea of "help to self-help" for the poor.[2]

Many of the first allotments were laid out on ground that the city could not use, in particular dumps. In a way the allotment is a product of the 'waste land' of the city, and at one time it was profitable to rent out this 'poor' soil temporarily to the poor people.

Since the first allotments were created the sheds have become bigger, almost small houses, where people often live for several of the summer months. In some cases whole allotment areas have been transformed into all-year-round properties.

The allotments in Copenhagen have undergone many changes in the past century, and have been particularly vulnerable to the planning policies of local authorities. Before the allotment reforms of 1976 most allotments didn't even have a lease for more than 3 to 5 years at a time, and in some cases the terms of notice were as low as three months. This meant that many allotments were removed from central Copenhagen between the 1920s and the 1970s.

In the 1970s, the Danish Federation of Leisure and Allotment Gardeners took up allotments as a political issue, in a struggle to prevent them from being eliminated. They became part of "Copenhagen's recreational areas", on an equal footing with parks and other green spaces. It was stipulated that a certain percentage of the green areas of the city were to be set aside for allotments, and most allotment associations now have a 25 year lease with an option to extend.

For me, the allotment is an example of how a practical arrangement has become a whole popular movement and lifestyle which has left its mark on the city, not only with its gardens and paths and traditions of social relations, but also in terms of overall city planning, since the city structure has had to find ways around the recalcitrant islands formed by the garden associations. In other areas it is difficult to have any influence on the overall formation of the city; it is dictatorial and authoritarian. I often feel powerless in the inflexible city space.

One could say that after the reform of 1976 the allotment associations should be viewed administratively in the same way as parks and green areas, but the various recreational areas are very different and fulfil widely different functions.

Ideally, the city parks are for everyone; they are open social spaces where people can meet, spend time, read, talk, play, or be simply somewhere to get a bit of peace, a pause in the rigidity of urban spatial relations. This is not least because the park is one of the few public spaces that has yet to become a consumer space. However in purely physical terms one can't do so much with a park, one can only choose whether to be there or not. For despite the immediate character of the parks as a 'pause' or 'free space', they are strictly regulated, not only with respect to their physical appearance, but also in relation to the ways they can be used. There are expectations of certain behavioral patterns to the exclusion of others. For example, Copenhagen City Council is at present trying to stop the "gay cruising" that goes on in the H C Ørsted Park.[3] Bushes are being cut down and fences are being built around the toilets to get rid of these "sleazy" meeting places.

Obviously, there are firm rules in allotment associations too; how high the hedge can be; how the soil is to be cultivated; what percentage of the garden should be for vegetables, what for flowers? These rules were laid down when the allotment was primarily a kitchen garden. The hedge mustn't be too high, so the neighbours can look over, and can keep an eye on one anothers' gardens. The allotment was not intended as a private garden where people minded their own business, but rather, as a social, utilitarian space, and the sense of solidarity in allotment associations was always an important aspect of its social function. Today these rules seem rather stifling, at least if I were to imagine myself living there. The allotment was formed according to an ideology that has a different meaning today. The Danish flag is very often seen in allotments, and refers back to a time when Denmark was occupied by the Germans during World War II, and some allotment owners had links with the resistance movement. Today, in my eyes, the flags reflect an unhealthy nationalism and a tendency towards xenophobia. Similarly, a garden plot in many associations can be handed down from generation to generation, and this in itself is a mechanism of exclusion. The chance of getting an allotment as a new owner today is very slim, and there are only enough plots for about 5% of the city population.[4] One is tempted to see some of these allotment associations as metaphorical microcosms of the nation state, where rights are predicated on one's place of birth. It is interesting to imagine the allotments and parks as more active places, allowing dialogue among different classes and ethnicities.

There are also many 'unused' areas in central Copenhagen. For example there is a long strip of poorly kept grass in the middle of the Sønder Boulevard, which is also known as "dogshit path".[5] Here people from the surrounding area could easily plant small gardens. These could be semi-private, or rotated, so that different people in the area could have an opportunity to cultivate them. The gardens could be freely accessible so people could spend time there and enjoy them. The same could conceivably be done with parks, where certain areas could be utilised as kitchen gardens; with free access, but with gardens that could be cultivated individually for certain periods. There are several places where small communal kitchen gardens have already been laid out in conjunction with housing complexes, but they are few in comparison to how many areas might be utilised this way. Extended functions for park areas and 'green' areas (which could go beyond gardening) might also change some of the ideas we have about what is possible in a city and what we can do in a public space.

So I suggest a reformulation of the allotment; a broader conception of what it is and what it can be used for, and on the whole an expansion of the concept of "recreational areas".

In the case of allotments one could begin with a few simple rules—for example rotating the ownership of the allotment every three to five years. This way it would not be private property, but could be used and exchanged among a greater member of people, thus becoming a more integrated part of city life. It would benefit both parks and allotments to have their functions changed, extended and discussed, just as it would be an experiment in itself to subtly shift the boundary between public and private places, boundaries that Danes in particular maintain zealously. Of course, one likes to have one's allotment garden in peace—after all, that's part of the point—without regulations about how tall the grass can be and without a neighbour always inspecting your flower beds. But the question is whether it might not be possible in a city to share recreational activities, time and property with others besides one's family and close friends.

Notes

1. Planstyrelsen, *Kolonihaver i Danmark*, Copenhagen: Ministry of the Environment, 1979, p. 10.

2. Planstyrelsen, *Kolonihaver i Danmark*.

3. Planstyrelsen, *Kolonihaver i Danmark*, p. 12.

4. A park in the city centre of Copenhagen.

5. Sønder Boulevard in a residential neighbourhood in Vesterbro, Copenhagen.

translated by James Manley

European cultural history is one long cavalcade of discoveries and inventions. Not even nature existed before it was invented. In a cultural paradox, the natural landscape, and especially *untamed*, wild nature is the great invention of Romanticism. The natural landscape arrived in Finland after a time lag, via the awakening of the enthusiasm towards the national that came about at the end of the nineteenth century. Since then, the National Romantic wilderness landscape has ingrained itself into the Finnish consciousness and tourist advertising for more than one hundred years.

Nature has, nevertheless, also had another side: in practice, the 'romantic' landscape was commonplace and familiar: fish from the lakes, and from the forest, game, berries, fuel and timber. All of these are associated with their own traditional practices. If he was to reach the remotest deep forests on his hunting trips, the hunter or the fisherman needed a knowledge of nature and a command of many skills. The forest had its spiritual aspect, its good and bad spirits. But all of this is a long time ago, attitudes to the forest have subsequently polarised into two main directions; romanticism, which is an import, and the practical, meaning exports. The modern European conception of nature is located somewhere between these two poles. It is a conception in which nature—whatever that means—is also otherness; the enemy, the conquering and subduing of which, just as much as the aestheticisation of some of its limited features, represents an all-embracing principle.

The little boys' forest

My own early "experiences of the forest" are of summer camping trips with my family in the 1960s and early 70s, and of adventures with others of my own age in the local suburban woods, where I went to drink beer and sit around campfires at night when a bit bigger. Of course, all this is a long way from the realities of nature and the everyday exploitation of the forest. But some of the enchantment of the backwoods, of the immemorial tradition of freedom away from social control and those in power, did survive.

As a child, I also read boys' adventure books, in which there were excursions into Finland's forests and wilderness, and onto its labyrinthine waterways. There were a lot of these books published in the 1930s and right up until the age of TV, at the start of the 1960s. A common feature to them was vigorous, wholesome outdoor life and the "freedom of the backwoods"! Nature was vast, clean and untamed, and above all it was fascinating: a forest full of secrets. True, the forests were copiously exploited in those days too, but in retrospect the crucial feature of the stories was specifically the environment; at that time the country still had extensive uncultivated, pathless backwoods, onto which the most astounding adventures could be projected.

Another object of enthusiastic perusal was the few volumes of *Suomi* (*Finland*), of black and white photographs, printed in the 1940s and 50s, that were on my grandparents' bookshelf, in which the main role was played by natural sights in the wilderness.

Trips to the forest

At the end of the 1970s my family moved to the outskirts of Helsinki, to an area partly covered with forest. I was 16 or 17 years old, and interested in the new surroundings, particularly the forest. My explorations began at the end of our yard, and reached further and further with time. I was looking for that vast, romantic forest, and since then I have pretty much roamed in all areas where natural forests can be found in Finland.

Certain places and areas have become very familiar to me. The character of these trips has also changed; as the forest has fragmented the vastness of nature has had to be found in the small. Since the beginning of the 1990s, I have been drawing maps. Initially of places for which I did not have a full 'proper' map. I drew the maps to clarify for myself the shapes of the terrain and the important places, I put into them every possible bit of information that I considered significant, I made more of them. In this form the map satisfied my need to portray the landscape. The ironic observations, just as much as culture or natural historical information, are of equal value on these maps. Alongside the maps, the trips have also produced a few plastic bags of film, texts and stacks of photographs.

Attempts to depict my experiences, and the splendid places I had been, brought these trips into the world of art. In the background gleamed romantic wilderness landscapes and adventure book nature. But it wasn't that simple, at times there was a contradiction, when the picture did not make sense. How do you express something that no longer really exists except in your own imagination, of which there remains in reality only a backdrop; small limited nature reserves, museumish exhibits and tourist spots?

The landscape of production

The image of Finland is still dominated by nature. This widespread country has a human population of about five million, with settlements concentrated in the south and coastal areas, and in a few growth centres. The countryside is being depopulated at an increasing rate. The forest dominates the land and the forest industry dominates the landscape. But still our mental pictures also incorporate the concept of vast, virtually untouched wilderness. The location of these mythical forests is mostly in eastern and northern Finland, regions tempered by National Romanticism.

But the reality is different; under global market capitalism the Finnish forest is principally a producer of raw materials. In practice, this means efficient exploitation taken to an extreme, and the ubiquitous, massive machinery that goes with this. Apart from minor remnants, proper wilderness and large areas of uninterrupted natural forests are only to be found up north in Lapland, where the forest is arguably more rugged, less dense, short and stunted. Elsewhere, the production landscape of intensive forestry crashes on, with its enormous cutting areas, saplings, and massive wetland drainages.

The construction of the vast, forest road network begun in the 1950s has lead to the breaking up of these areas, and nowadays the broad uninhabited wilderness, including its most remote corners, are ruled over by a dense network of forest roads. For the majority of people, however the extent of these changes have gone unnoticed. The propaganda of the forest economy—decades of forestry education and tourist propaganda—have done their job. But above all, people spend less time in the forest.

The campsite

The ideal camping ground has dry ground, is level and sheltered, there is drinking water nearby, and it is situated in a place that catches the sunshine. Quite frequently, these places are also aesthetically pleasing, precisely the kind where you feel happy to settle. Also associated with the camping place is a notion of the romantic—the campsite is almost a symbol of this—since the idea of stories around the camp fire plays an important role in this culture. A knowledge of the history of the landscape and nature in general can help us perceive more, including the way that nature is not just an empty aesthetic backdrop, a holiday paradise, or raw material and an arena for the technocrats' endless and deadly earnest games.

The study of archaeology lead me to discover many hitherto unknown sites of stone age dwellings. I still found the modern campsites of people living off nature, the reindeer herders, the hunters and the fishermen in the pathless wilderness of Lapland, equally interesting. This is, of course, part of a romantic image, of the traces of some ancient continuum. It doesn't bother me that the roof beams of the *kota* (a tepee-like structure used by the Sami people in Lapland) are covered in plastic, and that the camp in general doesn't comply with rigorous anthropological descriptions of the cultures of the northern wildernesses. In the wilderness, where man's visible influence is minimal, a kind of feeling of assimilation, of familiarity is linked with the campsite.

Although I do not want to live in the forest, and sometimes return from it tired, dirty and reeking of smoke, I always go back. This is not a question of a militant survival game, of hiking for sport or an exercise in meditation seeking for retribution for a sinful life. It is purely a concept of the romantic. I simply declare myself to be a total romantic, even my conception of the romantic is romanticised, based on intentions and on imagination.

Beyond the city

Romantic nature is construed as a kind of otherness, alien to modern urban culture; nature versus culture, and urban versus rural, and so on. In this manner the energetic and culturally varied metropolis, where the liberty of thought and manners apparently flourishes is the opposite to narrow-minded rednecks and their gossiping wives in the backwoods of the country. Modern urban culture is seen as the cradle of the pluralism and liberal tolerance. And where the city is fast and exciting, the country is slow and

dull. However, in its relation to "outside" nature, postmodern urban culture is—to my mind—narrow in its views, built on antagonisms and othering—creating a self-centred hegemony of its own superiority. Despite the flood of information it produces, it also produces massive amounts of lack of sense of relativity.

The essence of a seemingly open, but in reality fixed culture culminates in an area it defines to stand outside of itself, but which in reality is its borderland, i.e. the place where the sewers are drained, and from where nourishment, materials and energy are taken. The reticence and lack of a sense of relativity is most evident in how this outside "nature" seems strange and unfamiliar to the greater multitude, almost as if it didn't exist. And that is a good reason to distance yourself a bit from the city and its culture, and perhaps even to (re)acquaint yourself with the forest by visiting it at night.

ILLUSTRATIONS: JUSSI KIVI, MAP, LAKE KUTUJÄRVI, LAKE ALAJÄRVI, EARLY JUNE 1989, DRAWING, 1992
MAP, VIEW OF THE CAMP PÖTSÖPURO IN RAIN AND SLEET, DRAWING, WATERCOLOUR, 1996–97.
ROMANTIC GEOGRAPHIC SOCIETY PHOTO ARCHIVES NO. 40: KIRAKKAJOKI, HAMMASTUNTURE WILDERNESS, INARI (FIN) LAPPLAND, 2001

Kirakkajoen mutka - Ahvenjoki

Peggy:

My computer crashed and I lost your last email before I read it. Can you resend? I imagine it was a nudge about the copies. I keep thinking of more and more paintings for you to copy and I can't choose one! It's a terrible task you have given me. How do you feel about B's *Springtime*?

Matts:

I suppose that it is Botticelli's *Springtime* you mean? I am looking at a reproduction right now. It was a long time ago when I saw this painting. I am looking at the handsome young man who is depicted in the left hand corner of the painting and trying to remember the story behind the image. Why are you interested in this painting?

Peggy:

I am interested in her hair. When I saw it the first time, I thought that her hair was everything. And I also thought "O, it needs to be brushed!" Then I laughed, imagining Botticelli's brush strokes as a kind of failed hair brushing. When I was growing up, I was often advised by my older sister to brush my hair one hundred times every night before I went to bed. It was one of my first encounters with repetition, with copying, and with counting. When I became interested in painting as an activity, as something someone had done, I thought about this kind of repetition again. I know that copying is not the same as repetition, and yet they both involve a kind of "return to the first". I should probably also tell you that sometimes when I feel afraid in front of certain canvases, I try to reassure myself by counting. For example, Agnes Martin's painting, *Untitled (The Rose)*, inspires a kind of panic in me. To still my panic, I count the lines and "do the math" of the grid. The math consoles me because if I can count myself back to the present then I can withstand the pressure of a kind of limitlessness that her painting evokes. Sometimes I think she paints horizontal and vertical lines "beneath" her painting to expose painting's own surprising math—all that flatness and yet all that calculation.

When you paint, do you "do the math" of the 'original'? Do you measure the depth of the vanishing point? Do the geometry of proper perspective?

I know that in your pastorals the landscapes are, in the traditional sense, enquiries into the sublime. These enquiries are the ones that most panic me. Botticelli's *Springtime* is pastoral, but not quite in the way some of your copies are.

Matts:

Do you mean Flora? She's wonderful. But I wonder—are we thinking about the same painting, *The Allegory of Spring*? In my catalogue from the Uffizi Museum, on the same spread as this reproduction, is *The Birth of Venus*. Her hair fits your description even better, living a life of its own, and it does needs to be brushed.

Sandro Botticelli uses tempera on wood, and because of this the colours are still very bright, clear and strong. Also everything in these pictures happens on the surface; nature is painted like a stage set for these allegories and we can see the traces from every movement of the artist's brush. However, the pastoral landscape paintings described by Nicolas Poussin and Claude Lorraine are made using the techniques of oil painting. Layers of oil paint give depth to the colours, completely different from tempera. In these ideal landscape paintings you find dark areas—like black holes or gulfs, as made for disappearing into. Is it this force that makes you panic?

Today we are estranged from landscape as nature but the exciting darkness within the unknown (is it death) is still very present. Simon Schama writes in his brilliant book, *Landscape and Memory*: "There have always been two kinds of Arcadia: shaggy and smooth; dark and light; a place of bucolic leisure and a place of primitive panic".[1]

I am not sure what the notion of the sublime really means to me. In the Scandinavian tradition nature has been used as an escape from culture. When I was a kid I lived in the countryside, and there weren't any neighbours around. At the age of two or three—my mother must have been crazy to let me out—I would walk into the forest on my own, sometimes for a whole day. I had my dog with me and I guess it was thanks to him that I found the way home again. As an adult I found out that parks well known for gay cruising also have these dark areas were you can hide yourself, and I felt—still feel—intrigued by this.

I am not a skilled craftsman; because of this I have to exert myself when making my after-images. I need a good photo of the original, and then I use the classical grid technique to lay out the image. I need this grid so as to not go astray in the painting, as a measuring device to understand an underlying structure. Only in some cases have I completed my picture in front of the original.

I agree that copying is an attempt to repeat a painting; however, it is impossible to copy an image perfectly. This is because the original is painted in layers from the inside and out, while the copy will be built from outside and in. I believe the best copies are made in a time close to the original. When I make copies today, it is not so much about likeness as it is about difference. To paint a copy after Nicolas

Poussin or Claude Lorraine is an attempt to get closer to my thoughts about these landscapes—it is like taking a stroll in the forest again.

Peggy:
Yes, I meant Flora, although Venus interests me too. Putting them next to each other, one can see that there are two different ideas of modesty at work in the paintings, and two different ideas of erotic pleasure via the sublime. Flora is allowed to be beautiful because she is 'natural'—she has the putative innocence of nature. Venus is not innocent. She is beautiful not because of her closeness to nature, but because of her own power. A strange figure. In Botticelli's paintings, Venus is naked while Flora wears that wild dress, sheer artifice upon which 'the natural' is composed.

In your cruising landscapes, is innocence desired? Does it exist?

I am interested in what you say about your copies being about difference rather than sameness. Can you say more about this in terms of the attitude of the observer? When I think of your paintings, I think of them both inside a gallery and outside in a dark park. I guess what I am retaining here is this sense of two locations—the historical one, the so-called 'original' —and then the other "contemporary scene" which is infused both with gay erotic energy and the erotic energy of assessment in the art world. Both scenes are cruisings. But they each have, nominally at least, different languages and desires.

You called nature an escape, but from what did you want and need to flee as a young boy?

Matts:
The forest was a place to be with myself. Where I could just be. Outside the forest I felt exposed for and to other people's gazes. I think that cruising for me was for a long time related to an experience of being aware of my body.

It was for me related to the sublime in terms of giving up my body to be able to enter another zone of plain desire. At the same time I was only present as my body—it could be very dangerous and exciting to cruise in a dark park.

However, lately my interest has shifted more and more from what you might call "aspects of the sublime" to a more detached look at cruising space. What interests me is that we actually need areas in public space to disappear into. These areas are being used for other sorts of meetings and acts than the space was originally planned for. I also wonder how they came about and how to find them. I like to suggest to the spectator that my work could also be used in the same way, to function as such a space.

I mime when I copy and fantasise about the 'room' within the original painting. For example, I change the light, alter gazes, take away figures and/or paint the copy in a different technique from the original. However, I try at the same time to keep the original untouched—maybe innocent is a good word after all. I juxtapose my copies beside the original to show a difference. It is this gap between the two that creates the connection to history and to the different spaces.

And this points out that there might be an agreement between us about how to use space and see landscape.

Also in the *Returned* project I used this method of juxtaposition by leaving paintings made after Nicolas Poussin's *Spring or The Earthly Paradise* in what are now cruising parks. I selected those parks that have been modelled on the English Park. We know from art history that this type of park was highly influenced by the ideal landscape paintings executed by artists such as Claude Lorraine and Nicolas Poussin. The park itself is a copy. When a gay man who is cruising randomly meets my painting left there, a connection between the space of the museum and the park has been made. Both spaces sometimes host cruising or aspects of this activity. But in the park the left painting gives the spectator the opportunity to take it. He can take it out of its context and leave with it, or he can leave it as it was found.

I would like to ask you to have a look at Nicolas Poussin's *Landscape with a Snake* next time you are at the National Gallery in London. On the right side you can see a young man running into the painting—he has just witnessed the horrible scene that is being acted out on the left side of the painting. His hand is reaching out in the air (like he is touching the landscape) and his mouth is opened as if he is about to scream or as if he just has done. But this face could also be a face of desire. Also, Flora's mouth is open because she is smiling at us. The boy in *Landscape with a Snake* is like the other side of what Flora is for me. I have started to make a painting of his face. I have a good reproduction of Flora's face in a book about Renaissance paintings. I would like to put my painting, which I am painting on a panel, beside her face in this book.

This work for you excites me a lot.

Peggy:
Well there is so much to say now! First, let me just mention a very brilliant essay by Jean Laplanche and Jean-Bertrand Pontalis entitled, "Fantasy and the Origins of Sexuality". In it, they write, "Fantasy [...] is not the object of desire but its setting". Perhaps your attention to the setting on both sides of the frame—the historical setting

of the genre of landscape painting and the actual setting, the park itself, which stood in as the 'original' point of departure for landscape painting—becomes in your work the point of arrival. By placing your copies in parks, especially parks known as cruising sites, you 'return' to the scene of fantasy, the setting that first caught the painter's eye. Of all the things park and landscape design produced, paintings of them have been among the most persistent. Your 'returns' help us to see these parks and landscapes as productions of a kind of chain, a necklace of gazes, each linked to the site and sight of what was both glimpsed and missed in the 'original'. This aspect of having seen the thing and also missed it is part of what Lacan calls "the lure" of the gaze. It is what keeps us turning back. It is also related to Freud's idea that "every finding of an object [of desire] is a refinding of it", as he puts it in *Three Essays on the Theory of Sexuality*. One returns to what was in some sense incompletely seen, and in that return, one continually revisits the setting in which the in/sight hovers. Thus, part of what the genre of landscape painting allows us to see is indeed the fantasy of seeing fully, of not missing the visible itself.

This notion of the chain of seeing is surely at the heart of Poussin's *Landscape with a Snake*. It is a landscape that ripples with a series of belated sightings. The young boy running into the painting, as you put it, sees the snake too late to prevent death. And the woman toward whom he runs cannot see what he sees; she only sees the consequences for him. Behind her are two others who will soon see her distress, and to the right, some boatmen will soon turn and see the scene of reaction as well. Poussin, we might say in the language of contemporary theory, stages a drama in which the witness is forever belated, forever too late to prevent the trauma—in this case, too late to prevent death. The situation of the running boy captures the fundamental situation for the Post War spectator. No longer a direct witness to the catastrophe, the spectator is traumatised by the force of what was missed and that chain of missing reverberates across all the others adjacent to the 'original' event. The catastrophe, in other words, gains its status as 'original' event for the Post War spectator precisely because it seems to have been overlooked, unseen, in the moment of its enactment. The reverberating question of such immense blindness—how could this have happened without more people seeing it and preventing it?—constitutes the desire to return to the historical scene once more: to establish the facts, to retrieve empirical data, to preserve testimony.

This analysis is satisfying to a point. What it fails to address, however, is the supplementary details that constitute the core of Poussin's painting. The painting contains non-narrative and non-dramatic elements fundamental to the painting's lure. The blue of the sky and the water, the precision of the green leaves on the tree on the left, the white flowers against the wheat dirt of the small hill on the right— these elements produce a different kind of fantasy. The setting of the drama of belated sight is once again an elaborately beautiful pastoral scene. What, then, is the relation between the trauma of being a belated spectator, one who comes too late to prevent the catastrophe, and the calm serenity of the painting's pastoral setting? The immediate drama of belatedness is literally framed by a setting that bespeaks the possibility of timelessness. Is Poussin suggesting that the juxtaposition of two temporalities—urgent belatedness and ongoing timelessness—fuels the chain of reactions as if following a kind of natural law? In other words, the painting seems to suggest that looking entwines both the individual eye's encounter with the particularity of this scene and the history and future of other viewers' encounters with it.

Thus even at the moment of first apprehension, a sense of repetition within that encounter is also suggested. Perhaps *Springtime* continues to hold our attention because we continually need Venus to re-introduce us to Flora since we miss Spring each and every year. Something of this endless missing is at play in the space between Botticelli's and Poussin's paintings. I like the idea of including this running man's face in the painting you make for me. He helps focus something of the enigma of Flora's stillness, and the strange inanimation and vitality of her mouth and gaze.

Matts:

I would like to add something more to the painting. I don't know what yet. Maybe the answer is hidden in the background of the two paintings. I may put something behind the painting of the boy from Poussin's *Landscape with a Snake*—something you have to lift the panel to find.

I know that it is a man not a boy who is running—maybe I have called him a boy because he is also innocent, like Flora.

There is a witty play going on in these two different staged landscapes that interests me. Both paintings are filled with doubled meanings. Light and darkness are in both of them. Every time I look at the paintings the scenes are repeated. Flora meets us again and the boy runs into the painting, again and again. But always a little differently because that time has moved on for us.

Look at his right hand. I think that it looks as if it touches the landscape that is the painting.

I was in Chicago at the Art Institute to do a copy of a painting, *The Eruption of Vesuvius* by Jacques Volaire. This work became like a retreat for me: I was in the museum five hours a day, living in a hotel, looking at bad American TV, reading and taking long walks by Lake Michigan. Every day was repetition, copying the day before.

In the museum I had spectators behind my back all the time. I had to protect my working space and myself by using a radio Walkman and headphones. I was listening to the same classical radio station every day. Sometimes I looked back from my position to find a group of people looking at me and my copy. Some of them approached me to say that my copy looked exactly the same as the original painting. When I was sitting close to my work I just saw all the differences, small mistakes compared to the original painter's skills. I had to leave the painting and join the spectators at their distance to see that the copy actually looked pretty much the same as the original.

Peggy:

When you were copying the painting in Chicago, you were recollecting the previous day's painting as you repeated your brush strokes—brush strokes that were copies of his, of Volaire's. This aspect of your copying can be seen as a homage, a performance of the mimetic regard that we might think of as love. Copying can be distinguished from repetition as well; copying always involves a putative source or original—no matter how tentatively such an original is proposed. Repetition often seems to have no origin, in part because by the time consciousness of repetition occurs it is impossible to say what the first event was. Freud's axiom "every finding of an object is a re-finding of an object" captures well the psychic level of your 'returns'. Finding the landscape that gives the painting its body is always a re-finding of that landscape—inside and outside the frame of the painting itself. Therefore, by returning your paintings to natural landscapes, you acknowledge that act of re-finding; because one reason we know where we are when we are in parks is due to the history of painting that has shown us what a park is. In your 'returns', the observer is the one who literally finds the painting you re-found when you copied someone else's painting of a copy of a park.

I think also that the subject of Volaire's painting—the volcano—is telling. You say you 'retreat' into copying the painting. This retreat is a kind of burrowing in that also requires you to come away from it in order to see it. Similarly, the volcano's hole constitutes the focus of Volaire's work, but the painting also gives us all the surrounding 'scene' of that hole. I mention this because I think it is worth underlining the link between the libidinal drive within painting and the object that focuses that drive. Holes are holy. And often, as here, they are wholly busy.

ILLUSTRATIONS: MATTS LEIDERSTAM PAINTING A COPY AFTER NICOLAS POUSSIN'S *SPRING OR THE EARTHLY PARADISE*, THE LOUVRE, MARCH 1999. PHOTO: YVES BRETON
MATTS LEIDERSTAM PAINTING A COPY AFTER JACQUES–ANTOINE VOLAIRE'S *THE ERUPTION OF VESUVIUS*, THE ART INSTITUTE OF CHICAGO, JUNE, 2000. PHOTO: ROBERT LIFSON

Matts:

When I am copying in a museum, I am looking at the painting and the spectator is looking at me looking. To see someone copy in a museum is something we can relate to—it's something we expect to see when we walk into such institutions, even though it is rarely part of most artists' education anymore. But this is culturally specific. Once I made a copy of an English sport picture in South Africa, at the National Museum of Cape Town. Here I also worked at the opening of the show I was part of. The spectators came much closer to me—they asked different types of questions—they asked me more about the difference between my copy and the original. Here I became an image of something different and unknown, in contrast to my experience in Chicago. And when I was working in front of Nicolas Poussin's *Spring or The Earthly Paradise* at the Louvre in Paris two years ago, I became even part of an 'army' of amateur painters copying in nearly every corner of the museum.

Also when we are in the park we are looking at the image of the landscape and at the people we are meeting. These places are made for looking. And, yes, I agree, holes are holy. In eighteenth century parks (I return to this site and images again, and again) one could often find grottoes, and other wonders (holes) to enter. The image of Paradise needs to have unknown areas, a corner or two where one can find an entrance to the infernal regions.

Note

1. Simon Schama, *Landscape and Memory*, New York: Vintage Books, 1995, p. 517.

—Landscapes are connected to ideological projections, to desire, so how can we then describe Nothern landscapes and their evasive light without revealing ourselves? Should we proceed metaphorically, or seek a more down to earth, descriptive approach? Each viewpoint limits the view and determines the outlook. Each viewpoint sorts, fragments, and indicates a genealogy. There is no way to achieve a comprehensive and completely truthful description of the landscape and its tradtions. All we have at our disposal is a number of ideological and intentional positions and perspectives. We cannot separate the landscape from its histories, and our intentionalities inescapably merge with the specifics of the landscape, as is known from art historical categories such as landscape painting and land art.

—Maybe the time has come to think of location and tradition not only in terms of a identity of place, but also in terms of functionality, as suggested by James Meyer, who, in "The Functional Site", has outlined a difference between a literal and a functional site. The former implies an artistic, formal and sculptural understanding and intervention, while the other "may or may not incoporate a physical place; it certainly does not privilege this place. Rather, it is a process, an operation occuring between sites, a mapping of institutional and discursive filiations and the bodies between them."[1] Thus it becomes the responsibility of the artist not only to privilege the place, but also to problematise it, not least in its relation to other places and more or less accepted and understood regulations and legislation surrounding these places.

—One must ask when the traditional becomes the reactionary—places and assumptions about them not only supply and condition identity, but also restrict and hinder (other) identities. To be placed is also to be bound, and sometimes trapped.

Note

1. James Meyer, "The Functional Site", *Platzwechsel*, eds., Bernhard Bürgi and Bettina Marbach, Zürich: Kunsthalle Zürich, 1995, p. 27.

The Great Indoors

As Henry Lefebvre has noted in the introduction of his seminal book *The Production of Space*, it is not long ago that the notion "space" was understood in a strictly geometrical sense, and it is perhaps only recently that we have come to recognise spatial organisation as socially and technologically produced and thus ideological. Along with the implementation of institutional critiques' ideological analysis of the art space and a contextually critically engaged art practice during the late 1980s and through the 90s, many artists have extended those discourses to an investigation of spaces other than those exclusively of art. This interest not only suggests a usage of art (and the theories that goe along with it) as merely instrumental, but also explores our surroundings as informed by the notion of *staging*: Not 'staged' as in illusory, hollow or untrue, but quite the opposite: 'staged' as in the setting according to which our thoughts and actions make sense. Ideas of space, then, territories, borders, walls, doors, etc., not only recognise space as something constructed, but also as something that produces us, our behavior and understanding of each other. Thus, space is understood not only as a passive backdrop, but as a certain produced and producing technique for administration and control, in which, as we will see, it is, however, possible to insert personal narrations and fantasies. Lefebvre suggested that the moving about inside spaces and from spaces to spaces, could be characterised as "writing", a narration of movements and stops, usages and abuses of rooms, maintaining and deconstructing different consensus around those spaces.

A major consensus regarding the usages of spaces, is, obviously, the distinction between private and public spaces. "A man's home is his castle", as a popular saying goes, whereas, on another note, Virginia Woolf, in *A Room of One's Own,* articulated the need for a "private room", a room in which a woman can "be herself" as well as a room which is respected as hers, in order to be recognised and accepted as a 'whole' subject. A parallel to this notion can be found in the Nordic welfare states in which a room of one's own plays an important part: there is—ideally—an room of one's own for everyone. The "private" room—*my* room—is not only a place one occupies, but also a place one territorialises. In the private room certain actions and reveries can take place. For instance, teenagers retreat to their room, alone or with friends, and here a semi-exclusive zone is set up. It is in this zone that ideas and ideals of love, life, work, etc., take place (as well as artistic dreams). The room exists as a sort of fantasy space, a room for projections: a scenic space. This idea of the room as scenario, of the fiction and placement of privacy in regards to society, plays an important part in the many art installations of specific rooms, be it transformation of given spaces, the appropriation of spatial functions or the staging of personal, ficticious spaces.

In "The Mess of Life" Henriette Heise investigates different historic houses and the theories *and* practices spatially inherent in their construction. She walks us through different interiors and their stories, from the modernist to the mass-murderous. Katya Sander follows close behind with her essay "The Private Eye—Possible Clues for an Investigation", where she traces the history of modern interiors through the private detective in his search for clues, a search that finds it parallels in the psychoanalyst's investigation as well as in the contemporary marketing researcher's identification and location of desire. In "A Table, Which Might Not Be Understood as Clean in Modern Terms", Jakob Jakobsen instead goes through the trash, and investigates how trash is culturally defined, and can thus be redfined, as is the case in his construction of furniture made from discarded materials found in the streets of London.

Moving the gaze on objects of interiors even further back in history, we find Jan Hietala's tale of the opening of the ancient grave of Tutan-kha-men, entitled "The Gaze of Howard Carter". An opening of the grave and ensuing Egyptology that coincides with the advent of modernism, and that can seen as emblematic for not only the colonial gaze, but also as an allegory for the mind and the work of the modern artist. And, perhaps, for the spectatorship involved in modern art. Spectatorship and spatiality in contemporary art are the topic of Christine Melchiors' and Frans Jacobi's texts, both of which are statements on their own art practices revolving around the installation of scenarios, or rooms. In "The Flows of Intimacy", Melchiors writes on her efforts to establish a sense of intimacy between the room and the spectator. Following this idea, Jacobi writes about "the open work" as coined by Umberto Eco, and relates this notion to possibilities of working with scenarios for undefined actions and emotions, rather than finished works. He tries to define spaces that are ambient and that can evoke subjective, emotive responses and readings for the viewers/visitors. Last we get to follow Kerstin Bergendal and Eva Löfdahl in their continous correspondence on art and space, in their ongoing text project *Chamber Play*. The two sculptors/installation artists discuss and outline their concept of a chamber, and the identity involved in it through the objects inside it and its general spatial organisation. Theirs is a proposal for a possible space.

Red House

A "small palace of art of my own" was what William Morris called his house—the Red House—in Bexleyheath, Kent. He presumably conceived the idea to build it during a boating trip in France. He was rowing down the Seine together with his friends Charles Faulkner and Philip Webb. The latter was to be the architect of the Red House. At about the same time William Morris was toying with the idea of forming a brotherhood; an association of artists/designers/craftsmen, in which the work of mind, eye and hand would play complementary parts. The idea of building a house seemed to Morris to be a good combination of his need for a family home for himself and his wife Jane Burden and a place for the brotherhood to develop. He wanted to recreate a creative idyll—"very medieval in spirit", as he put it himself. To Morris the industrial revolution had made the present an unfair and cluttered place, so instead he pursued an idealised dream of medieval society and its products.

Jane and William Morris moved into the Red House at the end of the summer of 1860. The house was constructed of warm red brick and built in the middle of an orchard. As mentioned, Philip Webb was the architect of the house, but there is good reason to believe that Morris had a lot to say in the design of the house. One of the important driving forces behind Morris's creativity was a feeling of necessity. He thought it impossible to find appropriate furniture for the house, so he and the brotherhood set out to design the furniture and interior themselves. Morris's first biographer, J W Mackail recorded that "not a chair or table, or a bed; not a cloth or paper hanging for the walls; nor a curtain nor a candlestick; nor a jug to hold wine or a glass to drink it out of, but had to be re-invented". At the weekends the friends would arrive by train at Abbey Wood Station. They were then transported to the house by a wagonette designed by Philip Webb (to the amusement of some of the locals who thought they were the advance guard of a travelling show). The weekend visits became working parties—Webb designed most of the furniture with Edward Burne-Jones and Dante Gabriel Rossetti painting the furniture, glass and tiles. Morris designed flower patterns for the ceiling and murals for the walls, and the mathematician Faulkner painted the house's geometrical ceiling patterns, which were pricked out in the wet plaster. Jane and her sister embroidered the wall hangings in wool after Morris's design. Through this work the brotherhood became the firm Morris, Marshall, Faulkner and Co.—Fine Art Workmen in Painting, Carving, Furniture, and the Metals.

Lilla Hyttnäs

"Painters! Build your own houses—if you haven't had your imagination spoiled by endless studies of monuments", wrote the Swedish artist Carl Larsson in a letter to a friend in Sweden during a visit to Amsterdam in 1889. He was very engaged in "the burning question of the artist's new role as an all-around artist". Ten years later he published the illustrated book *A Home*. In it he portrays his own house as an ideal home and as part of a vision for a whole way of life. In colour reproductions of watercolours he showed his family and the house room by room.

Carl Larsson had met the Swedish artist Karin Bergö in France and they married in Stockholm in 1883. After living in France for a while, where Karin gave birth to their first child Susanne, the Larssons moved back to Sweden in 1885. In 1888 Karin's parents gave them the property of Lilla Hyttnäs in the village of Sundborn. In the beginning they used the house as a summer retreat, but in 1901 they left Stockholm to settle at Lilla Hyttnäs permanently. When Karin and Carl took over the house it was a quite small and rather plain old house, but during the years of 1890 to 1912 they designed and built several extensions to it. This was done without the help of a designer or architect and for the execution of the building work they relied entirely on local labour. During this process the house became considerably larger with a studio, a library and room for Karin and Carl's seven children and two maids. The Larssons decorated everything and anything in and outside the house in a pluralistic style, inspired by such different sources as Japanese drawings and patterns, Swedish folk art, English Arts and Crafts and eighteenth century Gustavian style. Some of the furniture was designed by Karin, others were antiques or simple old furniture painted in white or brightly coloured paint. Carl decorated the walls with portraits and patterns and Karin embroidered textiles for cushion covers, curtains, tablecloths, etc.. Lilla Hyttnäs was more than just design and architecture; it was a whole way of life that the Larssons consciously created. The many visiting friends, who were invited, took part in acting out the idyll of a healthy country life.

Rietveld Schröder Huis

Truus Schröder was discontent with the bourgeois lifestyle that she shared with her husband—a lawyer in Utrecht. She wanted to live a new kind of life. She asked Gerrit Rietveld to redesign the interior of her studio, which was part of the apartment she and her husband and three children lived in. At this time Rietveld was working as a furniture maker. By redesigning the interior, Frau Schröder believed she was restructuring the life that could be led within its interior. She wanted a room of her own—something she clearly felt she needed to be able to do so as to develop herself in an untrammelled way. Her husband died in 1923 and it was necessary for her to leave their apartment. First she wanted Rietveld to remodel an existing house, but they couldn't find anything suitable so she decided to build a new house. It had to be modest and inexpensive and at the same time Truus Schröder wanted the house to be a statement of intent of a new and modern life for her and her children. The house was built on the outskirts of Utrecht in 1924. It was Rietveld's first commission as an architect. In reality Rietveld and Schröder were joint designers, they worked on the house and much of the equipment and built-in furniture together. On the first floor Schröder insisted on sliding and folding partitions that would create separate rooms for her and the children. When more space was needed, the walls could be folded away. Another thing she wanted was a washbasin in every room. Most of the furniture was designed by Rietveld. Furniture and walls were coloured with the use of the three primary colours, white and neutral grey. The same colours were used for the vinyl on the floor. Truus Schröder and her children lived in the house from 1924, but she and Rietveld kept changing details of the house and the interior.

Rietveld once said that as a prototype for a new way of living, the house clearly placed enormous demands on its occupant and he believed that only Truus Schröder could live in the house. She later said he was probably right—living in the house for 58 years had taught her a lot and had given her considerable joy, but sometimes she felt that she couldn't live in the house the way she felt she ought to. In the late 50s the house became famous and had a lot of visitors. They were always welcome, but Truus Schröder didn't like it if they came unannounced—the place could be too untidy. She understood her own dilemma and said: "The mess of life. Nothing you can do about it."

25 Cromwell Street

Fred and Rosemary West moved to 25 Cromwell Street in 1972. They bought the house cheaply from Frank Zygmunt, who Fred worked for as a handyman. Frank had decided to look after them, so he helped them get a mortgage. This house became Fred's most precious possession, he worked on it whenever he had the time; digging, rewiring, building extensions, demolishing, replumbing, painting, decorating. It became a constant building site for 20 years. The Wests used every extra penny on the house and if they couldn't afford the materials, Fred drove around in the night and stole them. He really loved that house. Sometimes he sat on the wall outside and waited for somebody to walk by. He would then invite them on a tour of the house, and would be very pleased when they said it was a nice house. He had two plaques made, one for the external wall of the house: "25 Cromwell Street", and one for his wife's bed: "cunt". The cellar was his favourite spot. He had all sorts of ideas of what he could use it for: parties, orgies, a dungeon. When he and Rosemary took possession of the house in 1972 the cellar filled up with subterranean water and sewage. This gave Fred an excuse to stay there for hours or for whole days. Another room he was very attached to was Rose's room, where she had sex with other men. He had decorated the room himself and had made a small hole, through which he could look at Rose and her customers. Fred was already a murderer when they moved into the house. During the years at 25 Cromwell Street, he and Rosemary mutilated and killed several women and young girls, burying them under the bathroom extension, in the cellar, under the concrete in the garden. No. 25 was demolished a few years ago and only the cellar remains under the pavement.

Previously published in Infotainment, *1998*

The Private Eye —Possible Clues for an Investigation

"Oh... well... I am so sorry to bother you like this, but there's just one more thing..."

Seemingly at random and with no sense of direction, Columbo shuffles round the scene of the crime, visits friends and relatives of the involved and suspected, looking for possible motives. He chats, laughs, forgets, stumbles, makes detours, overlook and doesn't notice. Or so it seems. As we have learned from numerous episodes, Columbo shouldn't be underestimated. His eyes might seem easily distracted by glimmer and surface, and his mind appears slightly unsharp and unfocused. But at every end we know that he was bluffing and only pretended to be taken over by the rooms he visited; convinced by their appearance, reassured by their order, impressed by their luxury or embraced by their comfort. In the end we learn that his gaze was never resting; even the most minute detail did not escape registration. We learn that whenever he entered someone's room, his attentive eye was already scanning the interior down to the smallest detail while he pretended not to know even his way out. Watching Columbo perform his duty we follow in his footsteps (along with the camera) and we can try to guess at the direction of his gaze as it passes through the rooms, never bothered by the misguiding stories of their inhabitants: Only facts, objectivity and the cool, appraising gaze can find a way through the chaos of clues and everything else, and map them correctly in relation to each other. We learn that one object is never alone. Intentions are never far away, they cling to it, are invested in it, they order it, or they hide behind it.

For Columbo—and his colleagues in the genre—none of the everyday objects, their use or their position is insignificant. Columbo can make everything make sense. And precisely what apparently doesn't make sense, the details the rest of us have long since overlooked, are the things he is looking for. For it is almost without doubt here, in this seemingly innocent mess of life and surface normality, that the story as we know it must be changed and the events revised; it is through the careful and correct reading of these scattered lacunae and blind spots that we can gradually unravel the True Story: the story that on the one hand can explain the clues and retrospectively connect them into a single line of action, and on the other explain all the tangled, misleading explanations those involved have given, not to mention all the misleading traces in their wake.

Following Columbo in his efforts as they unfold on the TV screen reminds me of how the detective reads the rooms he travels through as if they were mindscapes, spaces with hidden corners and secret doors; forgotten deeds and well hidden events. It is within the logic of these rooms, behind heavy curtains and boxes hidden away at the back of old dressers, that the True Story lies concealed. So true, that it is perhaps not fully known even to the perpetrator.

In the innermost rooms

"To live is to leave traces", as the German philosopher Walter Benjamin remarked in connection with his studies of the bourgeoisie of the nineteenth century. Benjamin also wrote about the interiors of this period, about how "a surplus of coverings and protections, linings and encasings, wrappings and boxes grow together in the furnishing arrangements, on which the traces from the use of everyday objects can also be felt."[1] It is from amidst this manifold landscape of spaces within spaces within spaces, and from the contents of these spaces, their intertwinings and compactions, attempting to keep certain things apart from one another and others together, as well as from the interests to which their arrangement testifies, that the detective story arises and draws its sustenance. The early detective was born at the end of the nineteenth century from the ambivalent interior of the rising bourgeoisie, the variegated enfoldings, meanings and narrative potentials of these particular spaces.

    It is among the circles of gentlemen and cultivated citizens, for example, that Holmes and Watson move, and it is behind these peoples' closed doors, exclusive parlours and private chambers, that the two tireless investigators find their clues and evidence. From the same spacious interior of the bourgeoisie, the young Doctor Freud earns his living treating hysterical women, with a particular interest in these 'maladjusted' women's apparently incoherent dreams and messy narratives.[2] Freud, too, gets the idea that there is an 'interior' where the clues—if correctly decoded—can lead to the Story which, like a key, can explain all the other obscure actions and narrations into which these women spin themselves.[3] It is the idea that within the human being—as if in a continous mirroring of the outside—there are forever more rooms, and that an expert review of these rooms with attention to even the apparently most random traces, can lead to a different mapping of them: to a True narrative that lies behind all the other temporary stories; behind layers of drapes, doors and screens, hidden away and repressed in an attempt to avoid that which causes the story: the crime.

Clues from a story—out into the light

The rooms through which the detective story moves must similarly be constructed around a special story: there must be certain motives for them, they must be arranged around certain interests and inclinations. The rooms not only contain their inhabitants and trespassers stories hidden within them, they are also themselves clues to a story. The architectural theorist Beatriz Colomina has asked—since to every detective story there is an interior—whether one could write a "detective story of the interior".[4] It would be a story that snoops around in the hope of exposing some of the mechanisms that have produced the spaces and demarcations, these 'insides', 'outsides' and 'in-betweens'.

At the beginning of the twentieth century many architects tried to get away from the claustrophobic parlours of the bourgeoisie. The ambivalent and multi-faceted rooms with their thick curtains and stories of varying veracity were quite simply to be abolished. The aim was a 'truer' and 'purer' architecture whose immaculate honesty would first and foremost endure by virtue of the unraveling of hidden insides: the interior—the exclusive recesses of the rooms—was to be exposed and turned inside out. Large window sections and glass areas were not only to bring more light into the dark rooms, but also to a great extent allow the rooms to merge more with the surroundings outside. Pure, clear, white walls and simple geometrical forms recurred both indoors and outdoors, as if those were one and the same thing; as if there were no interspaces, no hidden chambers or hollow walls, no 'inside', only various degrees of 'outside'. As if by overcoming these interiors as such one could avoid the ambivalent stories they contained. As if it was solely the setting; the mere possibility of these narratives that caused them.

Discreetly I keep on shadowing the detective himself, from his first stirrings in the dim parlours of the turn of the last century to his way out of these. For, as we know, no matter how hard it tried, modern architecture has not yet succeeded in putting the detective out of a job. The modernists' plan to unravel the interior, to let it merge wholly or partially with the exterior, coincided with an extension rather than a restriction of the detective's field of activity. From the film noir of the 40s and 50s on, the urban space became an equally important—if not the most important—ingredient in the staging of the detective tale. Now the detective finds the revealing clues by following people and deciphering their movements through the city, staking out their homes from the street, waiting outside or in a building opposite, driving in cars, or hanging out at the suspects' local bars. The city takes over the role as the 'interior' stage over which the tracks of the narrative run and—not least—against which the subject (especially the dubious one) plays his or her role. Now it is the space of the city that is sifted for information and clues; indeed sometimes it almost seems as if it is this space itself, the city space, that creates its perpetrators.

The settings of film noir were not the cleaned up, well lit city of which some architects dreamed, but a city in the grip of the sprawling revisions of industrialisation. Separate spaces for production, distribution, traffic, consumption, and reproduction were defined and sometimes built up from scratch, while at other times—more often— these were imposed on an older city structure, whose existing spatial mechanisms, of course, resisted this: local interference, displacements, exceptions and overlappings were inevitable.

And indeed it was in the resistance to and the negotiations of these territorial systems that the inter-zones between the areas arose: behind the factory, on the street at night, down by the harbour in the fog, between waiting freight trains in the railroad yard.... It is in the blurring and erasures of the well-defined functions and ordering principles of the spaces that actions become suspect.

The Private Eye

As the spaces of the city became the new ambivalent interior of the detective story, the borderlines of the spatial categories of the traditional bourgeoisie began to crumble and were penetrated by the different territorialisations of other social spheres. The title of the "private detective" now seemed to refer to the very fact that he no longer represented an overall moral interest (truth and justice) but was engaged by a succession of employers with special personal interests and motives. Even the detective's right to invade and therefore transcend the various spatial categories became doubtful. From being a servant of justice he became an unshaven 'snooper' and 'the truth' was first and foremost his own. The 'public' in whose interest he should be acting was increasingly hard to define, as was its morality. The Private Eye was no longer objectively scanning, but now became a hired gaze entangled in it's own personal agendas as well as those of the customers—a gaze just as ambivalent as the city it frequents. Again the question arises: is it the detective himself who not only unravels the story but creates it, simply by his agency in these ambivalent spaces? And is it the spaces in which he moves that produces his gaze?

Different segments—different cities

Out of this idea of a modern, functionally subdivided city, a whole new form of urbanity arose: the growing middle class moved away and instead tried to define a different urban space—or perhaps rather an *anti*-urban space: the suburb. One very important relation for the suburban area was that there, contrary to the heterogenity of urban city space, was no mistaking the spatial definition in the way these spaces were articulated. The boundaries were strictly demarcated and unequivocal as to prevent any kind of 'interzones' arising, no areas open to interpretation, and thus no subsequent negotiation of them. This conception of space can still be read today from the overall planning of suburban projects: areas of detached and semi-detached houses do not give much emphasis to the signs and qualities of the traditional public spaces: there are rarely squares, market places or high streets and often there is not even a pavement— instead there are well-trimmed lawns all the way out to the road. The dense hedges, fences, bushes and flower-beds meant to keep the gaze of the outsider effectively outside are indicative of the view of 'the public' held in these urban spaces: there should preferably be none at all. 'The public' is somewhere else. The suburban space is conceived as the totality of a uniform set of small, private plots and not, like the city, a variegated space with intervowen functions and territorial discourses. The function of the suburban area as a spatial category is to be the 'private' sphere, on a mass scale.

Unlike modernism's dissolution of the interior in favour of different degrees of 'outside', the logic of these middle class suburbs seems to be the dissolution of the exterior in favour of various degrees of 'inside'. In the suburban landscape it becomes clear how the spatial system in itself provides a way of seeing: a special discourse that includes certain phenomena and effectively draws attention to those who fall outside them. The system of the suburban space is a tool of surveillance that screens off the elements it contains, and whose efficiency is zealously maintained by its inhabitants.

If, all the same, we sneak into one of these suburban houses, an interesting kind of spatial organisation emerges inside it: the functionally sub-divided urban plan, whose many partitionings, among other things, defined the suburb as a special space for "freedom, leisure and family" (reproduction), extends all the way into the interior of the single family house itself. As in a microcosmic reflection of the spatial system of the ideal city, each of the activities and functions of the private home is also partitioned off into its own space. The living room is the public space of this, the hallway its main street, from which all traffic is distributed rationally to the various separate rooms, which are rarely directly connected with one another, but lie as isolated cells along the traffic artery. And just as the space of the suburb is itself the parcelled-out private "freedom" cell of the urban machine, "work" and "leisure time" are also separated out within this home's own walls: kitchen, bathroom, wet room and back garden—the "workrooms" are hidden away; and front garden, living room and terrace—the representational "leisure rooms", are emphasised. (A paradox for the full-time housewife of the early suburban ideal: Her work thus consisted of perpetuating this idea of the house as the work-free space—in other words denying her own function.)

The mirror in the living room

The detective story is no longer watched on the big screen, but at home from the sofa, through the TV's "window on the world". Concurrently with the spread of the suburbs—in the 60s and 70s—the detective too underwent certain important transformations. First and foremost—especially in the USA, but later also in Europe—cop flicks became popular: never-ending series where we follow the police in their everyday work: their precinct, their colleagues, the daily crimes small and great. The detective is no longer the "private eye" but part of the police force in the service of the public. While his work is now governed by the justice of the system (and, often it seems, in spite of its unjust dispositions), the stories have no end—indeed the investigative work isn't that which is most important any longer, it's the detective himself that is—his personality and private story become pivotal. Hill and Renko, Simone and Sipowicz. The detective becomes an ordinary person with ordinary and not particularly enigmatic qualities. He becomes a person whose narrative consists of routinely investing his subject in the maintenance of the spaces around him, as well as can be done, however messy this may be. Just like ourselves. In the same way as the spaces of our private homes reflect the ideal organisation of a functional city, the matt glass of the TV screen seems to provide an axis for a reflection of ourselves within these homes.

Meanwhile, the windows of the suburban house also turn out towards our own world: unlike the idea of modernism's window surface, the terrace door does not open from the suburban family living room onto the surrounding 'outside' world, but rather out to equally private gardens, driveways, garages and flower beds.

The adman

Recently, on Danish TV, a very popular programme consisted in having a market researcher from a big advertising company in the studio, and a camera crew outside "on location". The viewers could volunteer to open their houses to the camera crew while they were not home. The adman would then impress us by sitting in the studio and from there solely through the eye of the camera excel in giving us exact characterisations of the occupants of the interior. Viewers, both at home in front of the TV as well as in the studio, were quite overwhelmed by all these Truths seemingly lying around in the form of old newspapers, unwashed dishes, paper bags and unmatching socks. These objects all seemed to be signs that were apparently easily interpreted by the expert gaze; signs and clues that reveal our identity, our 'innermost' being, to a degree we were hardly aware of ourselves. The audience shuddered with pleasure.

Of course, now this 'innermost' nature detected by the adman is not quite the same as the one Freud was working on putting into language, though the rhetorics of the show didn't seem to distinguish between them. What should not be overlooked is that the 'special knowledge' identifying the subject was here the expertise of the adman. It was his analysis that was being discussed, and his statements about how identity is "revealed by the interior"—as he put it—that were presented as being the closest we can get to the Truth today. But here too the detective himself and the logic of his gaze reveals more than his analysis: he is a market researcher, and thus we are first and foremost—and "deep within" (via the spaces we inhabit, it seems)—always already defined as consumers. Our inner spaces are not examined for clues to a crime in the traditional sense, but for clues to consumption. (Here, our being, in all its imperfection and impermanence, is in itself already an unfortunate crime). And we are identified not only through the purchases we have already made, but also with a view to the next one. Under these eyes, our home is not the private space and secure refuge that the modern urban system at first seemed to suggest; the space where "we can be ourselves"; but rather precisely the place that most of all identifies us in a system of capital. Our 'inside' is an interior whose story places us within a certain market segment and defines us as a certain target group.

The adman does not move around himself in the space he examines, but observes it from the placeless interior of the TV studio—an interior whose inside is a staged double in many senses: It is furnished as a "public home" (or a "homely public"); a comfortable couch and a coffee table arranged towards the audience in the studio as well as towards the cameras, mirroring our own homes and living rooms as we watch the programme. Like ourselves, the hosts and the visitors sit in front of the screens (constituted by resepctively the cameras and the TVs) reflecting each other. Our home is not only where we actually sit and watch, but also a generalised (normalised?) image which suggests to mirror our 'private' interior, addressing us through its spatial definition.

The outside of the TV studio (its backstage and surroundings) is of course never revealed. Thus, while talking about and addressing "insides", the marketing reseacher does not seem to articulate or speak from an own "inside" but rather a layer internalised "outsides". It seems as if "inside" becomes the very story we are told; the one we want to hear, again and again.

Like watching Columbo we can take on the expert gaze and search for something that doesn't fit, the blind spot or the little thing that is missing to make a story. And—along with a mutation of Freud's theories—the hopes for this story—if it is the True one, that is—is that it can solve the 'crime' or reveal the 'trauma': the hopeless repetition of everyday life, the bodies that bump into things and don't seem to fit as objects in these interiors, those unarticulated desires that don't find their corresponding rooms in the layout, and the fantasies that don't seem to make sense in these landscapes. Perhaps the hysteria of the maladjusted women whose bodies spoke about the pain and pressure they couldn't express consciously, but put into language in another way, can be used metaphorically: then maybe the repetetive buying which we are constantly encouraged to increase in order to maintain ourselves as valuable 'subjects' with healthy 'insides' can be seen as a hysterical symptom, a repetitive action suggested, promoted and articulated as the only way to express oneself in these spaces; of putting oneself into laguage.

Consumer culture and specatacle

The interest of market research articulates the subject as a space, an externalised interior which constitutes a certain system for ordering its objects (amongst others the body!) and their relations. The subject becomes a stage on which different spectacles about identity and desire can be set and watched. In capitalist consumer culture and the power of commercial address in this culture (due to number, size and colours) this has become not only the language of marketing but consequently also the language in which we are most often addressed, as well as the language in which we are encouraged to articulate ourselves. To quote Judith Butler:

> ... to be addressed is not merely to be recognised for what one already is, but to have the very term conferred by which the recognition of existence becomes possible. One comes to "exist" by virtue of this fundamental dependency on the address of the Other. One "exists" not only by virtue of being recognized, but, in a prior sense, by being recognisable.[5]

The address of commercials does however never seem to identify or reveal the Other: the voice never seems to have a face (apart from that of the model or the huge letters or the cute comic figure), it never seems to speak from a location and an identifiable space, but rather suggest that it exists only in its speaking to identifiable spaces, coming into existence as we hear it, identifying us and our different desires according to the different spaces we inhabit. It is a voice that always tells us about the objects and their place in our interiors; where they miss, where they should be, where they are too many and where they don't fit. Its address seems to be able to map out rooms we didn't even know existed, and fill them with objects, clues, traces and proofs of life which we hadn't even thought of. It narrates us onto a map which we will never be able to fully overlook and take charge of ourselves. It appears to speak with a knowledge we don't have—a subject who already knows—into which we can project our hopes for finding the one True Story; and thus finally be revealed as the perpetrator or cured of the trauma.

The Focus Room
A focus room consists of a simple but particular architectural system which divides a room into two by a large one-way mirror. On one side of the mirror the space is very well lit. There is a round table with chairs, maybe a few flowers, and generally the kind of requisites needed for constructing this certain kind of 'neutral' homeliness. There are also discrete microphones in the ceiling, often barely visible. The wall that is a mirror reflects the setup. In the other half of the room, behind the mirror, is a darkened, soundproof environment with single desks facing the window and discrete little reading lamps, facilitating note taking without the light beeing seen through the mirror. People in this room can survey and discuss the group sitting round the table without being seen or heard by them.

Focus rooms are hired on an hourly basis by companies who select and invite a group of people whose profile matches that of the target group in which they are interested. The people invited sit round the brightly lit table and are encouraged to talk about the various items the company seeks their opinions on. Sometimes the members of the group are told which companies have invited them, but most often not, since many people in focus groups seem to be so flattered by the sudden attention, that they might speak more positively about their hosts than they would normally. And for the company behind the mirror it is important to get "reality—direct and uncensured from the customer to you" as one advertisement for a focus room explains to its clients. The ad continues: "Be a fly on the wall, get familiar with your customers 1:1, directly, informally and in their own environment". Of course those who are being observed and studied are individuals invited because of their 'profiles' which again are defined in terms of market segments. Behind the mirror the firm's representatives are listening, observing and analysing what is being said about their products.

I am invited to join a focus group and I accept. The focus room is a space that in many ways resembles that of my TV: it also mirrors my home, my small talk with friends, my thoughts about everyday life and objects, my way of maintaining the order around me, investing my subject in my surroundings. I am also suddenly the protagonist as well as the subject under inspection. Both very exciting.

When the company hires a room they can also hire a detective in charge, hired by someone, a 'host' or a moderator leading me—the guest—through the many and confusing objects, helping me to make sense of them on my way—or rather helping my chaotic, unstructured and unscripted comments make sense in the framework I am subjected to. The moderator is the person in charge of the framing, someone who knows more than I do about the 'plot', about what is behind the stage sets, what interests are at play and what eyes are watching me as well as how I can make sense to those eyes; become somebody worth reading, somebody for whom I have a voice and a language. It is also the moderator who afterwards analyses my utterances and suggests what actions the company should take in order to address me better. While engaged in discussion of the various topics the moderator suggests (only she/he knowing what interest the people behind the mirror) I can survey myself in the mirror; it is huge as a movie screen, a whole wall, and I can see myself as I must look from behind the screen, as I am seen by my hosts. I can monitor, evaluate and assess myself just as the company can.

Notes

1. Walter Benjamin, "Paris, Capital of the Nineteenth Century", *Reflections*, New York: Schocken Books, 1986, pp. 155-156.

2. Gertrud Sandqvist, "Out of the Hysteria", *Paletten* 2-3/96, nos. 225-226, vol. 57, Gothenburg.

3. Until Freud and Breuer, it had been supposed that the misbehaviour and maladjustments of these women could be explained by the displacement of their ovaries. It was supposed that some ovaries had not found their right place in the female body; some even believed that they were wandering around inside the woman, homeless and disturbing. The ovary was an object out of place, and the restless motion of this object—which was thus never to be pinned down and clearly mapped— caused the unease: the female organs were not in place and messed up the patient. It was assumed that a restoration of the internal order would resolve the external order.

Freud made the link between narration and mapping, the conquering, the pinning down of the female body, and the crisis of this story. Wanting or not wanting, he pointed at hysteria as a *displacement*, though not of the female organs themselves, but rather of the external logic inscribing these organs. ("… that external events determine the pathology of hysteria to an extent far greater than is known and recognised." Breuer/Freud, *Studies on Hysteria*, New York: Basic Books, 2000, p.4.)

4. Beatriz Colomina, "The Split Wall: Domestic Voyeurism", *Sexuality and Space*, New York: Princeton Architectural Press, 1993, p. 74.

5. Judith Butler, *Excitable Speech—A Politics of the Performative,* London: Routledge, 1997.p.5.

This text is an altered version of an article previously published in Øjeblikket—Magazine for Visual Cultures, no. 36/37, vol. 8, 1996.

ILLUSTRATIONS: PETER FALK AS COLUMBO
(NEXT PAGE) KATYA SANDER, *SAFETY DRAWING*, 2000

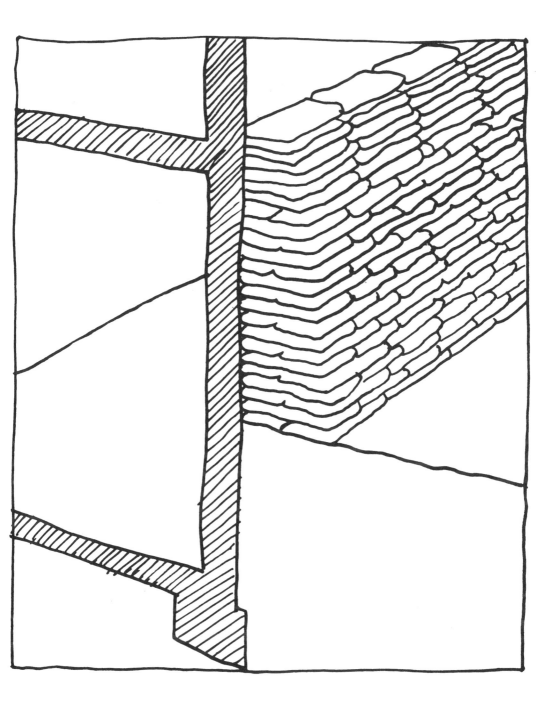

A new table, which might not be understood as clean in modern terms

For a project in a council flat/gallery (Sali Gia) in a modern block in South London I needed a table. The table was to function partly as a facility where people could sit down and read an information booklet and partly as a 'roundtable' for a series of meetings arranged as part of the project. There was not a suitable table in the flat, so I had to find one. Beyond the fact that I was interested in a functional and a somehow aesthetic piece of furniture, I was thinking in terms of economy. The spur to the project, relating to the modern environment of the block, was an analysis of the ideological space of modern architecture, city plans and object designs. Drawing upon a collage of ideas from key propagandists of heroic modernism and colliding the ideas with practices of late modern everyday life I was interested in engaging in a contemporary discussion of the 'new'. I decided that I would like to find a new table without having to buy one.

Health and hygiene were important issues for the modern pioneers and reformers. The discovery of the direct connection between germs and incidences of disease was brought forward by the French biologist Louis Pasteur *et al* around the middle of the nineteenth century. Antiseptics and an understanding of the need for keeping the operating theatres in the hospitals clean of germs were introduced in 1867 by the British surgeon Joseph Lister. These discoveries are crucial historical events, informing the analysis of the ideological background to the modern project. A scientific based division between the clean and the unclean was established. This distinction was an important part of the rationale behind the evolution of modernity, giving it a scientific base from its outset. The cholera epidemics, which caused havoc across Europe around 1850, are often said to be the main single event that spurred the hygienic shift. The disease devastated Hamburg and Paris in 1848/49 and in 1849 and 1854 respectively 53,000 and 20,000 people lost their lives in England. After the last epidemic in England the local physicist John Snow was successful in proving that polluted water was causing the spread of disease. From then on, beginning slowly due to the massive task and accelerating at the turn of the century, sanitation reforms, the centralisation of refuse collection and the layout of large landfills and waste incinerators outside the cities emerged hand-in-hand with the evolution of modern hygienic architecture.

At the end of the nineteenth century, practices of rag picking and recycling which were part of the underprivileged classes economic survival strategies, lost ground due to the new understanding of sanitation and hygiene. The scientific discovery of germs' disease causing abilities made waste into a health risk. Waste was harbouring germs. The resulting educational efforts combined with more effective systems of refuse collection removed much of the potentially disease-carrying material from the local communities. This impacted on the self-organising cultures of the trade in recycled waste which were an integrated part of urban life at the time. Rag pickers usually paid the refuse collectors to get access to the waste and they separated the usable parts and sold them on to ragmen for recycling and new production. Baudelaire described the rag picker of eighteenth century Paris as an archivist, a cataloguer who sorted through "everything the big city has cast off, everything it lost, everything it disdained, everything it broke". The leftovers from the rag picker functioned as food for pigs and chickens. Only dust and inorganic material were thrown away. These practices declined due to hygiene reforms, but traces of these cultures can be found today at car boot and junk sales.

Waste is socially defined. What is waste to one person is usable to another. There is nothing inherent to the material itself that will tell us whether or not it is waste. Waste is a quality that is imposed on various materials by a process that is wholly social. Vital for the development of the modern industrialised society was the imposition of a clear and universal definition of what is waste and what is not, and how to separate this potential threat to public health from life in the cities. A universal definition would make sure that impurities would not disturb the cycle of society, which had been upset so often before through epidemics of various diseases. Gradually waste became defined as a more or less homogeneous matter of negative value. The new definition cancelled the grey zone between waste and the usable through which rag pickers and economically underprivileged people were able to create value. Practices of recycling and creative maintenance and adaptation of objects for daily use were deemed unclean and the knowledge inherent to these practices lost ground. The doors were opened for the clean world of consumer culture.

This poses the question as to whether this modern conception of waste is just pathogenically based or whether it refers to a more fundamental system of value. If waste is socially defined and is to be understood as matter out-of-place rather than something fundamentally valueless, then a larger social system of valorisation comes into play. Generally speaking most of the modern pioneers within architecture, design and city planning were not revolutionaries in the political sense of the word. As Le Corbusier described himself, they preferred architecture to revolution. By morphological means the architects and planners overturned the old world through hygienic architecture and the health-centric environment they intended to realise. They valorised the new and the clean, as well as geometrical space and industrial production, as inseparable parts of the same package. There is no dirt in Euclidean space. But as the anthropologist Mary Douglas states: "In chasing dirt, in papering, decorating, tidying up we are not governed by anxiety to escape disease, but are positively re-ordering our environment, making it conform to an idea." This line of thought brings the whole discussion of modern waste and hygiene into a psychoanalytic field and opens readings of the treatment of waste as a practice referring to social hierarchies and symbolic systems; hierarchies and systems, hidden behind the imposed valuelessness and homogeneity of modern waste. The scientific based modern distinction between the clean and the unclean links, in various ways, the clean with the new and, generally, with life in modernity. And there is no way between life and death.

From my drifts around the streets of South London I have noticed that a considerable gap is still allowed to occur between the 'secretion' of rubbish from households and the collection of refuse. This grey zone between the private and the public space, between the household and the city is, for me, the source of a sort of unsystematic psychoanalytic gaze. The bodies of refused material mainly consisting of bin liners are frequently mixed with more or less crushed pieces of furniture. Sometimes the bin liners have been torn open and various signs of everyday practices leak onto the pavement: packaging, bits of food, sawdust, clothing, etc.. Often I have come across modern pieces of furniture dumped in the street: Marcel Breuer-style tubular steel-framed chairs or smashed up wardrobes and bookshelves made from easily cleanable melamine-laminated boards. I find it paradoxical to see these pieces of modern furniture, which were intended to manifest a new and clean world, lying as rubbish in the streets. They appear as ruins telling a story about a project which might have been an outright success, but which over time caused a series of side effects simultaneously undermining the project. The ideology of cleanness embedded in modern furniture somehow means that it shouldn't really be around disintegrating in a heap of rubbish. It should last forever.

I decided to collect pieces of melamine-laminated boards from the scrapped wardrobes and bookshelves I found in the streets. The boards could be recycled as raw material for the new table needed. In a week I had collected enough material for several tabletops. With glue I patchworked the pieces of board together into one big tabletop. It was cut into an appropriate shape with a jigsaw. Though a synthesis of dirty materials I produced a table... a new one which might not be understood as clean in modern terms.

This is a slightly edited version of a text previously published in Control Magazine no. 16, 2000 *.*

ILLUSTRATIONS: JACOB JACOBSEN

The decisive moment had arrived. With trembling hands I made a tiny breach in the upper left-hand corner. Darkness and blank space, as far as an iron testing-rod could reach showed that whatever lay beyond was empty, and not filled like the passages we had just cleared. Candle tests were applied as a precaution against possible foul gases, and then, widening the hole a little, I inserted the candle and peered in, Lord Carnarvon, Lady Evelyn and Callender standing anxiously beside me to hear the verdict. At first I could see nothing, the hot air escaping from the chamber causing the candle flame to flicker, but presently, as my eyes grew accustomed to the light, details of the room within emerged slowly from the mist, strange animals, statues, and gold—everywhere the glint of gold. For a moment— an eternity it must have seemed to the others standing by—I was struck dumb by amazement, and when Lord Carnarvon, unable to stand the suspense any longer, inquired anxiously, "Can you see anything?" it was all I could do to get out the words "Yes, wonderful things."

This is how Howard Carter describes the opening of the tomb on 26 November 1923 in his book *The Discovery of the Tomb of Tutan-kha-men*. Carter was working on commission from George Stanhope Molyneux Herbert, 5th Earl of Carnarvon. On 5 November Lord Carnarvon received a coded telegram at his family estate at Highclere Castle, and 18 days later he reached Luxor in the company of his daughter, Lady Evelyn Herbert.

Three days after the tomb was opened the official opening ceremony was performed. Not since 1323 BC had anybody breathed the air that the tomb contained. For over 3000 years it had been concealed in darkness. Like an unknown tale, yet to be told, the tomb had been hidden, secret and waiting. Something that until then had been completely unknown became in all its splendour reachable. Knowledge of a lost world was brought back to mankind.

Few phenomena have captured man's mind as have tales of lost worlds and civilisations: the Garden of Eden, Shangri-La, the continent of Sannikoff and the city of Atlantis. Myths and tales tell of valleys to which the road has been forgotten, cities that have become covered by snow, and worlds that have sunk into oceans. Western civilisation seems to rest on foundations of something lost. It's no wonder that psychology commonly refers to our subconscious, as a depth, wherein the answers of our impulses, needs and behaviour rest partly unseen, there at the bottom. With the discovery of the tomb of Tutankhamen a means of access, a key, was finally found to a lost civilisation—ancient Egypt.[1] *The Discovery of the Tomb of Tutan-kha-men* was published in three volumes between 1923 and 1933. Carter was not the author. Arthur Mace, an assistant curator at the Metropolitan Museum in New York, was appointed as co-writer. Mace was also a distant relative of Lord Carnarvon. The book is based on Carter's notes, and other sources. Due to this fact, the final version of the opening of the tomb is slightly different from what other sources claim actually happened.

According to Carter's notes, probably made on the evening of 23 November, what took place is as follows: "It was some time before one could see; the hot air escaping caused the candle to flicker, but as soon as one's eyes became accustomed to the glimmering of light, the interior of the chamber gradually loomed... with its strange and wonderful medley of extraordinary and beautiful objects. Lord Carnarvon said to me "Can you see anything?" I replied to him, "Yes, it is wonderful.""" The difference between the two texts is most obvious in the often-quoted line, a line that in the final version is altered from "Yes, it is wonderful." to "Yes, wonderful things." A third version of what was uttered on that glorious afternoon in 1923 was published in an article written for *The Times*, in which Lord Carnarvon was interviewed. Here Lord Carnarvon gives his impression of what Carter replied to his question: "Yes, there are some marvellous objects here."

Something that complicates matters even more is that the co-writer, Mace, had a third person help him write the book. Percy White, Professor of English Literature, with almost 30 novels to his credit, takes part in the process as a ghostwriter. White had recently finished a semi-autobiographical novel, *Cairo*. It is most likely that the transformation of the prosaic "Yes, it is wonderful", or according to Lord Carnarvon "Yes, there are some marvellous objects here" to the much more memorable "Yes, wonderful things" is the work of White. The complete notes of Carter to this day remained unpublished, and the version published as a document is an 'improved' and more literary one.[2] Whoever wrote *The Discovery of the Tomb of Tutan-kha-men*, the way of describing what was seen is reminiscent of a vision of something other than human. It is as if the discovered items suddenly appear in the focus of a camera lens, or even as if projected on a screen.

Carter's gaze sweeps over the objects, in the same way a camera would do in a panorama. It passes over the blurred images of gold, strange animals, statues and domestic artefacts. For a moment Carter even thinks that he is watching a wall-painting carved in relief. Then he changes focus and realises that the objects are three-dimensional. It is the flickering candlelight acting as a Laterna Magica, which strikes Carter dumb with amazement.

This experience is well known to anyone who has entered the auditorium of a cinema.

Out of the darkness something suddenly becomes visible. A moving picture takes form on the silver screen. It is as if the images on the screen were alive, and even more: in contradiction of all logic, it is as if the magic could become even stronger and more overwhelming, the more the projector light flickers, the more damaged the film's reality is.

There are several reasons for this method of description. Carter was accustomed to what at the time were regarded as the cheap thrills of the cinema, and most probably it colours his note taking. Another obvious reason is that both Carter and Lord Carnarvon had serious plans to sell the story to the film industry. In transforming Carter's notes into something already suggestive of a film sequence, a filmmaker could be encouraged to realise the cinematographic possibilities of the discovery.

But more than anything else, the way of describing what is seen and experienced is a description made by somebody who has devoted more time to pure seeing than to anything else in his life. For many years Carter had been economically dependent on what he can note with his eyes and transfer to paper. The gaze of Carter, at the moment he opens the tomb of Tutankhamen, is not the gaze of a scientist.

This is an astonishing revelation, since Carter's goal was to become an accomplished and well-respected scientist in the field of archaeology. When he wrote the notes of perhaps the greatest archaeological discovery of all time, and what he also certainly knew was historical evidence, he wrote like a creative writer, be it one ever so corrupted. In his last completed novel *The Golden Bowl*, Henry James makes a penetrating vivisection of a self-trained collector:

> Adam Verver knew, by this time, knew thoroughly; no man in Europe or in America, he privately believed, was less capable, in such estimates, of vulgar mistakes. He had never spoken of himself as infallible—it was not his way; but, apart from the natural affections, he had acquainted himself with no greater joy, of the intimate personal type, than the joy of his originally coming to feel, and all so unexpectedly, that he had in him the spirit of the connoisseur.[4]

The Golden Bowl was published 1904. It describes amongst other things, an age with a growing interest in collections, a world of museums and collectors. The description of the wealthy American collector Adam Verver could very well serve as a description of Lord Carnarvon.

Lord Carnarvon became interested in archaeology 19 years before the opening of the tomb, literally by accident. In addition to horseracing and photography, Lord

Carnarvon held a passion for motoring. He owned several expensive cars, and drove them himself. In 1903 he had a severe accident in Germany. On doctor's orders he moved to a climate said to aid convalescence. In Egypt he discovered another absorbing hobby, the excavation and collection of antiquities. By 1922 he was a well-known collector, amateur and self-trained, but nonetheless well known. He sometimes used Howard Carter as a dealer.

Carter's education was minimal. His family was poor, and he had to contribute to the family economy from an early age. This is probably the origin for the complex that would haunt him all his life, especially when he meets Egyptologists from the academic world. But he inherited something rare and precious from his father—an illustrator—an exceptional eye for detail, and the ability to draw.

In order to make a living he started to draw pets: parrots, cats and dogs. Through his work he was introduced to Lord and Lady Amherst of Hackney. Lord Amherst—a member of the Egypt Exploration Fund, and also the owner of the first mummy brought to England—helped Carter to get his first serious commission.

At the age of 17, Carter was sent to Egypt as an assistant draughtsman for the Egypt Exploration Fund. From 1891 to 1899 he worked for different employers, copying ancient works of art. In 1900 he was appointed an Inspector of Monuments for the French administered Antiquity Service. His job was to organise methods for the protection of the tombs. Later he combined this appointment with excavation work, obviously without conflict. In 1905 he started working as an art dealer and met Lord Carnarvon.

The combination of Lord Carnarvon's passion for collecting, the financial resources to do so on a large scale, and the eagerness of Carter to become famous and make a fortune, is most probably the reason for the success of their mutual dream; to find the tomb. What also united them, the aristocrat and the upstart, is the knowledge that they were both laymen. The only thing they had to rely on was their own will. Not unlike Adam Verver, in James' novel, they carried within themselves a belief that they had something unique.

The ignorance of Carter and Lord Carnarvon is probably the main reason why the mummy of the last Emperor of the eighteenth Dynasty Thutmos—Nebkheprure Tutankhamen—was so badly treated when the inner coffin was opened. In order to get some of the jewellery off his body Tutankhamen was decapitated and dismembered. The head was detached with a hot knife at the seventh cervical vertebra. With the same hot knife, the arms were also removed at the shoulders, the hands from the arms, the legs from the hips, and the feet from the legs.

In order to melt the pitch-like material that cemented the body and the golden mummy mask to the bottom of the innermost solid gold coffin, Carter also exposed Tutankhamen to the Egyptian sun for two days, in temperatures up to 65 degrees Celsius. Due to this treatment the skin of the Emperor became much darker than the first reported descriptions of a greyish colour, and the eyes collapsed. Apart from this, one ear disappeared, as well as the Emperor's penis.

Decapitated, castrated and sunburnt; could anything be more disgraceful to an Emperor? The only intact mummy of an Egyptian Pharaoh ever found was cut to pieces and scattered as if the Pharaoh had been so much offal.[3] Another ruler, of more modern antiquity, who Tutankhamen could be compared with is Vladimir Ilyitch Ulyanov (Lenin). Coincidentally, Ulyanov was embalmed only months after the discovery of Tutankhamen. In the process Ulyanov's brain was moved to one scientific centre, his skull to another, and the intestines to, well—who knows where. Immediately after the discovery an avalanche of commercial interest began to gather speed. A large-scale exploitation was planned from the very beginning. Photographer Harry Burton filmed every step of the excavation, and took the photographs that still stand as remarkable documentation of both the discovery with the content of the tomb and the brutal treatment of the Emperor. Goldwyn Picture Company Ltd developed an epic scenario from some notes by Lord Carnarvon, and The New York Times arrived to take photographs. In 1923, Hollywood director Cecil B De Mille, made the film The Ten Commandments with an Egyptian set, a theme De Mille would return to in 1934's Cleopatra.

The Tutankhamen craze touched every aspect of art and design. "Tutankhamen Rag" was played in ballrooms all over the world and luxurious interiors of Atlantic steamers were made in "Egyptian Style". Furniture, interior designs and fashion was also created. Van Cleef and Arpels made jewellery in the Egyptian Style. Lev Bakst unveiled an "Isis" collection. A perfume from Ramses of Cairo appeared on the market. This trend was apparent before the opening, but after the opening, it became fashion. Mass-production of Egyptian-styled items had begun, and the rights to the name Tutankhamen became an issue for patent lawyers.

The main difference between the 1923 to 1925 revival of Egyptian Style and the previous ones is that the new impulse came from mass media, cinema, photography and prints. Napoleon Bonaparte's expedition of 1798 and the publication of Description de l'Egypte, created a first wave of Egyptian Style, but it mostly appeared in architecture and furniture design, and did not reach wider levels of consumption. Meanwhile the actual investigation of the tomb, which took almost a decade to empty of objects, generated an enormous interest. Leading hotels in Luxor had to put up tents in their gardens. Every morning hordes of visitors crossed the Nile to watch the tomb being emptied.

The rights of ownership to the treasures were questioned. Should it be, as was the custom, divided between the Cairo Museum and Lord Carnarvon, or should it belong entirely to the Cairo Museum? The Nationalist Government was to get everything, or as mentioned earlier, everything apart from the Emperors ear and penis, on Lord Carnarvon's death. On 6 March 1923, near or in the Valley of Death, Lord Carnarvon was bitten on his left cheek by a mosquito. While shaving in his suite of rooms in the Winter Palace Hotel, he sliced the top off the small pimple which had formed and started to get inflamed, an infection developing into blood poisoning, which gave rise to pneumonia. Within a month he was dead.

The death of Lord Carnarvon, the man who initiated the search of the tomb of Tutankhamen, started the rumour of a curse, "The Curse of Tutankhamen". A few days before the opening, Carter's pet canary was killed in its cage by a cobra. Above the entrance to the tomb there was an inscription: "Death to Those who Enter". This became an omen, a prediction of Lord Carnarvon's death. Back in England Lord Carnarvon's favourite dog died at the exact moment as his master. A number of other people who had had something to do with the tomb died in strange ways.

Collectors all over England started to send their objects to the British Museum, anxious to be rid of them because of the superstition that The Kha had killed Lord Carnarvon. Only a few parcels received by the museum bore the senders' names.

In retrospect it is obvious that the casualties brought by The Kha were overestimated. Of those closest to the excavation, with the exception of Lord Carnarvon, Carter did not die until 1939, and Callender and the others, died un-dramatically. The last to die was Lady Evelyn in 1980. The average age at the time of death was 76.3 years. Prosaic reality, however, is not of any popular interest. The idea of a curse suited the image of ancient Egypt, then as now; an Egypt that has attracted European travellers, visitors, conquerors, and artists, from Herodotus to Dr Henry Kissinger.

Carter forced himself into the chamber, he penetrated it with his gaze and, piece by piece, he emptied the tomb of its secrets. When it was emptied and ceased to nourish Carter's hungry eyes, he left. What was left behind is forever devastated and gone. In this context, there was a moment worthy of comment from the opening of the tomb. The moment was brief, it passed quickly, and it could have passed unnoticed. The ostensible reason may have been the pursuit of knowledge, but just by watching, from simply moving his eyes over the objects in the tomb Carter, unconsciously or consciously, became the instigator of a process that has all the connotations of what could be described as rape. Both Carter and Lord Carnarvon, separately and in different ways, had for a moment the impression that there was something in the darkness and that that something was looking back. "If it is true that the whole world loves a lover, it is also true that either openly or secretly the world loves Romance", Lady Burghclere—Lord Carnarvon's sister—writes in her introduction to *The Discovery of the Tomb of Tutan-kha-men*. And she continues: "A story that opens like Aladdin's Cave and ends like a Greek myth of Nemesis cannot fail to capture the imagination of all men and women who, in this workaday existence, can still be moved by tales of high endeavour and unrelenting doom."

Sveaborg May 1997

Notes

1. Howard Carter and Arthur Mace, *The Discovery of the Tomb of Tutan-kha-men*, Mineola, NY: Dover Publications, 1977, (originally published in London, 1923-1933).

2. Lord Carnarvon and Howard Carter, *Five Years Exploration at Thebes*, Mansfield: Martino Publishing, 1998, (originally published in London, 1912).

3. D Forbes, *Abusing Pharaoh*, London, 1992.

4. Henry James, *The Golden Bowl*, New York: Penguin Putnam, 2001, (originally published in New York, 1904).

English language consultant Robert Connolly

ILLUSTRATION: JAN HIETELA *CORPSES FROM THE FINNISH CIVIL WAR OF 1918–67*, 1997. PENCIL DRAWING, ORIGINAL SIZE: 29,7 × 21 CM

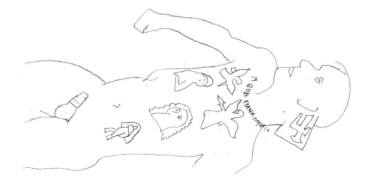

Where is Your Identity

Marc Augé, *Non-places*, 1995

1. House without Windows

White sawdust wallpaper for as far as the eye can see. Cheap grey wall-to-wall carpet and white fluorescent tubes everywhere. Walls, door openings, doors, corridors, more walls, little rooms and big rooms. A house without windows. Where is the entrance? I've been here for many hours now. First, an inquisitive attempt to orient myself. Futile. Then a longer period where I am elated and fascinated by the intricate architectonic structure. The spatial elapse is disposed in such a complicated fashion that it's almost impossible to find my way around. All the rooms look alike, only the size and the placement of the doors distinguishes them. The corridors are even worse: the cheap laminated plastic doors are completely identical and they only lead into new identical rooms or other corridors. I wander around a little, enthusiastically curious about the common aesthetics and the seemingly infinite variations on the very same simple spatial sequence. Everything is in place. My enthusiasm admittedly poses something of a paradox: it is an enthusiasm for absolute artistic consistency, even though the consequence of this particular consistency is a totally implemented lack of qualities and standpoints.

What follows now is a somewhat more confused phase. I sit myself down in one of the larger rooms and try to contemplate. Try to tune my mind to a level that corresponds to the mood in these rooms. Little by little I realise what's going on: irritation. I am unsettled by the uniformity; a notion that will not leave me alone. The lack of distinctive marks and clues is gnawing. Why don't I have something to write? I try to scratch marks where I've been and how I got there, but it's no use. By now, there are scratch marks everywhere, and I cannot recognise or distinguish one from another. The irritation grows and I have to admit that I am lost. I simply cannot find the door leading out of the house. Damn it! I sit down again and try to think the situation through. More worries. Then comes a strangely lethargic moment. Indifference sets in. I lay down on the bleak carpet in one of the smaller rooms and pretend to be asleep. It is a fragmented slumber, though: dreams about moving around in the labyrinth are combined with half-hearted attempts to wake up and figure a way out. Then, all of a sudden, a deep and dreamless sleep falls over me. Finally—rest. A long white trance. When I wake up, I have completely lost my sense of time. How long have I been in here? Why did I leave my watch in one of the other rooms? And why in the world can't I find it again? Time and place are dissolved in what has now become my perfectly diffuse consciousness. Muddled thoughts move through me in the same way as my wandering around the endless series of connected corridors and rooms; aimless. My thoughts and the surrounding spaces seems to have become one. It is as if the uniformity of the spatial structures reflects my inner monotony. It is my own self-referential confusion that prevents me from finding a way out. A loop of tedious escape attempts. Sawdust wallpaper for as far as the eye can see.

2. Six Fragments

The private is universal

There is a peculiar logic in the fact that the more private and personal a theme one presents, the more universal and easily recognisable it is to others. Of course, this is a point that mainstream culture has long since realised and made the most of. Ergo *Big Brother* and *Temptation Island*. Docu-drama. Docu-soap. In order to make any real impact, entertainment has to reveal something very private. The sphere of intimacy is invaded, and the private is bullied. The personal experience is always already public, reduced to mainstream cliché. Here, privacy means subjectivity, and subjetivity signals genuineness, 'real life', and thereby supposedly close to the viewer's trivial everyday existence—as a producible entity, a construction.

Art as identification point

The public is looking for identification. In visual art, however, instead of looking for this identification directly in the art works, as is most often the case in narrative film and literature, it is the artist himself that we identify with. The artist-myth, that is. The subjective artist. Many art works has become trademarks for this myth. They are read as statements about private life, about the artist as the extreme subject, who is living out life's problems to a further extreme than ordinary people with ordinary humdrum lives. The artist lives—supposedly—with more pleasure, more sorrow, more dejection—and more tragedy. Greater consistency, sharper thoughts. A considerable part of the indignation and thus the potential for provocation is possible because of this identification: "How can the artist allow himself to do this on our behalf?" is what a lot of indignation and dislike towards modern art seems to be saying. In this general identification with the artist lies an implementation of art as therapy—not for the artist, as is often assumed, but for the public which, through identification, has the opportunity to rehearse many different emotional modes. Therapy or affirmation.

Pleasure praxis

In the text entitled "The Poetics of the Open Work" Umberto Eco describes a type of art work which in many ways can be seen as similar to the above, with a few decisive changes though.[2] As a point of departure, Eco describes a number of musical experiments made by Stockhausen, Berio, Pousseur and Boulez. These composers were working very consciously with 'unfinished' compositions, where either the interpreter —the musician—or the listener puts together or arranges a number of sound structures. By turning the recipient into a participating protagonist in the process of creation, a new relation between artist, artwork and public is introduced. New "harmonic and concrete gathering relations".[3] Eco calls this new category of works "the open work" or "works in motion". "Motion" understood in the sense that in these cases, there is no definite conclusive artwork, but rather a successively variable quantity of equal variations, completed by different interpreters' or listeners' interventions. A field of possibilities. Eco consistently uses the word "pleasure" in connection with what it is to experience an artwork, and he demonstrates how this pleasure, the subjective experience of an artwork, has always been a part of the work's enunciation. With the appearance of the 'open work', this inherent openness has now become the central strategy and theme of art.

Proposal

A good storyteller tells his tales from the beginning to the end, as a dramatised progression in time, where the reader is guided, with a steady hand, through the phases of the story. One-way communication. For the audience, this can be spell-binding. One gets carried away; led through the universe of the narrative along a well-composed and appointed route. This is the responsibility of the narrative. The confirmation of the narrator. A dialogue, on the other hand, is more uncertain. Here, all the parties in the conversation are and complicit in the formulation of meanings. The outcome is far more unpredictable. Open. The conversation winds in different directions and a great many circumstances determine what is spoken about and with what intensity. Feelings and moods. The 'open work' has similar qualities. The meaning is found in a kind of conversation between the public, the artwork and the artist. The work is dialogic. And interactive. In France, they often use the term 'proposal' instead of 'work'. A suggestion. Etymologically, the term descends from the word for 'sketch': a temporary proposal for a work of art. But it serves as a suitable designation for the 'open' work category I am interested in. The work as a proposal for a conversation. The beginning of a story.

Improvisation

Similar improvised stories enter my own work. Partly my own improvisation, that of "the artist", in the sense that each work's idea and execution are determined in relation to their immediate context—whatever seems probable in the specific situation. And partly the spectator's improvised ideas or understandings of the fictitious relations and characters the work implies. In this fashion, the work functions as a fictionalisation of the given site. Some elements in the situation are accentuated while others are removed. Displacement. A piece of scenery. Something from a movie or a stage play. The exhibition place is turned into a potential stage, and the spectator imagines a course of action that might play itself out there. As she moves around in the scenographic tableau, she finds herself ambiguously positioned: both in the concrete exhibition building, and simultaneously in the fiction she imagines the scenery frames. As such, the work supplies a platform for the spectator's fantasies.

Identity as common fantasy

Accordingly, "The Poetics of the Open Work" could perhaps imply a more open form of expression. An expression for which potential is created in a concord between artist and spectator. Expression meant here in the sense of formulation of identity. The work offers an identification point within which the spectator not only reflects her/his own identity, but also invests it. The identity that the work expresses is therefore fictive. It is conglomerate of the artist's and the viewer's identity probings. Rendering possible a way running through a certain gamut of emotions. Identity as a game. Inasmuch as the game includes the spectator's identification with the artist, a fiction about the artist's identity is also created. The artist as a trademark for gamut of emotions. The fundamental principle, however, is still: the expressivity as a shared field of opportunity. Two minds with but a single thought?

Notes

1. Marc Auge, *Non-Places—Introduction to an Anthropology of Supermodernity*, London: Verso, 1995.

2. Umberto Eco, *The Role of the Reader—Explorations in the Semiotics of Texts*, Bloomington: Indiana University Press, 1979, p. 47.

3. Eco,.*Texts*, p.47.

Part two of this text was previously published in Øjeblikket—Magazine for Visual Cultures, no 41, vol. 9, Fall 1999.

translated by Dan A Marmorstein

The Flows of Intimacy

Experience within art is connected to experience in life. Art and life inspire each other, and the experiences of the individual subject depends on his or her sense of an own space, of intimacy. The notion of intimacy is like a spiral that—in endless shifts and displacements—turns from the central point of the subject. Intimacy is a frail line of demarcation in constant movement. In everyday life this can be traced along different boundaries: the walls of the house, the divisions between rooms, furniture, cupboards, clothes, skin.... Beyond these boundaries intimacy stretches into an immaterial, mental space. The scope of the intimate stretches from psychological depths to cultural conventions. But throughout life, however, this fragile space is continuously and simultaneously perpetuated and disturbed.

In art, I am concerned with reflections on the spaces surrounding us. I try to raise questions regarding the constructions of intimacy, and if the space of intimacy is an unfixed one, constantly in flux, then, perhaps, art (especially installation art) is placed between a "coming and going", being and becoming, closeness and distance. And as both the intimate condition and concept of art are in flux, they are also connected. Art can be seen as an intimate gesture, a communication of intimacy that is at once exposed and withdrawn in its own world. By questioning the space of intimacy I want to question art.

Personal, hand written letters are among the most immaterial things we consider intimate. The space of a piece of paper or a postcard can contain thoughts, travel descriptions, an important event or an insignificant occurrence. In this respect, personal letters constitute a multitude of smallish privatised spaces. They are moments without special significance and without a centre—at once too imprecise for statistics and too banal for history. To write to somebody is, in a way, to stretch the zone of intimacy beyond mental and physical boundaries. It is to immortalise a banal story: elevating the ordinary to something special and worthy of posterity. Catching fleeting moments of intimacy. Defining something by its surroundings.

To sense intimacy, you also have to integrate the feelings of others, their intimacy. In this respect, a work of art does not have to be the expressions of an individual, but can also be an atmosphere of the invisible presence of many subjects and objects.

Previously printed in the catalogue, Intimité, *Paris: Centre d'art contemporain, 1996.*

ILLUSTRATIONS BY CHRISTINE MELCHIORS, HABILLAGE URBAIN, LONDON 1999 INSTALLATION SHOT, CLOSE-UP, PRIVATE LETTERS CUT INTO LONG STRIPS

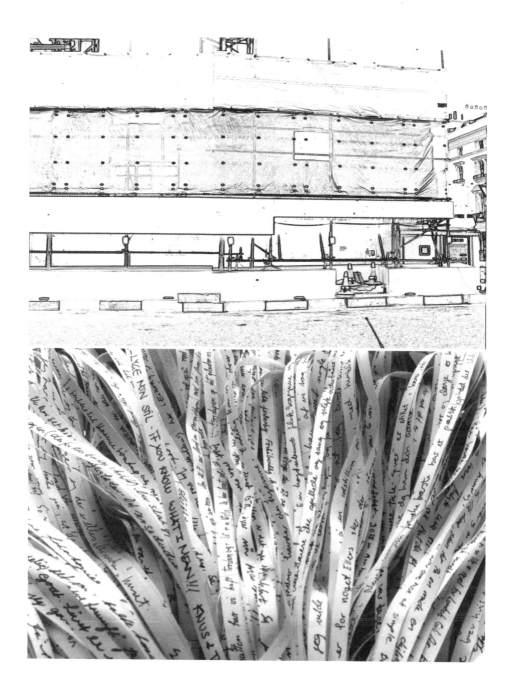

25/7/00

Dear Kerstin,

My, my, how it's raining. It never seems to stop. I started writing to you yesterday. Now, when I read your letter, I think about how what I've written will really confirm your view of things.

This is how I started:
—Here we are back again.
—One more push.
—They can't talk.
—This isn't a story.
—Filter.
—With different attitudes.
—Absolutely.
—Different natures.
—Absolutely.
—It isn't true.
—Well, it doesn't matter if you say the same thing one more time.
—The chairs stand there matter-of-factly, all along the wall. The will is there. Positive limits. Participator or observer, it makes no odds.
—Prickly, sulky, slender. Can you just sit there looking... Air, air! Hey!—The angle between wall and floor, between back and seat, an excellent arrangement. Cubic curse. Rotating disc. Sunbeam again. Tottering, dizzy with everything.

No, it won't do to go on that way.
The idea is that nothing should happen. It wasn't because time was short that more didn't come out of it. It's a strong, quite static configuration that we're showing. The reason there was a hint of mobility in some sketches and notes, is that it's so seductive to look at a proposal. Because you can take it all in at once, you imagine there are relations and combinations. It has a structural similarity to fortune-telling cards, in fact all practices are based on interpreting configurations. I think there's something attractive in that kind of mode of understanding, being able to keep the configuration in your head, being able to fiddle about with the parts. What makes such interpretations so repulsive is an over inclination to look for confirmation from "the outside", a kind of gambling addiction in relation to the oracle.

I think of the Chamber as a real room, and about the way we presented it at the exhibition. I've always wondered about the kind of furnishings. And life. Do you sit up against the walls? Can you permit yourself to stay passive for long periods? Be in a circle and make a few comments now and then? There must be an infinite amount of time. Is it a waiting-room? Or an ante-chamber? Is the arrangement just a neutral point of departure? You move around, grouping and regrouping, which you otherwise do standing, but here the conversations takes so long that you have to sit down.

For me the Chamber, the Play, or whatever you want to call it, is really a subject. I wouldn't be able to keep on with it if it didn't effect me. In addition it's a general field of tensions. *Chamber Play* (and the follow-up *Expedition*) are about choosing limits; about choosing the size of your world. Where is the focus, how is it distributed? When do you want expansion and when do you want moderation? Oh well you can't choose everything, but information and food are things we can choose much more than we care to.

What happens when you address a person?

I could go on here, but I'll send it now.

Eva

27/7/00

Dear Eva,

Proposal, I like that. As I see it, it's crucial that this whole dialogue has its origin in a (shared?) instinct for using correspondence as an effective proposal, as a free space. Compared with the exhibition spaces you otherwise work in, where you usually feel so fed up.

You once said, when we were going to place the chairs in the room, that it was "so you could sit there and dangle your legs as if in a waiting room". In the period between our two rounds of letters and when you were doing *Expedition*, I spent quite a lot of time in waiting rooms. Physical ailments, getting married at the Town Hall, or getting some business done at the tax offices—something common to all these waiting rooms is how democratically your own identity is reduced, and how a "place-specific hierarchy" arises among the people who happen to be occupying them at any given time. You hardly speak to one another, but still you're obligatory members of the same unit, you just belong to different sub-categories. You often manage to find out one another's names, you get to see other people's ailments, see family members etc.; each and every one acquires a status—as a case (he got in before me, must be more serious), as a couple, or as a fellow citizen. Each one becomes a kind of figure in the others' eyes. Each one defines himself or herself in relation to the other people who happen to share the space at the same time. Later when you come out again, for the most part you forget all about it.

The phenomenon has something to do with game rules. Rules of the game for a given space.

In an early letter you also talk about the Chamber as a fictive space, "a healing form". I've never quite understood whether you meant that the Chamber and the space of art are always the same, as a possibility. Or whether the Chamber, as in this last letter of yours, is quite simply a kind of non-art territory, populated by fellow human beings who are acting? A stage with a limited playing time? A space for ritual? And what is your role there?

Kerstin

1/8/00

Dear Kerstin!

[...] The ritual is a static construction and a healing form. As you say, I began by saying that "the Chamber is a fiction to step into. It isn't a physical space but a healing form". Recently I understood that I was probably mixing up fiction and ritual. Not conceptually, I hope, but emotionally. If you think that ritual is fiction, there is always something missing. It's meaningful to be aware of cracks, failures, openings and displacements in fiction. The rite is an option you can only fulfil. I can pour a splash of water into a plastic mug so that it has a meaning for me.

The Chamber and the space of art are not the same [...].

Eva

4/8/00

Dear Eva!

[...] What made me refuse to be primarily the (splendid) practical person was that I thought that otherwise some kind of explicit opposition of images might arise between the two of us here in Chamber Play—one spaced-out and whimsical (merely) and one practical and sensible (merely). Which wouldn't have been a fair picture of the dialogue or of us.

But from what was otherwise just a passing reflection (a corny attempt to be funny) the question arose of whether this second exchange of letters had itself in fact placed us—as differences/as dialogue partners—here in the Chamber Play. And this shifted the focus. Here comes a (highly randomly edited) fiction of a fiction about fiction.

Act One

Into the chamber come two people who don't know each other before they meet in the room. They are to spend time there together simultaneously, whether they want to or not, for quite a while.

First they look at each other surreptitiously, they don't quite know where to begin. Each draws a line on the floor to mark out their territory, then they sit down, each in a corner.

Silence falls.

One of them, E, says:

—The Chamber isn't a fiction to step into. It isn't a physical space but a healing form. The rope is a simple way to make a connection.

The other one, K, gets up, first kicks a ball of floor fluff, clears her throat and answers:

—Connections, to emphasise something about the space or in the space? To read a special meaning into simultaneity? Meaning requires pre-acquired, recognising, understanding. It's always me who chooses.

E turns around and says:

— The rope and the Chamber are both ways of relating to a space you can't encompass. They're answers to the question of how I think one can establish relationships now.

etc. etc.

They begin to play, first with words, then for a short while with concepts and later they start to play in earnest, choose to play out a whole series of pretend-situations, each sitting in her corner, together inventing and equipping what they call figures with different qualities... They have fun, they make suggestions, they approve or reject, they become happy and pleased.

Later they take a new step—they write down all the figures on cards. The cards are dealt out over the table, and E and K each pick a card three times. They are to use what is written on the cards to do something—anything at all to leave in the room.

Act One ends with both leaving, leaving behind new furnishings in the room. There are only a number of chairs around the room, and the playing cards lie in the window. On the walls hang a dialogue and a picture of each.

Act Two

Four years have passed. E and K are back in the room. They start by sorting the list of figures, each fiddling with their list. Then they swap, giving each other their versions. They sit down on the chairs...
K says:
How far could you get with these simple tools: the shared language and a kind of bench to sit gossiping on? "There are no practical problems", as you wrote somewhere. "Everything is just fiction."

E replies:
This is how I started:
—Here we are back again.
—One more push.
—They can't talk.
—This isn't a story.
—Filter.
—With different attitudes.
—Absolutely.
—Different natures.
—Absolutely.
—It isn't true.
—Well, it doesn't matter if you say the same thing one more time.
—The chairs stand there matter-of-factly, all along the wall. The will is there. Positive limits. Participator or observer, it makes no odds.
—Prickly, sulky, slender. Can you just sit there looking... Air, air! Hey!—The angle between wall and floor, between back and seat, an excellent arrangement. Cubic curse. Rotating disc. Sunbeam again. Tottering, dizzy with everything.

she turns around, and continues:
No, it won't do to go on that way.
The idea isn't that anything should happen. So it wasn't because time was short that more didn't come out of it. It's a strong and quite static configuration we're showing. At least as stable as an object.

K gets up and walks over to a fictive window...
—That's the difference between our two ways of seeing, working and relating to this Chamber Play. After all, I'm someone who likes to do big jigsaw puzzles, I admit it. But I don't think I'll take it upon myself to be the one who insistently picks out something usable from everything.

E: It's nice that it's going a bit faster and that we have more to talk about. It isn't strange that the differences come out now. At first we were so intent on agreeing. We had to do something together, in the same space. Now it's coming apart in a dialogue.

Sits down: You think I'm a bit too "spaced-out" sometimes, but remember that you've encouraged me. One of my first impressions from our work was that you thought it was great fun to use the Swedish language. I can really see that. It was the whole language, childhood, youth, the language of other generations, that welled up. It got me to use a more easy-flowing and flowery way of expressing myself. A bit affected. Old-fashioned. Something that has just lain there. It was in the Gothenburg of the 50s and 60s that language was formed. We found we shared it.
She continues:
Now the use of words/text in art is almost always objective, realistic and cool.
In other words, you mustn't be too poetically overwrought. In the letter writing we take up a female tradition that hasn't been established yet... *etc., etc.*.

Kerstin

6/8/00

Dear Kerstin,
I think we're both trying to create order. That's nice.
  I was talking to Catharina about language a while ago. She thought my way of expressing myself was 'rural'. In contrast to more 'streetwise' (possibly TV-like) ways of saying what you want to say and what you think as simply and effectively as possible, I suppose. I was puzzled about that 'rural'. Me—who have never been outside Sweden's two biggest cities except as a tourist. But I think what she meant actually has something to do with time. Yesterday I heard on the radio about a conversation recorded among Bushmen. The translation had taken an unusually long time because the conversation was so complicated and followed so many different strands. People seemed to be

talking about quite different things, and they got mixed together now and then. In the programme they thought that it took a long time to develop that kind of communication—not only in the life of human beings, but for a culture. Bushmen have lived in the same way and in the same place since the beginning of evolution. We who live in a changeable culture and have a written language to unload and deposit our experiences in, have no background for developing such a capacity for memory and simultaneity. This recalls the strange frogs and beetles they show in nature programmes, animals that are only found in marshes that have had a completely stable climate for millions of years. I won't go on any more about something I don't know anything about, least of all evolutionary history. What I mean is that *Chamber Play* is a bit of a reservation where you can communicate along several tracks.

[...]

You've referred several times to "a language parallel to our native language". That doesn't feel like my words. I don't understand it. I won't get bogged down in any issues of linguistic philosophy. "A non-linguistic figure" is something you can at best amuse yourself with. What you can communicate to someone else is the effects of this.

Experience outside language, tacit knowledge, the skills of the hand and body etc. are often described as a rhythmic understanding of sequences. I have a lot of difficulty with sequences. One possibility is that I have 'bunched things up in a heap' and that this is what I mean by "non-linguistic figures". But I don't think it's just that.

The first time I tried to describe something "non-linguistic" it was as a sequence: "In the dark on the ghost-train, straight ahead, go left and then stop". That was in a text for an exhibition about music—perhaps it had a meaning. Later I have tried to describe it as a certain kind of humour, "when the memory of repetition doesn't stick". When it goes around continuously, so to speak. An inner laughing.

It's amusing to read about how your perception of the Chamber has changed.

'My' figure "the rope" also changes its nature. First it is "a visible proposal". Rigorous and usable. Immediately before the exhibition I illustrated the figure with a drawing on a car with a rubber tail. Draining, channelling away. When I had to sit down and write the follow-up text for *Expedition* another part of the rope emerged. I started more or less like this: "For me the expedition involved stretching myself, extending myself. I miss those I wrote to. Now I do not address myself to any particular person. When the address/addressing is gone, I get all sorts of urges to (re)form the text, enlarge, reduce, make squares, arrows and columns."

The rope thus becomes the supporting form, what makes me able and willing to reel off meaning after meaning, something almost graspable, linear all the way from me to the other person. It is the conceived, perhaps invented contact.

The wall that was removed is also a rope, a supply of energy. Certainly, when we first invented the Chamber we devoted ourselves to creating determinations for it, while now we act as if we were in it.

A little digression:

I had to say something about public space at a seminar in Kalmar. I took an example, a Dutch project I heard of on *Out of Site*. An artist wanted to donate a sculpture of a lamb to the devotional area of a convent. I don't remember how it was going to look, but that doesn't matter. The suggestion resulted in a long correspondence between the artist and the nuns. They discussed it and meditated over the intended gift. In the end they refused the offer. The outcome was that it would in fact be distracting to have a sculpture in the devotional area. For them the imaginary lamb seemed so strong that no material thing could be clearer. In their enclosed space they could keep the lamb, they shared all the images and the memory of the event.

This was an example of what public space is not.

Six months later I was asked to tell the story again. I said that unfortunately I can't do things over again. In addition another lamb had got in the way. It was a TV advert, I thought it was incredibly amusing. It was about a Christmas dinner that never starts. The family manages to get through all the Christmas traditions, dance around the tree this way and that. In the end the father reads out the gospel for Christmas Day. He is forced to embroider a little on the text. It ends with "... and the little lamb looked at the baby Jesus". Somewhere in there the image of the pre-cooked Christmas ham came in. He has to get in all conceivable perspectives, even the lamb's—perhaps it's no coincidence that I think about it now.

So we act as if we were in the Chamber. It's an enclosed room. *The Chamber Play* is based on the illusion of the removed wall.

Eva

Dear Kerstin!

Now it's a year since we last wrote.

The Chamber is a demarcated space with a number of chairs to sit on. We showed such a room. It's an image of dialogue and instructions for dialogue. I read about the interest in the interior, the Nordic bedroom culture rather than the Latin café culture.

We chose an enclosed space but not intimacy. Why not? We both quickly agreed on that.

I pick out a word from the beginning of our dialogue: *"inutiheten"*. The word doesn't exist in Swedish. It was a translation of "interiority"—I don't know exactly what meaning it has. In more normal language one could probably say that "interiority" is the medium. You could also say that it's the mood, the atmosphere. The inward, coming from the inside, from the heart, from the insides. A focus on meaning and content. What's held inside and needed.

I write that interiority is the air of the Chamber; it could be a kingdom, odourless and supporting. Thickened and porous, slippery and stackable. The last was the first lines I sent. Yes, I suppose that's what we tried to create.

I think there is something inherent in the decisions, in the description of the things packed in; you take various things there which are gradually stored. And then all the repetitions. They are characteristic of the enclosed space. The marked thing is that we know they are repetitions. We notice small changes, with one purpose or another. In the open space, the café, the cocktail party, there are infinitely more repetitions, but you aren't supposed to notice them, at any rate you mustn't show that you're hearing something for the tenth time.

I wonder what significance you think the "strained" has in this project? As opposed to the relaxed, the intimate, the transparent. I think it's important that there is some sort of air. The worst thing, the most paradoxical, is that I have such difficulty when others are strained.

I read Fredrika Bremer's first novel a while ago. It was really unreadable. I must have thrown it away, I regret that now. It was fully of knotty forms, letters, interior monologues, direct speech: "Dear Reader, don't think that... have patience..."
As a matter of fact I think there is something that can generate such forms if one moves in the area of fiction/private/public.

Eva

22/6/01

Dear Eva,

Intimacy—as opposed to strain... good beginning.

What kind of intimacy can you get at all in a chamber?

The chamber could be a lift stuck between two floors, and you know you have to sit there until the lift mechanic comes. An indefinable space—you have to make the best of the situation. I got stuck in a lift with my father the other day. A lift of less than one and a half square metres, with pram and baggage. We weren't stuck for several hours, but long enough for the world to shrink in completely and be reduced to pure differences in the sounds from the stairwell outside—of encouraging shouts from worried staff, and with a time scale based on how long an old person can actually stay standing up.

An unexpected freezing of movement, and a mutually sensible handling of the new situation—all this together triggered a time of pure intimacy. Sounds from the other person that one normally doesn't register—breathing, sniffing, stomach rumbling. Thoughts that don't normally "cross the threshold of the teeth"* expressed at an abbreviated level with many meanings that precisely characterise an intimacy that must not go astray, become far too frank. One which used the metaphor, the joke, the hint for the unspoken.

Or the compartment on the long train journey south. You know you have to spend several hours in one another's company, and you have managed to start a conversation about why the conductor hasn't come, although you really intended to get that book read. These conversations can develop into pure situation reports on upcoming important decisions, about troubles and joys. All this woven into all sorts of small talk, and visits to the restaurant car. After these journeys obligatory addresses are exchanged although you will never use them.

Both conversations become relaxed and each becomes intimate in its own way precisely because they arise from an ambivalence—from a mixture of strained and sensible handling of the situation—and from room for repetition. The screw. The funnel.

The way I remember it, the beginning of our dialogue really lay in the decision to start it, so that the strain and the intimacy were basic requirements of the actual interiority.

The strain at the beginning was expressed by the terseness, the metaphorically ambivalent language. Now we are much more specific. But we both have the same resistance to re-opening the dialogue. I have, at any rate. It's a little tiresome to have to be so careful about speaking intelligently and clearly. But at the same time, with precisely all the repetitions we have already been through, it is one of the most intimate conversations.

But we've established, then, that the Chamber is pure fiction. That in fact it isn't a wholly enclosed space where we two sit and talk in peace and quiet. But a kind of lift with a built-in surveillance camera.

That's where the paradox lies, I think. And paradox is surely an important ingredient in content? Keeps content under control?

Kerstin

* Homer has Zeus say these excellent words to his daughter.

27/6/01

Dear Kerstin!

You interpret intimacy in a different way from what I first meant, but what you write is much better. I quite agree with you that everything you show, whether you want to or not, when you're close to someone, is very intimate. It expresses one's composite, unsorted life much more than for example if you make some physical or mental phenomenon a theme.

You write about more or less involuntary enclosures. The lift was awful. You enter the Chamber voluntarily if not without strain. I have difficulty being there now. Both in the physical sense—I have difficulty sitting inside—and as a mental state. The opposing force that the restriction can trigger doesn't come, the calm spreads, I just want to float around.

Eva

27/6/01

Hi Eva!

Thanks for your letter. You say you have difficulty being in the Chamber now; that the calm and the resistance spread. Can't we just go out then, but put on the Chamber—like a hat... I long to go out too—new streets, new sunglasses, and unexpected meetings. Can't we go this way, does it look good?

Promenades. The actual word: to promenade. My siblings and I had something—my children don't even have any idea what they are—"promenading shoes". There's a composite image in the concept: "particularly practical and aesthetic footwear for moving at a certain speed while one talks articulately about existence".

Is it by chance that we, as old Gothenburgers, choose the dialogue as form? I think about how often I walked through the city while I lived there, and how often one walked along with a friend. That's how one had time for that particular kind of conversation where the world got a bit bigger. Some of these exchanges of thoughts remain as if fixed, almost like spatial images, in the memory, and sometimes also in your conceptual world. Small packages, jigsaw pieces, or fragments that have become part of your overall picture of things. Like a virus, transferred from a narrator to a listener. Which you later, during another promenade, remember, tell, and thus pass on. But without breaking the connection, or the intimacy if you like, with the person you originally got the fragment from.

Just like a virus, a fragment of this kind can lie unnoticed in an unsorted corner of your consciousness, and only come into focus when you happen to pass the place where you received it. At the '7-ans' hot dog stand on Vasagatan in Gothenburg I heard for the first time about Arthur Koestler, about his work and above all about how he died. A consistent man, one has to say. At the '7-ans' hot dog stand I always used to order a chocolate milkshake. It was one of those I was drinking when I heard the story of Arthur and his investigations of "statistically non-reliable coincidences" and the possibility that the soul can survive the body in a different dimension. Each time I drink a milkshake my thoughts touch on that dimension.

Can a milkshake become a kind of Chamber?

The Chamber on your head—like a hat: when, like me, you live far from the places that can "activate a fragment", you have to develop other strategies for making contact with them. I have a well developed method that I often end up with when I have to get a work to end, to balance its equation, but one element is still missing for me. I go out to do something banal, and then I wander through streets and squares and shops. Drift around, expose myself to the influence of hours of casual encounters. This is not the promenade's moderate openness to the surrounding world, but a waiting and consciousness of a goal. More a kind of premonition of what one is searching for.

Method.
Resistance and calm.

Kerstin

Dear Kerstin!

I wrote that I would float around and that's certainly what I've done, and I've done a good bit of shopping, something I otherwise loathe doing. Amongst other things I've bought a cushion and ochre-coloured material—for sitting on too, I thought. So I am making efforts to sit. And to write to you. But I think above all I am searching for new spaces. I've tries a lot of places, both outdoors and indoors, busy and isolated.

Now I'm sitting writing inside a tree. The elm outside the window has grown unchecked, and neither Anders nor the person living below has complained. The branches press against the windowpane, when I open the window they come pouring in. A green sea, the wind is blowing strong and I am far below the surface. It isn't pleasant, and the violent movements at the edge of my field of vision make me feel queasy.

When I say I'm looking for spaces I mean, of course, for a number of purely practical purposes, but I am probably also looking for various hardly noticeable spaces. It feels like increasing activity among the imaginary spaces. That's vague, but I can't formulate it better. It isn't about the sort of memory spaces you describe, but I know what you mean. I'm not thinking of social fragmentation or tribalisation either.

I sometimes long for the promenade spaces too. I both walk and talk, but I have the experience of such concentrated promenade conversations now.

You can always go further.
The following is taken from Nicholas Crane's *Clear Waters Rising*. He writes about his hike across Europe from Santiago de Compostela to Istanbul. This is right at the start, and he is restless.

> *The maddest were the ones who had walked the furthest, which was a worrying omen.... My progress eastward was slowed by having to make headway against the current of pilgrims, united in their goal and bonded by alliances made during their shared weeks beneath the same sky.... They looked like the earth's last evacuees, escaping along the only open road. The blank expressions hid biographies whose latest chapter had sometimes been revelatory. 'Life's an open road!' exclaimed Werner, the Bavarian carpenter seriously. Another man had taken the Caminio to his heart and written a book about Galicia called* One Million Cows.

The author becomes very attached to his hat, as one does to good equipment when it has been with you for a while. I think this influenced me to buy a walking hat, wide-brimmed, but tied under the chin and at the neck, for my considerably more modest promenades.

There are plenty of examples of people who want to create or annex spaces. Annelie supplies me with addresses of websites of varying degrees of oddness. The latest one was the psycho-geographers. They're some kind of continuation of the squatters—amongst other things they want to establish a new calendar and they lived for a while in ancient monuments before they were brutally evicted from them.

Eva

Parts of this text were previously published in Pequod *no. 27, vol. 3, September 2000.*

translated by James Manley

—The establishment of rooms of identity, of scenarios, in contemporary art can be seen as a staging of fantasy spaces, of the suggestive and the private, as in the room of a teenager. It is the staging of mental spaces, of an arena for projections of possible selves; for self-pity or self-agrandissment, as well as for unspeakable acts and rituals better served by not seeing the light of day. Artists explore various usages of this room, as personal and ritual, as internalised and enclosing, as a workplace or, finally as a site for the enactment of fantasies and transgressions. To have and to occupy a room of one's own can indeed be said to be emblematic of welfare. To be without one is, perhaps, the greatest indignity of all. To have this room of one's own is in a sense becoming a subject.

—The notion of the interior points to issues of design, design of the self, as mentioned above, surely, but also of environments and surroundings (aka "machines for living"), and issues of inner spaces in the psychological *and* psychoanalytical sense. But if the staging and investigation of the room points to stagings and investigations of the mind, does the design of spaces then also refer to the design, machinations and control of the mind—a space for entrapment and manipulation (aka *The Prisoner* series)?

—The establisment of rooms are, though, not only a question of privacy, fantasy and self-hood, but also of transposure, of changing the identity of the gallery space—the white cube—into other representational and/or functional spaces (laboratories, shops, etc.), and, as such, engaging in a sort of comparative spatial analysis. This points to the possible formulation of an an expanded notion of space, that has moved beyond the geometrical notion of space into an investigation of its production, and, indeed, its products.

Interactions and Interfaces

A central issue for critical artists today, is the question of interactions with the apparatus surrounding art production; the parameters for reception (institutions, audiences, constituences, etc.) and the potentials and limitations for communication in different spheres (the art world, media discourses, the political field, etc.. How connections are made, and how they are, indeed, broken. This is discussed in both practical and political terms, ranging from methodological discussions regarding the use of space in installation to the construction of other spaces than traditional art spaces—that is, discussions on the formation of alternative public spheres, if not 'counter-publics'. Such concerns are not only focusing on the interfaces between the institution of art and the individual artist, from artistic as well as political perspectives, but they also touch on the relationships between the body and technology, and, furthermore, the establishment of networks, interfaces, lines of communication and, finally, attempts at escape.

In simple terms, one could also talk about the relationship between art production and reality, and, more specifically, the staging of this relationship through different viewing positions and contexts. In Peter Holst Henckel's essay "are you talkin' to me?—Dialogue, Mirror, Interface", he attempts to define a dialogic strategy for both the production and presentation of art works—both bodily, in installations, as well as in terms of identity, taking his cue from Jacques Lacan's theories of the gaze. Holst Henckel aims at establishing an art practice that is engaging as well as demanding, and that involves the spectator in a perceptual process of identification and participation, in which the art work itself is always unfinished and only partial, an art work to be extended, finished or rejected by the viewer. Mats Hjelm places the notion of the interface directly with technology in an introduction to, and employment of, Gilles Deleuze and Felix Guattari's critical theory, entitled "War, Art and Intelligent Machines—Humanist Criticism in the Information Society". Hjelm discusses the widespread use and developement of computer technologies, and their connection to the modern US military complex, and engages Deleuze and Guattari's notions of networks and rhizomes as ways to interact and criticise industrial structures—a critical practice to which he wants included contemporary art practices.

If Hjelm's approach to the interface between techonology and the subject is theoretical, the following texts are both examples of work within the realm of new media. In a conversation with media theorist Geert Lovink, Marita Liulia discusses her work in digital media, based, as she is, in a country renowned for its technological production. In "Art in the Age of the Mobile Phone—Text Messages from Finland", Liulia describes her practice with virtual networks, and the problems and potentials in working with a non-traditional artistic media in other contexts than those familiar to the traditional art world. The establishment of networks and platforms, as discussed by Liulia and Lovink, is also the goal of Kestustis Andrasiunas, who delivers his "Institutio Media Manifesto", a virtual 'media institute' on the world wide web. This institute is an attempt to create an interface with the public sphere through the circumvention of known academic institutions for other ends than are ordinarily associated with them. This is a notion also found in the manifesto by the committee for Copenhagen's Free University (at the time of writing consisting of artists Henriette Heise and Jakob Jakobsen), "All Power to the Copenhagen Free University". As is the case in Institutio Media, Copenhagen Free University is an attempt to create a platform where theory and practice merge. Both texts are, obviously, manifestos, and repre-sent concrete models of intervention and interaction. Despite these shared intentions, however, there are also major differences between the two 'institutions', where the former might be termed an alternative public sphere, the latter can be better characterised as a kind of counter-public sphere in the political sense.

The last text in this chapter, Knut Åsdam's "Heterotopia—Art, Pornography and Cemeteries" returns to the description of methods of installation art practice, while trying to establish new networks of engagement. However, he dismisses the Internet as a critical forum, and focuses instead on those real and marginal spaces in society desribed by Michel Foucault as "heterotopic" and "other". Here, Åsdam sees possibilities for ruptures and resistance. It is not coincidal, of course, that Åsdam brings up notions from Foucault—just as Hjelm brought up Deleuze and Guattari: the artists in this section all use theory *instrumentally* in relation to art practice, or as a "toolbox" as Foucault and Deleuze themselves once famously described it.[1] They use critical theory as an integral part of their practice, and view art and theory as parallel forms of knowledge and critique that should be employed in order to interact with society, its categories and institutions, its political problematics, and in order to produce critical practices in relation to these issues.

Note

1. Michel Foucault and Gilles Deleuze, "Intellectuals and Power", Russell Ferguson, William Olander, Marcia Tucker and Karen Fuss, eds., *Discourses: Conversations in Postmodern Art and Culture*, Cambridge, MA: MIT Press, 1990, pp. 9–16.

… are you talkin' to me!?
—Dialogue, Mirror, Interface

ILLUSTRATIONS (PREVIOUS PAGES): PETER HOLST HENCKEL, STILLS FROM THE VIDEO …ARE YOU TALKING TO ME, 1996

About half-way through Martin Scorsese's famous film *Taxi Driver*, 1975, there is an unforgettable scene that helps to accentuate the whole theme of the film and at the same time distills and encapsulates a number of the issues that have concerned the visual arts in recent years. I am thinking, of course, of Robert de Niro's mirror scene, which in the narrative structure of the film functions as a turning point and culmination of the main character's, Travis's, increasing introversion and paranoia, and at the same time heralds Travis's transformation from passive 'voyeur' to 'actor'. The scene can thus also be seen a problematisation of the dialogic as such; of the actual relationship between art and observer, art and public. The film, and the mirror scene in particular, can therefore be used to illustrate some of the aesthetic, social and political issues that have been put into circulation by the visual arts lately. The Travis figure epitomises some of the contradictions that can also be found in the neo-avantguardist artists' role of today. As in the 1970s, the schism between contemplation and active participation has again become topical, although the issue now appears more differentiated and subtle than in most of the straight forward pro-contra dialectics of the 70s. One important reason for this is that contemporary art actively involves the spectator in the play of meanings that art sets off. Thus art has increasingly come to function and understand itself as an interface where particular types of experience, knowledge and questioning are made communicable and thus open to dialogue. In a similar manner, the artist here also takes on more of a role of active mediator between various aspects and spheres of the life-world, than he did in the role of otherwordly, mysterious oracle.

… are you talkin' to me!?

Travis has come back from Vietnam and gets a job as a taxi driver. His days flow into one another, he drives around in the streets of New York, eats junk food, watches TV and goes to porn flicks. He drives his taxi, etc.. His monotonous life goes hand in hand with increasing introversion and a growing conviction that he is the chosen one who at the right time will wash away "the scum of the streets"; an idea that clearly originates in Travis's own isolation and egomania—a condition that the film's camerawork intensifies. We see, as if with Travis's own eyes, the rainy streets of New York glide by on the (wind)screen of his taxi. On the whole his access to the world is second-hand, filtered, either through film and television or the growing number of pills he consumes every day. Travis is in other words a typical product of atomised modern Western societies that seem to have found a destabilised balance in the shared myths of popular culture. He is helplessly stuck in this network of images and has gradually become the slave of repetition and apathy. Spurred by the urge to action he makes contact at one point with a well-stocked gun pusher. The scene where Travis buys a small arsenal of handguns makes clear, in a meta-filmic loop, how he seems trapped in the simulated reality of pop and media culture: he buys a PKK (James Bond films), a snub-nosed Smith and Wesson (Mike Hammer), a pocket model .25 (also 007) and a .44 Magnum (Dirty Harry films and the most popular gun throughout the 70s). Immediately afterwards comes the scene that ushers in Travis' transformation into actor. The scene takes place in front of a mirror and can be seen as a grotesque reversal of Lacan's concept of the mirror-stage. Travis stands facing the camera. As in a John Ford western he practices drawing his .25, which he has carefully fixed to a slide-bar attached to his arm. The camera lens functions as his mirror, and as a spectator one is drawn in as witness and third party to the diabolical dialogue Travis holds with himself: "... are you talkin' to me!? ... you're talkin' to me? ... you're talkin' to me? ... then who the fuck do you think you're talkin' to!? ...."

The Other

As I have said, the scene can be viewed as an introverted distillation of Lacan's mirror stage. Lacan sees this stage as fundamental to the formation of the ego, since in the mirror-image the child identifies in the imagination with 'the Other', while the subject is constituted in a split between a 'perceiving' and 'perceived'. It is a precondition of this, says Lacan, that the child perceives the picture of his own body as a totality, while the motoric does not yet exercise total control. In the first half of *Taxi Driver* Travis is characterised precisely as being incapable of acting; in other words he has not yet achieved full motor ability. In the mirror scene he sees himself as an actor, using his motor abilities, but not as part of a positive 'development' of ego formation. In the mirror scene, on the contrary, the situation is turned on its head, since the mirror /camera lens perceptually captures the spectator and makes him or her an accomplice and witness to Travis's mental, social and political collapse. The picture is thus reversed, mirrored, and we as viewers are wrenched into the meaning-structure of the narrative. As in Foucault's reading of *Las Meniñas* the perceiving and the perceived have entered into an endless and unresolvable game of rejection and attraction, of action and passivity, criticism and affirmation.[1]

The space of dialogue

Thus, as viewers, we are implicated in an interfacial space where our basic political/ideological attitudes are challenged by being played out and concretised on a bodily scale.[2] That the observer in this way, through the perceptual, becomes a kind of accomplice in a play of meanings that extends beyond the traditionally aesthetic and into the social and political, is something of which one can find many examples in the art of recent years, where the observer is sometimes snapped out of his or her passive observing role and becomes active, either directly as a physical actor or as part of the dialogical exchange of meanings for which the work functions as initiator and focus. The usual modernist distinction between the perceiver and the perceived, between subject and object, is thus undermined and replaced rather by a circulation principle where one is reflected in the other, and together they make up an open, interwoven and continuous field. The individual 'work' is then no longer primarily qualified by its character as object, its way of being an object for a subject, but is characterised more by the dialogical space it unfolds. The context of the work, understood as the, in principle, infinitely complex physical, social and political interfaces presented by the work, of course, become very important to the relevance and success of the work. By contrast it is so to speak only in the use of the work in the world, in the concrete interaction with it, that one understands it as anything other than an object among others. One could say that it is in the dialogue with the context that 'the work' finds its form and in the dialogue with the viewer that it finds its content.

Interface

Whereas work and context in a classic modernist definition could be categorised as distinct formal and content stable preconditions of the meaning of the work, art is now intervening more as a kind of spatial interface or point of contact that enables an interaction with the world on the basis of particular, fixed orientation points. Just as the encounter between water and air—surface tension—has a number of special properties that differ from those of the respective elements that meet, the interface has properties that extend beyond, influence and reciprocate with the categories 'work' and 'context'. Art, thus, does not imitate reality, nor does it become one with it—in that case it would simply disappear, but as an interface we can rather understand it as an independent space or relational sphere in which it only makes sense to behave as an actor or user. The spatial organisation of the interface constitutes a scaled architecture in which we have precisely this possibility—to see ourselves as actors in terms of the various spatial relations made up by our placing in the world. By establishing such interfaces art can so to speak spread out a surface that makes a dialogue possible between user and system, between human subject and world.

Utopia and heterotopia

In Foucault's "Of Other Spaces" he operates with two fundamentally 'other' types of space: the utopia and the heterotopia.[3] While utopia is by definition a non-place and therefore a non-existent distortion or idealised picture of society as we know it, heterotopia is a real place, a displaced or radicalised other place. But as Foucault points out, there is between these two types of space a third, mixed or hybrid form of experience that is associated with the mirror. For with the mirror we are dealing with both a utopia and a heterotopia. If we stand in front of the mirror we experience ourselves in a virtual non-real space which opens up behind the surface of the mirror, while at the same time the mirror really exists and is connected with the same spatial reality as our own body. Such a mixed experience, at once real and virtual, utopian and heterotopian, is equivalent to what many visual artists today attempt to capture via their projects.

Representatives

An example of this type of artistic practice is Gerwald Rockenschaub's *Catwalk*, which was part of the Austrian pavilion at the Venice Biennale in 1993. Rockenschaub was one of the three artists brought together by the curator Peter Weibel under the umbrella title *Representatives*.[4] As an overall manifestation *Representatives* took its point of departure in Austria as a nation and Austrian as an identity, and the historical, cultural and political questions that this inevitably raises; questions which become visible and are represented in other ways through the Austrian pavilion, the overall history of the Venice Biennale and the geopolitical organisation of the Giardini Park. The exhibition *Representatives* was an effort to try and identify and mediate what one could regard as different layers or scale levels of the total Austrian identity issue.

Catwalk

Rockenschaub's *Catwalk* took its point of departure in the Austrian pavilion's architectural and cultural-ideological meaning—inasmuch as it spatially represented an Austrian cultural value-set within the framework of the micro world order of the Biennale. The pavilion was designed by the Austrian architect Josef Hoffman and was finished for the opening of the Biennale in 1934. Architecturally it appears with its two large rectangular exhibition halls as a classical, but also a very modern, rationalistic building. The two exhibition spaces get their light from a window strip placed at the top of the enormous wall surfaces. The spaces thus close in perceptually on themselves, since the observer cannot look out of the space, but is urged to simply contemplate the exhibited art objects. In this way each room functions as the perfect 'white cube': the place where the viewer meets the authentic artwork, and which is at the same time suspended from the outside world.

Rockenschaub took on the role of mediator as opposed to artist as Creator. Rather than creating a number of object-works he constructed a giant "scaffolding staircase" which ran through and symbolically broke down Hoffman's white cubes. This drastically changed the character of the pavillion, that went from being a historical, museum-like space to being an arena for a critical view on Austrian national identity formations. The stairway gave the spectator the opportunity to move up to the high window strips, so that the view of and relationship with the 'outside' was re-established. In a highly concrete way *Catwalk* thus exposed and enabled the direct interweaving of art and the lifeworld that a large part of modernist formalism of the twentieth century has constantly tried to eliminate. *Catwalk*, in other words, unfolded in the crossover between the analytical dialogue with the context and the interactive dialogue with the viewer; precisely a work understood more as a spatial interface than as an autonomous object. Work, observer and context had here merged and constituted something more—a relational sphere where particular experiences and meanings were activated, clarified and brought into play. Thus *Catwalk* became a field of possibilities which, depending on our active participation—physical as well as intellectual—opened up an avenue where we could enter into a dialogue with the life-world that we have such difficulty viewing and grasping as a whole because we are either too far from it or too close to it to understand it. In this sense *Catwalk* can be seen as a good example of an artistic practice that is all about using art as an interface space where we reflect ourselves in the world in a way that makes it a little more real and a little more unreal to be a part of it.

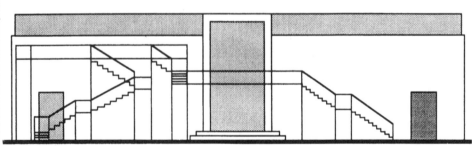

ILLUSTRATIONS: THIS PAGE: FLOOR SECTION, CATWALK, NEXT PAGE: FLOOR PLAN, CATWALK

Notes

1. Michel Foucault, *The Order of Things*, London: Routledge, 1991, p. 3-16 (original: *Les mots et les choses*, Paris: Éditions Gallimard 1966).

2. *Taxi Driver* must, in this context, also be understood in terms of a political/ideological 'frame tale'. As Susan Buck-Morss has pointed out, Lacans mirror theory can also be seen as a theory of Fascism. See Susan Buck-Morss, "Aesthetics and Anaesthetics: Walter Benjamin's Artwork Essay Reconsidered", *October* no. 62, Cambridge MA: MIT Press, 1992.

3. Michel Foucault, "Of Other Spaces", *Diacritics* 16-1, London, 1986.

4. Besides Gerwald Rockenschaub, Christian Philipp Müller and Andrea Fraser each contributed a project.

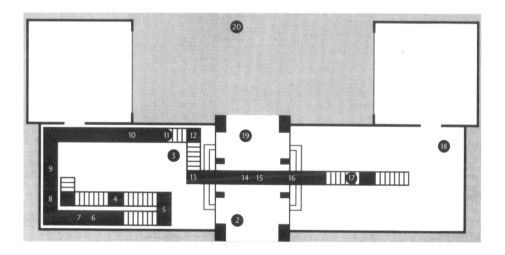

Government is the Entertainment Division of the military-industrial complex. [1]

Frank Zappa

In 1973 the United States of America, the world's leading military power, was forced to sign a peace treaty with Vietnam, a small country in Indochina. The USA didn't only lose the war in Vietnam, but also the struggle for both international and domestic opinion. The development of the modern war machine from the Vietnam War until our own day is indicative of the fast growth of the information society and its influence on society as a whole.

The strength of the Vietnamese military structure was its short chain of command and its ability to adapt to the specific situation that pertained at any given moment on the battlefield. Vietnam may have had a politically totalitarian ideology, but in practice guerrilla warfare is very decentrally organised and every individual or unit has a very high degree of self-determination. On the other hand America's high-technology war apparatus required unprecedented logistical work and a very far-reaching control system. This meant a non-transparent information apparatus, with enormous resources being necessary to process and analyse information. When a hierarchical structure meets a high technology war apparatus the system becomes paralysed, uncommunicative and inflexible.

30 years later, when the American war machine was shown in direct transmissions from the desert war in Iraq, we saw a new kind of military apparatus where the most important weapon was not missiles but information technology. [2] With unparalleled precision and, ostensibly, without bloodshed the USA not only won the war but also the struggle for international opinion. The USA's present day war machine is the result of dramatic developments in recent years in information and communication technology. The military efficiency is the result of the ability of information technology to leach out relevant information from enormous quantities of unstructured data quickly. Besides military efficiency, the modern war machine has gained a completely different kind of control over mass media. In the past everything was done to prevent the media playing any part in what happened on the battlefield; today the military does just the opposite and integrates mass media in military operations so much so that we can watch live transmissions from a battlefield on CNN.

The rapid growth of information technology in recent years may seem like something without a history, something that cannot be placed in a wider historical and humanist context. But writings of French thinkers Gilles Deleuze and Félix Guattari in the 70s and 80s can give us a deeper understanding of the enormously impenetrable and heterogeneous complex constituted by power, politics and information technology. They can help us to create a starting point for how a critical, artistic and humanist practice might look in an information society.

This information is top security. When you have read it, destroy yourself.[3]

Marshal McLuhan

The computer as an idea was born in 1936 when Alan Turing, its inventor, specified the logical conditions for the functioning of a computing machine without regard to how they could be implemented in practice. The original aim of the machine was to attempt to answer a number of abstract questions in meta-mathematics. Turing had the idea that any conceivable mathematical function could be reduced to a number of memory positions that were either in the state of "AND gates" or "OR gates". Since Turing did not speculate about how this machine could be constructed or function in practice, he could devote all his attention to reducing the machine as far as possible, making it purely speculative.

The Turing Machine continued to exist as an idea only until the middle of World War II. The needs of military intelligence to encrypt and decrypt information soon made it necessary to try and build such a machine in reality. Turing himself worked as a cryptologist during the War and was for example involved in cracking the Nazis' Enigma Code, making it possible for the Allies to monitor the Nazis' radio communications in detail. Machines that Turing and others used for cryptological and ballistic studies were not complete Turing Machines, but they included several of the functions that were to make the future computer possible.[4]

The true Turing Machine, as conceived in Turing's idea of 1936 or in the computers of today, is a universal machine. This means that it can simulate the function of any other machine that works with symbols or representations, for example a piano or a calculator. The Turing Machine itself does not behave as a car or aircraft, but *reproduces* this behaviour. This means that any other machine that can be explained or described with the aid of symbols can be reproduced by means of a Turing Machine and a number of external operating systems. This, of course, also applies to the car or the aircraft in the example above. Today's industrial robots and 'smart missiles' are examples of exactly this.

The remarkable thing about the Turing Machine is that it cannot only simulate any other machine; it can also exist at such a high degree of abstraction that it can take the form of a code in memory or on paper. This code can later be moved and used in any other Turing Machine and thus make it possible to simulate the whole course of events without needing to carry out any form of physical construction. This abstract part of the machine is what we call software.[5]

> 'The matrix has its roots in primitive arcade game', said the voice-over; 'in early graphics programs and experimentation with cranial jacks.' On the Sony, a two-dimensional space war faded behind a forest of mathematically generated ferns, demonstrating the spatial possibilities of logarithmic spirals; cold blue military footage burned through, lab animals wired into test systems, helmets feeding into fire control circuits of tanks and war planes. 'Cyberspace. A consensual hallucination experienced daily by billions of legitimate operators, in every nation, by children being taught mathematical concepts... A graphic representation of data abstracted from the banks of every computer in the human system. Unthinkable complexity. Lines of light ranged in the nonspace of the mind, clusters and constellations of data. Like the city lights, receding....'[6]
>
> William Gibson, *Neuromancer*, 1984

The Internet was born from ARPANet, a decentralised data network developed for the American Defense Department's advanced research programme ARPA at UCLA in 1969. The idea of ARPANet was to secure the military communications apparatus in the event of a nuclear conflict. By using a technique called 'packet-switching' to break data down into their elements and then not reassembling them until they had reached their precise destination, ARPANet could make itself invulnerable to conventional attacks. If part of the network was knocked out, information was automatically re-routed to another part. In 1983 ARPANet was divided up into a military and a civilian network, Milnet and ARPA-Internet. Shortly afterwards, the administration and maintenance of the cables and equipment that formed the backbone of ARPA-Internet were transferred to the US National Science Foundation (NSF). The American Defense Department had only granted institutions funded by the Pentagon access to the network, but under the auspices of the NSF the network became accessible to all American educational institutions. This change became the starting point for the development of ARPA-Internet into the enormous, formless, anarchistic information space that is the Internet of today.[7]

The Internet itself is only part of an even larger complex of interactive networks called The Matrix. This is the overall network structure which, besides the Internet, also includes UseNet, FidoNet and BITNET. By 1990 ARPANet had ceased to exist as an independent unit and had been totally subsumed by the Internet.

Even though the Net developed into a civilian form when the NSF assumed responsibility, the aim of building it up was not to give individual users access to an anarchic, non-hierarchical communication tool. The structure of the Net instead has to do with the American war machine's experience of hierarchical battle command systems. The strict hierarchy that formed the basis of the Allies' war machine during World War II turned out, against the background of conflicts like the Korean and Vietnam wars, to be an impossible war doctrine for a belligerent high-technology power. What was needed instead was an information system that was flexible and decentralised, and could withstand attack.

The network structure of the Internet not only permits individual packets of information to take different routes to reach their goal; it also allows these packets to carry with them their own potential for analysis. These intelligent code strings, so-called 'robots' or 'agents' can travel on their own across the network and gather up information, then come back to the sender with the information required. Examples are search engines such as Alta Vista or Lycos, which have the ability to go out and gradually bring order to the infinite, unstructured information space that the Internet has become.

What, then, has happened to the individual's potential for influencing his own situation? Has the new kind of information processing brought us increased insight into power structures and military systems? Unfortunately, I believe that the feeling of access to all the information in the world that the Internet provides is an illusion. Access to information no longer determines who holds power; power is rather determined by access to tools for leaching out reliable and relevant information. These tools require considerable economic and technical resources. Tools for retrieving relevant information from a great mass of information are called 'filters'. These filters can be anything from a simple search function in a word processor to incredibly sophisticated systems that use artificial intelligence to retrieve exactly the relevant information from gigantic volumes of unstructured data. The sophisticated filters of today not only work on logical, mathematical principles; they also use behavioural and psychological models to pin down the relevant information. Since the filters are built up with artificial intelligence, unstructured and inexact search concepts can also be used to produce relevant answers. Such filters develop their performance as they are used, and can themselves learn from the experience of earlier searches.

It is the access to sophisticated tools for information-filtering and the ability to extract relevant information quickly that constitutes the real effectiveness of the war machine into which we gained some brief insight through the Gulf War. The Western military powers no longer need to worry about mass media gaining access to unfavourable information, since the information processing of the media is, quite simply, not fast or powerful enough. Instead, mass media queue up for access to the efficient information apparatus the military has at its disposal. These apparatus create exactly the news value the media want—but on the military's terms. Another important consequence of using agents for information gathering is that command structures no longer need be dependent on loyalty and reliability in their sources; the information is retrieved without any human involvement. The risk of the military itself being misinformed has decreased dramatically. Weapons, as such, have not changed to any significant extent since the Vietnam War; instead it is communication tools that have changed their appearance. The modern war machine can control without appearing to control, and communicate without being interrupted. The information space created by the Internet is the perfect gameboard for the war machine of the 90s in what Gilles Deleuze calls the society of control.

Food for the mind is like food for the body; the inputs are never the same as the outputs. [8]

Marshall McLuhan

If the data networks are controlled by the military and the military in turn controls the media, what resources exist for expressing oneself in the society of control? The society of control is the term used by Gilles Deleuze for the society that follows Foucault's society of discipline. Foucault placed the society of discipline in the eighteenth and nineteenth centuries, and this society reached its peak at the beginning of the last decade. Deleuze asserts, in his text "Postscript on Control Societies", 1990, that the old forms of resistance no longer work in the new society; resistance must take new forms to be able to take on new power structures. [9]

The twentieth century was the century of film and mass media. This development was closely related to the transition between the society of discipline and the society of control. Already in the infancy of film, directors used the camera to capture the world around them with a view to initiating change. It is a fact that the very first films made by Louis Lumière at the end of the nineteenth century were kind of documentaries. The public were shocked to see a train coming towards them or to see the workers leaving Lumière's factories. During the 1920s and 30s John Grierson's GPO Film Unit in England made a series of films documenting everyday reality. Among other works their film *Housing Problems*, 1931, had a strong effect on the British Government's housing policy.

In the turbulent climate of 1930s political debate there was lively discussion amongst philosophers and other intellectuals as to whether film had a positive or negative effect on social development. These discussions exhibit poignant similarities to today's debates concerning the Internet and the influence of digital technology on the human potential for self-determination and freedom of expression. Central figures in this discussion were Walter Benjamin and Theodor W Adorno, both of whom were important forces in the German Frankfurt School. Benjamin asserted that film could be used to educate the masses and thus become a tool of social change. Adorno claimed, on the other hand, that film might be a powerful tool, but that it could be used by anyone, not only left sympathisers, and presumably more effectively by those who already had power, as they also had access to more resources.[10]

The 60s later became the starting point for a new body of theory about mass media and communication with its origin in a discussion of the medium of TV. One of the central figures here was Marshall McCluhan, who coined the well known slogan "the medium is the message". McCluhan asserted that the medium itself is meaning-bearing; it influences both us and the message independently of the intention of the message's sender. This means that the choice of medium is just as important as content. This was an important argument for the video activism that developed during the 60s.

The development of video technology in the 70s dramatically increased the potential for documentary, independent film work. The new video cameras were small, simple to use and relatively cheap. Unlike film, video tape could be re-used and the camera need only be operated by one person. Another reason for the development of video activism was the laws that came into force in the USA in connection with the development of cable TV networks. In order to run a TV cable through a residential area the company was obliged to furnish the area with a TV studio that was freely accessible to the public. These "Community Television Centers" became a unique opportunity for the distribution of alternative programmes and the beginning of a wealth of different activities with the video camera as the connecting link. A new group of guerrilla videomakers arose, first in the USA and later throughout the rest of the world. This was also the beginning of video art, where a central part of the expression was precisely the relatively poor image quality. Now people also began to experiment with different forms of real time, live-transmitted video and new forms of narrative.

In the 60s and 70s artists began to question traditional forms of expression in the visual arts. They experimented with performance, site-specific art and installations. The first pioneers of computer graphics arose at this time too, but as yet the computer was far too expensive and unmanageable to make an impact on artistic life. For a long time the artists who worked with computer technology were closely tied to various computer manufacturers and commercial TV companies—the art created using computer technology was surprisingly traditional and uncritical.

It was not until the Apple Macintosh and the Amiga computer appeared at the end of the 80s that the personal computer was inexpensive and user-friendly enough for a large number of artists to take an interest in it as a medium of expression. During the 80s the computer made its impact on video editing, thus the most common form of computer-based expression were videotape animations. A few artists associated with research centres or computer manufacturers could experiment with what were, at the time, sophisticated graphics, and three-dimensional worlds, largely inspired by William Gibson's novels describing computer networks and cyberspace. At the same time continental philosophy made its definitive breakthrough in the art world. The French philosopher Jean Baudrillard gave us the idea of 'simulacra'—that is, copies without originals. At the same time Paul Virilio offered a gloomy vision of technological development that had got out of control. Despite the fact that these new ideas were themselves dependent on new technology, the artists who worked with it were still, for ·the most part, rather uncritical.[11] Instead, these ideas were applied to photographic art and installation. The discussion of simulations along the lines of Baudrillard's thinking was expressed by means of conventional photographic techniques and many artists, Barbara Kruger and Jenny Holzer for example, worked with media-oriented projects. The appearance of the expensive art catalogues of the 80s was to a great extent the result of work with the new computer-based printing and desk-top publishing techniques.

The 90s became the decade for global networks, when information technology became a national and political concern. Computer technology began in earnest to compete both visually and in terms of price with other forms of expression. The dreams of interactivity, downscaling and global communication in the 60s and 70s suddenly became technologically and economically feasible. Today artists can have complete video editing facilities in their personal computers with picture quality that is wholly compatible with that of TV. The tools for image processing and three-dimensional imaging have also become an option for artists with relatively few economic resources. And, of course, access to the Internet is today as inexpensive as talking on the phone. With the artists' opportunity to use sophisticated information technology without depending on the computer companies supplying them with equipment, an artistic practice has emerged that is more interested in people's conditions of life and their potential for self-determination. The picture quality of today's consumer cameras is so good that the independent filmmaker or artist can compete with big production companies, nor is it any longer quality without content that is the norm. If large glossy Cibachrome photographs were typical of art exhibitions of the 80s, the video monitor or video projector was typical of the 90s.

From the beginning of the 90s we also witnessed a new form of media-critical activity on the Internet, with everything from pure image-creating visual arts projects to discussion groups. This discussion often takes its point of departure in "cultural studies", a rallying point for a number of currents of thought that attend to issues of sexuality, gender, ethnicity, media theory and cultural theory. A fine example of this new critical Internet culture is the Spoon Collective, which is administrated by the Institute of Advanced Technology in the Humanities at the University of Virginia.[12] This Internet site is an association of "net citizens" who support free and open discussion of philosophical issues. The Spoon Collective has a number of interesting email lists in subjects like film theory, art theory, continental philosophy, media theory and gender issues.

> *A schizophrenic out for a walk is a better model than a neurotic lying on the analyst's couch. A breath of fresh air, a relationship with the outside world.*[13]
> Gilles Deleuze and Félix Guattari, *Anti-Oedipus*

Gilles Deleuze, 1925-1995, studied philosophy at the Sorbonne in the 1940s and later became a Professor at the University of Vincennes, a new and experimental institution founded by François Chatelet and Michel Foucault in the spirit of the student revolution of the late 60s. Deleuzes's Tuesday seminars in Vincennes, held at the beginning of the 70s, were a well-attended attraction for activists and anarchists as well as other intellectuals.

Over a period of 40 years Deleuze published 20 significant philosophical works. His writings ranged from monographs on individual philosophers and artists to studies of film, capitalism and philosophy. Deleuze once approved the term 'vitalism' as a description of his philosophy. It can be said to describe both the currents with which he felt an affinity in the history of philosophy and the ease with which he moved between different disciplines and idea traditions. Any attempt to sum up his life's work or categorise his philosophical project becomes almost impossible, not only because of the enormous range of his work, but because of its experimental aspect. Deleuze's work differs from that of the more text oriented French post-structuralists inasmuch as he draws his content from several other important French traditions of thought. His work is informed by theories of science and mathematical philosophy as well as ethnology, theatre and music.

Deleuze was perhaps above all a thinker who emphasised the small and the local in opposition to the usual philosophical currents which stress abstraction, generalisation and universalism. This small-scale approach and interest in the local also explains his sympathy for the political currents that were a result of the 60s student revolt. This does not mean that Deleuze was an anti-intellectual, but rather that he thought we should be prepared to abandon abstraction in favour of the concrete and the distinctive, that we should not search for the abstract and general applicability of concepts but, instead, should confront each specific concept with the actual reality from which a concept is derived. It is only at this level that the distinction between the small and the large finally becomes irrelevant. Philosophy becomes no longer an object for observers but a situation for actors involved in a course of events.

What might seem inconsistent in Deleuze's work is the fact that he spent such a long time writing monographs about established academic philosophers, while his later more independent works are a direct critique of traditional philosophy. Deleuze himself responded to this criticism:

> ... I suppose the main way I coped with it at the time was to see the history of philosophy as a sort of buggery or (it comes to the same thing) immaculate conception. I saw myself as taking an author from behind and giving him a child that would be his own offspring, yet monstrous. It was really important for it to be his own child, because the author had to actually say all I had him saying. But the child was bound to be monstrous too, because it resulted from all sorts of shifting, slipping, dislocations, and hidden emissions that I really enjoyed.[14]

As a public figure Deleuze was best known for his participation in the movement that followed the student revolt of Paris 1968. This was where he met his friend and lifelong co-worker Félix Guattari.

Félix Guattari, 1930-1992, was a practicing psychoanalyst and political activist. He worked from the mid-50s at La Borde, an experimental psychiatric clinic founded by the Lacanian analyst Jean Oury. Guattari was himself one of Lacan's first pupils.

Although he never formally distanced himself from Lacan's École Freudienne, the work at La Borde gave him a very different orientation. This was directed to abolishing the hierarchy between analyst and patient in favour of an interactive group dynamic. This dynamic aims to strengthen human relations so that they do not fall into stereo-types, opening up instead to fundamental metaphysical relations. These relations carry forward the most radical and basic forms of madness and neurosis and channel them into a revolutionary praxis. Guattari's anti-hierarchical ideas anticipated the events of May 68 and made him an early partisan in the movements that were being established at this time, amongst others the feminist and gay movements.[15]

In 1972 Deleuze and Guattari published the world's best selling philosophical work, *Anti-Oedipus*. This was the first book that Deleuze and Guattari wrote together and can be seen as a critique of both dogmatic Marxism and scholastic psychoanalysis. Anti-Oedipus should be viewed in the light of the intellectual dominance the dogmatic left exerted in the 70s. In 1993 the American Deleuze expert Brian Massumi wrote in *A user's guide to Capitalism and Schizophrenia* that "the most tangible result of Anti-Oedipus was that it short-circuited the connection between psychoanalysis and the far left parties". In the new parties of the left Deleuze and Guattari saw the danger of a powerful new bureaucracy based on analytical reasoning.[16]

In the preface to the American translation of *Anti-Oedipus* Michael Foucault described the book as an *Introduction to the non-fascist life*. Foucault was referring not only to political Fascism but also to the Fascism within ourselves that makes us long to be dominated. With this point of departure in the book Foucault sums up a number of important principles for a "manual or guide to everyday life": "Develop action, thought, and desires by proliferation, juxtaposition, and disjunction, and not by sub-division and pyramidal hierarchisation". [...] "Withdraw allegiance from the old categories of the Negative (law, limit, castration, lack, lacuna), which Western thought has so long held as sacred as a form of power and an access to reality. Prefer what is positive and multiple, difference over uniformity, flows over unities, mobile arrangements over systems. Believe that what is productive is not sedentary but nomadic."

Political action should be liberated from all kinds of demands for unity and totalitarian paranoia: do not demand of politics that it should re-establish the individual's 'rights' in the way philosophy has defined the individual. The individual is a product of power. What is needed is a 'de-individualisation' with the aid of doubling, displacement and manifold combinations. Foucault ends his description of this anti-fascist lifestyle with the advice: "Do not become enamored of power."[17]

Deleuze's and Guattari's experimental mode of writing and their ability to break out of the hermetic world of modern philosophy have made them sources of inspiration—almost cult figures—within various currents of thought in contemporary media theory. Common to most of these currents is the way they in one way or another resist power concentrations and hierarchies. Deleuze and Guattari have generated several concepts that explain complex psychological and cultural phenomena and which have become central to the discussion of new media technology. One of these concepts is 'rhizomes', which has its origin in the special form of root-like underground survival system found in a number of plants, including ferns and wood anemones. Deleuze and Guattari write, in the first plateau of the book *A Thousand Plateaus*, 1980:

> *A rhizome as a sub-terranean stem is absolutely different from roots and radicles. Bulbs and tubers are rhizomes. Plants with roots or radicles may be rhizomorphic in other respects altogether: the question is whether plant life in its specificity is not entirely rhizomatic. Even some animals are, in their pack form. Rats are rhizomes. Burrows are too, in all their functions of shelter, supply, movement, evasion and breakout. The rhizome itself assumes very diverse forms, from ramified surface extension in all directions to concretion into bulbs and tubers. When rats swarm over each another. The rhizome includes the best and the worst: potato and couchgrass, or the weed. Animal and plant, couchgrass is crabgrass. We get the distinctive feeling that we will convince no one unless we enumerate certain approximate characteristics of the rhizome.* [18]

This odd metaphor, which is one of the key concepts in *A Thousand Plateaus*, has also been used as a way of describing the diffuse cloud of information that is the Internet. There are innumerable examples of projects that have had their starting point in the rhizome concept, and I have selected one: *The Deleuze & Guattari Rhiz-o-mat*, a project by Jason Brown. [19] The Rhiz-o-mat is a website that generates randomly chosen quotes from Deleuze and Guattari, primarily from *A Thousand Plateaus*. The odd thing about this project is that despite the fact that it simply throws up random quotations, it still manages to create a very credible text. The reason the Rhiz-o-mat functions so well is, of course, Deleuze's and Guattari's way of writing, where the text can be and is read in a number of different ways. In a short note at the beginning of *A Thousand Plateaus* Deleuze and Guattari even point out that the different plateaus can be read independently of one another. The book as a project and what it represents is at the same time a sub-text to the whole work. It strikes me, when I have looked at the

Rhiz-o-mat for half an hour and have almost lost myself in time and space, that this is perhaps the only natural way to experience Deleuze's and Guattari's work. The *Rhiz-o-mat* constantly creates new cross-sections through the relative and complex world of thought made up by Deleuze's and Guattari's work—and automatically provides the opportunity for new readings that a book, with its closed form, has difficulty providing. Nor does the *Rhiz-o-mat* give you any illusion that the observer can participate. The illusion of user interaction that so often occurs in a multi-media context is given a real beating here. The *Rhiz-o-mat* creates a meaningful content through a random presentation of information, while on the other hand all the pointing-and-clicking in most 'interactive' projects does not lead to any intelligent information being transferred at all.

    A Thousand Plateaus, which was written by Deleuze and Guattari over a period of seven years, can be seen as a developed adaptation of schizophrenic or 'nomadic' thinking. This nomadic thinking opposes traditional philosophy's hermetic and self-sufficient world in favour of a kind of thinking that moves freely in a constant 'outsideness'. This thinking requires a new assemblage of tools to describe lines of development and sequences, as it is not about generalisations and hierarchies, but concentrates instead on the specific in each situation and opposes logical-deterministic conclusions. Deleuze and Guattari, therefore, invoke the aid of concepts like 'line of flight', 'stratum' and 'becoming'. An example of such a concept is *becoming* instead of *being*. Deleuze and Guattari write, in the tenth plateaux of *A Thousand Plateaus*:

> *Becoming is a rhizome, not a classificatory or a genealogical tree. Becoming is absolutely not imitating, or identifying with something; nor is it regressing-progressing; neither is it corresponding, establishing corresponding relations; neither is it producing, producing a filiation or producing through filiation. Becoming is a verb with a consistency all its own, it does not reduce to, or lead back to 'appearing', 'being', 'equaling' or 'producing'.*[20]

In the world of Deleuze's and Guattari's thought this becoming is a path away from an absolute terminology that gives each individual a closed meaning in the very instant of naming. There is a considerable difference between being a woman and becoming-woman or between being a man and becoming-man.

    Central to Deleuze's and Guattari's work, too, is the term "machine". But they do not use machine in the way we would intuitively understand it. Guattari says in the second chapter of the book *Chaosmosis*, 1995, that "The machine would become the prerequisite for technology rather than its expression."[21] He has made the machine something that is superordinate to technology and thus turns upside down the Aristotelian relation between man and machine. He further writes that "the goal of *techne* was to create what nature found impossible to accomplish", and in this way a new line of thought is formed with its origin in the machine, where *techne* is only a part. In order to understand Deleuze's and Guattari's work one has to be able to see the breadth of this line of thought. Deleuze himself says that:

> ... we give the machine its greatest extension: in relation to the fluxes. We define the machine as any system that cuts the fluxes. Thus, sometimes we speak of technical machines, in the ordinary sense of the word, sometimes of social machines, sometimes of desiring machines. [22]

This wide area of application for the term machine creates a whole world of possible extensions and lines of development, and leads us on towards a technological lineage or in Deleuze's and Guattari's words a "machinic phylum". The word phylum, from the Greek for 'family' or 'tribe', is used in a biological, hierarchical system to describe a lineage or kinship group. In Deleuze's and Guattari's work this concept has to do with the inherent line of development in matter, a kind of immanent will in matter to develop different functions. This way of thinking, of course, provides a brand new and partly frightening perspective on technical development. Deleuze and Guattari write in the twelfth plateau of *A Thousand Plateaus*: "We may speak of a *machinic phylum*, or technological lineage, wherever we find a *constellation of singularities, prolongable by certain operations, which converge, and make the operations converge, upon one or several assignable traits of expression.*"[23] A phylum implies an inherent line of development, but Deleuze's and Guattari's description of this lineage avoids in a very precise way the issue of determinism. They stop at the description of the phenomenon, while an abstraction or a generalisation would have had absolute implications.

This technological lineage has also been the point of departure for the book *War in the Age of Intelligent Machines*, 1991, by the American artist and writer Manuel de Landa. The work is an important key to the linkage between digital technology, the war machine and the transfer of cognitive structures from humans to machines during the latter part of the twentieth century. In the first chapter of his book De Landa uses the metaphor of a robot historian who looks back at his own evolution: "... when this robot historian turned its attention to the evolution of armies in order to trace the history of its own weaponry, it would see humans as no more than pieces of a larger military-industrial machine: a war machine." [24]

De Landa later uses this technological lineage as an explanatory model for an odyssey through the history of war which results in a discussion of hunting weapons. De Landa's analysis of this technological lineage leads to a frightening world where weapons systems reach such a high degree of autonomy that they become hunters who make their own decisions and create a battlefield on their own terms. Here mankind is at best a small part of a war machinery that has its origin before mankind and its final destination after mankind.

War. The possibility at last exists that war may be defeated on the linguistic plane. If war is an extreme metaphor, we may defeat it by devising metaphors that are even more extreme. [25]

J G Ballard

Today we have access to the technological communication tools that people dreamed about in the 60s, but what should we do with them? The question should, perhaps, be asked in a different way: the established power apparatus and the military have drawn specific conclusions from the political events of the 60s and acquired a communications apparatus that is more efficient than before, while at the same time this apparatus lulls us into a notion of increased individual self-determination. How then would a critical practice that considers human needs look?

If we look at the new technology in this way the possibilities of the technology for the ordinary human being are rather a side effect of its real aim. This point of view requires a critical practice that aims at the exposure of hidden power structures rather than an aestheticising use of an array of new tools.

Deleuze's and Guattari's critique of modern science's focus on the general and the abstract takes on a new meaning in the light of digital technology. The search for the abstract has not only applied to modern science but has also been a hallmark of modern art. In art, modernism has been about capturing or abstracting from nature. The artist has been the link between the civilised modern human being and our primitive past. The art of the twentieth century exhibits many examples of this, from Cubism to Surrealism to Minimalism, etc..

However, it has always been the natural sciences that have developed the most sophisticated models for the understanding of reality. Abstract thinking has been a way for limited human reason to understand multi-dimensionality and complicated phenomena. We have created models for the origin of the universe and the smallest elements of things—medicine and psychoanalysis have mapped the human body and psyche. This quest for general explanatory models has compelled us to find increasingly complex formulae and systems where we try to explain every nuance of existence. The problem, simply, is that the complexity of these abstract models is so great that the initial specific situation can no longer be explained or derived. Science and academic philosophy have created their own self-generating world of abstract models functioning independently of, and better than, reality.

In order to re-orient ourselves and regain the initiative in a world where we can no longer tell whether what we see is real or a perfect simulation, we need to reconquer the specific. We can no longer rely on the idea that an abstract model is true just because our minds experience it as correct.

A critical practice requires a position outside the normal value system with an orientation from the general towards the specific. Paul Virilio describes this by saying that our own technology has become an unknown 'dark continent' that we must rediscover. To orient ourselves in the universe we must learn to deal with our own technology rather than discover the natural world.[26] We have already come to the point where the representations created by machines are as powerful as our own sensory impressions. The next step will be that technological evolution continues humankind and creates a new race of the predatory machines to which De Landa refers in his book.

Before mankind loses its 'mastery' of reality we need to create strategies for our survival. We have to train ourselves to discover how the new technology manifests itself and to decode hidden power structures and the inbuilt ideologies of the technological systems. To do this we need a new type of critical cultural activity, one not concerned with trying to find elegant aesthetic or logical mathematical models for existence, but instead reads and explores each factual, individual situation. This activity cannot be limited by academic philosophy against which Deleuze and Guattari polemicise in *A Thousand Plateaus*, but must be typified by free, nomadic thinking. This new form of politico-philosophical resistance is at once artistic and intellectual, and it restores to art its function as an integral part of the human community.

Notes

1. Frank Zappa, *The Real Frank Zappa Book*, New York: Poseidon Press, 1989.

2. General Accounting Office Report, "Operation Desert Storm Air War", GAO/PEMD—96-102, Washington, DC: 1996, pp. 3-9.

3. http://mcluhanmedia.com/mmclmoo3.html, 1997.11.17.

4. Manuel De Landa, *War in the Age of the Intelligent Machines*, New York: Zone Books, 1991, p. 129.

5. De Landa, *War*, p. 130.

6. William Gibson, *Neuromancer*, London: Harper Collins, 1994, p. 67.

7. Mark Dery, *Escape Velocity: Cyberculture at the End of the Century*, New York: Grove Atlantic, 1997, p. 5.

8. http://mcluhanmedia.com/mmclmoo3.html, 1997.11.17.

9. Gilles Deleuze, *Negotiations 1972-1990*, New York: Columbia University Press, 1995, pp. 177-182.

10. Thomas Harding, *The Video Activist Handbook*, London: Pluto Press, 1997, p. 3.

11. Richard Wright, "More Power. The Pioneers of British Computer Animation and their Legacy", *History of British Experimental Video*, Knight, Julia, ed., London, 1996.

12. http://jefferson.village.virginia.edu/(spoons/index2.html, 1997.12.26.

13. Gilles Deleuze, and Félix Guattari, *Anti-Oedipus*, London: Viking Press, 1977, p. XVII.

14. Deleuze, *Negotiations*, p. 6.

15. Brian Massumi, *A User's guide to Capitalism and Schizophrenia*, Cambridge, MA: MIT Press, 1993, p. 2.

16. Massumi, *Capitalism*, p. 3.

17. Deleuze and Guattari, *Anti-Oedipus*, p. XIII.

18. Gilles Deleuze and Félix Guattari, *A Thousand Plateaus—Capitalism and Schizophrenia*, Minneapolis: University of Minnesota Press, 1988, p. 6.

19. http://www.arts.ucsb.edu/(messiah/rhizomat/rhizomat.html, 1997.12.30.

20. Deleuze and Guattari, *A Thousand Plateaus*, p. 239.

21. Felix Guattari, *Chaosmosis: An Ethico-Aestetic Paradigm*, Bloomington: Indiana University Press, 1995, p. 32.

22. Félix Guattari, *Chaosophy*, New York: Semiotext(e), 1995, p. 98.

23. Deleuze and Guattari, *A Thousand Plateaus*, p. 406.

24. De Landa, *War*, p. 3.

25. J G Ballard, "Project for a Glossary of the Twentieth Century", *Incorporations*, Zone 6, eds. Jonathan Crary, and Sanford Kwinter, New York: Urzone, 1992, p. 279.

26. Paul Virilio, and Sylvère Lotringer, *Pure War*, New York: Semiotext(e), 1983, pp. 137-138.

Previously published in Tom Sanqvist, ed., Nomadologin, *Stockholm: Raster Forlag, 1998.*

translated by James Manley

The Finnish multi-media artist Marita Liulia once described her country of origin as "a one idea nation". With one company, Nokia, now bigger than the Finnish state, one giant telecommunications firm, Sonera, and one media company owning the only daily national newspaper, the *Helsingin Sanomat*, with its one art critic, etc., etc.. Having been isolated and colonised in previous centuries, being squeezed by both Sweden and Russia, Finland is now going through its 'Golden Age', with unprecedented prosperity, at least for those who own Nokia stocks or work for Nokia, which is an increasing number of people. The process of urbanisation and post-industrialisation is vibrant, with people and resources concentrating on the south coast. Also, as a member of the European Union, Finland will soon introduce the Euro. It even has a growing population of immigrants and refugees. But Finland has still only five million citizens who continue to suffer from cold, dark, lonely winters and celebrate the long warm days in summer. Population wise it does not amount to more than North London, as one critic used to say. Or maybe Greater Berlin. A population which is not very big for a country of its size.

How do these demographic, political and economic facts effect the cultural climate in this country? I met Marita Liulia briefly in 1996 and got to know her better during my stay in Finland for two months in 1999 when I was working on the Temporary Media Lab at the Kiasma Museum (http://www.kiamsa.fi/temp). During the winter of 2000 we did an online interview which developed step by step into a collaborative text.

GL: How does the economic and geographic condition of Finland effect your work? It seems that you are being thrown back and forth between the village type of cultural policies on the one hand, and on the other the unique opportunities of five year long state grant for artists. Please introduce us to your version of Finland.

ML: Finland is a nation where only one idea rules at a given time. We are just five million people (and not growing), with a long history of self defense. The Russian 'bear' has always been a threat, and the Swedes are not so loved either. The Finnish are not conquerors but defenders by nature, so we turn the new millennium page as a pure white, deep clean and nature loving, extremely well organised country with straightforward, rather equal people who just have one big problem: long and depressing winters. Maybe that is why we have such a bad record for committing suicide.

Since World War II Finland has been surprisingly culturally Anglo-American. Before World War II the third language after Finnish and Swedish, which was compulsory, was German. Now as we are a member of the EU, and our standard of living and degree of democracy is top of the league world-wide, we could afford to loosen our "only one idea at a time" policy a bit. After World War II we had proportionally the largest migration from the country-side to the cities in Europe. Spiritually Finnish culture has not yet arrived from the countryside to the city, and culturally people tend to look backwards—just think about the very nostalgic Aki Kaurismaki films (the last one, *Juha* was a silent one!). The 50s are still considered to be the Golden Era of our culture. However, this doesn't mean we don't have good and original artists, it is just difficult to find (popular) art connected to contemporary urban life. New media hasn't (yet) brought very much change, which is surprising. The Finnish are not as technophile as they are made to be, they are just keen users. Exactly as you told me about that other techno nation—Japan. The generation which will slowly change this attitude is still in its early 20s. But we are getting there. Mentally I fit better into that younger generation than in my own, which I think is why my audience in Finland is rather limited. In recent years I have mainly focused on issues in contemporary (fe)male roles and identities that are not specifically Finnish *per se*—I could have done it anywhere. Actually I did. I am constantly on the move.

At the end of the 80s I was very frustrated about the art and media world (I worked for years as a journalist/photographer) and—more than anything else—about my own ideas about the arts and the media. I grew up with Marx, Hegel, Kant, Dostoyevski, Marcuse, Sartre, Nietzsche—a company of rather gloomy men, that is. Plus artist bohemians, from Baudelaire to Burroughs. Very inspiring for a young and passionate woman artist, isn't it? In the late 80s I started to study postmodern and gender theories with great appetite and ended up combining my old skills with new ideas and new technologies. It was at this point that I finished writing the concept for the *Jackpot* CD-ROM installation. After talking with technicians I realised that there was no other way—I had to start working with computers. In the 80s I had already used computers for making sound and light installations, and by the early 90s I had started to direct a team of professionals. I began producing large multi-media programmes.

GL: Both of your CD-ROMs, *Ambitious Bitch* and *Son of a Bitch*, deal with (female and male) sexuality.

ML: Sexuality is just one of the issues, including changes in feminine and masculine identities, excerpts of recent discussions about (fe)male gender roles, psychoanalysis, social relationships, biological discoveries and fashion. I am interested in changes and I am fascinated by the ways people express themselves; by words, by body language, by thoughts, by clothes.

GL: I know you do not like to be identified as a feminist, because of its limitations concerning the fixed and narrow identity politics which go with this term. Still, it would be justified to say that the sexual politics of art and new media are playing a dominant role in your work. Would you consider yourself a cyber-feminist?

ML: Me a cyber-feminist? Why not! It depends what you mean: does it mean one is a feminist? For me this simply means a person who wants equality. Even in cyberspace. Let's add cyberspace to the list (laughter). Some feminism is needed there, too.

GL: How are these issues played out in Finland? Your country is well known for its strong women, and perhaps also for its slightly tragic and disaster-prone male culture. How do you turn your explicit theoretical and political (psycho)analyses into a sexual esthetics?

ML: The field of the new media developed simultaneously with the high tide of feminism, with lots of (young) women getting involved—expecting to avoid patriarchal hierarchies typical of 'old media'—like film. I considered studying film in the 80s but quickly realized I would be 50 before the guys in power would allow me to make my first feature film—and by that point I would have run out of ideas. None of my female friends who are film directors have ever made a feature film. In multi-media nobody knew much about how to play boss. These days I think that a female director is not a strange creature from outer space… but you do have to be 'a bulldozer', as you put it once. No mistakes allowed.

In new media and technology, despite a promising start, the number of female students has declined rapidly. The field of the new media is heavily engineer-oriented. Even in Finland where the whole state (our new president is a woman), the bank system and the cultural sector are run by women, we have to be worried again about the fact that girls do not find information technology a very seductive subject. I have worked together with engineers for about 12 years now and I take care that my teams are built up so that both sexes feel comfortable and safe. It is a hard, sometimes full time job, but I enjoy it. The more the people are mixed, the less prejudice there is. When I did the research work and wrote the manuscript for the *SOB* (*Son of a Bitch*) CD-ROM I wondered how I could realise it in Finland. If a woman creates a work about men with such an outrageous name, the consequences are obvious. I took a risk and operated with a sense of humour. I guess in Nordic countries women can afford to laugh about dumb blonde jokes, but male roles are surprisingly rigid. Male identity is not something to poke fun at. It is also possible that the timing for *SOB* was wrong. It was too early, but I had to do the work anyway. In general sexual and gender identities have been a popular issue in Nordic (cyber) art and culture over the last ten years but not so in popular culture. If I compare Holland and Finland, our popular cultures are quite apart as far as sexual/gender issues are concerned.

GL: Throughout your art career you keep coming back to your own body, visualising it, taking pictures of it, morphing it through Photoshop, dressing up, metamorphosing your face into other faces, other personas. What makes you so fascinated by this? Your biography seems to be full of big changes. You have gone from journalism, through performance and installation works to multi-media, and now the Internet, with projects becoming ever larger in scale. How would you describe these phases, this drive to move onwards, the cycles in your works which lead you into a creative crisis in order to reach the next level? Were does this capacity to change, to transform into somebody else originate from?

ML: This is a very simple and therefore tricky question. It is curiosity that drives me. I want to see what is behind things. I have always felt that the only real limits I have are body and time. I spent my childhood in hospitals reading and making plans about what I was going to do if I survived. When I got better, around the age of 15, my hunger for life was insatiable. I wanted to see and experience as much as possible. I could call that my artistic-intellectual role as a hunter of hidden meanings behind self-evident truths—I am constantly playing around with ideas and testing them. I also play around with myself. In a way my body is material, a model which is always available. By changing styles and characters I find out about different attitudes. I also change my character according to my work. Projects have grown naturally bigger because with more experience I can handle more—I need challenges. I cannot repeat myself—I feel drained out if I have to, so my next project always differs a lot from the previous one. My art projects are research projects as well. That is why it takes three years to finish each one.

GL: You have been part of the multi-media industry from its very beginning, in the early 90s, and you founded your own company, Medeia Ltd., employing a flexible number of freelancers depending on the project. So far you have been very successful, but there is still the fundamental problem of how to distribute multi-media titles, especially when these are art works. You are now setting up a Finnish version of the Paris-based Moebius prize for multi-media, the "Prix Moebius Nordica". How do you look at the recent developments in this industry? It looks like it is a tough business for artists with ambitious ideas about interfaces, complex content and non-linear ways of telling stories. And where does the Internet fit into this? Much of the money these days is going into e-commerce and not so much into (CD-ROM based) multi-media. CD-ROM production, with its large budgets—somewhere between a thick catalogue and a film—might, in the long run, be too difficult a proposition, with so little return on sales. Or do we just have to be patient and speculate on the ever-growing number of computer users?

ML: I am operating somewhere between the art world and electronic publishing. My main problem during the 90s—and I am not alone in this—has been (international) distribution. The art world still lives in video time (even today many big museums are not equipped to deal with computer-based art!) and electronic publishing companies are only just building up their systems. Also, high quality content is expensive and demanding to create, so it isn't appealing to cash-crazed marketers. At the moment I am preparing my next multi-media title called *Marita Liulia Tarot*, which will be produced for four different platforms: printed cards, CD-ROM, the Internet and wireless mobile format (WAP). By now it has been translated to Dutch, English and Italian. It was quickly adapted in countries like the Philippines and Singapore.

I am interested in current developments in telecommunication systems and I believe in multi-platforms at the moment. We will go on working with CD-ROMs and DVDs because the Internet's development towards multi-media is slower than I thought four years ago and audiences want their techno utopias to be fulfilled at a push of the button—just because salesmen told us everything was going to be possible... I am dreaming of distributing my work for free—but who will pay for the high costs of production? It might be a nightmare—or a real challenge for a producer.

Somebody said that future audiences will not be willing to pay for content—that would be something the advertiser would take care of. Will commercial companies control the content in future? Will a banner in a website pay for the content? What kind of critical, intellectually demanding, challenging stuff could that be? This raises many interesting questions. (Noam Chomsky's lurking behind these lines). The best solution for distribution problems is located in the Net itself, as those who produce content should build up a network in order to distribute the work. The first steps in that direction are being taken now.

GL: Could you tell us something about your way of working? To what extend do you think artists have to become engineers and technicians? What is your relationship to the computer software and to the programmers you work with? Do they influence the final result, or do you keep control over the whole process? How would you describe the digital images and the interactive environments you design? It seems that you are still 'drawing' images, in the handicraft way; but this time with a computer.

ML: I am doing my best to try to bring members into my team who are going to be genuine contributors. For years I have been looking for an outstanding programmer who has a degree in philosophy. Seriously. Many programmers I have worked with tend to be too young; nerdy types with too little experience in other necessary fields (those legendary social skills...) to work in a team long term. But then I have worked with so many good ones recently that I should shut up. In a team I am the director and sometimes also the producer so I always carry the responsibility for the project as a whole and I am the one who takes control if somebody's not able to do the work or has problems in the team. Of course once you have a team you've got problems too! I have written a mini-manual of sorts for my students about the main problems they will probably encounter. One has to foresee upcoming problems. Male and female roles are an endless source of problematic situations. Creating a good, respectful atmosphere seems to be essential—and that is my main job as a director. No wonder I feel like an alien when the work period is over! I have to leave the studio for some months and get really pissed off in Paris or Bangkok or somewhere else faraway, as I cannot afford to bring my moods to work.

All my work is based on photography, even *SOB*, whose interface is realised with Quick Time Virtual Reality. We manipulate digital photos or video images (we might even paint them one by one, and there are 24 images in a second!) The amount of stills I have to work with is so large, approximately 4 hours to browse in one programme, and the body and mind really do have their limits—both my hands have had to be operated upon. But I really adore working with images. That's my greatest enjoyment. I could perhaps manage without writing but I really would suffer if I could not create images. It is a basic need for me. My works are based on (manipulated) photos because of the quality. And it's more economic. Maybe later on I will start to work with 3-D and artificial graphics. I do like to combine real images with artificial ones, and the result should not be documentary.

The way we work in a team is as follows: first I present my idea (manuscript) and my (philosophical, estethic and political) goals to the team. I also prepare images and some examples of the multi-media realisation. Then we start working together and I do my best to encourage the team to bring their own ideas and criticisms to the fore. It is sometimes hard work, especially if people have been employed in companies where they are not expected to have an overview of all aspects of the work. It is extremely difficult to generalise but I have noticed women have to be encouraged to defend their ideas whereas young men... well, I mentioned the lack of social skills before. What I like best is to work with multi-skilled, hard-working people who are curious about their own capacity.

GL: Can you say something more about the relation between the artist and the engineer? This relationship does not seem ideal at the moment. Is the only solution that artists become technicians of sorts? If not, what are their skills—to tell stories, to draw what they imagine? Artists these days have to be, more than ever, project managers, administrators, therapists and PR strategists in order to operate successfully in the market.

ML: To be successful in the market has always been demanding. It helps a lot if one is multi-valent—and also an attractive person. Artists have always worked with other professionals (though their names are hardly ever mentioned), including engineers. I am aware of the deep divide between artists (or people from the cultural field in general) and engineers. They approach work differently, and understand their capacities very differently. The problem is how artists who are interested in technology/new media will manage to find engineers who have a desire for art and culture. Generally it depends on one's contacts and one's attitude. I think we have to co-operate and learn to communicate with different professionals. The present situation forces artists in that direction, as one cannot handle all the professions which are needed for realising the larger kind of multi-media works.

GL: The relation between so-called contemporary artists and so-called electronic or new media artists seems complicated. Over the last decade these groups have become separated from each other. Due to the rise of the net and the arrival of computers in artists' studios and in art schools, we are now heading for a clash. I am not sure if it will be a productive 'accident'. You are active in both worlds. Would you like to see the electronic arts 'ghetto' disappear?

ML: In my surroundings—in Finland and in France—these groups are not so far apart. The number of artists that have started to operate using the Net is growing fast. Like in any other profession, the computer is just the tool of this epoch. I think this tool needs to be demystified. The audiences and the art world need guidance with electronic arts. The main problem is one of availability—how to distribute and present the works in the art world. The time we live in now is a time of images. Artists should benefit from that instead of being afraid of the new professional tools. Then again, younger generations have different attitudes but their encounter with the slow and conservative art world has not been a very successful one. They have to make their own rules.

I expect that the new crop of curators, organisations, exhibition spaces, magazines, activities and even schools will make the change—but it is a slow process, partly because commercial image making, the advertising business and TV has succeeded in monopolising the pool of young talent for a long time now—with money.

GL: What do you expect of new media critics? Can you remember a good piece you have read recently which might indicate the way to go? Should criticism be more based on hyper text or should we direct ourselves towards the level of the "Tres Grandes Theories" ? (to become the Sartres and de Beauvoirs of the Internet, as it were....)

ML: Maybe the speed of technical development has been so breathtaking that the grande theories are still on their way. It always takes time to build up a comprehensive view of a period in history but after all the hype I'm eager to see it. In our era sociologists (Castells, Bourdieu, Zizek) and linguists (Chomsky) seem to be doing the most interesting work. Recently I have concentrated on gender issues in order to understand what was happening to concepts like 'woman' and 'man', but the necessity for me to understand rapidly changing conditions in society and economics is growing.

Consumerism (which has replaced former ideologies) is something we are embraced by in our everyday life, and it obviously brings with it a certain kind of "revolution" which has been going on for some time: Nokia's annual budget is bigger than the government budget of Finland. Who controls Nokia? The main shareholders. But who are they? What are their interests? Who controls a country, we could also ask. Since the the 80s intellectuals have been surprisingly silent on these issues, though they have changed radically in the same period. For a long time now it has not been fashionable to criticise society, the media—or individual companies. Instead, it has been fashionable to chose between brands. There is so much to observe and analyse. Media critics could offer some interesting views.

GL: How do you interpret the mobile phone mania and where do you fit critical and artistic content and interface design in the current explosion of telecommunication? Will everybody be a mobile WAP artist in the time of the telephone call?

ML: I find it interesting how our ideas of communication are changing so rapidly. Availability and accessibility are changing our self-understanding and way of life faster than we care to notice. We want to be anchored in time, which is why we buy the latest tools. The drive of the market is astonishing.

Wireless communication creates an odd combination of distance and intimacy, which seems to be immensely seductive. Especially among youngsters: SMS-text messages are extremely popular in Finland, as are mobile phone desktop images. I don't know if this will bring new art forms, but I am interested in the code language that it has produced. Artists can use whatever medium but the medium itself doesn't make art. It has always been difficult for the art world to accept new mediums for artistic expression. It is again a question of power, as in any system. Those who have it, tend to keep it out of reach of others. Newcomers have to prove their plausibility. But if I were a poet, I would immediately start a 'Poem Phone' where one could get 400 character haiku's to the screen of a mobile phone and the money would go in the poets' own pocket, with no publisher involved. As I already mentioned, I am planning to use wireless WAP/third generation technology as one of the four platform for my next work. My reasons to use wireless GSM/WAP were merely experimental but then they turned into a real product. Nowadays I turn my gaze towards digital TV and wonder how to make it interactive in an intelligent way. How other media, like Internet and mobile phones could be connected to TV. If the manuscript I'm working on at the moment actually fits the new platform, I'm curious to see how it will function and how the audience will response. The most attractive thing about new media for me is the new and unexpected audiences that are to be found with it.

The works of Marita Liulia can be found at http://www.medeia.com

edited by Patrice Riemens

ILLUSTRATION: MARITA LIULIA, *TAROT WAP ICONS*, 2000

HAAVEILIJA
DREAMER

TAIKURI
MAGICIAN

NOITA
WITCH

HALLITSIJATAR
EMPRESS

HALLITSIJA
EMPEROR

GURU

RAKASTAVAISET
LOVERS

VAUNUT
CHARIOT

OIKEUS
JUSTICE

ERAKKO
HERMIT

ONNENPYÖRÄ
WHEEL OF FORTUNE

VOIMA
STRENGHT

HIRTETTY
HANGED MAN

KUOLEMA
DEATH

KOHTUUS
TEMPERANCE

PIRU
DEVIL

TORNI
TOWER

TÄHTI
STAR

KUU
MOON

AURINKO
SUN

TUOMIO
JUSTICE

MAAILMA
WORLD

Institutio Media Manifesto

INSTITUTIO MEDIA has been designed as an attempt to transfer an institution onto the Internet and to study the way it functions on the Web.[1] Its address is www.o-o.lt. An academic institution was chosen for this purpose since we have the broadest knowledge of the activities of such institutions at the present time. We also wish to explore the relationships between physically limited and virtual spaces. In real space and time the functioning of an institution is restricted by its physical premises and the regularity of its activities, which are necessary for the interactivity and existence of that institution. In contrast, a virtual space is restricted by technology and the quality of the Internet connection. The Web makes it possible to avoid the expropriation of the physical location—it is replaced by a 'site' on a server—as a quantity of magnetic memory.

This project was initiated by writing a manifesto and then drawing a scheme of the institute. We chose to write a manifesto because of its compact and expressive form, and to represent the project with a graphic drawing because it is more clear, less ambiguous. The Internet radio, magazine and mailing list depicted in the scheme are considered as continuous projects. The chain of these projects is INSTITUTIO MEDIA—a mediating institution. The basic aim of this institution is not original, but is instead to create new forms of data: projects, communication links and a data bank. We are only altering the place of the action. This shift in itself is the object of our interest.

The crisis of academic institutions as described by J F Lyotard was based on the emergence of a new medium that became a mediator between the accumulated information (data banks and archives) and the user (student). Therefore a professor's situation radically changed: he/she no longer has the monopoly of being a mediator (and commentator at the same time). If you work as a catalogue compiler or information collector-reteller, i.e. do mechanical work, you can be substituted by a machine. It will do your job better. If you produce new knowledge, it can be found in data banks. It is no longer necessary to visit certain places to obtain information. Information is not limited to a physical location and form. The chain of mediators started to break up and be replaced by quicker ones. On the other hand, transmission (and, partly, data production) is a new form of narration if information is selected and transmitted in a certain way. Therefore listening to a professor can be considered aesthetic—although you can obtain the same information elsewhere and in a quicker way (an exception being if the professor does not write), but you can admire (or not admire) the means and quality of transmitting. Choosing a mediator has thus become a matter of psychological and aesthetic comfort.

We can recall the ancient Greeks—peripatetics, their walks and discussions in small groups, which had already started with Plato's Academy. A mobile group of thinkers used to walk in a garden without clear limits or an obvious structure, except, perhaps, a network of paths. None of them was solely a listener or a narrator. Listening was merely a means of participating in a conversation. An interlocutor became listener and narrator in turn. One can act using the Internet in a similar way— both in real and unreal time. You can create structures and communities whose nucleus is on the Internet, able to survive without large financing and premises, but comparable to those existing in a physically limited space by the quality and quantity of data. This is because in the Internet you can pretend to be anybody you wish, choose means of narration, and compile your image from excerpts of other narrations. You can present yourself as either a unique or regular data base. INSTITUTIO MEDIA's data base would represent a kind of memory important to the identification of the institution—a collection showing the consistency and reasonableness of data selection rather than taste and education.

The INSTITUTIO MEDIA site consists of text, audio, video (writing/sound/image), links sections, and a search system. The first component of the data base requires precise complementation. The contents and the form of search depend on each other. The structures of data bases becomes a kind of data transmission. Not only what data you receive, but also the way you receive it, becomes important. In this respect the means of interpreting the data is a search system as well. However, data without selection and structure turns into noise. With that in mind we are going to create a logical and convenient search systems (or, a data base interface) that will act as a mediator. An institution's building and administration are not indispensable to its function, but the communications network, without which a group and data base could not function are: the pure form of an institution is a group of researchers who analyse problems and produce data.

Note

1. The Latin name INSTITUTIO MEDIA—the intermediate institution—defines both a social action and the character of activity on the Internet.

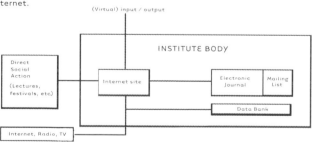

All Power to the Copenhagen Free University

Of all the affairs we participate in, with interest or without interest, the only aspect still impassioning is the groping search for a new way of life. The aesthetic disciplines have proved blatantly inadequate in this regard and display the greatest detachment, but the way forward is not to disband these disciplines—the way forward is to demand more from them. In our search for new ways of life the chemistry of unhappy consciousness and surplus energy is still making us establish experimental institutions and still making us reformulate a discourse within which we apply the word 'aesthetics'. Copenhagen Free University is one such institution/discourse.

Living in a society ruled by the stomach of the ever-expanding middle classes—obsessed with security and order and consensus—the unhappy consciousness tends to implode with the suicidal feeling of there being no exit. With a tradition of truce and consensus politics within Danish society the aesthetic disciplines have been predominantely playing along the lines of the State in the reproduction of cultural values. The state explicitly states that cultural politics have nothing to do with social politics, and is convinced of the 'single' common good that can come from the integration of the aesthetic disciplines with the nations general production value. Both in terms of cultural and monetarian capital, that is. Synchronously the state is encouraging all, including the cultural producers, to be critical, to behave with social responsibility and in general expects people to express themselves and promote individualised subjectivity. This strategic double bind is the technology of power—a technology for creating and controlling the voices present in society. Conflicts are explained as misunderstandings and mediated through the panacea of 'dialogue'. Using words such as Communism, Class Struggle and Revolution in a Danish context will qualify you for a free consultation with a psychiatrist.

Copenhagen Free University is one voice in a mumble of voices. We are not two or three individuals, we are an institution drifting through various social relations, in the process of being produced and producing. We are the people in the house. This position establishes an ever-changing formation of new contexts, platforms, voices, actions but also by inactivity, refusals, evacuations, withdrawals, exodus. According to the Situationist Asger Jorn, subjectivity is a point of view inside matter, "a sphere of interest", and not necessarily that which is equateable with the individualised ego. Our subjectivity (what is said and what is done) rises from the material conditions of our everyday lives and subtracts from the mediated rationale of the public sphere. In the public sphere any arguments are caught up in and filtered through the rationale of the individualised citizen. What if you do not feel like a sensible citizen? Copenhagen Free University is a 'sphere of interest' arising from the material life we experience and will always already be politicised before any citizenship. Our scope is both local and global, looking for fellow travellers around the corner and around the world.

Our point of departure is now and here: the circulation in and the consequences of the present day political knowledge economy and the desires distributed, accumulated, redirected or blocked in the flows and networks of that landscape. The fact that higher education is not an exclusive domain of the bourgeoisie and its children anymore and the generally highly skilled workforce of today have brought us mass-intellectuality. The mass intellectuality and today's immaterial mode of production that demands a workforce that is able to work in an environment producing abstract products characterised by knowledge and subjectivity, has, in particular, caught our interest. Not that we would like a job, but we recognise that this development is influencing our emotional lives.

Based on assembly lines and machinery, the Fordist mode of production demanded a manual effort from the worker and did not invade the nervous system in any way other than through boredom. In the Western world this mode of production has been left behind. Work is knowledge and the centre of productivity has moved inside the body of the worker, colonising not only the muscles, but the nervous system as well. Production increasingly involves, at various levels, an ability to make decisions among different alternatives giving a degree of responsibility through this decision making. To be productive in the knowledge economy, the worker is expected to become an active subject: one has to express oneself, one has to speak, communicate, cooperate, etc.. The mode of production is becoming immaterial and is related to processes of communication which require that the worker is critical and expresses subjectivity. It comes as no surprise that the ethos of the state regarding citizens has become almost identical with the ethos of capitalist production regarding the worker. The present day political knowledge economy is taking shape.

When we turn our attention to the mode of aesthetic production we have to recognise that the artist is becoming the role model of the worker in the knowledge economy. The artist is traditionally investing 'the soul' in the work, which is exactly the qualifications modern management is looking for when looking for a new employee. The entrepreneurial, self-employed independence and the sacred individuality of artists are the dream qualifications of the knowledge worker of tomorrow: An unorganised, highly skilled individual with no solidarity selling his/her living labour as a day-labourer. The heroic avant-garde artist of yesterday will become the scab of tomorrow. We see it around us and are doing it ourselves, with or without interest.

Another aspect here is the fact that much aesthetic production today is instrumental in the reproduction of the ideology of the knowledge economy. This often happens when artists are engaging in new technology, when artists are engaging in social regeneration, when artists are making art in public space. In general when artists are engaged in good and edifying causes. Artists are, with intent or without intent, affirming the current hegemony: spearheading new market standards or sweeping up where the state and capital are missing out. Copenhagen Free University is setting out to develop other strategies; strategies of withdrawal and contestation. 'Withdrawal' to indicate an activity not based on direct opposition, but on a refusal of power, a refusal of obedience. 'Contestation' to indicate an activity engaged in exposing the antagonisms, which, under the surface, characterise society and allow them to crystallise.

Copenhagen Free University was established to explore and intensify the forms of knowledge and subjectivity that we see withdrawing from or being excluded from this increasingly narrow-minded circulation of the knowledge economy. Our primary aim was not to throw sand in the machinery, but to valorise the stammer, the poetry, the disgust, the schizophrenia, etc.. For that purpose we needed a university. Even without any permanent internal structure the Copenhagen Free University is the body, which guarantees our valorisations.

It seems that the knowledge economy is working with an understanding of aesthetic disciplines solely as products within a superstructure. When a city has been planned, a building built, a product developed, it is then that artists are called for. This understanding is the currency amongst the State, art institutions, and many of the artists. Art is a social practice, but is it solely a construction to the good of public health? We intend to reconnect the discussions of aesthetics to the base. The mass-intellectualism and the globalisation of today offer a potential to re-introduce avant-garde tactics not based on the universality of the heroic avant-garde, but unfolding as collective and polymorphous creative forces in the production of social relations. Aesthetics beyond disciplines. Aesthetics as a fact of life.

All power to the Copenhagen Free University.

The Commitee of 17 July 2001

ILLUSTRATION: COPENHAGEN FREE UNIVERSITY, PUBLICATION NO.2 AND NO.3

Heterotopia

—Art, pornography and cemeteries

If one considers the primary obsession of the twentieth century to have been about time and place, like Michel Foucault did, then it is possible to draw on the notion of *heterotopia* in relation to contemporary art, contemporary culture and the migratory society. Connected to this, as we will see, is the question of identity—which also has to do with space and place—since space (in which the subject is known) is never something neutral, but a linguistic and historic dimension, which simultaneously privileges and impedes various subject-formations.

Like utopia, heterotopia is a place/space which has the property of being outside of the society which produced it, while at the same time carrying a relation to all the other remaining, 'external' spaces. Heterotopia suspects, neutralises or inverses the relations which it signifies, mirrors or reflects.

The difference between a utopia and a heterotopia is that a heterotopia possesses a material reality. If one says that the reflection in the mirror is a utopia, then the mirror as object and as medium is a heterotopia. Or, to be more precise: the mirror is a heterotopia when it reconstitutes you as standing and looking at yourself being reflected.

At all times, societies have had their heterotopias, and they have often been among the most interesting and revealing sites in their societies. Historically speaking, we can divide heterotopia into two main categories (and several sub-categories): heterotopia of crisis and heterotopia of deviation. These are places for individuals in crisis or deviation in relation to the society to which they belong, i.e. places for menstrating women, adolescents, the elderly, the mentally ill, and sexual deviants. But these spaces could just as well be places for purification, privilege and knowledge as places that were meant to prevent its subjects from that kind of access.

In "Of Other Spaces", Foucault lays out certain principles for heterotopia:
— All societies constitute heterotopia.
— A heterotopia can change its function because of changes in the society that occur over time. Any heterotopia has a specific function with regard to the society to which it is related.
— A heterotopia can, at one and the same place, layer several different places that in of themselves seem incompatible.
— Heterotopia is usually linked to slices of time and these open up to heterochronies (either accumulative or transitory).
— Heterotopia always presupposes a system of opening and closing, which both isolates and makes it penetrable. A heterotopia is not accessible for everybody as a public space, but rather poses certain criteria.

— Heterotopias always have a function in relation to all the places/spaces that remains (outside). Either in terms of creating an illusional space (heterotopia of illusion) and which reveals all the 'real' spaces as built on illusion, or by creating a space that is another, another real space—which is just as perfect as our places are messy and disjointed (heterotopia of compensation).[1]

Some examples of heterotopia are cemeteries, movies, gardens and carpets, boarding schools, bordellos, toilets, pornographic spaces, holiday camps, mental institutions and saunas. (Gardens are among the oldest of all heterotopias and were originally a representation of a microcosmos. Foucault also demonstrates how carpets were initially like gardens which could move across space.)

A more recent example are the motel rooms situated along the highway, where people go to carry out illicit activities, and besides, the heterotopic principle also provides a good characterisation of the incipient years of the Internet.

A heterotopia can also change its meaning through history (in much the same way that a signifier acquires a new signified), like for instance the porn-theatres in Times Square in New York. Following the new regulations governing the district, the traditional stomping grounds for the sex industry in New York have been transformed into Disney entertainment centres for the "whole family". From being a space that reflected the surrounding society through the investments of sexuality or "perversity" as such—the area is being turned into a heterotopia of compensation, constituted by an over-perfect representation of American middle class and working class ideals.

Another historic example of a heterotopia which has altered in character over time are the balconies in the movie houses in the segregated United States: the balconies in the movie houses come from a legacy of the theater and were originally isolated and privileged spaces for nobility or specially selected guests. Through the politics of segregation in the United States, the function of the balconies was shifted to become the only seating allowed for coloured moviegoers, as they were denied acess to the main hall. This turned upside down the historic conventions—where the balconies had previously been a place of privilege and privileged distance/withdrawal—whilst simultaneously confirmed the existing political priorities. Through this—albeit reprehensible—subversion of the conventions of the theatre, the entire economic and political structure in the United States became linked to a space that was meant to be isolated from a notion of the State as a whole. As a phenomenon, this shows a main point of the notion of heterotopia: how space and place are always agents for processes of subjectivity, and stand in a political relation to the society that produced them.

It's not easy to be aware of a heterotopia in your own time, but I think examples have emerged in art, both through its own activation of heterotopic spaces for the viewers, and through the continued interest within contemporary art for spaces and places within our contemporary and historic culture. Throughout history, the heterotopias lie there like fine networks and folds, revealing the structures of every day politics in the societies from which they arose. Often, but not always, their main purpose was to exclude and make sure that society was safeguarded from symbolically threatening quantities like puberty, menstruation or senility. But precisely from having different investments in terms of identity and politics, these places also came to acquire an intensely subversive potential.

One of the first visual artists who outlined the notion of heterotopia—and let it unfold within his work—for the sake of a historic understanding of both political investment and identity-formation, must have been Dan Graham. Graham picks up on the historic framework from Romanticism's English gardens and the Renaissance's Italian gardens through to modern urban planning, and reveals the bourgeois subject's construction—through a representation of a hyper-perfect understanding of reality.[2] His work becomes an accommodation of a historic and discursive subject, displaced from—but also in direct contact with—the surrounding environment. Often, he reduces this function to a minimum and allows it to determine the entire work. We see this in his recent pavilions, where one of the few things that happen is that the viewer is placed inside a filtering of reflections of him/herself and the surrounding milieu, inside of a historical and socially specific architectonic situation. His pavilions are also simple socialisable spaces, where you can "hang out" and reflect on the more political and social-psychological themes that are being discussed in the videos or in the architectonic and social situation itself. (i.e. the rooftop café at the DIA Center for the Arts in New York.)

Dan Graham was also one of the first artists who had an immediate connection to the youth—and popular-culture of his own time (in an entirely different way than pop art's aestheticising of youth culture). With Graham, one can see a problematisation of the subject which takes punk as seriously as suburbian housing. It is not a matter of adopting the aesthetics of punk, but rather of valuing it and treating it with a taken-for-granted seriousness (and humour).

Dan Graham also picks up historic heterotopic strategies, in order to elicit a discussion around contemporary social structures of power and subjectivity. One example would be the video *Rock my Religion*, where Graham presents parallels between the practice of spaces of deviation and crisis of punk and the religious Shaker movement. Another example is the article comparing Eisenhower and the hippies. His articles in the *New York Review of Sex* and the ads in *Screw Magazine* also constitute examples of this kind of activated space.

In recent years, artists like Jocelyn Taylor and Lovett/Codagnone have made multi-page projects in porn magazines. Whilst these projects had to fulfil demands from the publisher in terms of sexual content, the projects did not have a particular focus on—or function as—promotion of the artists. Rather they functioned as an active overflow of the term and the function of 'pornography'. They confronted the reader directly with discussions and themes concerning spaces of identity, (and created a non-space within a non-space).

It comes as no surprise that women have been central to the creation of several heterotopic spaces. From special places where the menstrating woman was kept apart from society—either because of her overwhelming spiritual powers (as historically in the Urba culture in West Africa), or because she was considered to be soiled—the honeymoon also constituted such a place: a non-space in relation to its society. Just as important as the celebration of a union of families was the de-localisation of the "woman's deflowering"—which "was carried out by the man"—and which was something that would preferably take place on a ship, in a train or in a hotel room; non-spaces in relation to her or his home society.

Representation of sexuality has been central in relation to the creation of many heterotopic spaces, and it is interesting to think about the role the stage has had in this context. The theatrical stage was a place/space that brought together supposedly incompatible spaces (such as the bourgeois public and street realism), and also functioned as a place where female sexuality was symbolised, masculinised as expression, and made fitting to the public. This is similarly the case with the cinema. Things were never so given though, and both cinema and theatre also provided a space for the transgression of the masculine gaze—a plane of deviation in the meeting between expectations and representation.

Camille Norment's installation, *Degas' Dancers*, 1995, touches on this. In a heavily theatrical, black painted space, the surface of the floor is filled with point shoes with attached high heels. They are arranged in pairs, but in order to fit into the different positions that they suggest, one would have to have a perfect mastery of the body. Classical dance becomes coupled with Chinese toe-binding, extreme physical regimentation, fashion and a fetishisation of both the shoes and the woman as phallic. Besides, it steals up on you that the scene or rehearsal space you are standing in is

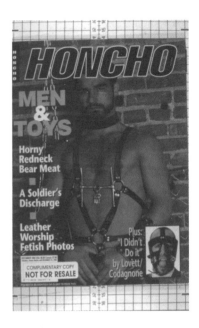

ILLUSTRATIONS (OPPOSITE PAGE, FROM TOP): JEFF WALL AND DAN GRAHAM, MODEL FOR CHILDRENS PAVILION, 1989, COLLECTION: VILLA GILLET, FRANCE
DAN GRAHAM: CLINIC FOR A SUBURBAN SITE, 1978. MODEL.
COURTESY MARIAN GOODMAN GALLERY
LOVETT & CODAGNONE, COVER OF HONCHO WITH ARTISTS PROJECT.
XAVIER LA BOULBENNE GALLERY

402

ILLUSTRATIONS (FROM TOP): CAMILLE NOURMENT, *DEGAS' DANCERS* (DETAIL), 1995
GLENN LIGON, *END*, 1995. GLENN LIGON, *COLONIAL*, 1995
GLENN LIGON, *TWIN*, 1995. COURTESY MAX PROTECH GALLERY

not in a theatre, but rather a strip club.

Classical ballet, the shoes and representation (as such) of 'woman' are Western cultural fetishes of the most traditional kind, and they possess a European ethnicity: *these concepts of 'fetish' and 'function' are solidly based in Freudian economy of desire. Furthermore, the masculinisation of the representation of the woman and the skin colour of the shoes show everybody that what is at play here is a delineation of, or a claim to, the European woman.*

However, the shoes as fetish object also engages an economy of desire for a contemporary feminine gaze, as a *female fetish*; and here opens up to us the possibility of a field of desire, which transgresses the patriarchal, capitalistic twentieth-century notion through which everything is defined in terms of lack.

In an installation at Max Protech in New York in 1995, Glenn Ligon had problematised the spatiality in which the viewer finds him/herself, and that which the viewer recollects and constructs his complex of identity around. The first thing that met the visitor, was the sound of Al Green songs—laid as an 'ambience' in the room, and which moved between foreground and background (depending on whether or not you focused on it). Spread around in the space stood a fragmented reconstruction of an African-American home from the 60s or 70s, with small sets of furniture that outlined differ-ent rooms within the family space. Together with knick-knacks, were photo albums and magazines in which family photos were combined with porn pictures, and weekly family magazines were strewn about with gay porn magazines. The gallery space and the family room were 'shifted' and queered, and thus the anticipated sexual signi-fication or sexualisation of the family was bypassed.

In this connection I use 'queer' as the political term brought forth from 'queer theory', which again grew out of a meeting between post-structuralism, gay, lesbian and feministic thinking and activism. 'Queer' is here not necessarily bound up with sexual praxis (bi, homo or hetero), but is a quantity of identity for one's subjectivity which is in deviation from the—historically speaking—patriarchal, authoritarian and compulsory heterosexually dominating structures of power. ('Queer' is then, as it were, also a deconstruction of historic, heterosexual masculinity.)

'Queer' is what Deleuze and Guattari would have called "a line of flight", a "becom-ing minority", and "to always be in the room next door". This is not a matter of avoid-ing conflict, quite the contrary. It is rather a project for finding the points of conflict (the discussion between powers of conformity and deviation)—to move right there in the area of crisis; to just manage to escape—just evading being turned into a cell of the law. So-called 'queer space' is—per definition—heterotopic, because of the power strata of sexuality and its investments into all social, public and personal spaces.

In Glenn Ligon's *Twin* from 1995, one sees a bed with an extra pull-out mattress. The extra bed is pulled halfway out under the top mattress and reveals a large number of magazines which are hidden from the upper bed which is neatly made up. The magazines consist of a mixture of *Jet* and porn magazines with pictures of men in various constellations. Already in the title, it is clear that the bed and the space have another character than what is evident in their more representational surface. Like a ghost, or a double of the family's anonymously representational son, the orientation of puberty lies there—and which hidden from view tries to spin an identity from the accessible sources in relation to race, class and sexuality.

Ligon's installation is interesting from several perspectives: the work is doubly heterotopic—through the boy's room as such, and through the theme of homosexual sexualisation of that room and the family architecture. On the one side, there are the articulations and the activation of a so-called 'queer space'. On the other side, you have the teenage room, the homosexually sexualised boy's room and the 70s (as a cultural signifier) as other strata of the heterotopic spaces. Besides, the African-American middle class home is also situated in a very special political relation to the representation of norms and social structures, although it is not heterotopic in and of itself.

Heterotopia is not restricted by the classical opposition between individual and society, and by that the prevalent (Freudian-Lacanian) model of the unconscious is disrupted. (A heterotopia is far from being something politically correct in itself—that is a relation that does not enter the picture. As we have also seen in some of the above examples, a heterotopia can be a forcibly suppressing space or a space of pleasure, and can be a 'good' or a 'bad' place for different individuals.)

Félix Guattari knew how to utilise the possibilities given in a heterotopic situation. Until his death in 1992, he worked not only with philosophy and political activism; his chief occupation was with the experimental psychiatric clinic, La Borde, in Paris. For Guattari, the clinic embodied a possibility for finding other therapeutic forms of treatment for people with at times considerable mental difficulties—based on his notion of schizo-analysis. Like Foucault, Guattari was preoccupied with employing the notion of 'subjectivity' instead of the notion of the 'subject'. He was also intensely interested in breaking away from the dominance of Freudian-Lacanian models of desire and from traditional psychoanalysis in general—based as they are on patriarchal and capitalistic models. Guattari understood them just as much as functions for the production of subjectivity as analytical models. Moreover, he was opposed to psychoanalysis' universalising claim.

In its inception, the La Borde clinic might very well have been defined as a heterotopia of crisis. But internally, it possessed a self-awareness and the activity of a heterotopia of deviation.

One could say that in their incipient years, the World Wide Web and the Internet constituted heterotopic spaces. Perhaps they were heterotopia *par excellence* in much the same way that the ship was to Foucault. (To Foucault, the ship was a perfect example of a heterotopia: a floating space, a place without place, a society that closes up around itself but which is, at the same time, changeable in relation to its surroundings.) But perhaps this is to let the term thin out a bit—the Net has always had so many sub-spaces. Moreover, it is now undergoing intense changes, and the power structures to which the Internet relates are not really all that clearly defined; the site of power—as well as the site of resistance—are situated in an ambiguous zone without borders in the conventional sense. Nonetheless, it appears that the Internet's investments are rather easy to spot and that, for the most part, it is merely reproducing a space of liberal capitalism which we know so well from before. Even though the power structures have become nomadic and deterritorial, this does not mean that they cannot have a segmentary and conservative effect. However, it is still difficult to say what the position of World Wide Web or the Internet is, and it is not a very helpful question, since the Internet is not one thing but rather a structure that is creating its own heterotopic spaces, points of deviation and assault groups.

As a way of concluding or enveloping this article, I'd like to refer to Alessandro Codagnone's installation, *Mean-Room*, from 1994; an installation as a heterotopia *par excellence*. The present article is indeed also something like a public toilet; full of anonymous graffiti and references, with glances at other subjects in the text.

A CODAGNONE: MEAN ROOM, 1994, INSTALLATION DETAIL

Notes

1. Michel Foucault, "Of Other Spaces", *Diacritics* 16-1, Spring 1986.

2. See, for instance, Dan Graham's text "Garden as Theater as Museum", Dan Graham, *Rock My Religion*, Cambridge, MA: MIT Press, 1993, pp.286-307.

Previously published in Øjeblikket—Magazine for Visual Cultures, no. 42, Vol. 10, Spring 2000.

—How can we conceive and construct specific platforms and networks for art production and communication, and, additionally, positional or participatory models for spectatorship as opposed to modernist generalised ideas of artwork and spectator? Does this entail a reconfiguration of the (bourgeois) notion of the public sphere into a different arena and/or into a mass of different, overlapping spheres? Or, put in other terms, what can be put in the place of the public sphere? Private zones, clubs and salons, (more) institutions, sub- and/or counter-publics? And what are the different arenas and possibilities and methods for interaction within and between them? When thinking about art production and representation, it is therefore crucial to negotiate such terms both individually and in relation to each other. And just as contemporary art practices have shown that neither the work nor the spectator can be formally defined and fixed, we have also come to realise that the conception of a public sphere, the arena in which one meets and engages, is likewise dematerialised and expanded. We no longer conceive of the public sphere as an entity, as one location or formation as suggested in Jürgen Habermas' famous description of the bourgeois public sphere. Rather, we have to think of the public sphere as fragmented; as consisting of a number of spaces and/or formations that are in conflictual and contradictory relations to each other. And we have come to realise, through the efforts of Oskar Negt and Alexander Kluge, that our interactions as subjects with the public spheres are dependent on experiences. There not only exist public spheres and ideals of such spheres, but also counter-publics. This means, on the one hand, that the artwork itself (in an extended sense) is unhinged from its traditional forms (as material) and contexts (galleries, museums, etc.), and on the other hand, that it is made contingent on another set of parameters that can be described as 'spaces of experience', that is, notions of spectatorship and the establishment of communicative platforms and networks in or around the artwork that are contingent on and change according to different points of departure in terms of spectatorship.

—The Nordic welfare society can in many ways be seen as a realisation of this century's early emancipatory projects, but as a high-tech, democratic vision it also embodies Deleuze's dystopic vision of a society of control. In this predicament of welfare, we are apparently dealing with a complete and totalising system of social control that is not only marked out by grand societal structures, but also internalised in each subject— we are all the state and all social democrats. The replacement of the disciplinary society's spaces of confinement with open spaces and electronic, virtual control challenges not only the traditional institutions, but also classic forms of resistance, to which art sometimes belongs. Throughout their history, the resistance forms we know have been linked to the struggle against disciplinary suppression in the form of institutional and confined spaces. Now, it is rather a matter of analysing which problems arise in welfare states, where not only is the state thoroughly institutionalised, but also the institutions themselves function as representatives of a democratic and egalitarian ideal for society.

—This strange relationship between openness in society and its institutions on the one hand, and the internalisation of social control in the individual subject on the other, is, perhaps, best analysed in the open and egalitarian Nordic version of the welfare state. In these states we find relatively easy access to public institutions, benefits and records, but access that is contingent on acceptance of the registration, mapping and ordering of the subject: to find your file, you must, obviously, not only know your number, but also accept its use as a means of communication and participation. The rights bestowed on the subject—i.e. the right to be a subject—is however also limited to certain subjects: despite the Nordic countries' supposed and idealised openness, they also have some of the world's strictest immigration laws and smallest refugee quotas. The existence of welfare and openness is becoming more and more dependent on nationalist policies. Openness only exists within national borders, and subjects and society only interface through a geographical and nominal delimitation of interaction with so-called 'others' and other spaces. Thus it is increasingly becoming an area of particular artistic-theoretical interest how we are to understand this ordering of society, and how we are to establish dialogical forms of critique and forums within this understanding.

Kestutis Andrasiunas is a media artist and initiator of INSTITUTIO MEDIA. Lives and works in Vilnius.

Søren Andreasen (born 1964). Artist. Lives and works in Copenhagen.

Asmundur Asmundsson is a visual artist and writer. Lives and works in New York and Reykavik.

Magnus Bärtås (born 1962) is a self-taught artist based in Stockholm. In his work he has focused on storytelling, biographies and marginal architecture. One of his latest works, "Satellites", is dealing with kiosk models from former communist countries. He has published a collection of essays entitled "Orienterarsjukan och andra berättelser" ("The orienteer-disease and other stories") (2001). Magnus Bärtås is also a tutor at Konstfack (University College of Arts, Craft and Design, Fine Arts Department) in Stockholm.

Kerstin Bergendal (born 1957) is a sculptor and installation artist. She is a founding member of the artists' curatorial group Tapko. Lives and works in Copenhagen.

Ernst Billgren (born 1957) is a painter and writer. Works and lives in Stockholm. Attended Valands Art Academy, where he later became Professor. His art explores different techniques and media: mosaic, painting, sculpture, photo, etc.. He moves between art, architecture, film and set design, and literature like the fox some people see him as.

Margrét Blöndal is a visual artist with a special interest in nature. Lives and works in Reykavik.

Ingrid Book (born 1951) is an artist, organiser and writer. She is a former Professor of painting at the Statens Kunstakademi in Oslo and at the Art Academy in Umeå, Sweden. She has been collaborating with Ingrid Hedén since 1986. She lives and works in Oslo.

Bjørn Bjarre (born 1966) is an artist, writer and editor of *UKS-Forum for Contemporary Art*. A collection of his comics made in the late 80s was recently re-published by Jippi Comics. For more info go to: www.bjarre.org. Lives and works in Oslo.

Claus Carstensen (born 1957). Artist and writer. Professor at The Royal Danish Academy of Art from 1993 to 2002. His most recent books include *Poems (Compilation)*, d.t., 1999, *The Semiotics of Drawing*, 2000 (an anthology), and *99/00 (poems)*, 2001. Lives and works in Copenhagen.

Ingar Dragset (born 1969) is an installation and performance artist. Has been collaborating with Michael Elmgreen since 1995. Lives and works in Berlin.

Anders Eiebakke (born 1970). Artist currently working with painting and drawing, Chairman of Young Artists Society in Norway (UKS) and independent curator. Lives and works in Oslo.

Michael Elmgreen (born 1961) is an installation and performance artist. Has been collaborating with Ingar Dragset since 1995. Lives and works in Berlin.

Anja Franke (born 1962). Installation artist and tutor at Det fynske Kunstakademi, the Art Academy in Odense, Denmark. She is an associated member of the research group Freja: Cyborgs and Cyberspace. See: www.cyborgs.sdu.dk She lives and works in Copenhagen.

Tone Hansen (born 1970). Artist and curator. Editor in Chief for the yearly magazine project *Frottefactory*. Currently working on a book about the future of the Norwegian art scene. Lives and work in Oslo.

Carina Hedén (born 1948) is an artist, organiser and writer. She is a former art critic at *Göteborgsposten* in Gothenburg and a former Professor at Umeå Art Academy in Sweden. Since 1986 she has been publishing Hong Kong Press, an outlet for artists' books. She has been collaborating with Ingrid Book since 1986. Lives and works in Oslo.

Minna Heikinaho is an artist working with different social projects. She runs the art gallery Push Firma Beige in Helsinki. In her gallery side by side with art exhibitions take place numerous art projects in co-operation with different social groups.

Henriette Heise. Visual artist. Co-founder of the Copenhagen Free University. Lives and works in Copenhagen.

Karl Holmqvist (born in the 60s) is an artist working mostly with writing and live readings. He is the founding editor of esoteric wall journal *Aesthetic Movement*. Lives and works in Stockholm.

Peter Holst Henckel (born 1966). Installation artist, member of the interdisciplinary project platform Globe, tutor at the Jutland Academy of Fine Arts, Aarhus Denmark. Lives and works in Copenhagen.

Jan Hietala, born in Stockholm, has for the last decade worked with video, film and theatre. His writing has been published in Russia, Finland and Sweden. Recent projects are the video installations "Liquid" and "Win". He teaches at colleges in the Nordic countries, is writing a PhD on the subject "Homosexual Aesthetics", at The Royal University College in Stockholm, and is also working on his first full length feature film.

Mats Hjelm (born 1959). Artist and filmmaker. He currently lives and works in Stockholm. Recent solo exhibitions of his work have been held at Gallery Index in Stockholm (1997 and 2000), Gallery Kari Kenetti in Helsinki (1998 and 2000) and Baltic Art Center in Gotland (2001).

Jakob Jakobsen (born 1965) Installation artist and organiser. Lives and works at The Copenhagen Free University (www.copenhagenfreeuniversity.dk) and the Infopool Network in London (www.infopool.org.uk).

Frans Jacobi (born 1960). Visual artist. Exhibitions in Scandinavia and abroad since 1983. Member of the artist-duo CoLab and co-founder of i-n-k /institut for nutidskunst, a venue for contemporary art. Teacher at the Royal Danish Academy of Fine Arts since 1994. Lives and works in Copenhagen.

Sara Jordenö (born 1974). Artist-writer. Co-founder of the independent gallery space Signal in Malmö. Is currently pursuing a MFA degree in the Interdisciplinary Studio area at The Department of Art at UCLA in Los Angeles. Forthcoming projects includes the artist book/documentation project *Persona* (2002) and co-arranging the symposium *Radical Time* in Los Angeles in January 2002. She lives and works in Malmö and Los Angeles.

Jussi Kivi is an environmental artist, who lives and works in Helsinki.

Gunnar Krantz (born 1962). Narrative artist. Works with comics, video, installations and web projects that focuses on autobiography and politics. He is a teacher at "Serietecknarskolan", a school dedicated to the art of making comics in Malmö. Homepage: www.seriekonst.net

Heta Kuchka is artist, who works mostly with photography and video. She lives and works in Helsinki.

Peter Land (born 1966) is a visual artist working mainly with video and drawing. He lives and works in Copenhagen.

Matts Leiderstam (born 1956) artist, lives and works in Stockholm.

Marita Liulia is called the Finnish pioneer of multi-media art. She is currently working with a performance that combine traditional art forms with new technology in ARS 01 exposition in Kiasma, Museum of Contemporary Art in Helsinki.

Geert Lovink is a writer and theorist specialised in net culture. He is an ambassador for the Society for Old and New Media/Den Waag in Amsterdam, where he also lives.

Annika Lundgren born in Sweden (1963), based in Copenhagen. Works mainly with a kind of 'public events' and activities outside the art institutions.

Eva Löfdahl (born 1953) lives in Stockholm. Artist, working with installation, sculpture and writing—at present preparing a work in public space in collaboration with CarusoStJohn Architects.

Lars Mathisen (born 1958). Installation artist and filmmaker. Lives and works in Copenhagen and New York. He is currently working on a new film.

Jørgen Michaelsen (born 1961) is a conceptual artist and writer, working with text, imagery and video. He lives and works in Copenhagen.

Deimantas Narkevicius (born 1964). Artist, curator, filmmaker and writer living and working in Vilnius.

Christine Melchiors (born 1963 in Denmark). Installation artist, lives and works in Paris, regularly coordinates projects taking place outside art institutions.

Anneli Nygren works with film, video and drawing. She is also a writer and art critic. Nygren lives and works in Turku.

Peggy Phelan is the author of *Unmarked: the politics of performance* (Routledge 1993); *Mourning Sex: performing public memories* (Routledge 1997); and the Survey essays for *Art and Feminism*, ed. Helena Reckitt (Phaidon 2001), and *Pipilotti Rist* (Phaidon 2001).

Arturas Raila (born 1962) trained as a sculptor, is now working with human relations and social issues in the medium of video. He lives and works in Vilnius.

Khaled Ramadan (Born 1964). Lives and works in Copenhagen and Vancouver. Installation artist, architect, Ph.D candidate in Art History and tutor at Copenhagen University, Consultant for the Ministry of Culture's Development Fund in Denmark and Mobile Curator for the Nordic Institute for Contemporary Art, NIFCA. He is the editor of the anthology *Peripheral Insider* (forthcoming).

Kirstine Roepstorff (born 1972). Visual artist and she is a member of the feminst group Kvinder på Værtshus/Women Down the Pub. Lives and works in Copenhagen

Pia Rönicke(born 1974). Artist, is currently working on a film project for Moderna Museet, Stockholm, dealing with the problematics of Stockholm suburbs encountering issues of segregation and local democracy. Lives and work in Copenhagen.

Beathe C Rønning (born 1968) is an artist working with fragmented, narrative installations and multi-media projects. In addition, she works on the lifelong social concept called "Liftings" where people are being physically, literally lifted by the artist. Lives and works in Copenhagen and Oslo.

Katya Sander (1970) is a conceptual artist working with architecture, film, memory and desire in relation to consumer culture. She also writes and is the editor of the magazine *Øjeblikket* as well as a member of the feminist group Women Down the Pub/Kvinder på Værtshus.

Jyrki Siukonen is a conceptual artist and researcher. In 2000 he finished a Doctoral degree at the Academy of Fine Arts, Helsinki. Siukonen writes, lives and works in Tampere.

Heidi Sundby is an artist and writer. Lives and work in Oslo.

Jan Svenungsson (born 1961). Artist, based in Berlin. During 2001 exhibited in the Biennale de Lyon, and built a 15 m brick chimney sculpture on the edge of a forest for the Skulpturbiennale Münsterland. Professor at the School of Photography and Film Gothenburg University 1996-2000.

Inga Svala Thorsdottir is a visual artist and a founder of Thor's Daughters' Pulverization Service (TPS). Lives and works in Hamburg.

Thorvaldur Thorsteinsson (born 1964) is an artist and writer living in Los Angeles and Reykavik.

Sophie Tottie is an artist working with painting, video, photography and drawing. In her works she investigates existential questions in their relation to political and historical events. Tutor at the Malmö Art Academy. She currently has the DAAD artist grant in Berlin, and lives and works in Berlin and Stockholm.

Elisabeth Toubro (born 1956) is a sculptor. Lives and works in Copenhagen.

Elin Wikström (born 1965) is a conceptual artist. Lives and works in Gothenburg and London.

Måns Wrange is an artist and professor at the Art Department of Konstfack (University College of Arts, Craft and Design) in Stockholm. At present he is working with a think-tank consisting of people from among other fields the Swedish Government, the university system and the business world with a view to the discussion and presentation of solutions to a wide range of social problems. As a curator he has among other things organised *The Stockholm Syndrome*—an international art exhibition in the form of a documentary computer game on CD-ROM.

Knut Åsdam (born 1968) utilises sound, video, photography and architecture to work with the politics of space and the boundaries of subjectivity. Often these concerns are related to themes of dissidence, remnants of utopic practises, and an analysis of space in terms of desire, usage and history. Lives and works in New York.

The publishing of this book was made possible by a grant from NIFCA, The Nordic
Institute For Contemporary Art in Helsinki. NIFCA is an institution under the Nordic
Councel of Ministers.

Published in collaboration with the Danish Art Foundation.

With generous support from FRAME and Norsk Kulturråd.

FRAME
FINNISH FUND FOR ART EXCHANGE